SUCCUBUS: SHADOWS OF THE BEAST

NOCTURNAL TRINITY: BOOK ONE

LEONARD D. HILLEY II

CHAPTER 1

ailey Yates knew that her brother Vincent would never have killed himself had it not been for his new wife, Cassie. And yet, Kailey stood at Vincent's graveside while the workers prepared to lower her brother's casket into the cold ground ... his final resting place.

The gray overcast Seattle sky with its chilly swirling mists set the mood for the burial and the gloom that also possessed her broken heart. The towering leafless oaks in the cemetery were sinister skeletons forewarning that the dangerous kiss of winter's death would soon settle over them, harsher than ever before.

One never escaped death, but sometimes death came too early with an unfairness that made Kailey want to scream at the heavens from her inner rage and loss. After all, her brother had been a successful attorney in his early thirties and destined to become the first in their family that had graduated from college to live a prosperous lifestyle. He was a man who had never entertained suicidal thoughts.

The workers and his ritzy friends from the Langston Law Firm had come out in great number. She estimated no less than one hundred people had arrived. Never had she seen so many expensive suits and vehicles. Coming from a modest middle-class family, she never imagined she or her brother would rub elbows with the upper class of society, but he had been adamant that they would be wealthy and had worked painstakingly to get them there.

While the priest gave the eulogy, the men and women stood stoically silent, their eyes staring at Vincent's casket. The priest finished speaking and led the audience in a proper prayer, praying that Vincent's soul found forgiveness and mercy for leaving this world by suicide.

How fitting, Kailey thought, wringing her hands. *Blame the innocent for what the murderer did.*

While the others respectfully closed their eyes, she gazed around, trying to see Cassie, but the two men standing in front of her sister-in-law blocked Kailey's view. Moments after the priest finished his lengthy ill-placed prayer, the wealthy people mingled to hug, shake hands, and chat.

The slight breeze swirled Kailey's long reddish-brown curls, forcing her to pull her hair back and letting it fall onto her back and shoulders. Her jaw suddenly tightened, hiding the wrinkles that deepened into cute dimples whenever she smiled. Her hazel eyes suddenly blazed with anger and vengeance.

Across the grave Cassie stood dressed in a form-fitting black skirt that accentuated her perfect curves and perhaps distastefully revealed more leg than what was suitable at a funeral for one's husband. Her tight long-sleeved jacket cut off at her midriff, revealing her well-defined abs. She wore black-netted hose and velvety black high heels.

Hell, streetwalkers wore more clothes in this cold weather. Kailey fumed.

Cassie hid her pale face behind a white handkerchief and sobbed. Kailey understood how a man might be immediately drawn to Cassie's exquisite beauty. Her slender oval face with high cheekbones gave her a regal presence even at this dismal funeral. She carried herself with the utmost grace, in spite of her poor choice of attire, but she also had a seductively dark energy radiating from her.

When Cassie's dark eyes met Kailey's, Cassie lowered her hands and meekly folded the handkerchief. Her tearless eyes weren't even slightly tinged red. A bit of amusement curled Cassie's pouty lips. An odd flicker of recognition blazed in her eyes and hinted slight detestation, even though they had never met in person. Kailey felt the resentment and didn't understand why, unless Cassie had somehow figured out that Kailey suspected her of murdering Vincent, which Kailey did. Perhaps Cassie read it in her eyes. Or worse, perhaps this she-devil could read Kailey's thoughts.

Moments later, Cassie broke their connection and returned to her fake sobs, wiping at her eyes with the cloth in a way that demanded pity from the solemn onlookers.

One of Vincent's former attorney friends wore a gray pinstriped suit and overcoat. He approached Cassie to console her. He was trim with brown hair, a firm jaw, and offered a tender smile as he spoke to the widow. She buried her face against the man's chest. Obviously surprised by her approach, he gently patted her back from an awkward distance, but Cassie aggressively wrapped her arms around him. To lessen his discomfort in the situation, he finally leaned in closer and embraced her.

She nuzzled against his chest, reached beneath his jacket, and clung to him. Her body shook with what people nearby might have considered violent heaving sobs. He rested his chin atop her head and whispered. His hands gently rubbed her back, and she seemed to calm at his touch and gentle words. She stopped sobbing and became less broken.

Can't you see that those tears aren't real? A slight breeze rustled Kailey's long flowing brown hair. Instead of remorse for her brother's death, she felt a growing resentment toward his widow. A bitter taste came to the back of her throat, and she fought the rising gag reflex from seeing this woman's blatant slutty behavior and utter disrespect for her husband. *What did Vincent ever see in you?*

Kailey also battled the growing urge to march across the cemetery and rattle the woman with several jabs to her face and a few swift punches to her stomach.

Another place. Another time.

Kailey's sister-in-law, even now, wore little makeup. Her lipstick was a bright red hue, which made her pale reflection appear even lighter. Her raven hair was neatly styled with silver pins and sprigs of Lady's Breath. Her pretend *tears* had not smudged the dark mascara around her eyes, and with her ashen complexion she resembled a corpse better than her brother probably had at his viewing. To others, even the hundred or more attending the funeral, she appeared stately, reserved, and the *perfect* widow.

Well played, Kailey thought. *You've fooled them, but not me.*

Cassie was a cold parasite that had preyed upon Vincent, seduced him into marrying her, and then had taken his life to possess his wealth and million-dollar estate. Kailey couldn't act on her suspicions alone. She needed proof. The coroner had ruled her brother's death as a suicide, but she believed it was not. Relevant details had never been disclosed to her, and she wanted answers.

Vincent had been murdered. Cassie had killed him and made it *look* like a suicide. Kailey was determined to prove it.

Vincent had been the most optimistic person Kailey had ever known. He had been the perfect role model and mentor. He encouraged her to pursue her dreams and to never allow them to die. He helped pay her college tuition and let her stay at his house during her summer breaks, but that was *before* Cassie entered his life.

During the final semester of her senior year at college, Vincent had called and told her that he had finally met the woman of his dreams. He emailed her several pictures of them together. Kailey was excited for him and asked when she'd get to meet Ms. Right. Vincent promised that after she graduated, she could come meet Cassie, and stay with them while Kailey searched for a job in Seattle. Until then, she could Skype with him.

But after Cassie moved in with him, his demeanor changed. Kailey noticed it via their live chats. His enthusiasm dwindled. His zeal for life vanished. He looked thinner, disheveled, and no longer shaved regularly. His haunted expression and fearful eyes clued her that something wasn't quite right, but whenever she questioned him about his relationship with Cassie, he averted his gaze, quickly changing the subject. He became uncomfortable and paranoid whenever she mentioned Cassie's name. He almost seemed to hold more fear toward her than the love and affection he had shown months before.

She and Vincent had always been close siblings, but after his engagement to Cassie, the woman became an invisible wedge between them. Their Skype video chats became fewer and fewer. Kailey emailed, texted him, and left messages at his office, but seldom did he respond. He simply shut her out. Since she attended college at Boston University, she couldn't take a quick weekend trip to visit him, especially not during the final semester of her senior year. But his lack of communication frightened her. Sudden silence was not his nature.

Something wasn't right.

She directed the blame toward Cassie.

And now, Kailey watched the funeral attendees disperse and head back to their vehicles. Her stomach soured. She predicted antacids in her near future.

For her brother who had worked so hard, *this* was the end of all his good deeds and his life.

She closed her eyes and fought heated tears. She wished her graduation had been a week earlier. Perhaps then ... no, nothing she could have done would have prevented this. However, the timing seemed odd. For him to die on her graduation day was more than a coincidence. She felt that in her gut. Cassie knew Kailey was coming to Seattle to stay with them after graduation. Vincent had told her.

The attorney trying to comfort Cassie escorted her to Vincent's midnight blue BMW. Her brother had owned several luxury vehicles but the BMW had been his favorite. He referred to it as his *baby*. The man opened the driver's side door but Cassie shook her head and pressed herself against him. Her feigned loss wasn't worthy of any notable acting award, but this attorney bought and believed it. The awkwardness he had shown earlier had lessened. He hugged her closely, trying to comfort her.

"I ... I don't think I'm in the right frame of mind to drive, Frank," Cassie said in a pathetic tone, shaking her head. She dabbed at invisible tears with the handkerchief but her hungry eyes flirted her need for him to console her and become her savior. Perhaps even more.

"I can drive you home," he said with an assuring smile.

Cassie smiled and playfully placed her hand on his and squeezed. He seemed partly taken back but also greatly flattered by her closeness.

Kailey shook her head and rolled her eyes. *Dear God!*

"Oh, no, Frank," Cassie said, shyly. "I can't ask you to do that."

"You didn't ask. I offered."

She gave an adoring smile and an intense flirty stare. "What will you do with your car?"

"I'll have my stepson follow us. He can drive me home from there. I want to make certain you get home okay."

Cassie beamed a smile. "That's so sweet of you. Thank you."

"Not a problem. Vincent wouldn't have it any other way."

Score one point for the attorney.

The smile faded from Cassie's face at the mention of Vincent's name. Her eyes narrowed and she lost the vulnerable, needy persona she had shown only moments before. Her voice became icy. "Never mind. I can manage the drive back *just fine*."

"Seriously, Cassie, it's not a problem," he said in an almost pleading tone. "I'd be happy to drive you."

Kailey couldn't believe that this man, who held every bit of confidence a successful man could possess, had quickly turned into a desperate soul. He acted like pleasing this woman was the most important deed on Earth.

Pathetic.

"No," Cassie said, brushing past Frank and slinking into the driver's seat. "I'll go visit one of my friends instead. I don't want to be *alone* in that big house tonight."

"As upset as you are, it's not wise for you to drive even a short distance. Really, please let me help."

Deduct two points for fawning.

No longer acting the vulnerable, sorrow-filled victim, her eyes narrowed and grew fierce without any trace of her former flirtiness. Coldness echoed in her voice. "I won't impose on you. There's no sense having *your stepson* drive to my estate to pick you up. That's too much trouble."

Frank held the door open, standing between it and the car. Although extremely uneasy, his voice remained calm and rational. "Honestly, I don't mind. Besides, how else would I get home?"

"I would have driven you home after we shared some wine and talked. But *no*, I can see that's not something you're interested in. Now *move!*"

The bitch wins.

Kailey hurried toward the BMW, hoping to introduce herself and disrupt the embarrassing scene before it further erupted. Cassie's sudden mood swing and dominant behavior caught the attention of the others heading toward their cars. They stopped walking and turned to see what was happening. Her dangerous tone of voice echoed across the cemetery.

Frank raised his hands in surrender and took a step back from the BMW because of her erratic attitude. He looked uncertain of whether he should keep talking or head to his own car. Before he did anything, Cassie slammed the door, started the car, and sped down the narrow blacktop that meandered and cut through the cemetery.

"Damn," Frank whispered, turning. He nearly walked right into Kailey. "Sorry."

Kailey forced a smile when she looked at the shattered expression on his face. Cassie had crushed his ego in less than a few minutes.

Wow. What misery had Vincent endured with her?

Kailey turned to watch the BMW leave the cemetery and turn onto the highway, speeding away. "What was that all about?"

Frank ran a hand through his hair, shook his head, and then rubbed his chin. His eyes searched as he thought. "I wish I knew."

She extended her hand toward him. He gently took her hand and squeezed slightly. Not quite the firm handshake she expected from a man.

"I'm Kailey. Vincent's sister."

He frowned, expressing his sorrow. "I'm Frank. I'm so sorry for your loss. I worked with your brother."

"I know."

"He was such a great guy. He has pictures of you on his desk. He talked about you a lot, but not so much lately."

Kailey lowered her gaze. Her eyes moistened with tears. "It had been over a month since I last heard from him."

"My condolences for your loss. He was a man of great character and good to work with. Does Cassie act like that a lot?"

"I can't say. I never had the ... *pleasure*."

"You never met your sister-in-law?"

Kailey shook her head. "No. Not even before they married."

He offered a nervous laugh. "I can't say that you missed out on that. She went from friendly to spiteful within a few minutes. I don't know what to make of it. What did I do wrong? Maybe I should call and apologize to her."

"Why? You didn't do anything wrong. You certainly don't *owe* her an apology."

He shook his head. "I don't know why, but I feel like I do."

"From what I gathered from your conversation, she wanted you to spend the night with her."

Frank seemed genuinely shocked. His eyebrows rose. "She just lost her husband, your brother. I don't think she'd ..."

Kailey nodded and forced a weak smile. "Unfortunately, I believe it's exactly what she was insinuating."

"I thought you didn't know her."

Kailey almost burst into laughter at how naïve he was, but she managed to prevent the laugh from surfacing. "I don't know her, but I do know her *type*."

Frank rubbed his wedding band. "But I'm married."

"I don't think she minds. In fact, that might be why she targeted you."

In disbelief, he simply shook his head and ran a nervous hand through his hair. "Wow. I never even picked that up on my radar."

Oblivious. Naïve. Groveler. How'd you ever pass the state bar?

Kailey smiled, flashing her cute dimples. "Can I ask you something?"

"Sure."

"How long did you work with my brother?"

Frank straightened his tie. He started walking down the narrow blacktop, and she followed alongside him. "For the past four years. We were both hired by the Langston Law Firm at the same time."

"Were you close friends?" she asked.

He shrugged. "We had a beer every now and then. Played racquetball once a week until he got married. We were friends, but I wouldn't say that we were ever *tight*."

"Did he act differently lately?"

"Yeah." He nodded while his eyes deepened in remembrance. "Yeah. I suppose you could say that."

"How?"

"He was often late to our morning office meetings or for his court hearings at the courthouse. He had always been prompt until just these past few months. But more often than not, he was too distracted. He had dark circles and bags beneath his eyes, like he hadn't slept much. Very fatigued."

Kailey wiped a tear from her eye. "The last time I spoke with him via Skype he didn't look well. He was pale and much thinner."

Frank shook his head and glanced toward Vincent's grave where a well-dressed elderly gentleman stood. Two shapely young ladies that could have easily been his granddaughters clung to his arms like intimate lovers. "You think you know a lot about a person when you work with them. He never seemed like the type of person that would kill himself."

"I don't believe he did."

Frank looked into her eyes. "Are you implying foul play?"

She shrugged.

"The news said that he committed suicide," he said. He gave a nod toward the old man at Vincent's grave. "And that's what Mr. Langston told us, too."

"That's the owner of your law firm?"

He nodded.

"The media is known to lie or not supply all the facts. Usually, they'll say anything that helps their ratings."

"I agree. But no one had any reason to kill Vincent. He was a public defender and got the majority of his clients' sentences dismissed or greatly reduced. Who do you suspect killed him?"

"She just drove away in his BMW after you unknowingly declined her invitation to spend the night with her," Kailey replied.

"You think Cassie killed him?" he asked in a near whisper.

"I have strong suspicions."

Frank frowned. "Why? You said that you have never met her."

"I know. I never have."

"What makes you suspect her?"

"For one, she spent a lot of time today trying to gain sympathy from everyone else but she never shed a single solitary tear."

"But—she *was* crying."

Kailey shook her head. "No. She pretended to be crying, but look at your shirt."

Frank glanced down.

"She left red lipstick on your shirt, but there's no mascara. No wetness from tears. I know some mascaras are water resistant but I watched her closely. She kept her face covered with a handkerchief most of the time, but her eyes never moistened. Hell, even after all of her performance, her nose wasn't even runny. You ever *really* cry?"

He nodded. "Of course."

She didn't doubt that at all. "Then you know what I'm talking about. Your eyes water. Your nose runs uncontrollably even after you have stopped crying. Think about it. Did she ever actually do either?"

Frank's eyes narrowed as he thought. He shoved his hands into his pockets. "Now that you mention it, I never really saw any tears. Damn, how could I have been so blind? She started flirting with me, and I guess I didn't pay attention." His face flushed red from embarrassment.

"See? She's trying too hard to play the part of the grieving widow, which is why I believe she killed him. She wants the pity and attention from everyone. She tried to make you feel like a knight in shining armor, so you'd rescue her. You almost fell for it."

"Unfortunately, I almost did," he replied, loosening his tie.

"Did you ever meet her before today?"

"Yeah. She was never a stranger at the law firm. She even came to the Christmas party last month, some other functions, and popped in for lunch almost every day. But I never really spoke with her privately though. Do you know where your brother met her?"

"A nightclub. Nocturnal Trinity?" She frowned as she said it. "I think that's the name."

Frank nodded. "Probably so. It's only a few blocks from the courthouse."

"You go there often?"

"No. I've never been there. With a wife and a teenage stepson, I'm not frequent to the partying scene but I hear that it's a nice, if not an *odd*, place. Easy to lose yourself inside from what I hear."

Kailey frowned, studied his eyes, and crossed her arms, trying to keep from shivering in the cold. "What do you mean?"

"Several large dance floors with lots of people inside. Most of the patrons are friendly, but this place attracts a lot of dark people."

A slight breeze scraped brown leaves across the narrow road. She pulled her thin jacket tighter, and rubbed her arms for more warmth. Frank eyes shifted with a bit of uneasiness. They glanced back at the gravesite and the elderly gentleman no longer stood there.

Kailey scanned the area and found the old man getting into the back of a silver limousine with the help of his driver. The two young women got into the limo, too. The rear tag stated: Langston.

She turned her attention back to Frank. Crossing her arms, she looked up at him and asked, "The people are dark? In what way?"

Frank ran his hand through his hair. He lowered his voice. "Underground club activities. Some refer to that nightclub as a den of deviants. Every major city has at least one club like that, from what I *hear*."

She knew what he said was true. She had known of similar places in Boston. She and her college roommate took the train to Salem once a month to visit one. But those clubs were located in the darker districts of those two cities where most authority figures seldom frequented and where the orthodox feared to explore.

"Why would they have their nightclub so close to a courthouse?" she asked.

He shrugged. "Sometimes the best way for someone to become invisible is to be right out in the open. It draws less suspicion."

True.

"I can't imagine the local officials allowing such a place to operate."

Frank smiled and headed for his Rolls. "Those living on the dark side tend to be found everywhere. Attorneys, police, and even judges are amongst them."

"In Seattle?" she asked in a near whisper.

Frank's face grew grim. With nervousness in his eyes, he simply nodded.

"So if my brother met Cassie at Nocturnal Trinity, I wonder why he went there in the first place?"

"There's no telling. He may have gone to talk to one of his clients. Not too long ago, he represented a client who had connections to the occult and witchcraft. Perhaps he was invited for a drink and while there, that's when he met Cassie."

"I suppose. But there's a world of difference between someone in the occult and those who practice witchcraft."

He studied her with curiosity and uncertainty. "I honestly don't know the difference between the two, but from what I've been told, the club does discriminate on who they allow to become a member."

Kailey cocked an eyebrow. "One has to be a member to get inside?"

"No," he said, shaking his head. "A member or one of the Founders can invite someone as a possible initiate, but a pledge enters under complete scrutiny."

"I see. Might be harder for me to get inside than I had imagined."

"Why do you wish to go there?"

Kailey sighed. "I want to find out why Vincent went and how he met Cassie."

"Be forewarned, they have been known to prey upon the innocent."

She shrugged. For a man who had never been to the club, he seemed to know quite a bit about it. But with his pansy nature, someone had probably already scared him shitless about the place. She didn't imagine it took much to horrify the man.

Frank stopped at his car. The majority of the attendees had already left. The remaining few were in their cars preparing to go. He glanced around and then he said, "Where's your vehicle?"

"I don't have one. I flew in last night and got a hotel room. I took a cab here."

"Where are you staying? I'd be happy to drop you off."

Kailey shook her head. "No. I want to stick around here a bit longer. I'd like some quiet time at my brother's grave. I wasn't able to with the large crowd earlier."

"I understand." He reached into his vest pocket and took out a business card. "You can reach me at this number anytime you need to talk to me."

"Thanks. Could I ask a favor of you?"

"Sure. What do you need?" he asked.

"Is there any way that you can let me look around inside my brother's office before Cassie does?"

He frowned while he thought about the request and nodded. "I don't see what harm it would cause for you to go into his office. Do you mind telling me why? I mean ... is there anything in particular that you're looking for?"

Kailey shrugged. "I'd just like to see if he left anything that might explain why he stopped keeping in touch with me."

"I don't see a problem with you looking around, but Cassie has already been there."

"When?"

"The day your brother died."

Kailey became uncomfortable. "Why so soon?"

"To get a copy of his will."

Her eyes narrowed. That seemed a bit untimely. "Already?"

"Yes. I suppose that adds to your suspicions as well?"

"Wouldn't it you?" she asked.

"It does now."

"Since he's my brother, I'd like a copy of his will."

Frank offered a grim smile. "I tell you what. Stop by the law office tomorrow morning, and I'll let you into his office and get you a copy of the will."

"Thanks."

Before he got into the car, he said, "Are you certain I cannot drop you off somewhere?"

"I'm fine. I need some time to process everything."

"Okay. See you tomorrow then?"

Kailey nodded. "Yes. I'll be there at nine."

Frank got into the Rolls, said a few words to his agitated stepson, and then drove slowly down the narrow cemetery road.

After he turned onto the main highway, she returned to Vincent's grave. Hot tears of sorrow, loss, and anger meandered down her cheeks. No head-stone had been set, and a mound of dirt was piled on top of the plot. Due to the soggy ground, and the current off and on showers, she assumed the headstone would be erected after the soil firmed.

Never had she felt so alone. Vincent was dead, and she had no friends in Seattle. Her closest friends lived in Boston. Her childhood friends in the modestly rural area near Sweetwater, Tennessee, where she had grown up, had probably moved to other parts of the country like she had. Even with the modern social media age, she had not heard from any of them. She doubted any of them remembered her.

The gray mists ceased, but the heavy fog remained. The bleakness strangely comforted her. Today was not a day for the sun to shine, and respectfully, nature had obliged her. She saw no celebration in death. Finding the actual truth, however, was a victory dance in the making, but the finish line was nowhere in sight. Hell, she wasn't even certain where she needed to start.

"Nocturnal Trinity," she whispered. She wondered if Frank was correct and that her brother had gone to talk to a former client at the nightclub, or had something more sinister occurred there?

The nightclub seemed the most logical place to visit first, since the night was approaching. She wasn't able to stop by the attorney's office until the next morning anyway. Being a stranger in Seattle, she realized that any investigating she did into her brother's death possibly brought direct danger to her life. It was essential for her to tread carefully and be vigilant at all times because she didn't have anyone she could absolutely trust to rescue her if dire circumstances arose.

"Whatever happens," she said, standing at the edge of his grave, "I'll be back. Either to tell you of my success or they'll bury me in the spot beside you."

Kailey took a deep breath. She called the taxi service that had brought her to the cemetery. With determination she walked away from the grave and headed down the narrow blacktop so the taxi driver could easily spot her whenever he arrived.

With all the events that had transpired over the past few days, she needed something strong to drink to help ease her nerves, which also provided the best excuse for going to Nocturnal Trinity. She'd rather become dead drunk than end up dead, but mixing alcohol with anything often caused more problems than it was worth. To get to the truth, she needed to take some risks. That was how investigative reporters dug up the grit for their news stories, which was why she had pursued that field. Everyone had skeletons in the closet or some dirt that couldn't be washed away, and for some unknown reason, discovering the dirty laundry of someone else was always worth tossing a few bucks to read, even if there was no real relevance in knowing. Gossip was always hot.

Nocturnal Trinity might prove to be the place where she could unlock the mysteries to her questions or quite possibly end her curiosity forever.

Kailey looked around the cemetery. Normally people felt uneasy about being alone in the midst of all these graves, but she liked the quiet and brief bit of isolation. She crossed her arms and closed her eyes, listening to the wind whistle through the branches. She didn't know of a more peaceful place.

When she opened her eyes and turned, she noticed the taxi cab approaching. She stepped to the side of the blacktop and waited. Once she left the quiet of the cemetery, she believed nothing in her life would ever be peaceful again, not until she became a permanent resident in this cemetery like her brother.

CHAPTER 2

*R*iding in the back of the cab, Kailey stared out the window. Her cell phone ringtone played, "Abracadabra" by the Steve Miller Band. She quickly answered.

"Hey," Kailey said.

"How are you holding up, hon?" Raven Hawkins asked in her throaty voice.

Kailey loved to hear her roommate talk. Her unique voice resulted from years of singing in her high school choral group. Once she enrolled in college, she fronted a Goth punk band for about a year before she strained her vocal chords and had to quit. "The best that I can, Raven. It's not been easy."

"I know. I'm so sorry. When are you coming back to Boston?"

"Not for a while."

"Why not?"

Tears welled in Kailey's eyes. She remained silent for more than a minute. Finally, she said, "I have some things that need to be taken care of."

"Like what? Wait ... you still don't think she killed your brother, do you?"

Kailey explained how Cassie had acted at the burial and the scathing look Cassie had given her. She also mentioned what she had discussed with Frank, too.

"Did you even get a chance to talk to her?" Raven asked.

"No. Not that doing so would change my feelings about the situation. I'm certain she's the one responsible."

"Don't you think that you should at least talk to her first? I mean, a lot of times we learn a lot more about a person by her expressions, especially eye contact."

"Eye contact? Raven, if looks could kill, I'd be dead."

"Talk to her."

"Oh, I plan to talk to her," Kailey replied. "Just ... the cemetery didn't seem the appropriate place, especially after the way she flew off the handle. If she reacted like that toward me, they might have been looking for a place to bury *her* body."

"You're right. It wasn't the best place. But—"

"Raven, a face-to-face conversation with her probably won't change my mind."

"Hon, I know how upset you've been over the past two months ..."

"Raven, you saw my brother the last time I Skyped with him. His eyes were sunk in. He was so tired looking. He never even hinted of a smile."

"Yes. His aura was being drained. By what, I'm not quite certain. That's why I'm concerned about you being there all alone."

"I'm going to be okay."

"I suppose the possibility of you staying at your brother's house is out of the question now?"

Kailey half chuckled. "Oh, definitely."

"Where will you stay?"

"Tonight I'm still at the Hilton. I will go shopping for an apartment tomorrow."

"Without me? That's sounds like fun. Maybe I should free up my schedule and come out?"

"As much as I'd love to have you with me, I really need to sort through all this."

"Alone?" Raven asked, disappointed.

"Yes."

"That's not healthy or safe."

"Why not?"

Raven replied, "As your roommate, I've come to know you quite well over the past four years. You won't let up on this until you know the truth."

"No, I won't."

"See? Then you need some outside help, and I freely offer my services."

Kailey smiled. She loved how Raven always wanted to protect her. Since

Kailey was only five feet, three inches, she believed Raven viewed her at a disadvantage and treated her like a defenseless little sister. That was something Kailey had come to love about Raven.

"I'm not going to allow myself to get into trouble," Kailey said.

Raven gave a breathy sigh through the phone. "Trouble tends to find you."

"Since when?"

"I'm *joking*! I know you've always acted prim and proper."

"I can take care of myself," Kailey said. "I may be short ..."

"Don't even remind me about your kickboxing and MMA wannabe contender dreams."

"Those dreams aren't dead. I'm still young enough to start my official fighting record. I've won amateur bouts already. Besides, I pinned you down, remember?"

Raven laughed. "And I enjoyed every second of it, hon."

Kailey blushed, closed her eyes, and placed her palm to her forehead.

"Do you have any leads?" Raven asked. "I mean, other than just your *suspicions* about his wife?"

"Actually, yes. I'm going to the nightclub where my brother met that ..."

"Soul-leech?"

"I was actually thinking of a word that starts with a capital B."

Raven burst into loud laughter, enough that Kailey took the phone away from her ear until her friend quieted down. "Call her what you will, but someone was leeching Vincent's soul and draining him of his energy. I can't really fault you for believing she's the guilty party. So what's the name of this nightclub?"

"Nocturnal Trinity."

"Hold on, one sec."

"Why?"

"Googling."

Kailey shook her head. She watched the sidewalks as she rode to her hotel. A lot of people were headed in different directions. None seemed glum about the gray misty evening. She figured people here were used to the lack of direct sunlight and probably never gave the damper days a second thought.

"Oh, you have me *sooo* jealous, hon," Raven said.

"Why?"

"Nocturnal Trinity is definitely a club I'd love to scope out."

Kailey laughed.

"Damn," Raven said with a gasp. "I spoke too soon."

"What?"

"I don't think you should venture there alone."

"Why not?"

"Their symbol. It gives off some bad vibes. *Very* bad vibes."

"I'm only going for a couple drinks and to look around. No major snooping."

"No. I'm getting a sick feeling about this, dear. You definitely *don't* want to go there alone, especially not tonight."

"Why not tonight?"

"We have a full moon," Raven replied. "Well, technically it's actually completely full tomorrow."

"With the rain and overcast sky, it's doubtful anyone here will see it."

"That makes no difference."

"I *know*, but I'll be fine all the same."

Raven sighed. Kailey was certain her friend had included a dramatic rolling of the eyes like she always did. "Kailey, do you still have the protective amulet I blessed for you?"

"Of course. It's on the silver chain around my neck."

"Don't lose it. Keep it on you."

Kailey swallowed hard. "Raven, you're starting to scare me."

"I hope so."

"Don't do this to me."

"I'm strictly trying to warn you. That place isn't for someone like you."

"Like me? What the hell do you mean by that? And this place *is* ... for you?"

"You know what I am and how long I've practiced."

"I know."

"Even I wouldn't want to go in there alone, but if I did, I'm much more prepared for handling it than you are."

"I just want to look around."

"Kailey, I'd wait until you have someone you trust to go with you."

"Like you?"

"Yes! Especially me," Raven said gleefully.

"I understand your concern, but this is too urgent. Besides, if I don't find anything that helps me tonight, I will go visit Vincent's office tomorrow morning and take the first flight back to Boston."

"You promise?"

"I promise."

"Okay, but keep your phone where you can dial me should anything go wrong."

"You know that I will, but with the distance between us, what good will it do?" Kailey asked.

"So I can keep my sanity? I'm worried about you."

"Then light a candle and say a prayer for me."

"One has been lit ever since you boarded the plane. But hon, the distance between us makes me less effective."

"How so?"

"My nerves, for one thing. It's harder for me to concentrate when I know you're not nearby."

Kailey shook her head. "You're exactly like an overprotective sister."

"Really? That's all?"

Kailey started to reply but remained silent.

"You know I love you, right?" Raven said.

"I know. I love you, too."

"No. I really still *love* you."

Kailey sighed softly. "Raven, we've talked about this many times before. Why are you bringing it up ... *again*? Now?"

"Because I miss you. With you being away, my feelings for you are stronger than ever."

"You understand that the love I hold for you is different than what you hold for me. You're like a sister to me. Because of that, I can never step past that threshold. I treasure you as my closest friend, but it can never be romantic love."

Raven broke into quiet sobs, which made Kailey ache inside. She always knew that Raven was attracted to her and wanted to be intimate. Kailey had told Raven upfront that she didn't feel the same way, but what Kailey had said wasn't exactly true. She had tried to convince herself that her feelings were what she felt for a close sibling and nothing more because she liked having Raven as a close friend and a roommate. However, she worried that once they ever became intimate that relationship might somehow sour, and if so, she'd lose Raven altogether.

Early in their first semester they had gone to a sorority party, gotten tipsy, and started kissing. After a few seconds, Kailey pulled away from Raven and shook her head. The fear of losing Raven washed through her. So Kailey lied and told Raven that she didn't feel enough passion to proceed to be anything other than friends. But deep inside, she really loved Raven and often she had intimate dreams about them passionately kissing and petting one another.

Raven had looked hurt, but the following day, she acted like the incident had never even happened. Kailey suspected this was to ease the tension until they knew one another better, and perhaps that Kailey would have a change of heart. Inside of giving in to her true emotions, Kailey kept the wall between them.

"Am I the reason why you're staying there?" Raven asked in a sobbing, broken voice.

"No-o-o. But mentally, I have a lot to sort through. Please don't cry. You know I hold you as my dearest, most important, friend. I always will."

"I know, dear. I only wish that you ... felt what I do inside for you."

Kailey bit her lower lip. "I honestly wish it could be more from my end. I really do."

"Maybe one day?"

"I can't promise that."

"I know."

Kailey watched several individuals wearing hoodies walk down the sidewalk. Hoodies seemed commonplace. But three individuals in particular caught her attention. She turned and studied them through the rear taxi window. One man with two young women. Because of their hoodies, their pale faces were only visible from the nose down. Prominent piercings decorated their cheeks, noses, and their black painted lips. The man wore black tattered jeans and the two women wore skin-tight yoga pants, the equivalent of body paint, in her opinion.

She did a second take because she thought her eyes were playing tricks on her. The two girls appeared to be tethered to him, and they were. Hemp ropes were tied around each woman's waist and tied to his wrists.

Damn role players.

"Are you still there?" Kailey asked.

"Yes, dear. Always for you."

"What is it about Nocturnal Trinity's symbol that bothers you? Do you know what it represents? Is it occultic or pagan?"

"It's an odd combination. They're blatantly bold to prominently display it on a sign where the entire downtown can see it. Of course, the majority of people that see it won't even have a clue as to what it means."

Kailey said, "Vincent's colleague told me that some of the regular patrons are judges, attorneys, and even police."

"Then those people are probably members, which isn't a good thing for you since you're looking for information they probably want to remain secret."

"What does the symbol represent?"

"It's a complex insignia but if what it represents is actually true, it is very dangerous combination. For one, the nightclub has trinity in its name, which at first glance lets you know that three things are united into one."

"Oka-a-ay. Can you just cut to the chase, please? I'm nervous enough as it is. *What three things?*" Kailey asked.

"Demons, witches, and the undead. Three separate orders that for some reason have chosen to join into one faction."

Kailey rolled her eyes, and huffed. "Raven ... Seriously?"

"I *am* serious. You just did my eye-roll, didn't you?"

"Yes," she replied, somewhat embarrassed and trying to suppress a smile. She missed Raven more than she cared to admit. They had been roommates long enough that she was picking up Raven's habits and even across country, Raven called her on it.

"Look," Raven said. "I'm telling you exactly what this symbol represents, and if that's accurate and not merely my speculation, that's a dangerous place to enter. For you, me, or anyone that's not a member."

"I'll be careful," Kailey said.

"Hon, can you tell me one thing?"

"What, Raven?"

"How do you even plan to get into the club when it's members only?"

"I don't know. I'm sure there has to be a way."

Raven exhaled an aggregated sigh. "Of course there is, but not a *safe* one."

"You worry too much."

"You, dear, don't worry *enough*. Here's the thing, sweetie. Let's say that you find someone who takes you inside as a pledge. Do you understand what that means?"

"I have to buy him a drink or dance with him?"

"No," Raven replied. "It means that you owe that person something. Now, he or *she* might accept a drink as payment, if you're lucky. But I doubt anyone will settle so cheaply."

"And if I'm not lucky?"

"That price might be your life."

"Don't over exaggerate."

"I'm not."

Frustrated and growing even more anxious, Kailey glanced up at the back of the taxi driver's head. His head was tilted to the side. He was obviously eavesdropping on her conversation. She lowered her voice into a whisper. "Why do you suspect such a huge price for being invited into this particular nightclub?"

"There's a hierarchy in establishments like that. In order to rise in rank and prove their loyalty, sacrifices are often made."

"I went to some pretty dark clubs with you in Boston and Salem. We never encountered any problems like that. I've never heard of any club like this."

"Every place we visited paled in comparison to the culture that thrives inside Nocturnal Trinity. I would have never taken you into such a dangerous place. You know that."

"How do you know so much about them? You got all that information from Google?" Kailey asked.

"No, dear. Being a witch, I'm always studying and seeking information. Not just from the Internet. But in my coven, there are elder witches that help keep us informed, especially when new groups emerge."

"And have they ever mentioned Nocturnal Trinity?"

"No. This group is new to me, but their symbol is the biggest clue. It's not simply a marketing logo. Power oozes off it. Some pretty bad mojo."

"Like a curse?"

"No, it's a warning as well as the leaders flaunting their power. You're not mentally or spiritually equipped to handle these folks. Hon, please go to the airport and get a ticket to Boston. Come home. You *don't* belong there."

Kailey gritted her teeth. "If I come back to Boston without knowing the truth, I'll resent you for the rest of my life. You know that, right?"

Raven became silent.

"I know that you love me," Kailey said. "I understand that you have my safety at heart, but I need to find out if that bitch killed my brother or if someone else did. Can't you understand that? If you don't, that tells me that your feelings toward me are based on selfishness and *not* love."

"You're right. I am selfish. But I do love you and will never give my heart to another person. My heart belongs to you. I constantly worry about you. I need you in my life, even if we're always *just* friends, but I've always hoped it matures into something more. Unfortunately, with what you're seeking to uncover, you'll learn firsthand that all these dangers are very real. I'm too far away to help you so please be safe."

"I didn't mean to sound so harsh," Kailey said softly. "I'm on edge as it is.

I will question everything I see and hear. Skepticism is my game. Following my inner voice has protected me for many years."

Often she talked to herself. Her skeptical nature caused a tiny voice to whisper inside her mind, sometimes chiding her through cynicism and at other times, silently berating those around her for their inherent stupidity.

Raven sniffled. "That might be enough to get you through tonight."

"I know how to defend myself, Raven. I've trained for years."

"In a physical fight, I'd bet on you every time. But when you're dealing with the supernatural, you're the underdog. Don't forget that."

"I understand. But you know I always carry Sparky."

Raven laughed softly. "That's better than nothing. Make sure that Taser has fresh batteries."

"It does."

"Please be careful, Kailey."

"*Okay*. But would you please stop worrying?"

"Not until you're back here, safe and sound."

Kailey groaned and shook her head. "You're still acting like you're my mother. God! We're the same age."

"*Goddess*, dear. And I'm sorry. Look, I will talk to some of my sisters in the coven about the symbol and see what advice they give. You call me if you get inside that nightclub and again after you get back to your hotel room."

"I will."

"Promise."

Kailey groaned. "I promise."

"I truly hope that you decide to return to Boston tomorrow."

"Let's see what happens tonight."

"Be careful."

"O-k-a-a-y," Kailey replied with a long exasperated sigh.

"Blessings to you, my dear. I love you," Raven said softly before quickly ending the call.

Kailey stared at her phone. Raven's picture covered the main screen. Her photogenic twenty-two-year-old friend winked and puckered her red lips in a kiss. Her short black hair was spiked with pink tips at the ends. She wore a silver witch's pentagram and the symbol was also tattooed on her left wrist. Her dark complexion came from her Italian heritage and wasn't something Kailey could ever match with a spray tan, even though she had once tried. In every respect, she thought Raven was the most beautiful young woman she'd ever seen. Already she terribly missed the sound of her voice.

Even though Raven was in her early twenties, she acted much older. She was mature and level headed, except when it came to how she expressed her obsessive love for Kailey. Kailey hoped that the distance between them might lessen Raven's infatuation. Raven fretted over her like a mother would a daughter, and for a while, because Kailey's parents had died when she was twelve, she liked having that type of security—that someone watching over her best interests. And, at other times, like now, she felt like a rebellious teenager trying to break free of that stern motherly grasp.

Whether Raven would accept it or not, Kailey needed to be on her own for a while. No matter what transpired at the club, she believed that she would still look for an apartment the next day. She needed some independence without the chokehold of *love* Raven kept exhibiting.

Kailey glanced up and caught the gaze of the driver in his rearview mirror. She wasn't certain how long he had been looking at her. His eyes made her uneasy, but at the moment, she didn't believe it mattered who was driving. After all the talk about Nocturnal Trinity, its possible supernatural ties, and the types of people that frequented the nightclub, she was apprehensive, almost on the fringe of becoming borderline paranoid.

"You need help getting into Nocturnal Trinity?" he asked. His voice was deep and gravelly. With the heavy overcast skies and a gloomy fog settling, she wasn't able to see his facial features clearly, just his eyes.

"Nah," she replied, "I'm cool."

"Wasn't trying to eavesdrop, young lady. Honestly. But it does kinda come with the job." He waved his hand showing the open space between the front and back seat.

"That's okay."

"Seems your friend must have advised you not to go?"

Kailey nodded and stared out the window. "Yep. That's her call."

"You might want to listen to your friend."

"Why? What do you know about the place?"

"As a cab driver, you hear and see a lot of strange things. Let's just say that I avoid that area after midnight. Most cab drivers nowadays do."

"Why's that?"

He cleared his throat of what sounded like thick phlegm. The thick smell of cigarette smoke stuck to the cab's upholstery, indicating that he was a heavy smoker. He voice was coarse when he spoke. "Well, for me, I don't like cleaning up blood out of my backseat."

She cringed and scooted closer to the door, looking at the seat. "Blood?"

He nodded. "Yep. The last person I picked up from that place had suffered a stabbing or something. Not rightly sure. The man was holding his throat and blood was seeping through his fingers. A lot of blood. Messed up my vinyl seats. I'm surprised he hadn't passed out or died. I swore after that I'd never take late calls for pick ups from that area again."

The taxi slowed and turned into the Hilton's parking lot. She was greatly relieved. She quickly paid the fare and tipped the driver, and started to turn away.

"Wait a sec, missy."

"What? Did I not pay enough?"

The hotel lights illuminated the man's face, and he didn't appear sinister at all. He smiled in such a way that she thought of her deceased father. This man's deep dimples revealed that he smiled a lot. "Here. Take this."

Nervously, she extended her hand and opened it. He placed a silver cross pendant onto her palm. She looked uneasily at the cross and cocked a brow. "What's this for?"

He shrugged. "For good luck."

Kailey studied the cross for a moment and shook her head. *Really? Luck?*

He eased off the brake. He smiled through the open window. "Take care of yourself, kid. Not trying to scare you, but I don't want to read about you in tomorrow's paper."

Those words hung in her mind. Chills shot up her spine.

She watched him circle through the parking lot, and once he drove onto the street, she hurried through the sliding front doors of the hotel. She went to the desk to reserve the room for another night until she decided whether to hunt for an apartment or to return to Boston tomorrow. Between the warnings Raven had given her, and now a stern admonition from a complete stranger, she wondered if she had taken on more than she could handle alone. But justice for Vincent outweighed these subtle underlying fears. She wasn't ready to leave until she discovered what had really happened to Vincent.

Once Kailey was inside her room, she brought up the Internet on her laptop and found Nocturnal Trinity's webpage. Glancing through various pictures of the dance scenes at Nocturnal Trinity, she realized almost all of the people wore dark clothes and Gothic makeup. She still wore her dark clothes from the funeral. Other than her dress being overly fancy, she thought she might be okay. Suitable makeup to blend in might be more difficult.

She didn't realize how tired and stressed she was from the long flight and laying her brother to rest. After calling a car rental service for later in the evening, she stared at the nightclub website photos until she drifted off to sleep.

CHAPTER 3

*A*fter Kailey awakened from a nap, she glanced at her phone. She'd slept four hours.

"How?" she groaned, rolling off the side of the bed.

She stood, straightened her dress with her hands, and hurried to the restroom. She needed to check her makeup.

Since the cab driver had expressed that most drivers refused to go anywhere near Nocturnal Trinity after dark, she had called a car rental place before she had accidentally dozed off. She expected them to deliver the car at any moment as the man she spoke with said that he'd bring one out after they closed for the evening.

The last thing she wanted was to leave the nightclub on foot. The streets were unfamiliar to her and walking after dark for several blocks was out of the question, regardless of which city she was in.

Looking in the mirror, she noticed her hair-sprayed hair was twisted. She grabbed a hair pick and made it less unkempt. Sleep had lessened her building fear of entering Nocturnal Trinity alone, temporarily at least.

Bravery wasn't an inherent trait for Kailey, but to bury her suspicions and perhaps discover the truth behind her brother's death, she'd face whatever evil resided inside Nocturnal Trinity. Of course, dying after learning the truth seemed a wasted effort that she didn't plan to undergo.

She wasn't ignoring Raven's stern warnings; but deep inside, Kailey's gnawing fear struggled to break through her determination to make her cower and flee Seattle's dark underground society. She refused.

Thinking about her conversation with Raven, she knew her friend was right. Physically, she might be able to defend herself from an attacker, but not against someone that might have powerful supernatural abilities.

Looking at the mirror, she applied another layer of mascara to darken her eyes a bit more. This was when she needed Raven's help. Her friend could transform an innocent looking girl into a dark Marilyn Manson sideshow freak by using her makeup artist abilities. Kailey, on the other hand, barely succeeded in making herself look like a caricature from one of Tim Burton's animation movies.

Another thing Kailey lacked was having tattoos of any sort. She had entertained getting one when Raven got the witch's pentagram inked on her left wrist. Now, she wished she had. At least something. No tattoos made her stand out to the others, especially at this nightclub, according to all the pictures on their website. They'd know immediately that she didn't belong.

Of course, any members associated with the three orders would probably sense her presence immediately. She had learned about demons from religious students that frantically begged that she attend church to save her soul from the devil and his demons. Since Raven was a witch, she understood that members of the craft were probably worldwide. But the undead wasn't something that she understood. What did Raven mean by that? When she talked to Raven again, she planned to find out exactly what an undead was.

When her cell phone rang, she jerked and gasped before reaching to answer it.

"Kailey?"

"Yes?"

"It's Donnie. I'm here with your rental and the paperwork you need to sign."

"Thanks. On my way down."

K ailey drove the black four-door sedan. Rain sluiced the windshield in between the swipe of the wipers. The interior lights were light blue. She played pop music on the radio at a low volume so she could hear and properly follow the dictated GPS directions to Nocturnal Trinity from her phone. It had been several months since she had driven. She had forgotten how pleasurable and empowering it felt to drive without sharing a bus or train seat. She wished that the rain would slack because she'd love to ride with the side window partway down. Being hot natured, the winter air was refreshing. With the overcast sky, the night seemed darker than most, but she guessed her slight paranoia made her draw such a conclusion.

She slowed when the GPS indicated the nightclub was only a block away. As luck would have it, there weren't any parking spots on either side of the street. She was forced to enter the parking garage and didn't find a parking place until she was on the third level.

So much for a quick exit.

After Kailey parked the car, she memorized the spot number. Level 3. Slot 47.

Nervously she listened and glanced around. Hearing no one, she hurried to the elevator, hit the button, and waited for the doors to open.

On the ground floor, she paused and looked out. Droves of darkly dressed, overly pale-skinned individuals walked out of the parking garage and headed across the street where two long lines of people waited for the club bouncers to check their IDs. When she reached the closest line, however, she found out differently. This long line was for the hopefuls, the ones who *weren't* members. These individuals hoped to catch the attention of incoming members that might invite them as their guests. They were either skimpily dressed or flaunted bizarre occult tattoos and jewelry. Prominent zippers and buckles seemed to be the norm on almost every leather and vinyl jacket and skirt. Almost every individual had painted his or her fingernails black. Tiny chrome crosses twinkled beneath the faint streetlights. She assumed a Hot Topic store must be nearby and these interesting people kept them overflowing with business.

Regardless, she felt underdressed and exposed. At first glance, she wondered how anyone could be an ugly duckling in this crowd, but she was the misfit and the one out of place. Even if she had matched the others' attire perfectly, she knew she would still stand out as an imposter. If nothing else, her eyes revealed it.

A half block away was shorter line. **Members Only**. Security checked ID badges with the utmost scrutiny, but that line kept actively flowing through the door. Perhaps it was due to the misting rain, but none of the members seemed interested in visiting the guest line and choosing someone to enter with them.

Kailey stood in the last spot of the extremely long murmuring line, wishing she had brought an umbrella and her jacket. The blowing mists grew heavier. Water dripped off the awnings. Other people were still streaming their way toward her line, fighting past the homeless dirty beggars, so she didn't believe she'd be at the end of the line much longer.

A third door beyond the active line displayed a large black plaque with crimson letters that read: **Founders Only**. No one other than the oversized muscle-bound bouncers stood near that door.

A silver limo pulled to the curb in front of the door. The bouncers at that door smiled and opened the door for those she considered to be *The Chosen* while the limo driver courteously pulled open the back limo door.

Three men and three women emerged elegantly dressed. No tattoos. No piercings. At least none that were visible. The well-groomed men sported expensive suits and the women wore fancy ball gowns. The way they carried themselves expressed aristocratic royalty. Their haughtiness made them appear to be above everyone else, and those in the long line were the lesser souls, and possible enthusiastic servants.

Everyone in the line hushed, unable to turn their gazes from them. She almost expected flashes from cellphones and cameras to ignite, but none did. Several signs on the wall forbid the taking of any pictures. Doing so was an automatic lifetime ban from Nocturnal Trinity. Knowing the short attention span of most social media-lytes, she was surprised to see the crowd's obedience.

Kailey had never seen people so beautiful. Even from her distance, she was attracted to them, wanted to be closer, to touch them, and like those pleading for their attention with their fixated eyes near the front of the line, she actually hoped one of them chose her. She didn't understand this sudden urgency and undying desperation to want to please them. Her heart raced. She felt faint. These unexpected sensations frightened her for a moment, and then she found herself with a fixated need tugging at her heart, her mind, and her soul. Never had she craved anything more than wanting to see what was *beyond* the **Founders Only** door.

Kailey wondered why Raven had insisted the place was such a danger. These six people didn't appear to be individuals set out to inflict damage upon anyone else. From the crowd's reaction, they weren't any different than famous actors and actresses. Hot models. She didn't detect anything evil in nature about them at all. She was captivated by their overwhelming charisma and eroticism that seemed to ooze from them.

Her building lust waned and almost turned to immediate sorrow. She thought her opportunity to enter Nocturnal Trinity was gone. Five of the six had passed through the door with hardly a glance toward the hopefuls.

The last woman—a tall slender brunette—dressed in a royal blue gown stopped at the foot of the stairs. She took a step back and faced the line of desperate faces. Her alabaster skin was flawless. A smile curled her full lips. She left the stairs and walked toward the line. Her fluid-like movements made her appear to hover slightly above the sidewalk as she approached.

Her prominent plucked brows, high cheekbones, and narrow-bridge nose made her stately and elegant like a princess destined to take a throne. The men and women gasped at her alluring beauty. Their pleas for her attention silenced, and they slightly bowed their heads with humility, hoping she chose them.

The woman paused beside a man wearing a black hoodie. Her mouth formed a delicate smile. She gently placed her hand upon his, nodded, and he lifted the rope to leave the line to stand next to her. She nodded, and his two tethered girls joined him.

Kailey took a quick breath. She recognized the trio as the ones she had passed during her cab ride hours ago. How long had they been standing in line?

The brunette continued down the line of people, studying each with intense scrutiny, gazing into their eyes, and she appeared to be reading their facial expressions to know their true thoughts. Occasionally, she placed a gentle finger beneath one's chin, lifted it, and frowned, passing on to the next person. None complained about her choosiness, but a couple of individuals fainted from her gentle touch.

Midway down the line, she chose a young blonde girl with high pink-dyed pigtails, pink net stockings, and pink platform shoes. She wore a black miniskirt and a shredded tank top. The girl stepped from the line and joined the trio that continued tagging along behind the member.

The lady glided farther down the line, and when she was fifteen or so people away from Kailey, their eyes met. The female founder ignored those that stood between them and hurried to where Kailey patiently waited. The closer she came, the faster Kailey's heart beat. The woman's powerful aura thrust forward in a wave that pushed against Kailey and the people nearest her. Kailey righted her feet to prevent toppling backwards.

"And you," the woman said to Kailey with a wide smile. "You're … different than all the others. I sense it. You'll do *lovely*."

The lady winked at her. Excitement rushed through Kailey and made her lightheaded. Everything around her seemed to spin momentarily, and she thought she'd lose consciousness like some of the others until the lady gently touched her hand. Power jolted and rushed through her, forcing her to take a sharp breath from the elation.

The lady headed back to the **Founders Door** with her chosen pledges. Once she turned her back to the faithful people in line, they immediately beckoned for her attention. When she reached the two huge bodyguards, she waved a hand in the air. "Enough!"

Everyone went silent. Kailey's ears rang.

"These are all I choose for the evening!" she said.

Seconds later, one bodyguard opened the door, and the lady passed through with Kailey and the other guests. When they entered, she saw no light. A strange empty silence enclosed them. Darkness. And suddenly all the warnings Raven had given her came to mind. She became extremely nervous, and mentally put herself on guard.

ailey hesitantly followed the lady through the dark narrow corridor, wondering why no laser lights flared various colors. No loud music thundered. The darkness prevented her from even seeing her hand in front of her face. She was reminded of those funhouse enclosures where one wandered through complete darkness, constantly worrying about what might leap out to scare her. The uncertainty of where she walked frightened her more than one of those mazes.

Her heartbeat thudded in her ears, and she wished Raven stood beside her.

The air seemed thicker, warmer, and scented with jasmine and perhaps cinnamon. The old floorboards creaked beneath her feet. Where was the woman taking them?

For a moment she wondered if they were even inside the nightclub. She wanted to ask where they were, but since the others remained silent, she decided not to ask. All sorts of bizarre thoughts crept through her mind. Human trafficking was one of them.

The lady stopped suddenly. Kailey bumped into her, lost her footing, and almost tumbled face first to the floor. But the thin lady grabbed Kailey's arm with incredible firm strength and with hardly any effort, prevented Kailey from falling.

"Careful, dear," she whispered in a rich foreign accent. "Don't want you bruised. We're almost there."

Kailey wanted to ask, "Where?" but the soothing tone of this lady's voice lulled her. But it was more than just her voice that tugged. The woman's touch was like a drug, immediately easing Kailey's worries.

The flowing waves of the woman's aura wrapped around and embraced Kailey, urged her forward, but she wasn't certain what might be happening to the others the lady had chosen from the line. Were they still behind her? She wanted to reach back but couldn't. An invisible force coaxed her to keep moving.

She didn't like the surrounding darkness. She wanted to see where she was walking. She slid her hand into her purse to grab her cellphone so she could use her flashlight App.

Her cellphone was gone.

"Where are we going?" she finally blurted out.

The woman stopped. This time Kailey didn't bump into her. She wasn't certain what had let her know the woman had stopped and stood directly in front of her, but she sensed the woman's presence. She guessed this woman's aura provided some sort of buffer radiance. Behind her the floorboards creaked. Weaker energy pressed against her back. She assumed this was from the others that had been chosen from the line.

"Young lady," she replied. "Were you not in line *hoping* to be invited?"

"Yes. Of course," Kailey said in a soft whisper, not certain if the woman had spoken aloud or directly into her mind. "But I thought this was a nightclub with dancing, music, and drinks."

"It is. Just we're going to one of the elite VIP sections."

"May I ask your name?" Kailey asked softly.

"Flora." The aristocratic tone was cold. She imagined the woman's gaze was even colder.

Flora apparently returned to walking because Kailey gently reached forward but found nothing except air. She took several steps. The floor rattled slightly, causing Kailey to reach out to the side where her hand touched the wall.

A burst of faint light shone into the narrow corridor, forcing her to shield her eyes. She became disoriented. Sweet smoke and incense drifted on the air.

Squinting, she stepped from the narrow corridor and let her eyes adjust to the light. The hoodie man and his two female companions stepped out, followed by the pink-streaked blonde.

With a gentle swipe of her hand against the round light switch, Flora dimmed the lights even more. As the lights lowered, neon purple halos glowed around the metal lampshades, which made the plush carpet appear thicker.

A half dozen black leather couches lined one wall. Fresh drinks sat on coasters at the end tables. Smoke drifted from abandoned cigarettes and incense sticks. Several crumbled joints set amongst the ashes. Round bronze tables with ice bucket insets held bottles of champagne and rich red wines.

A bald man wearing a trench coat sat on one of the couches and peered out the large windows that overlooked one of the dance floors. His solemn expression resembled someone under deep hypnosis. In the odd lighting his face resembled a corpse's. He didn't seem aware of their intrusion into this VIP room.

"Andreas," Flora said. "Where did the others go?"

He rose slowly, stretched, and when he faced them, the odd glow from the lights gave him an even more menacing appearance. He towered at least six feet six inches tall. His scarred face was stern. His cold eyes hardened. He looked like a person that got into fights a lot and probably never lost. Perhaps he was one of the founders' personal bodyguards. Or, a hit man.

"Down on the floor," he replied in a low monotone.

"Why? They were supposed to wait for me and our new guests."

"Problems arose."

Flora walked to the panoramic window and peered down. Her eyes narrowed, and she shook her head. "Guests?"

Andreas shook his head slowly. "No."

"I see. We're still at this, are we?"

Andreas gave a solemn nod.

Flora turned to Kailey and the other hopefuls. "Guests, my apologies. Please, follow Andreas. He'll lead you downstairs where you'll get free drinks of your choice. Dance. Socialize. Have the time of your lives. Perhaps at a later date, we can sit and get to know one another better."

The hoodie man and his tethered slaves headed toward Andreas.

Kailey approached Flora. "I have lost my phone."

"You left it with the man at the door," she replied.

Kailey frowned and shook her head. "No. I never did. I'd remember doing so."

"Trust me. It's there."

"I need it."

Flora shook her head. Her dark eyes were frightening to behold. Her glare peered into Kailey's eyes with such force that Kailey took a quick breath and swallowed hard. There was an unspoken threat in her harsh icy gaze. "You'll get it back when you're ready to leave. Not a moment sooner."

Kailey nodded, but she didn't like not having her phone. Without it, she had no way to contact Raven or the police, if that became necessary. A bigger problem dawned upon her. Whoever had her phone could get all of her information, her contacts, and later use the information to track her. And worse, she thought, cringing. What if Raven called to check up on her?

Dear God.

Raven would be enraged for another person to answer, especially if a man answered. She'd demand answers and want to know where Kailey was, expecting the worst. Of course, if no one answered at all ...

She hoped Raven was too busy to call because either outcome meant Raven was on the next plane out to Seattle. Kailey really didn't want to deal with *that.*

Kailey tried remembering when she entered the door with Flora, but the memory of stepping past the threshold seemed blocked from recall. She certainly didn't remember handing her phone to anyone. How could she forget someone taking her phone?

A slight tinge of pain throbbed momentarily at the base of her skull. She felt the warmth of being watched and turned.

Flora gazed into her eyes. "You've lost someone recently, haven't you?"

Tears welled in Kailey's eyes. She tried to fight them, but they came anyway.

"Someone close," Flora stated. "And *that's* why you're here."

Kailey found the strength to break eye contact and stared through the window down at the crowd. Everyone dancing seemed taken by the music and the crisscrossing rainbow laser lights. Whatever problem Andreas had indicated, she didn't see any disruption or what the commotion might have been. The crowd of people was lost in their own little worlds.

"Loss heals with time," Flora said without waiting for an answer.

How did she know?

Until Flora had mentioned it, Kailey had been more nervous than she was grieving. Her curiosity and memory loss caused her mind to shunt away the death of her brother temporarily, so how did this lady that she'd never met before know?

Raven often joked that Kailey didn't have a good poker face. Perhaps it was time she discovered how to keep her emotions hidden and bury them deeper. But most people she knew capable of doing that were cold and callous. She never wanted to be like that.

"Ah, no matter," Flora said. "Right now, follow Andreas and I to the lower floor. Enjoy yourself."

"I need my phone," Kailey said softly.

"You'll find much more suitable things here than your cellphone can possibly ever give you." She sighed and headed to the door. "This younger generation's obsessive need for technological things ... "

Andreas stood patiently waiting and holding open a narrow door. He smiled. The expression looked alien on his face.

After Kailey reached Andreas, she stepped onto the wrought steel spiral staircase and followed the blonde down. She felt isolated, and she wasn't certain what to expect when they emerged onto the dance floor. Kailey glanced back once more before exiting. She could have sworn that she saw coffins in the far corner of the room.

Six of them.

CHAPTER 5

*A*s loud as the electronic dance music pulsed, Kailey was surprised she hadn't heard or felt the slightest sound in the upstairs VIP room. Apparently they had built incredibly soundproof walls, which was good for those choosing to relax upstairs. An ominous thought occurred to her. Noise impenetrable walls also provided the opposite effect. Any gunfire, explosion, or scream, for that matter, would be muffled within those walls. Murders could go unnoticed by the guests on the lower floor.

Whatever the Founders chose to do upstairs couldn't be heard by anyone outside the room. And if Cassie was a member here and truly responsible for draining Vincent of his soul energy like Raven had insinuated, what worse things might occur inside Nocturnal Trinity? Were the Founders like some strange supernatural mafia?

A week ago, she wouldn't have entertained such a thought. But tonight, she realized she had stumbled upon some kind of mystical force. How else could she forget handing a stranger her phone? And Flora ... she could read her thoughts, and the odd tingling sensation she had felt made her wonder if that was an invisible tendril Flora sent to pry into Kailey's mind, lurking for information.

Flora and Andreas separated from Kailey and her other invited guests. Kailey watched them vanish into the massive wave of Goth dancers and was relieved to see them go. A low cloud of cigarette smoke hung over the heads of the dancers. Fog machines pumped more visibility obstructions, making it difficult for her to navigate. She carefully avoided people's swinging arms and their wild shuffling dance moves. Occasionally, hands with bright glowing rings came surprisingly close to striking her face as she squeezed through the mob.

Seeing mirrors reflecting the array of lights, she kept making her way toward the bar. A strong shot of something alcoholic might help reduce her uneasiness, but she didn't plan to get drunk. Not here, and certainly not now. Taking Raven's warnings to heart, she couldn't allow herself to have her senses numbed. She needed to keep her wits sharp.

Kailey couldn't shake her suspicions that Flora possessed some sort of mental magical power, but it was different from any type of magic she'd felt Raven use. She never believed in telepathy, but now she wondered. Flora had definitely pricked into her mind to read her loss and her emotions. A mysterious power flowed around the lady, which seemed to make everyone within her presence become infatuated with her.

Kailey found Flora intoxicating and craved being near her, but after Flora had disappeared through the dancing throng, Flora's power had lessened. Or had Flora simply directed her attentions elsewhere? She also noticed that she suffered a mild headache since the lady's absence.

Finally, Kailey reached the bar. She found a swivel barstool, climbed up, and sat down. The overhead lights were dim, which made seeing anything on the bar beyond a few feet quite difficult. She looked at the mirror behind the bar, hoping to see Flora moving somewhere within the surging crowd. No sign of her. The bartender approached from the shadows.

"Whadda it be?" The wiry man asked, cocking a heavily pierced eyebrow. His narrow lips tightened but didn't tease the slightest hint of a smile. Most bartenders she had seen were friendlier than this because tips were something they favored. Of course, anyone noticing the gruffness of this man would be terrified *not* leaving a tip.

"What's a common choice in Seattle?" she asked.

"Ah, new to the city, are ya?" His voice held a British accent, quite different to Flora's.

She nodded.

"I thought so."

Kailey smiled nervously. "Is it that obvious?"

The man looked at her clothes, lack of tattoos, and her nervous smile. "It's more than obvious. No tats ... a lacy black dress? I'm surprised with your lack of enthusiastic art and piercings that anyone even chose you as a guest."

"Actually, so am I."

"What brings you to Seattle?" he asked.

Kailey glanced down. "Funeral."

"Ah, sorry. You left that to come here? This place reeks of death as well."

He slid a drink to her. The glass contained pink-tinted liquid with a stemmed cherry in the bottom.

"What is this?"

"Betty Paige. It's what most of these Goth punk girls request."

She sipped it and gave an approving nod. "It's good."

"Do you know who chose you as a guest?"

Kailey nodded. "Flora."

His eyes widened slightly, but only for a second, and he rebounded with a sly grin. "I see."

"Is that not good?"

He shrugged. "Based upon your clothing, it seems about right."

"What do you mean?"

"She has a strange sense of humor."

"That she does, Nigel," a deep-voiced man said from behind her.

Kailey spun the stool around and sat face-to-face with the broad shouldered man. His long curly hair was tied back in a thick ponytail. He wore his neatly trimmed blondish brown beard like a Viking. Black tattoos of skulls, iron crosses, and mutilated corpses covered his sleeveless muscled arms. On the inside of his forearms were strange runic symbols.

The barkeep took a glance at the giant of a man and walked to the next customer. His eyes reflected resentment and fear.

"I'm not sure what you mean?"

"Her sense of humor?"

She nodded.

He chuckled and waved off the question. "Not an important matter. Just stick close to me, and you won't need to worry about her."

Kailey studied his tattoos. Between the dark tattoos on his upper arms were symbol scars that had also been carved into his flesh. The rugged marks indicated that they were cut into his flesh with a jagged blade and not a razor.

"My name's Jinn," he said. His eyes flickered, resembling a Tiger's Eye gemstone being turned in the bright sunlight. The mesmerizing effect captivated her and she didn't wish to look away. He smiled and extended his hand.

She offered hers, and he pulled it to his lips, kissing the back of her hand gently. Surprised, she gasped and her face turned bright red. "I'm Kailey."

"Pleasure," he said. "Mind sharing a booth with me? I'd love to know more about you."

"She's Flora's guest," Nigel said.

Jinn shrugged. "So?"

"You know her temper."

"Settle down," Jinn said with a sly grin. "Flora's nowhere near. Besides it's quite rude to invite a guest and then totally abandon and ignore her."

He took Kailey's hand and helped her down from the barstool. Offering his arm like a true gentleman, she looped her arm in and around his, allowing him to escort her through the crowd. The strange rune scars were smooth to touch, but also hot with fevered heat.

Jinn led her to a small booth. There was only room for one person to sit on each side of the table. After she seated herself, he sat opposite her. Even though they weren't too far from the dance floor, the music dramatically lessened in its intensity but the lighting wasn't any better than at the bar. She liked the quieter atmosphere, but the shadows still disturbed her. She felt like someone was watching her.

A waitress set a large pitcher of dark beer in front of Jinn. He smiled his approval. Looking at Kailey, he said, "So what are your impressions of Nocturnal Trinity thus far?"

"It's different. Apparently they took my cellphone when I came in."

He nodded.

"Flora said that I gave it to the man at the door, but I don't remember doing so. I should remember that, shouldn't I?"

"Damn vamps," he said.

"Excuse me?"

"You were compelled. Mind control. She made you give up your phone and then erased it from your memory."

"What? So she's a vampire?"

"Yes."

Kailey laughed. "That explains the coffins in the VIP room."

"It does actually," Jinn said without the slightest grin. His stern facial expression offered no suggestion that he was jesting.

She sipped her drink and looked toward the bar. "Are there other vampires here?"

Jinn nodded.

"*Real* ones?"

"Blended in amongst all the overly dressed wannabes and dreamers, yes. They're here and very real."

Her brow tightened into a frown.

He laughed with a deep hearty roar. "You don't believe me?"

"I suppose there are werewolves, too?"

"Phht. Not in Seattle. They wouldn't dare enter our city, but if they ever did, they certainly wouldn't seek coming here. Although a pack of them live near Salem, Oregon, which is well south of us. "

She studied his face and his eyes, waiting for him to admit he was kidding. "You're serious."

"Very much so," he replied.

"Okay. I've heard strange things have happened at this nightclub. I can't say that I don't believe she's something more than human. She has power. So why did she compel me?" she asked.

"No cellphones are allowed inside Nocturnal Trinity. No cameras either."

"Why not?"

"Keeps our privacy and increases the outsiders' curiosity. Prevents our competition from trying to copy the club's layout. Not to mention that some of our members hold high offices in Seattle and wish to keep the public from knowing they frequent our place. We help ensure that by not allowing cameras. Then it becomes a nonsense game of he said, she said, which isn't front-page news for any newspaper or even the Internet media. People want pictures. Proof. They believe those, even if someone doctors them up."

"I wouldn't have taken any pictures," Kailey said.

Jinn shrugged. "Doesn't matter. It's one of our rules. We strictly enforce our rules without prejudice."

Kailey bit her lower lip and shook her head. "She could have just asked. She didn't have to compel me."

"Flora likes to display her power to our guests. You might check to see if they took anything else."

Kailey dug inside her tiny purse attached to the side of her belt. "Damn, my Taser is gone, too. So's the silver cross I had."

"Of course. No way they're going to allow *that* in here."

"Because she's a vampire, right?"

"Still not a believer?"

She shrugged and placed a hand to her chest. The silver necklace and blessed pendant Raven had given her were still there.

"You got to keep that," he said with a slight nod. "What is it?"

"A friend of mine from Boston gave it to me."

"May I see it?"

Kailey gently pulled the chain up until she tugged the pendant through and let it rest on the front of her dress, but she didn't dare take it off.

"Interesting. And this friend of yours ... she's a witch?"

She nodded, surprised that he knew. She quickly redirected the conversation. "You're certain Flora's a vampire."

"Yes."

"What makes you ...?"

Jinn crossed his muscular arms and shook his head. "Why do you still question this?"

"Because no one talks ever about vampires except in movies or books."

Jinn nodded toward the dancers and laughed. "Yep. Thousands of people believe in them. Otherwise, they wouldn't be here."

"They believe in the hope that they exist."

"No. Vampires have survived throughout the ages. Low profiles have been the key to their survival, which is why they are so protective of a club like this. And if someone breaks the trust or threatens to expose their whereabouts, that's really when compulsion benefits them the most. Of course, there are ways to make traitorous humans disappear entirely."

Kailey glanced around the club a bit uneasily, wondering how many in the crowd were vampires. If what Jinn said was true, she wondered why her brother had come to Nocturnal Trinity in the first place. She needed to find out whom his client had been and *why* he had chosen to meet here. Were there no other options?

Jinn took a long drink of the dark beer, set it down, and said, "So, Kailey, answer this for me."

Her nervous eyes flicked to his. "Sure."

"Was it dark outside when Flora arrived at the club? I'm sure you were standing in line then."

"It was dark, but I hadn't been here long when the limo arrived."

Jinn smiled. "Who was in the limo?"

"Her, two other ladies, and three men."

"Those are her siblings. All vampires. They never arrive until after sunset. And did she take you through a dark corridor?"

Kailey nodded.

"She avoids the main entrance and seeks to hide in the shadows until they are safely inside their VIP room or they hit the dance floor to mingle with potential *recruits*. It's all about image, or lack thereof, depending upon where the mirrors are." He gave a shrewd grin, and his oddly colored eyes blazed for a moment.

"They really don't have reflections?" Kailey asked.

"Depends upon the mirror."

She frowned. "How?"

"Antique mirrors contain silver to cast a reflection and most vampires can't be seen in those."

"Why not?"

Jinn shrugged. "We don't rightly know. However, modern mirrors, like the ones we have here, use aluminum so vampires can be seen in the mirrors and blend readily into the crowd. We do that purposely to conceal their identities."

"So there's more vampires here than Flora and her siblings?"

"Yes. A few dozen."

Her uneasiness increased. Not knowing who were the vampires concerned her. This place was more unsettling than Frank had insinuated and hindsight prodded her that she probably should have waited before entering the nightclub alone. Raven had warned her that the symbol for the place represented unforeseen dangers, and other perils existed here that Raven had never mentioned to her before. However, admitting it would allow Raven's, 'I told you so,' and Kailey hated those moments.

Her friend was a witch with ever-growing powers and intuitions, but even she had never brought up the subject of vampires. Of course, Salem, where she and Raven often frequented on the weekends, was where witches openly thrived and congregated in great number, taunting the tarnished past injustices of the innocent people wrongly executed because of religious intolerance, false accusations, and control.

A white-haired gentleman passed their table. On each arm a voluptuous woman clung to him. Their skin was a reddish tint. Each woman held such exquisite beauty that Flora paled in comparison, which Kailey never imagined she'd see during her lifetime. But since Flora was capable of compulsion, was she deceptively beautiful and blinding people into awe?

These two women's ears were pointed, and small horns protruded above their foreheads. Their skirts were extremely short, revealing the lower curve of their buttocks. Black fishnet hose hugged their perfectly proportioned legs. Scaly long tails protruded through their black chemises at the base of their spines. At first she thought these were costume prosthetics, but when she noticed how the tails curled and swayed effortlessly back and forth as these *women* walked, her eyes widened. She held no doubt that the tails were real. The women playfully intertwined their tails as they walked.

The elderly gentleman talked to the beautiful creatures and laughed softly. Occasionally one smacked his butt with the pointed tip of her tail, making him smile and squeeze her buttocks. He turned in Kailey's direction, and she gasped. It was Mr. Langston, the elderly man she had seen at the cemetery. A devious smile curled his lips. He recognized her. She quickly turned and looked down at the table.

Jinn noticed her alarm and glanced toward the trio. "You know him?"

She nodded. "My brother worked for him."

"Mr. Langston?"

"Yes."

"You're brother's an attorney?"

"He was. He's dead."

"I'm terribly sorry," he said in a low tone that expressed no emotion at all. His strange eyes narrowed as he studied her.

"His funeral was today." She suddenly worried that perhaps she had said too much. Revealing that she was Vincent's sister in the very place where he had met Cassie, gave away her cover of simply an out-of-town tourist seeking an interesting nightclub to get a drink. Once word got out that she might be here to investigate the place, more scrutiny fell on her.

Langston disappeared through emerald curtains into a dark room with the ladies. On the other side of the curtain the two women giggled and squealed.

Kailey's stomach quaked with sudden nervousness. She wondered what took place behind the curtain where Langston had gone. Had Vincent ever been back there? Were any other attorneys, judges, or high officials already back there? If so, exactly what were they doing?

She wanted to peek through the curtains to see if Cassie was there, but wondered what she'd do if the woman was.

Rather than saying anything more, Jinn motioned toward the nearest waitress. The waitress hurried to their booth and smiled.

"Bring Kailey another drink," he said. "And put it on my tab."

"Your tab?"

Jinn replied with a wink. The waitress giggled and headed toward the bar.

"That's not necessary," she said.

"Nonsense. It's the least I can do. We try to create a club type atmosphere here where people have a sense of belonging and feel safe, which is why a lot of these participate every night. They have no unity outside of our establishment."

"So they are delinquents?"

He shrugged and smirked. "Some are, but the majority are not. More often they are just former victims from dysfunctional families, hoping to find a place to fit in. This place is where people who believe they don't fit into society can come and find acceptance."

The waitress returned with another drink for Kailey. This one looked dark and was not a fruity drink. The strong scent of alcohol hit her nostrils. She slid it aside and gazed at him. She reminded herself that she needed to keep her faculties, and suddenly she wondered if Jinn was deliberately trying to get her drunk or worse.

Kailey studied his unique eyes. The shifting gold, brown, and yellow colors were beautiful and difficult to look away from. She kept wondering what his ties to Nocturnal Trinity were since he kept referring to "*we*." He acted strong, protective, and authoritative like someone who was there to help others. Like Flora, he possessed a strong aura. He spoke with a smooth, deep voice that she found soothing, pleasant, and almost hypnotic. Her curiosity had built.

"Are you one of them?" she asked.

He laughed. "A vampire?"

"Yes."

Jinn opened his mouth to speak but was interrupted.

"No, dear," a woman said. "He's *not* a vampire. He's a demon."

Startled by the revelation, Kailey shuddered and turned in surprise to see a dark haired woman dressed in a delicately laced gray gown. Her green eyes hinted of mischief and a smile tugged at her narrow lips. She wore an emerald necklace that mimicked the color and twinkle of her eyes. Small silver pentagrams accentuated her earrings. Her pale smooth skin seemed blessed by a kiss of soft moonlight.

Jinn laughed. "Ah, Eva, so nice of you to give away the surprise!"

"No surprise from you since you'd have never told her until *after* it was too late, if ever."

Kailey's brow rose in question. "Too late?"

Eva nodded. "He's a seducer, luring you to fall in love with him, so he can *drain* every ounce of dignity and integrity you possess. He's an incubus."

Jinn frowned and sneered. Then he laughed heartily. "Well, when you word it like that, it sounds so dirty and vile."

"That's because it is," Eva said evenly. She glanced at Kailey and said, "You didn't drink any of that?"

She shook her head.

"Good. Don't. Or else, you'll do his bidding for an entire month. Longer if he continues sneaking the concoction to you without your noticing. I'm fairly certain you don't' wish to be his love slave."

Kailey was appalled. She glared at Jinn. His gentle smile was no longer pleasing but perverted and offensive. He offered a slightly embarrassed shrug. Clarity of mind helped her see through the facade. Seconds later, horns appeared on his forehead. She shook her head and blinked several times. She questioned whether she had taken a drink or not. The longer she stayed inside Nocturnal Trinity, the more she regretted having come in the first place.

Jinn sighed. "What brings you to my table, Eva?"

"I sensed strong magic from this direction."

Jinn laughed. "You know that's not my style."

"Yes, I know. The magical flow comes from her and beckoned me."

Kailey looked confused.

"She's not a witch," Jinn said.

"No. The magic comes from her pendant and the power called for my assistance."

"Odd, don't you think?" he asked.

Eva nodded. "It is since I don't know her or the witch that cast the spell."

Jinn looked to Kailey and back to Eva. "I never sensed any such thing."

"That's because the request was masked to protect her from *you*." She glanced at Kailey. "I suggest you keep your distance from him."

Kailey slipped out of the booth, frowning at him.

Jinn's eyes blazed. His anger flared his nostrils and his jaws tightened. He rose with tightened fists and faced Eva. Eva tilted her head with a stern frown. She raised her right hand with her palm directed at Jinn. He frowned, looked at the faint glow around fingers and grumbled. Then he marched away.

"He's pissed," Kailey said.

She shrugged. "No matter."

"You're not concerned about angering a demon?"

"Come with me," Eva said, ignoring the question. She extended her hand to Kailey. "We should speak privately."

Kailey took her hand and a tinge of warmth shot up her arm. Eva led her to a hidden stairwell on the opposite side of the bar. Various scents of incense loomed.

"Whoever gave you that pendant loves you very much," Eva said, releasing Kailey's hand.

"My friend, Raven, gave it to me."

"I see. The spell she cast on it is meant to protect one's spouse. Does she hold a deeper love than you do for her?"

Kailey nodded. "She does, and she has told me often. Even tonight."

"And you don't feel the same way?"

"No. I love her, but not in a romantic way."

Eva frowned. "Never lie to a witch, young lady."

"I—"

Eva raised her index finger and shook her head. "Your words cannot hide the true feelings in your eyes or your heart. Why do you fear giving into your love for her? I don't think uncertainty is the reason for your bridling your real passion." Eva studied her carefully. Her eyes softened. "You've suffered great loss?"

Kailey nodded.

"That explains so much, but you cannot stay in fear forever. If you do, you'll never know true love."

Kailey's heart beat harder. She didn't like how Eva and Flora were able to read into her thoughts. What was their intent and purpose for doing so?

Eva smiled. "So you're not a practitioner?"

"No."

"Interesting. Then why are you here?" Eva asked, stopping on the stairs to gaze at her.

"To find the person that killed my brother, Vincent."

Eva frowned. "What makes you think that you'll find the person here?"

"This is where he met her."

"You think she's here? Tonight?"

"I don't know. Possibly."

Eva gave an odd smile. "Nocturnal Trinity is such a bizarre place. No telling what you'll discover. Some good. Some bad. Few have died here, and then there's always tonight."

The cold words shot straight to Kailey's soul. The iciness of Eva's tone brought chills to Kailey. The gleam of the witch's cold stare was frightening. Then she turned toward the stairs.

CHAPTER 6

*E*va continued up the stairs. At the top, she headed to the right, opened a door and gently offered her hand to invite Kailey to enter first. Once inside, she closed the door and mumbled an incantation. Runic symbols were painted on the back of the door. She turned and faced Kailey.

"That will bar anyone from hearing what is said inside this room," Eva said. "Please. Take a seat."

Kailey sat in a plush chair with cushioned armrests. Glancing around the room, she knew this was a different VIP room. She assumed the factions had a private room for each of them.

A large window overlooked one of the dance floors, chilled bottles of wine set in ice buckets, but the décor was witch symbols. A glass fronted bookshelf of old books against the far wall. Its doors were locked.

The room didn't have any lamps or overhead lights. Dozens of candles flickered. Incense oils scented the room. Most of the symbolism she recognized because of Raven's books and drawings. Her friend would relish visiting this room.

"Who chose you tonight?" Eva asked.

"As a guest?"

"Yes."

"Flora."

Eva shook her head. "Typical."

"Why? Jinn stated something similar about how she had a strange sense of humor."

"She does. I'll admit that. And no telling what her intentions were for you this evening."

"Like what?"

Eva shrugged. "She probably would have placed you under a hypnotic trance and humiliated you. Lucky for you there was a major distraction tonight."

"Is that why she abandoned me?"

Eva crinkled her nose. "I'd say so."

"What happened?"

"Let's just say that there's a slight rift within our organization right now. Lots of practical jokes lately. Nothing serious, but a few of the recipients are more perturbed than others. Perhaps it will smooth over. Perhaps not. Of course, no one wishes to take the responsibility. No one has lessened the blows, either. We have a strong system of checks and balances but some are ignoring them. Power struggles never end pleasantly."

"So Flora is an actual vampire?"

"Of course. Jinn filled you in on that, right?"

"Yes."

"One word of advice," Eva said.

"What's that?"

"Avoid eye contact with her at all costs."

"Compulsion?"

"Yes, dear. It can be a costly mistake. Worse than losing your phone."

"How old is her vampire family?"

Eva smiled. "Her *clan* is a bit over two and a half centuries old. They are quite powerful, but they have their limitations."

"Where did they originate?"

"They came from Europe. Croatia was their homeland before they migrated through various war-torn countries until finally settling here."

"Are there other cities that have these ... clans?"

"Most major cities have hidden vampires. Most relish their privacy and are glad that society views their kind as fictional. It makes denying public accusations so much easier." Eva smiled broadly. "However, none of the vampires are as bold as these who live in Seattle. Of course, they are better protected and barely a whisper rises about them outside of Nocturnal Trinity. The invited humans seldom know they've danced with a vampire, demon, or a witch."

"But they hope to?" Kailey asked.

"Of course." Eva handed her a chilled glass of wine. "Young people are so naïve. Seeking for the fictional aspects blinds them to what is actually surrounding them. Easy for them to become unknowledgeable prey." She sighed heavily. "Now, tell me more about the one you believe killed your brother."

"Her name is Cassie." Kailey said the words, expecting Eva to immediately recognize the name.

Eva shrugged and shook her head. "Can you be more specific? Names as common as that with the hundreds of people passing through the club every night doesn't help. I know no one by that name."

"I don't know much about her."

"She was married to your brother and yet—"

Kailey said, "I live in Boston. He married but I never met her. I was to spend the winter and spring with them after my graduation to look for a job here."

"So you plan to reside in Seattle?"

"Yes. I was going to hunt for an apartment tomorrow."

"I see. And what makes you think Cassie had something to do with his death? His ... *murder* as you insist." Eva swirled her wine in a crystal goblet, smelled the aroma, and took a sip. Her green eyes glowed like a cat's.

"After their marriage, he drastically changed from the positively minded person I knew into someone that was fearful and paranoid. Whenever I mentioned her name, he looked paralyzed by terror and disconnected our chat soon after."

Eva pursed her lips. "Not all marriages are bliss, my dear. To borrow an old cliché, 'Marriage changes people.'"

"I understand that, but this was different."

"In what way?"

Kailey took a sip of the wine, trying to think of a way to adequately describe Vincent's demeanor. Instead of adding more, she said, "Raven called her a soul-leech."

Eva's eyes widened with interest. She set her wine goblet on the table and leaned forward in her seat. "Why?"

"Raven sat with me during the last conversation I had with Vincent via Skype. His eyes were sunken in. He had lost a lot of weight. She told me over the phone today that someone was sapping his soul, draining him of his energy."

Eva sat in a chair facing Kailey. Her emerald necklace and eyes sparkled in the flickering candlelight. "What made you think to look here?"

"I saw Cassie at the funeral. My brother told me months ago that he had met her here. His friend and colleague mentioned Vincent had come to Nocturnal Trinity to talk to a former client. I guess that's when he met her. His friend told me more about this club, so I wanted to check it out."

Eva smiled. "I see. What did Raven say about you coming here?"

Kailey stared at her wine. "She warned me not to come."

"Seems she is a witch blessed with wisdom."

"She is."

"And yet, you failed to heed her tender advice," Eva said sternly. "Your love for your brother must have been very strong."

Tears spilled from Kailey's eyes without warning. Angrily she fought this flood of emotion. She wanted the anger more than the sorrow of loss. For now. Once she avenged his death, then she'd welcome the tears. She nodded. "Yes. He was the only family I had left in this world."

"Family doesn't have to be bloodline. Friends ... *close* friends are family, too."

"I know." Kailey wiped away tears with the back of her hand. She tightened her jaw. "I'm sorry for crying."

"Don't be. Release of sorrow heals the soul. Now, tell me more about this Cassie. What did she look like?"

Kailey described how the woman looked at the funeral.

Eva shook her head. "I don't recall seeing a woman that fits that description, but with the dress code here, that doesn't mean anything. People are known to dress up rather outrageously. Some never repeat a costume, either. However, what your friend said about your sister-in-law being a soul-leech ... we have creatures at Nocturnal Trinity that can do that. You mentioned that your brother came here to meet a client?"

"Yes."

"Who?"

Kailey shrugged. "I don't know. My brother worked for Mr. Langston."

Eva's eyes narrowed. "The attorney?"

"Yes. My brother worked for him as one of his law firm associates."

"What is your surname?"

"Yates."

Eva's brow furrowed. Her eyes raced as she thought. She set her wine glass on the small table and gently tapped her index finger to her lips. "Vincent Yates. Yes. Yes, I remember him. Such a polite young man. He was your brother?"

"Yes. Do you remember seeing him here with his client?" Kailey asked.

"No. Like I said, child, so many people come and go."

"Mr. Langston was with two women that had tails earlier."

"Yes." Eva nodded. "He has a strange fetish for the succubae."

"What exactly are they?"

"Demons. Like Jinn, they seduce and feed off of their servants. And we have more than two hundred willing souls here tonight."

"Mr. Langston is a servant?"

Eva laughed softly. The pleasant sound flowed like the song of a siren, making Kailey's heart beat faster, making her sit forward in her chair to get closer to Eva.

"Oddly," Eva said, "Mr. Langston *believes* they serve him, and that is the greatest deception any demon can blind a human with. During the ecstasy of sexual pleasures the succubae feed from their humans. The exchange of sex for blood appeases these demons. Langston and other men don't recall the feeding, but they cannot ever forget the euphoric sex. Such pleasure overrides minor pain and they eagerly come back for more."

"What about bite marks?"

"Succubae have healing properties in their saliva to make the marks disappear."

Kailey frowned, thinking. "Perhaps Cassie is a succubus?"

Eva smiled. "Quite possibly she might be. It can be hard to prove."

"Why?"

"Succubae are shape-shifting demons, constantly changing their outward appearance. But, if what you say is true, such an accusation is not something to be taken lightly. If she is a succubus that seduced him into marriage and killed him for monetary gain, she has violated the one rule our organization deems the most evil with the highest penalty for a demon. Once murder occurs and is proven, the guilty party is banished."

"That's it? Banished from Nocturnal Trinity?"

Eva shook her head. Her lips tightened into an even smile. No humor danced in her eyes or on her lips. "No, the demon is banished from this world forever. And for her, if she killed him, death would be so much more pleasant. There is no returning from the abyss."

"Oh."

"Let me ask you something else."

"Sure."

"Jinn approached you fairly quickly, didn't he?"

Kailey nodded. "Yes."

"Perhaps you should have taken your friend's advice and not come here."

"Why?"

Eva sighed. "With the turmoil our establishment is currently experiencing, they chose you for a reason. Clearly you're not dressed like any of the other hopefuls that wish to enter our nightclub. Sure, you're wearing all black, but with the trinkets and clothing accessories you lack, you stood out rather obviously. The innocence in your eyes clued them, too. The vampires often scoff at the likes of you. The majority of our members would have never taken you seriously as a prospect and simply ignored you. Flora *purposely* chose you, brought you in, and abandoned you at a moment's notice. Jinn picked up from there."

And you after him ...

Kailey frowned. If she was indeed being set up, she doubted that only two of the three would be involved. This witch was Part Three of whatever they had in store for her. Perhaps Kailey was naïve on the surface, but what she knew on the inside from her researching skills, she understood she couldn't trust any of them. She could play the game, too. "What are you saying?"

Eva's eyes narrowed. "They are working together. They know *who* you are and that you're here to find out about Cassie or whoever she really is."

"By your tone of voice, I take it that's a bad thing?"

"Worse than you can imagine."

Kailey swallowed hard. "How?"

"To put it bluntly? They want you dead."

CHAPTER 7

"Dead?" Kailey asked.

"Yes."

"To protect a demon?"

"Of course. But more importantly, to cover their tracks."

"Why? Are they close-knit like family?"

Eva shook her head. "No. Losing one to banishment lessens their strength. With our alliances already disintegrating, such a thing would cause further division. To prevent that, they'd rather eliminate you than sacrifice her."

Her assumption that Eva was working with the other two was confirmed. Being locked inside one of the VIP rooms was a fatal mistake. Fear claimed Kailey's eyes, even though she had tried to hide it.

Dammit! I need to learn to hide my emotions.

Kailey glanced toward the door. "What can I do?"

"First, we need to get you out of here. Alive is preferable." A smirk formed on her face.

"That's not funny."

"It's not intended to be, but you should have understood the danger you put yourself into by coming here. Raven even warned you."

"I know," she replied, catching the underlying threat in the witch's words.

"I'm curious as to why a devoted witch like your friend has taken to you with so much passion."

Kailey shrugged. "I don't know. We were roommates our freshmen year. We *clicked*. She continually tries to protect me."

"Nothing about her practice of witchcraft interested you enough to pursue it?"

"It fascinates me. But ... I'm not certain of my path in life." She gritted her teeth and winced. *Learn to hold back such information. Stop revealing your weaknesses.*

"I see." Eva's devious smile spread wider.

Kailey was beginning to think she was in a bad play recital of *Hansel and Gretel.*

"Let's concentrate on getting you out of Nocturnal Trinity," Eva said. "They know that you left the dance floor with me, so they will be watching for us to re-emerge."

Kailey bit her lower lip, wondering how the hell she had managed to walk blindly into such a trap. "Do you think they'll try to kill me here?"

"Doubtful. I don't think we'll have a problem getting you out of the club, but it's what happens *after* you are on the streets. Did you take a cab?" There was more amusement ringing in the woman's voice than precaution, almost as though she wanted to see bloodshed and pain.

What's your hand in this?

"No. I was told they don't pick riders up from this place."

"Unfortunately, that's true. You didn't *walk*, did you?" Glee resonated in her tone.

Still fishing.

Kailey shook her head. "No. I have a rental car."

"Good. Where'd you park?"

"In the parking garage across the street."

Why don't you just draw her a map? Invite all the friends and neighbors. Damn ...

Eva sighed. "Not good. Walking might have been better."

"How?"

"At least you would get a running start."

Uneasiness coursed through Kailey. How she wished she had listened to Raven. Sometimes, she just wanted to prove her friend wrong, and now she realized this hadn't been the best opportunity to do so.

"Okay," Eva said. "Do you remember where you parked in the garage?"

Kailey nodded. "Level 3."

Her emerald eyes flickered and narrowed. She shook her head. "Damn. You've made certain that all of your options are completely unfavorable, haven't you?"

Check. Did that.

"I suppose so, but not intentionally."

Kailey fretted. Her eyes resembled a frightened rabbit that had no place to hide from its predator. Nervous sweat dampened beneath her armpits. At the present moment, nothing she did could reduce her fear. Taking a huge intake of air, she adjusted her dress and nervously ironed it with her hands. If what she faced were only a physical threat, she wouldn't have a problem fighting. She had trained for those types of confrontations. However, the threat she faced wasn't flesh and blood, but supernatural. Creatures she never believed existed. She wasn't prepared or trained to combat those.

Eva studied Kailey's behavior and pursed her lips. "Calm down. Acting worried will place the advantage in their court. You won't be able to think clearly and your reactions will be untimely. Trust me, they capitalize on mistakes."

No kidding.

"How am I supposed to feel, knowing that a vampire and demon want to kill me?"

"There's one thing I don't understand about you," Eva said.

"What's that?"

"You're a mere human without any magical abilities of your own. You've entered a bar unarmed against demons and vampires."

"I had a silver cross."

Eva smiled. "Are you a believer of the cross?"

"You mean a Christian?"

Eva nodded.

"No. A cab driver had given it to me earlier in the day."

"Then the cross benefits you none at all. You came in here unarmed and unprepared. Only true fools do that."

"I didn't even know vampires and demons *existed*. I certainly never thought such things would be here."

Eva shook her head. "Tsk, tsk. Such ignorance gives you no justification. Yelling that you don't believe they exist only makes them laugh a few moments longer before they *kill* you. So if you're not a Christian nor a practitioner, what do you believe in?"

"Only what can be proven with evidence."

Eva frowned. "In a world with so many gods and religions, you choose none?"

"No, not any particular god."

"You're a naïve mortal with two immortal groups that want you dead," Eva said.

I'm betting three groups.

"Not quite the welcome you expected in Seattle, is it?"

"No," Kailey replied.

"Sadly, there may be no need for you to look for an apartment. You might retain your permanent residency in a Seattle cemetery."

Tears burned the edges of Kailey's eyes, but she prevented them from escaping. She had hoped for a different outcome when she had entered Nocturnal Trinity. She wanted to avenge her brother's death, and already two immortal individuals that she had never met before tonight were set to kill her. Three actually since the witch didn't seem able to contain her growing excitement about Kailey's possible death.

Kailey hadn't even seen Cassie since the funeral. Was the woman even in the nightclub? By the way her brother's widow had acted in the cemetery, she doubted Cassie was grieving or if she had even shed a tear.

She wondered what Cassie was doing, if not here. Was her sister-in-law a succubus? She had no way to really tell. Remembering how Cassie had flirted within minutes of the priest's eulogy, her anger rekindled and burned inside her heart. Her jaw tightened. She refused to die easily without knowing the truth. Above all else, she wanted vengeance.

So if the three factions of Nocturnal Trinity wanted her dead, she'd not die without at least kicking and fighting with everything she had.

Kailey stood, set down her wine glass, and crossed her arms. "You said that Jinn was an incubus."

"Yes."

"Why do those succubae with Mr. Lancaster have tails, and Jinn does not? And if Cassie is a succubus, why doesn't she have one or horns?"

"Demons work to make themselves overly attractive to those that they may gain the most from. They can cloak themselves, disappearing entirely, or they can make their claws, tails, pointed ears or horns disappear. If she truly is a succubus, she's hidden her succubus characteristics. Of course, they can also hide them if their servant prefers them to. They can look ever how their human lover wishes for them to appear. Doing so requires sustenance by drinking blood from their host. And since Jinn loves to seduce women, he usually tries to appear as humanly as possible."

Kailey frowned. "Does that mean that Mr. Lancaster prefers them to look like demons?"

"Apparently so."

"Why?"

"Fetishes vary from person to person. You'd have to ask him."

Kailey's face expressed severe disgust. "I'll pass."

Eva smiled. "Some things are best left unasked."

"No argument here. After you revealed to me that Jinn was a demon, his horns appeared, but nothing else became visible."

Eva smiled. "Since I exposed his deceit and what his plans for you were, his mantel shattered somewhat. However, he rebounded quickly and was able to keep the rest hidden from you."

"Otherwise I wouldn't have seen his horns?"

"Probably not. Well, not unless he wanted you to see what he actually is."

Kailey relaxed and lowered her arms. "Are you able to detect demons apart from vampires and humans if they are cloaked? I mean, see them as they actually look."

"Most of the time. Powerful demons conceal themselves quite well. But these aren't things you need to worry about at the moment. We need to get you safely out of here and to your car."

Kailey said, "How do you plan to do that?"

"We walk you through the front doors."

Niiiice ...

Kailey gave Eva a suspicious glance. "That's not safe."

"I can take you out through an underground tunnel that leads to the other side of the street, but for your safety, the more witnesses that see you leave, the less chance that they will try to harm you in view of others."

"Okay. But I need my phone."

"We'll get it."

Someone rapped at the door.

Kailey frowned and glanced toward the door. "How?"

Eva went to the door, peered through the peephole, and gently pulled it open. A slender woman slinked through the door with the grace of a cat. Her eyes were a deep sapphire blue. Her skintight black clothes revealed her perfect figure. She probably didn't have an ounce of body fat. She slid something into Eva's hand and made her way to the sofa.

"Thanks, Tabby," Eva said.

Eva returned to Kailey and handed her a cellphone.

Kailey's eyes widened. "This is my phone. How'd *she* get it?"

A sly smile crept across Eva's face. "She's been listening."

Kailey turned the phone on, scanned through the messages, and her call list. Apparently Raven had not called. Yet.

Good.

"I thought no one could hear us?" Kailey asked.

"She's my familiar. When I brought you here, I mentally requested that she bring whatever belongings of yours they had checked at the door."

"What about the cross?"

Eva shook her head. "That one's a bit more difficult. Besides, you said that you're not a believer, so it really does you no good to have it. Now, we need to get you out of here."

When they reached the door, Eva opened it. A cat mewed from the sofa. Kailey turned and saw a Siamese cat sitting on the arm of the sofa. Tabby, the woman, was nowhere to be seen. With a raised brow, she faced Eva. Eva nodded.

"Tabby?" Kailey asked, tucking her cellphone behind her belt. "How?"

"No time to explain. Let's go."

CHAPTER 8

*K*ailey felt like every eye in the nightclub watched her as she passed through the center of the dance floor with Eva. She assumed it was her paranoia more than actually being true. She didn't doubt that Flora and Jinn were watching her. She expected them to keep track of her. Quite possibly those closely associated with her two newfound enemies were keen to not letting her escape their sight, either. Devoted people often did dangerous things to prove their blind loyalty, and for those seeking immortality, murder was not outside their limitations.

While she walked, she kept to one side to keep an eye on Eva. She didn't trust this woman any more than she trusted Jinn and Flora. Eva had acted at first like she wanted to help her escape from Jinn, but she was unable to rein her optimism about Kailey getting attacked. There wasn't any "Good Cop, Bad Cop," actions occurring. They were all *bad*.

Midway through the crowd, she suddenly wondered how many vampires were in the nightclub. How many demons?

The blinding lights kept her from trying to look over the crowd. Dancers wearing black clothes within the drifting machine-produced fog were simply shadows without details. No faces were recognizable, and even if she could actually see them, their pale makeup and dark mascara obscured their true identities. Cassie could very well be masked and concealed within this dance assembly. The sudden advance from either group of immortals wasn't something she'd notice until after it was too late to even try to defend herself.

Vampires and demons were immortal. Witches, as far as she knew, were not. How did Eva plan to protect her? Magic, she supposed, could be a powerful weapon, but was it enough? Surely it must be or else the witches were at a great disadvantage. She didn't believe witches would house themselves with two clans stronger than themselves. Eva had mentioned a system of checks and balances, but Kailey didn't have enough details to know who kept whom in line. But again, this witch didn't seem too intent on actually helping her, so Kailey knew she was basically on her own.

A small prick of pain needled at the base of Kailey's skull, causing her to flinch involuntarily. She felt an invasion into her mind, her thoughts.

Flora?

Kailey searched the dance floor with her peripheral vision, looking for the vampire, checking to see any sudden gliding movement came toward her. She saw nothing except the mob of uncoordinated Goth dancers. If corpses danced, she now knew what that would look like.

"Why are you in such a hurry to leave?" Flora asked. *"The party is just beginning."*

The whispered voice came inside her head.

Stern.

Clear.

Threatening.

Kailey stopped walking and looked around. Where was she?

Kailey realized that Flora's mental interruption had distracted her enough that she lost sight of Eva or Eva had simply slipped away, abandoning her to whatever folly Flora intended to do. Kailey's only hope to exit Nocturnal Trinity safely had disappeared into the half drunken mob that reeked of cigarette and marijuana smoke. In a room full of mindless wannabe servants, she was alone. Isolated. Eva was gone. Purposely, Kailey believed.

Kailey possessed no weapons to protect her from the vampires or demons. The only safeguard she had entered with was the pendant blessed by Raven. She thought it odd that it had not been removed, but they had taken the cross. Perhaps the protection spell upon the silver pendant thwarted their confiscation. Doubtful. But for some reason, they had let it pass and Eva had located her through its magic.

Secluded and alone inside a dancing crowd, she missed Raven and worried that she might never see her again. She wished Raven ...

I'm sorry, Raven. I should have told you how I truly feel.

The thundering music lessened. The beat decreased into a more steady rhythm, much like a beating heart. She slowly turned a three-sixty, hoping to see Eva. Instead, she realized that the crowd was pressing toward her, closing in, and they were trying to box her in. Blank expressions hung on their faces. Their eyes were empty. They weren't deliberately doing the actions. Well, at least not on their own. They were spellbound and didn't have control of what they were doing.

As the young men and women pressed in toward her, the mixed smell of alcohol, sweat, and smoke-saturated leather and vinyl nauseated her. She covered her nose with her hand while searching for a partial path through the crowd.

Kailey's main priority was no longer vengeance.

It was survival.

Escape.

Playful laughter rang softly in her ears like crazed undulating whispers.

"Damn," Kailey said, trying to sidestep the advancing, mind-controlled crowd.

No doubts came to her about these people being controlled due to mass compulsion. If Flora was the one controlling the entire crowd of a hundred or more, the woman possessed even greater power than Kailey could comprehend. Of course, she didn't have any way to know that this was all Flora's doing. It could be a combination of her with her siblings and whatever power the demons offered. Currently, knowing the specifics didn't interest her. She only knew that she was in trouble.

Seeing the glowing EXIT sign, she squeezed through several people, but the human wall thickened between her and the door. The dancers stiffened, and wedging between them was no different than trying to squeeze through a narrow stone passage. She didn't think she was going to be allowed to leave. The barrier of people stood side by side without any gaps between them.

With desperation she looked into their eyes, hoping to reason with them, perhaps plead for compassion. Their eyes held blank stares. They had no recognition of her or any thoughts of their own. An outside force had kidnapped and controlled their minds. Whatever they did from this moment forward, they probably wouldn't recall their actions and would never be held accountable if ever question by authorities. Hundreds of potential witnesses who honestly didn't see anything. That was a frightening thought.

Without any sign of Eva, Kailey wondered why the witch had deliberately abandoned her. Perhaps Eva couldn't aid her. Doing so pitted the witch against the demon and vampire forces. How that affected the nightclub's politics was beyond her. A human woman might not be worth the risk. And since she didn't really know Eva, there was the greater possibility that the witch was in league with the others against her. That was something Kailey needed to consider since she was the outsider.

Why not stick around and have some fun? Flora taunted.

Kailey stared at the encircling crowd. While she might not have the tools necessary to combat supernatural creatures, she had trained in Taekwondo and Aikido martial arts since she was a small child, earning black belts in each. And after her parents had died, she became obsessed with training. It was the only thing that alleviated the weighted burden of loss.

Raven had often teased her about her kickboxing, whenever Kailey headed to the gym; but at other times, Raven informed her that such defensive tactics were great for women to protect themselves. She stopped wrestling with Raven for practice after Raven began enjoying it too much and for other reasons other than for Kailey to increase her grappling hold techniques. She couldn't convince Raven there were times when she might actually need to defend herself.

Like now.

However, she didn't want to attack or hurt these people unless she was forced to do so. They were only doing what they were compelled to do. And yet, they moved closer. Under this hypnotic control, did they experience pain or would they continue coming at her?

The clumsy way their bodies unevenly jerked in their staggered approach with their obvious absence of mental thought spooked her. They were under someone else's power, but at least she could see them. She feared the demons more since they could vanish and cloak themselves to attack her without her ever seeing their approach. It was impossible to fight an invisible enemy.

Kailey didn't have much room to move. The people approached from all sides. Slipping from her shoes, she ran a few steps, jumped, and planted both feet against a man's chest. No cry of pain came from the young man. The impact sent the man backwards against the wall of lurching men and women behind him. Their swaying bodies prevented him from dropping to the floor, but she continued with the momentum and leapt again. Her right foot landed on the shoulder of another man, she pressed off quickly, and dove forward.

Like she hoped, the controlled crowd was being manipulated to box her in because none of them tried to grab or yank her into the crowd. Their movements were painstakingly slow, possibly because it took the controller too long to filter into the correct mind to try to take her down, which worked to her advantage. They were only to provide an obstacle until whoever was in charge revealed what he or she wanted.

Kailey clasped her right hand firmly on a woman's shoulder and her left on a man's. These two individuals grunted, shook their heads, and suddenly awakened. Flora must have released her control. Frightened by her touch, the man and woman stepped aside and allowed Kailey to drop to the floor on her stomach.

The pain was instant, knocking the air from her lungs. She groaned and rolled to her side, gnashing her teeth from the pain. She coughed several times before taking in a deep gulp of air, so she could rise to her feet and make a mad dash for the door.

Before she rose, a blur of brilliant blue like a metallic butterfly shot along the outer wall and headed directly at her. She shook her head, trying to see what was approaching. An inch from her nose stood Flora. The vampire stared down at her with a narrowed smile.

If Flora's intent was to frighten her, she'd done one hell of a job. Jinn should be proud, if not envious. But strangely, Kailey's fear was waning and her annoyance was taking over.

Sometimes when she was getting ready to fight, she looked at her larger opponent with fear and uncertainty, but once she entered the ring, that dread disappeared. She tapped into her inner strength and thought of nothing else but taking down her rival. Because she had lost so much during her short life, she hated to lose, so she refused to back down.

"You're a quick thinker," Flora said. "I like that, but unfortunately you're not quick enough."

Kailey pushed herself up, slowly stood, then straightened her skirt and brushed away dust and debris. Her abdominal region still ached, but she used the pain to her advantage, letting her anger grow.

She was careful not to gaze directly into Flora's eyes, although she was angered enough that she wanted to. Her hands balled into tight fists. Her pumped adrenaline made her want to hit something. She was only a few feet from the door. She thought of darting toward it, but two muscled men stood there with their huge arms crossed and their faces twisted with an *'I dare ya'* look. She clenched her jaw and almost took them up on it. As heated as she was, she didn't see the two men winning the bout. But this battle wasn't their doing and not their fight.

Flora eased closer. From the corner of her eye, she noticed Jinn approaching. A second later, Eva pushed her way through the crowd that had resumed dancing and rather oblivious of the raucous only a few feet away. The trio stood before her with expressionless faces.

"What have I done?" Kailey asked. Her fists ached from holding them so tightly.

Eva's stern gaze broke. She burst into a small fit of laughter and glanced toward Flora and then to Jinn. She waved her hands and shook her head. "Sorry, Flora, but I can't do it any longer."

Jinn roared in laughter, too.

"Do what?" Kailey asked, her jaw tightening.

Confused, she looked from Eva to Jinn, and then her eyes settled on Flora's throat. Flora laughed softly. "I'm sorry, child. *Welcome* to Nocturnal Trinity! We simply couldn't help ourselves."

"What?" Kailey's brow creased with uncertainty. Although partially relaxed, her hands remained balled into fists. Just in case. Her anger was hinging toward rage.

Eva fanned her face with her hand. "We generally do this to some poor unsuspecting soul around Halloween. Someone that's a virgin to the knowledge of demons, witches, and vampires."

"You were too innocent to our cultures. We couldn't resist," Flora said.

"This was all a joke?" she asked, fuming.

"All in good fun, child," Flora said.

"How *dare* you!"

Kailey's eyes focused on Flora's chest, directly above the vampire's left breast. It was good thing she didn't have a wooden stake. With her burning anger, Kailey would make every effort to drive it through the woman's heart. Whether or not if it actually worked, she'd be satisfied at least temporarily.

Flora's eyes narrowed as she read Kailey's thoughts. She slid toward Kailey. Her hand wrapped around the girl's throat and squeezed tightly. "That's not something you need to dwell on."

Kailey's face reddened. Her eyes bulged. Eva grabbed Flora's wrist.

"Careful, witch," Flora said. "The ties between us are strained enough as it is."

Jinn placed a hand on Flora's shoulder. "Let the girl go. We did carry our prank out a bit further than we agreed, even more than we do on

Halloween. She has a right to be angry. Is there any one of us who wouldn't think vengeful thoughts over something less trivial?"

Flora took a deep breath and gazed at Kailey. Kailey refused to make eye contact, staring instead at the woman's chin. "I could snap your neck without much effort, girl. Know that."

Kailey closed her eyes, gasped for air, and gave a nod.

Flora released her. Kailey took a deep breath of air and leaned forward.

"One thing I admire about you is your courage," Flora said. "Instead of staying afraid, you were determined to fight your way to escape. Most cower and cry. I commend you for bravery. Jinn?"

Jinn smiled and pulled a laminated tag from his shirt pocket. "Here."

Still panting, Kailey took the tag and said, "What's this?"

"You're a honorary member of Nocturnal Trinity. No need to stand in the line with the pathetic beggars ever again. Consider it a conciliation prize."

Kailey gritted her teeth. She fought to keep her mouth closed.

Conciliation prize? You bastards!

She had come to Nocturnal Trinity for a purpose. A serious reason. She wanted to find her brother's killer. Instead she was made the butt of some sick joke because she wasn't dressed a *certain* way. Even after she had revealed to each of them what her mission was, they still carried out their distasteful prank.

Jinn stepped toward her. His eyes shifted through various colors. "Look, Kailey. Our timing was perhaps bad."

"*Perhaps?*" she said in a near hiss of a whisper through clenched teeth.

"But the person that you're looking for, this Cassie, she's not here. I've combed the place, Flora has, and Eva did too. We don't know her. Please forgive us for ... what we put you through. That's why we each looked for her while giving you a *tour* of the place. That's why we offer you the membership. Feel free to return any time if you believe she'll return."

Kailey dared a defiant glance into Flora's eyes. The woman's gaze was cold, much like the vampire's corpse and heart. Her fear of the vampire had foolishly vanished. She wished to make the vampire pay for making her endure such humiliation.

Flora tapped into her mind. *Beware what you seek, for you may well find it.*

With the silent threat, Kailey turned and headed to the door. The two bouncers saw the heated rage in her eyes and backed to the side. She brushed past them. Pushing the door outward, she stepped onto the sidewalk.

As her current luck would have it, the mists from earlier had turned to cold rain. No umbrella. No jacket.

Peachy.

Her shoes were still on the dance floor, and she'd be damned to make a re-entrance to go get them. She braced the cold with anger, disgust, and determination. Adrenaline pulsed through her unlike any time before. If she could willingly tap into that, no fighter or supernatural creature would ever intimidate her.

But like luck, she knew it was only a matter of time before it waned.

Exhaling her frustration, her breath streamed a long white cloud. Trying to calm herself, she scanned the sidewalks. The faint streetlights cut through the forked branches of the leafless trees. Several cars lined the far side of the street, and the heavy shadows that hung over them were enough to make her wonder who or *what* might be lying in wait.

The lingering line of hopeful people was perhaps half of what it had been when she had entered Nocturnal Trinity. For a moment she entertained the thought of throwing her membership tag onto the street to watch the line turn into a crazed fighting frenzy, but she realized that keeping the card might prove beneficial in the future, especially since she expected she'd need to return.

Although the trio had played a cruel joke, and perhaps Kailey had unknowingly set herself up for it since she didn't truly know the type of subcultural atmosphere she was trying to sneak into. But now, she knew. She understood better what these death painted people sought. However, they were blind to what they were actually setting themselves up for, too. They were willing to sacrifice blood to become one of the chosen. The privileged. Yet, they didn't comprehend the exact cost that came along with submitting one's will to another's desire.

Of course with how these *Founders* had treated her, there was the possibility that they never expected her to return, which may well have been their true intention all along. Eliminate a problem before she *became* a problem. Their nonsense gag might have frightened away others, but she viewed their actions more like taunting bullies hoping to make someone submissive to their threats. Bullies pissed her off.

It made no difference to her that these bullies were supernatural creatures. Surely they had weaknesses. Almost everything did. When she discovered what those weaknesses were, she'd capitalize on them. She was determined to turn the tables on them, especially if she ever discovered they knew who Cassie was and where the succubus was hiding.

Kailey crossed the empty street, cold water splashing across her nylon stockings. Traffic was dead. She pulled her cellphone out from behind her belt. She half expected a rectangular bruise on her abs the next morning after landing on it when she fell. The cellphone screen was a spider web design of glass fragments from where it had shattered beneath her.

"Shit!" she said, increasing her pace toward the parking garage. Carefully, she scrolled the screen, hoping not to cut the tip of her finger. No calls. *Good news.* The bad news was she'd have to replace her phone tonight or the following morning.

Kailey figured Raven would have been calling or texting repeatedly since her roommate always acted like Kailey couldn't survive without her. She hoped the distance between them would allow her friend to mature a bit more. Kailey was being forced to grow up quicker than she expected, especially after the ordeal inside the nightclub.

Before entering the parking garage, she glanced back at Nocturnal Trinity. Two bouncers stood at each door. A few of the people still waiting in the line with a lost look of rejection finally stepped out of the line and walked away. She wondered how they felt—wanting to belong to a club and being denied on a daily basis. Outcasts of the outcasts. One couldn't get any lower than that. With what Jinn had mentioned about most of the members not having an outside life or a family to flee to, what did the others do who were not members in the club and held the same depressing reality. Where did they go after the line ended and Nocturnal Trinity closed for the evening?

Movement atop the nightclub's roof caught her attention. Two tall individuals stood in dark trench coats. The only reason she saw them was due to their extremely pallid complexions. Otherwise their clothes allowed them to blend perfectly into the shadows.

She paused and turned at the parking garage entrance, watching them, which proved to be a grave mistake. Apparently realizing she had seen them, the two leapt off the roof, landing on the sidewalk in a squatting position, rose, and tore into a sprint straight toward her.

Kailey didn't waste the time or energy to scream. She wasn't the screaming type. She simply ran into the garage as fast as she could, hoping to get to her car before they got her.

CHAPTER 9

For Kailey there was no better high than adrenaline. When it increased in the bloodstream, people were capable of doing extraordinary things that they normally couldn't. This was no exception for her, either.

Still slightly pumped from the adrenaline during her altercation in the nightclub with Flora, Jinn, and Eva, her body reacted quickly. Now that she had active pursuers, a second burst of adrenaline pulsed through her.

She ran. The cold wet nylon wedged around her toes squished with each thudding step. Her numb feet pounded against the frigid concrete. Sparks of pain permeated through her cold feet, radiating all the way up to her ankles, but she didn't slow her pace. Her small feet pattering the ground made strange echoing sounds and left deformed footprints on the dry concrete inside the parking garage.

The abrasive surface shredded the hose off the bottom of her feet as she ran. She was a fast runner, but even with the grace of adrenaline, she didn't see herself running up three levels of ramps to get to her parking spot. Depending upon what these men were—vampires or demons—they were blessed with supernatural speed and strength, which gifted them with an increased advantage. She couldn't outrun them for long, and she certainly didn't have the time to wait for an elevator door to open if the lift needed to descend from a different floor.

Kailey sprinted toward the winding ramp and noticed a Goth girl and guy standing outside the elevator holding hands. The floor light above the door lit up. She changed her direction slightly and ran toward them.

The doors opened with a loud *Ding!*

The couple stepped into the elevator and turned, facing her swift approach.

"Hold the door!" she shouted.

The guy placed his hand across the door sensor to prevent the doors from closing. Slowing as she ran through, she thrust her hands against the back wall of the elevator. They smacked hard. She squinted from the pain and groaned. Panting, she turned and hit the close button repeatedly.

The two men in black trench coats sprinted toward the open elevator. Their thin pale faces were nothing more than tight skin stretched over their skulls. They had no body fat. Their wicked, violent eyes glowed a strange green and were filled with hunger and desire to inflict horrid amounts of pain. Prominent fangs protruded from their wide mouths. The backs of their trench coats caught the air, slightly resembling capes as they ran.

"Are you in trouble?" the young man asked.

"Not if these damn doors close fast enough."

He looked outside the elevator and noticed the two vampires. His eyes widened, and he pulled his girlfriend behind him bracing himself for their rushing blow.

"Shit!" he shouted.

The doors moved slowly toward one another. The gap was getting smaller, closer. For a moment she believed the doors would meet before these two men reached the elevator. In a blinding rush, the two men suddenly thrust their clawed hands through the narrow opening. They growled and snarled like crazed beasts. The Goth girl shrieked, grabbed the back of her guy's jacket, and pulled herself snugly against him, shutting her eyes tightly. Kailey shoved at the men's long-clawed hands, trying to force the two men to retreat their attack. It wasn't working.

The vampires blindly reached for her, grabbing air, hoping to snag her or someone. No words came from their mouths. Angered grunts and hisses breezed toward her.

With her right hand Kailey kept pushing the close button, but as long as their arms prevented the doors from closing, the elevator was not going to move.

"Dammit," Kailey said, shoving at the hands, pushing the button. "Close, close, close ..."

The Goth male reached into his coat pocket and took out a small glass bottle. He plucked the wooden cork from the opening, and approached the grabbing hands. He peeled back the sleeve of one intruder and poured the liquid onto the man's arm.

Immediately the ivory skin smoldered with rising steam. Pinkish purple blisters puffed on the vampire's pallid arm. The arm yanked back and the attacker howled in a fierce shrieking scream. He splashed water through the open doors, striking the vampire's face, and then he poured the remaining contents on the other attacker's arms. Welts formed on his pallid flesh, too. A moment later, the door closed and they ascended.

With a marveled expression on Kailey's face, she asked, "What the hell is that stuff? Acid?"

He shook his head. "No. Holy water."

Shit! Could this night get any stranger?

Already her mind was overwhelmed by the new knowledge of demons, vampires, and the great possibility that her sister-in-law was a succubus. Apparently figuring out how to stay alive was rising on Kailey's educational list.

"So they … were vampires?" Kailey asked, leaning over, resting her hands on her knees while trying to catch her breath.

"What else would they be?" He offered his hand. "I'm Blaze. This is Luna."

Without standing, Kailey reached and shook his hand. Sweat crested on her brow. Her breathing was starting to regulate. Her mouth was dry and pasty. "Thanks, Blaze. I'm Kailey. It's good to meet the two of you."

Blaze ran a hand through his sleek black hair. She wondered how much hair gel the guy used. A streak of Kool-aid red divided his long bangs. Two silver rings pierced his lower lip. He shrugged. "It's the least I could do."

"How'd you know they were vampires?"

"We've stood in that line for three weeks now. Not once has either of us been chosen to enter the nightclub."

"Then why keep going?"

He grinned. "It's the *in* place where everyone wants to be."

Kailey sighed. "They made me an honorary member tonight."

"Lucky you," Luna said, crossing her arms. A sneer curled her upper lip and her eyes revealed her bitter envy.

Luna's short hair was a variety of brightly dyed blue and red spikes. Her face was alabaster and beneath the fluorescent lighting, she glowed like a small moon. Luna was a fitting name. Her blue eyes sparkled. Her tight black corset pushed up her powdered white cleavage. Her right ear was pierced with at least a dozen or more small silver rings. Several chrome crosses were stitched into her corset.

Kailey shook her head and glanced toward Luna. "Trust me, it's not worth all the hype you've been told. The rumors aren't worth the sacrifice. At least not for me."

The elevator slowly rose.

Blaze chuckled. "Apparently not, since two of their Psi-vamps came after you. What did you do to upset them?"

"What do you mean?"

"The Psi vampires are the ones directly above the freshly recruited. Hell, you should *know* since you are a member now."

"No, sorry. No manual or codex. They didn't inform me of anything like that. Hell, they really didn't inform me of anything at all."

"Basically, The Psi-vamps have earned some stripes, so to speak. Those vampires are the ones that are mentally linked to the Founders in the nightclub. They are the outside *eyes*, more or less, but I've never seen them *ever* leave their posts on the rooftop. What did you do?"

"Nothing that I know of, except for leaving the club and that had been quite mutual," she replied. "Tell me, where did you get the holy water?"

Blaze reached into his pocket and took out a business card. "Here. It's a little shop on the north side of Seattle. They sell a lot of ritual supplies. Stakes, crosses, etc."

"So you knew about the vampires?"

Luna nodded and gave a wry smile. "Who doesn't?"

"Yes," Blaze said, laughing softly. "Most all of the Goths know. That's why they wait in line regardless of the weather."

"And you brought holy water to their nightclub? Why?"

He shrugged. "A precaution. You never know."

"I suppose it's good that you were never chosen," Kailey said.

"Why's that?" Luna asked.

"They compelled me at the door and took my silver cross, my cell phone and my Taser. No telling what they might have done to you for bringing holy water into the club. Looks like it's a more dangerous weapon than a cross since you can splash it from a good distance."

Luna's worriedly glanced toward Blaze for reassurance. Her radiant eyes dimmed. She looked broken and frightened. His confidence waned, too. He frowned, deep in thought. Must have something to do with the two vampires that had tried to attack her.

"We can't go back now," Luna said.

Blaze nodded. "I know. You're right."

"Why not?" Kailey asked.

"Because I assaulted those two with holy water. They saw us. Believe me, they *won't* forget our faces either."

Kailey frowned. "How do you know so much about them? I didn't even know any of these creatures existed until today. How do you know about the Psi ones?"

The elevator reached the third floor. Before the doors opened, Blaze hit the emergency stop button to prevent the doors from opening. "You have that business card. We have a secret group that meets at that shop on Thursday nights at midnight. Whenever one in our group is fortunate enough to be invited into Nocturnal Trinity, they fill us in on the details at the next meeting. I only tell you this because it looks like they have marked you."

"Marked me?"

He nodded. "For some reason, you've done something to offend them. I can't say that they *won't* kill you, but sending those two after you, it's a clear sign that they want to scare you away. Or perhaps not."

"I don't understand."

Blaze sighed and combed his hair to the side with his fingers. "They gave you honorary membership. They may only be testing you."

"In what way?"

"They might want to see if you're brave enough to return after those psi ones chased you." Blaze hit the emergency button again.

The doors opened. Blaze and Kailey cautiously peered out. No sign of the two reconnoiter vampires.

Blaze took Luna's hand and stepped outside the elevator. Kailey followed.

"Some advice," Blaze said.

"Yeah? What's that?"

"Stop by the shop and at least get yourself an iron crucifix for protection."

"Iron? I thought silver ..."

He shook his head. "No. The Founder vampires are old world vampires. Iron from their homeland is the best cross you can use. The shop owner has them. He can also fill you in on other valuable information that may well save your life if ever you decide to return to Nocturnal Trinity again."

"And what about those crosses you're both wearing? Most of the people in line wore those."

Blaze laughed. "Chrome crosses? No one takes *those* seriously. They're just useless trinkets. You might as well sprinkle glitter on yourself and call yourself a fairy. Doesn't make it true, and a chrome cross is like glitter. It's only for decoration."

"What more do you know about these vampires?" she asked.

"We're still piecing it together. So few of us ever get inside the club. Even though Nocturnal Trinity's security is tight, we do have a couple of undercover members inside. As for the rest of us, we keep hoping to be chosen. No one should ever try to force his way inside though. Even if you could get past the huge bouncers, you won't get past the two that just came after you."

Blaze stopped by a beat up station wagon with heavy metal rock group stickers all over the rear door. He unlocked the passenger side door to let Luna in.

"Thanks again, for your help," Kailey said.

"Until sunrise ... be safe," Blaze replied.

He opened the other door, sat down, and started the engine. She continued walking, counting parking spaces. Blaze slowly drove past her, nodded, and then Kailey walked alone.

Trepidation swept around her like an invisible cloak. With her adrenaline diminished, she watched her shadow stretch and change direction each time she walked beneath an overhead light. She glanced down at her aching, cold feet. Shivers shot through her body, partly from the cold and a bit because she wasn't certain if or where those two psi-vamps might reappear. The fear of the unknown and unexpected was worse than fighting a visible opponent. She didn't like being alone in a city she knew so little about.

Kailey got inside the car, locked the doors, and watched the aisle of parked cars on each side of her. Nothing moved.

She put the key into the ignition. Before starting the car, her phone lit up. Raven's crystallized photo shone on the broken screen. Her ringtone went off.

Thankful to talk to a familiar voice, Kailey answered. "Raven?"

"How could you do this to me!"

The panic in Raven's voice made Kailey recoil and sit back. She was jolted by sudden fear. Her stomach twisted. She'd never heard Raven use an accusatory tone with her before. "What's wrong?"

"How could you, Kay? *Why* did you?"

Raven sobbed heavily before the call disconnected.

Kailey carefully pushed the redial number. Several chips of glass dropped off the screen. A sliver of glass stabbed the tip of her finger, causing a crimson blood droplet to swell and after a moment, meander into a thin line down her index finger.

An automated message said, "You don't have permission to call this number. If you think—"

You blocked me? Why?

Kailey ended the call.

Chills crept up her spine. Her stomach sickened. More than three thousand miles separated them, and she didn't know what had upset Raven so much. Whatever it was had occurred in Boston, and Raven was blaming her for it?

Kailey started the car, backed up, and drove slowly toward the descending ramp. She had never felt more alone.

CHAPTER 10

*R*aven's words still rang in Kailey's ears. She wiped away tears. Driving past Nocturnal Trinity, she expected the two holy-water-scalded vampires to attack her car.

They didn't.

The waiting line was empty. She guessed they had left due to the heavy onslaught of cold rain. Even the bouncers had gone inside. She didn't dare glance toward the rooftop, just in case the two Psi-vamps were there.

Her insides quaked from nervousness. She cranked the defroster to high, hoping the heat would dissipate her chills. Her mind raced, trying to figure out a way to get in touch with Raven.

What had she done to upset her?

Kailey sobbed. "God, I miss you, girl."

She reflected a moment before correcting herself like Raven would have done. "*Goddess*, I miss you, Raven."

Kailey sighed.

Four years of classes to earn her degree in investigative reporting had constantly kept her questioning everything. To be a great reporter, she needed to dig for the evidence. Often she compared what she did to how an archaeologist worked. They exhumed artifacts from the earth. Sometimes, they were fortunate enough to get a relic in pristine condition. Other times, the artifact was shattered and the pieces were strewn over a vast area. Until they found all the pieces and put them together, they generally weren't satisfied. She had a lot of clues, but a lot of the information was still missing. The gaps left the puzzle unclear, without proper direction. She needed to dig for more information. Like artifacts seldom lay on the surface for anyone to find, the evidence she needed was not superficial. Entire cities were buried underground. Likewise, the facts she sought were not out in the open. She hoped Nocturnal Trinity was the most dangerous place she'd ever have to investigate.

Her gut told her otherwise. Should she continue pursuing whom she thought had killed her brother, she was destined to search much darker places, which might introduce her to even more dangerous people and creatures than Flora and Cassie. Of course, she had to survive the vampire and succubus first.

Kailey neared the hotel where she was staying, but instead of turning into the parking lot, she pulled alongside the sidewalk into a parking spot with a meter under the streetlight darkness. For some reason she didn't feel safe going back to her hotel room. At least not yet. She glanced into her side view mirror. As best she could tell, no one had followed her from the nightclub.

Flora, Jinn, and Eva probably had gathered enough information about her after she had been mentally compelled to hand over her cellphone. They had access to all of her information and her emails since everything automatically loaded on her phone without needing an encrypted password. So they knew exactly where she was staying. The possibility that they had not scoured through her phone and email messages was slim. And while under Flora's mind control, she had no idea what other information she might have unwittingly given the powerful vampire. How close did she have to be for Flora to gain control of her mind? Was Flora still able to use mind control on her from a great distance?

Kailey typed an address into the car's GPS mapping system that she had memorized long ago. Her brother's address. She wanted to know what Cassie was doing. Had she gone back home or had she gone to a friend's house like she had told Frank that she would?

She hoped the woman had done the latter. If she wasn't home, Kailey still possessed a key that her brother had mailed her. She'd love to look around the house to see what information she could find. His house would be the most difficult place for her to get clues.

For some reason Kailey didn't believe that Flora and the others did not know Cassie. Vincent would not have lied about where they had met. He had no reason to lie about something so trivial. Frank had even insinuated they had met at the nightclub. She believed Cassie frequented the place often and was possibly inside when Kailey was earlier. Nocturnal Trinity was an obvious link to her brother's death. She believed that wholeheartedly. Proving it, however, was another matter.

Their practical joke was more a threat in the hopes that she'd go away. Leave town. As disturbing as the situation was, she refused to give up until she discovered whether or not Cassie had something to do with Vincent's death. Should evidence prove that Cassie was indeed innocent, Kailey didn't have any problem getting on the next flight to Boston and leaving Seattle forever. Seattle held nothing for her except her brother's grave. And now he was gone.

Forever.

Seeing Mr. Langston strutting around with the two succubae troubled her. He openly accepted their demonic appearance without prejudice and almost rewardingly walked around with them like prizes on his arms. His eyes reflected a wealthy overconfident man empowered by the love of his two sexy demons. But, as Eva had told her, he believed they served him. In his blindness, he didn't understand that the grim circumstances of their relationship were quite the opposite.

A half block ahead emergency lights flashed at the side of the road. As she came nearer, she recognized the battered station wagon to be the one that Blaze and Luna had left in. The hood was up. He was bent over the engine shining a tiny penlight. Luna hugged her arms and stood huddled partway under the hood, trying to keep out of the drizzling cold rain. Kailey slowed and parked in the spot ahead of them.

She stepped from her car. "Do you need any help?"

Blaze turned and nodded. "Yeah. We could use a ride. I think this piece of shit has seen its last day."

"Come on and get in."

The Goth couple hurried toward her car and got into the backseat. She turned the heat to high again. Once they were inside and shut the back doors, Kailey glanced over her shoulder. "Where are you heading?"

Blaze rubbed his hands together and blew into them. His lips trembled from the cold. "We're sorta out of a place to stay on our own. That card I handed you earlier?"

"Yeah?" Kailey replied.

"The owner allows us to sleep in the basement. If it's no problem, could you drop us off there?"

"Sure."

"Where are you staying?" Blaze asked.

"A hotel a few blocks back, not far from Nocturnal Trinity." Kailey read the business card and typed the shop address into the GPS mapping system. She stored her brother's address into the computer's memory. Perhaps fate had altered her plans for the rest of the evening. She was partially relieved to take this detour.

Blaze chuckled. "Why the hell are you all the way out *here?*"

"I don't feel safe returning to my room right now." She considered telling them about her plans to drive to her brother's estate, but then decided that it was too premature since she didn't really know them. Besides, she had told the trio inside Nocturnal Trinity more information about herself than she should have, and that hadn't work out too well. She needed to learn how to hold back until she was certain she was speaking to trustworthy people.

Blaze leaned forward, resting his chin on the seat. "Why? Did those two vampires follow you?"

She shook her head. "No."

"Someone else?"

"No. But since they had taken my phone, I'm pretty sure that they know what hotel I'm staying at. Daytime seems like a better time to go there now."

"You're probably right," Luna said evenly.

"Besides driving soothes me," Kailey said. "It's been a few years since I have driven. I didn't own a car when I lived in Boston."

"Boston?" Blaze asked.

Kailey nodded. "Yes. College."

Luna perked up. Retreating from her sullen attitude, she leaned up beside Blaze. Her face beamed. She caught eye contact with Kailey in the rearview mirror. "That's so close to Salem. Did you ever go there?"

Kailey smiled. "Yes, my roommate and I went at least one weekend a month. Sometimes more often than that."

Luna faced Blaze with raised eyebrows. "I'd so love to go there."

He kissed her cheek and smiled. "One day. I promise."

Kailey looked at Blaze in the mirror. "So tell me why you and your group have so much interest in Nocturnal Trinity?"

"That's something you should talk to Micah about."

"Micah?"

"The shop owner."

Kailey smiled. "Surely, you can tell me something more than that?"

"You're right. I could."

Luna nudged his arm and gave him a frown.

"What?" he asked.

"She's giving us a ride in this bad weather, Blaze. Besides, it's apparent that she's not in favor with the league at Nocturnal Trinity. She needs to know."

"League?" Kailey frowned.

"Their hierarchy," Blaze replied.

Kailey sighed. "Luna's right. They're not too keen on me being there."

"In spite of that *honorary* membership, right?" Blaze asked with a wry grin and a quick wink.

Kailey laughed softly. "Not so much honorary as it was a *conciliation prize*. And yes, that's *exactly* how they termed it."

"What the hell is that supposed to mean?" he asked.

"As a practical joke, they tried to scare the hell out of me since I didn't believe demons and vampires existed before tonight."

"Really?" Luna asked.

Kailey nodded.

Blaze shook his head. "That's strange. The majority of our American society doesn't believe in such creatures, either. People are blind to the supernatural, even those most hopeful in finding them to become one. Give thanks to Hollywood and books for keeping their existence nothing more than fictional lore. Of course, the fanatical will always believe and those are usually the ones *not* chosen to enter Nocturnal Trinity."

Kailey shook her head slightly. "I wish I *still* didn't believe in them. But if you two have been trying to get inside to research what's going on, there must be a reason why."

"Presently, the best I can tell you is that there has been a major shift in energy in Seattle. Some great evil has arisen that wasn't here before."

"In Nocturnal Trinity?"

"We cannot say that for certain, but it is likely that nightclub is the source of its origination in Seattle."

"How does Micah know so much about these paranormal influxes?"

Blaze shrugged. "That's something you need to ask him. To Micah, this evil energy flux is personal, but I'm not certain why."

"He's never told you?"

"No," Luna said. "Right, Blaze?"

Blaze shook his head. "Not entirely. We're a small group. Thirteen, counting Micah. We spy for any suspicious activities in and around

Nocturnal Trinity and some other ... not so pleasant areas. We report our findings to him."

Kailey looked into his eyes with intense interest. "And you're willing to help him ... why?"

"He's a cool guy. Plus he's taught us a lot about the supernatural beasts and how to survive," Blaze replied. "According to him, darker things are coming to Seattle."

"Much darker things," Luna whispered.

"Then why doesn't he tell you more?" Kailey asked.

Blaze shrugged. "For our safety?"

"You have thirteen members?"

"Yes."

"So a coven?"

"Some might think so, but we don't consider it as such," Luna said.

Kailey chewed her bottom lip for a moment. "My roommate is a witch. Has been since she was very young. That's why we went to Salem a lot. She'll probably move there eventually. But there's nothing in Salem like what I saw at Nocturnal Trinity tonight."

Luna smiled. "No. There's not. That's why I *want* to go to Salem. The witches dominate what powers come into their city."

"Are you a witch?" Kailey asked Luna.

"A novice, but thanks to Micah, I'm learning a lot."

Luna's voice of reverence toward Micah disturbed Kailey somewhat. Either he was generally a great person with good intentions to help people avoid evil, or he was a powerfully charismatic person that charmed others to claim his dogma as their own. Charmers were often more dangerous than people gave them credit for, and by the time followers understood that, it was too late. One didn't have to go too far back in history to see the results of cult leaders.

On the chance that Kailey got to meet Micah and discuss his goals, she'd remember not to drink the philosophical Kool-aid. Her interests to talk to him lay more in finding out what secrets Nocturnal Trinity kept hidden from the city.

Blaze smiled into the mirror at Kailey. "Given that you are new to knowing vampires and demons do exist, Micah can give you lots of beneficial advice. He also has a small library of ancient books about supernatural creatures that he loans out."

The GPS computer indicated that they were approximately two blocks from the Metaphysical Ritual Supply Shop. Traffic seemed a bit steadier here than near Nocturnal Trinity, which she liked. She felt safer.

Following the automated, computerized voice on the GPS, she turned into a narrow alley into sudden darkness. No street lights. She slammed the brakes. The headlights revealed several rusted dumpsters and bent up aluminum trash cans. Hard bits of sleet and rain bounced off the windshield. She hit the auto-lock mechanism for the doors.

Kailey glanced over her shoulder at Blaze. "Is this the right street?"

He nodded.

"Here?" she asked.

"Yes. You have to drive about a half block farther down the alley."

Kailey took a deep breath and held it while she thought. Her night had been bad enough with the vampire, witch, and the demon. For some odd reason, she didn't believe she was completely free of danger.

And now ... this? A dark alley where she could easily get pinned in and surrounded by newly gained enemies? She'd seen horror movies with premises that ended better than this.

Kailey didn't like the thought of driving into an unlit alley. She wanted to tell them to get out and walk, but she could never bring herself to do that. She'd hate to read in the paper the next day about someone finding the bodies of these two in an alley dumpster. Of course the headlines could be about the three of them being murdered, but she'd be dead and unable to read it. That made the situation even worse to imagine.

"It's okay, Kailey," Blaze said. "We can get out here."

Kailey sighed and lifted her foot off the brake. "Nonsense. I'm not going to let you walk in this weather. I'm just a bit uneasy about dark tight places right now."

"I can understand that," Luna said. "But trust me, there aren't any bad vibes in this alley. None to us."

"She's right," Blaze said. "It's our home."

Kailey drove slowly. Golden eyes reflected in the headlights. A black cat slinked from the alley and behind a dumpster.

"It's Midnight!" Luna said with excitement. She looked at Kailey in the mirror. "That's my cat."

Kailey gave a slight smile, turned back toward the alley, and rolled her eyes. The longer Kailey was around this girl, the less she believed Luna actually sought the Goth lifestyle. She still acted like a twelve-year-old. Her nature seemed too jolly and she was not a drab downer. Her outfit and makeup were merely an extension she could use to spy for Micah. Doing such favors granted her more spell and ritual training. Easy trade for an eager soul.

Midway down the alley the right side widened into a small parking lot. The magic shop. Candles burned inside glass lanterns. The shop wasn't what she had expected it to look like. The storefront was modest with various posters taped on the glass about various meetings, concerts, and readings. She had expected the place to be darker and perhaps more sinister.

She shook her head, softly chiding herself. Nocturnal Trinity had left a bad image in her mind, which might take adequate time to shear the grime from her soul.

Kailey put the car into park. Blaze and Luna got out. Before he closed his door, he said, "Hey, you're free to spend the night here with us. I'm sure Micah won't mind."

Kailey smiled and shook her head. "I appreciate the offer. Really. I can't impose."

"You're not," Luna said with an eager innocent smile. "We have plenty of room."

"No, really. I have a lot of things on my mind. It's been a trying day. But, I will come by tomorrow when Micah is here. He might be able to help answer some of my questions."

"You're sure?" Blaze asked.

Kailey nodded.

"Thanks so much for the ride," Luna said.

"Not a problem."

Blaze closed the car door, waved, and fumbled with some keys as he headed to the side door. She waited until he got the door opened, and they stepped inside before she backed the car up and drove back in the direction she had come.

Kailey thought about everything that had transpired since she had left the cemetery. Although she had seen a lot of new disturbing creatures that possessed supernatural powers, the one incident still bothered her the most. The way Flora had penetrated her mind and read her thoughts. The vampire alarmed her. Flora possessed the ability to control what Kailey had done and afterwards, erased it from her memory. That was a dangerous power. A power Raven had never mentioned, and Kailey believed Raven might never have heard of anyone capable of such control.

Blaze had mentioned that Micah had knowledge of an evil entity that had made its presence known. She didn't know exactly what the significance was, or whether Cassie had any role in the sudden shift of power. Perhaps even her sister-in-law was a victim under Flora's mind control and all. She wondered if a vampire could hold such power over a demon.

But when it came down to Cassie, Flora and the others didn't seem to be forthcoming, only that they had expressed they didn't *know* her and had *looked* for her during their mischievous game. They knew more than they were telling. But she didn't know how one might pry such information out of a vampire and demon or if one even could. Being mortal, she didn't have any true means to ward off their powers. She fought with words, which might be good for a journalist, but combatting vile soul-seeking creatures ...? She didn't see how she could use her meager skills to her advantage. She doubted martial arts aided her against a vampire capable of taking full mental control of someone else.

Kailey disliked how everything in her life was unraveling. She had just buried her brother, failed to find the essential information about Cassie that she needed, and apparently had done something critically wrong that had damaged her friendship with Raven. Their friendship was the last cherished possession she clung to in this life. That meant she had to fix it, even though she didn't know what had upset Raven to such a drastic degree.

She drove until she came upon a twenty-four hour drugstore. Pulling into the lot, she hoped that they sold disposable cellphones. Since Raven had blocked Kailey's number, she might send a short explanatory text from a new number. She might only get one chance to communicate, but at the moment that was all she had.

*A*fter Kailey activated her new phone, she added Raven's number to her contacts. She typed: *"Raven, I don't know what I've done. Please talk to me. You're my best friend. Please respond. Tell me what's wrong?—Kailey."*

She held her breath several moments while her thumb gently rested on the "send" button. With tears forming in her eyes from the fear that she might not get any response at all, she closed her eyes and pressed the button. Now came the wait.

An extremely long thirty seconds passed, which was at the edge of eternity in a texter's world. She didn't receive a text, but the phone rang. "Raven?"

"Kailey? Why do you have a new number?" Raven's voice crackled as she spoke. She sniffled. Kailey wondered how long Raven had been crying. She assumed since she had called and erratically yelled at her.

"My phone got smashed. I will transfer the SIM card later, so my old number will be active again."

A long sniffle came over the phone. "Oh."

"Raven, what's wrong? You're very upset."

"You called and left me horrible voice messages."

"No, Raven. I didn't. Honestly," Kailey replied. She went on and explained how they had taken her phone at the door when she went inside Nocturnal Trinity. "Hon, you know I'd never say anything bad about you. You're like a sister and you *are* my very best friend."

"I had a half dozen messages while I was with my witch friends. You know they frown on bringing a phone to any meeting. So when I got back to the room and saw messages from your phone—"

"It wasn't me. *They* had my phone."

"It certainly *sounded* like you."

Kailey wiped away a tear. "It wasn't."

"I miss you," Raven said. "It hurts inside."

"I miss you, too. It's frightening here without you."

"Come home."

"I can't. Not yet. Did you get a chance to talk to your elder?"

"I did."

"What did you find out about that symbol?" Kailey asked.

Raven cleared her throat and blew her nose. "I told you it had some bad vibes, remember?"

"Yes."

"It's worse than what I had even thought."

"In what way?"

Raven sniffled. "There is a unification of three forces, like I had theorized when we talked earlier. This synthesis is between ... are you ready for this?"

"Vampires, demons, and witches."

"You know?" Raven asked.

"Yeah, I *met* some of them. One from each faction. My guess is that each is the leader of their group."

"Ah, I see."

Kailey sat in her car, watching the parking lot while she talked. As she thought about the nightclub and Flora, she became uneasy. Almost paranoid. "You knew vampires existed?"

"Yes."

"And you didn't think this information was something I *needed* to know?"

"Would you have believed me if I told you?"

"Probably not."

"See? Kay, you have no belief toward any deity, either, which is unusual. You know I am a witch and you've never ridiculed me about my lifestyle. I was afraid if I told you about vampires, you'd think I was crazy and our friendship would be over. Right?"

Kailey laughed softly. "I already *think* you're crazy, but I love you anyways."

"I'm in good company then."

"Tell me more about Nocturnal Trinity."

"There's so much to talk about. I wish we weren't so far apart. It's easier to talk face to face."

"I know. But we're not. This is important to me."

"Well, most people have no idea about what the symbol represents. To many the artwork is part of the show, their trademark, but Skye wanted me to tell you to stay away from them. The evil flowing in that circle isn't something to take lightly."

Kailey sighed. "The research I've done today—"

"Oh, the reporter in you! HLN will be lucky to hire you."

"Be serious, Raven. I met a young couple today that told me that something evil has emerged in Seattle recently and it possesses a great deal of power."

"Really? Do you believe them?"

Kailey checked her mirrors and rechecked the door locks. She didn't like sitting in the near empty parking lot this late at night. She felt exposed and watched. "They believe it wholeheartedly. They live in an apartment beneath a witch supply house, and the owner, Micah, is the one who gave them the information. Now the witch, Eva, at Nocturnal Trinity felt the power of your spell on my pendant."

"Do note, my dear. The witches in that nightclub aren't like the ones here in Salem. They are of a fiercer lineage. They are dangerously powerful and use blood sacrifices to cast their magic. Black magic, which means they do not honor, 'Harm no one.'"

"I sort of got the feeling that the witch I met wasn't all warm and friendly. Then she is definitely in the right place."

"What do you mean?" Raven asked.

"The nonmembers are willing to do whatever is necessary to be selected by the Chosen in order to enter Nocturnal Trinity, which means giving blood."

"You saw that?"

"It was inferred. The Red Cross should be so lucky. People line up outside the nightclub's doors for hours to get in."

Raven blew her nose again. "And you got picked the first time?"

"Yes, to teach me a lesson obviously. But, hey, I'm now an *honorary* member."

"Look at you!" Raven said. "Stepping up in Seattle after only one day."

"Hardly."

Raven replied, "I'd be leery of ever returning there."

"Oh, trust me, it's a last resort. The only way I will go back there is if I can't find the answers elsewhere. I am going to the attorney's office where my brother worked tomorrow morning. Maybe there's some clues there."

"Okay, hon, but here's where I drop some critical information in your direction. So listen carefully."

"I'm listening."

"Kay, the symbol represents a mutual binding between six demons, six vampires, and six witches. Their bond, well ... circle, has enhanced their powers into one force, giving them frightening power."

"Flora's the one that frightened me the most."

"The vampire?"

"Yes," Kailey replied.

"Why?"

"Mind control. Not just compulsion. She could telepathically reach across the room and tap into my mind. She can control people. The entire dance floor was under her control, blocking my exit." Recalling that, chills ran up her arms. She started the engine and checked all the mirrors again.

"If she has that kind of mind control, you probably *did* leave those hateful messages to me."

"You really think she could do that?" Kailey asked.

"Do you remember anything during the time they took your phone?"

"No."

"Then yes, it's possible."

"Damn."

"I know, right? They are strongest inside that building and when they are all together. Never forget that. It's their turf. Mortals stand no chance trying to fight them there."

"I will talk to this Micah tomorrow. He knows a great deal about them."

Raven sighed. "Apparently not enough if he's still snooping around there."

Kailey glanced at the console clock. 3:33 a.m. Damn. *Where had the night gone?*

"Beware and be safe."

"I will."

"I want you to return to Boston, but I respect what you seek."

"Thanks, Raven. I will probably look for a place to rent tomorrow."

"Seriously? Why?"

"Just for a week or two. It'd be cheaper than a hotel."

"That's probably true. When you get an address, let me know, okay?"

"You'll be the first person I tell. Probably the *only* person I tell."

"Hold on a second," Rave said in a quick whisper. Her voice tinged with uneasiness and fright.

"What is it?"

"Shh!"

Kailey felt her stomach twist.

"There's something here," Raven whispered.

"A person?"

"No. A spirit or a demon."

"Stay on the phone."

"Shh! I'll try. I need to set up a warding spell. *Oh, Goddess ...*"

"What's going on, Raven?" Kailey whispered.

"I see its shadow outline through the curtain. It's on the outside of our apartment, Kay. I need to go."

"No. Don't hang up."

"I need both hands, dear, and I need to get to my altar."

"Please ... don't hang up, Raven."

Raven whispered, "Some advice for you."

"What?"

"Start believing in a deity. It's for your own protection. What you're up against is dark. They fight on a spiritual level. Arm yourself."

"I'll be okay. Really."

"I'm getting off here now," Raven said evenly. Her serious tone disturbed Kailey. Seldom did her friend ever keep stillness in her voice. She was usually too giddy, but not now. She was dead serious.

"Raven, don't hang up."

"Sorry, love, but I can't have outside distractions. Love you, honey. Be safe."

And with that, the call ended.

Kailey felt numb. She had no doubts that whatever was trying to intrude into their apartment had found Raven because Kailey had gone to Nocturnal Trinity. For the first time since her parents had died, Kailey wished she believed in prayer. But she had blamed God for the death of her parents and refused to ever seek His help or guidance. No matter what she did, she was too far away to assist Raven. The distance was nothing compared to the emptiness inside.

Calling the police did no good. What could she tell them? And if they did go to the apartment to find Raven in a ritual prayer, they wouldn't react to the situation too well. Raven would never forgive her for such an intrusion, either.

Kailey didn't know the names of any of Raven's coven friends, so contacting them was impossible. There was nothing she could do except hope and wait. After all, when she had denied every possible deity, why should any of them bother to listen to her now?

Worrying wasn't going to change the present situation. Raven was a strong, brave woman. She had ways to protect herself that Kailey did not. All she could do was to wait until she heard back from Raven, so rather than worry, she thought it best to search for facts and evidence to keep her mind off of it. The quicker she discovered the truth, the sooner she could leave Seattle.

Kailey placed the new phone in the cup carrier. She pressed the recall address button on the GPS map. When her brother's address came up, she backed up and drove out of the parking lot. Before she returned to her hotel to get her belongings, she wanted to see his estate. She hoped Cassie was elsewhere, so she could look around the inside of the house. Perhaps he had left clues for Kailey to find.

～

The drive along the bay to get to Vincent's vast estate might have been more enjoyable on a moonlit night. As it were, with the rain and thick fog, the drive was treacherous. Several times along the road she believed a blind person had as good a chance of seeing the road as she did.

Her mind raced through all the new information the exceedingly long day had surrendered. Things she had never imagined existed except in fiction, legend, and folklore, had presented themselves to her. For some reason the news of dark creatures didn't disturb her. Perhaps she was simply numb from the shock that had yet to register in her mind. After this phase passed, she might become more apprehensive. Their existence, however, made her exploration desire arise. She wanted to know where they came from, exactly how old they were, and most importantly, what their weaknesses were.

Other than having to drive through the fog, she found its thick obscurity comforting. It blocked out the rest of the world and shrouded her. She was a vessel of emptiness. Loss had taken its toll on her throughout life.

Losing her parents at a young age had left her and her brother to face the world together. They had died during Vincent's first year of college. He moved out of his dorm and took what little inheritance money they had received to rent a small apartment for the two of them while he worked on his law degree and she continued toward her high school diploma.

Their parents' mysterious deaths made her delve into criminology and investigative procedures. She wanted to find the truth behind what had happened, but that mystery continued to elude her. Vincent sought being an attorney because he wanted justice to prevail when very seldom it did. She often imagined how strong a team they'd have made if they worked together on various cases that he represented. He would handle the legal side while she did the undercover investigation to help free his clients of their charges. But his murder robbed her of that dream.

The details surrounding the death of her parents weren't ever revealed to her. Because Vincent was older he was given the details, but he never disclosed them to her. Even after she turned eighteen, he denied her the information that she wanted to set her mind at ease. And now, he was gone, too. She'd never know what had happened.

Suddenly, she wondered if his death was somehow inadvertently related to theirs. Why had they died? What facts had he possessed that she might now need to stay alive? Did their family have enemies in high places?

Dammit! Stop overthinking everything or you'll go insane!

She tightened her grip on the steering wheel. Her mind constantly churned through various scenarios until she arrived at logical conclusions, but when it came to her parents' deaths, she never found logic or any closure. She spent many sleepless nights, staring at the ceiling in the darkness, trying to find reason. She counted on more endless nights without sleep after her brother's death, too.

That's why she needed to find Cassie. She needed to know the truth, and if the woman proved to be the succubus that had drained him of his life force before finally killing him ... she'd end the demon's life. Somehow. She didn't believe it would be murder since Cassie wasn't human.

Driving along the winding road, she came to a place where the fog was broken, making everything on the road suddenly visible. The GPS computer informed her that she was approximately one hundred yards from Vincent's estate. Her heart raced.

Kailey slowed the car. After the supernatural encounters at Nocturnal Trinity, she thought about turning around in the next driveway. Coming back at a later time would be better. Daylight. No, she couldn't come out this way during the daylight hours. Cassie might not recognize the rental car, but should she see Kailey's face, Cassie would know who she was.

Even with the darkness and thick fog, she felt more exposed the closer she came to her brother's estate. If Cassie was a succubus like Kailey suspected, what powers did her sister-in-law possess? Could she detect Kailey's presence like Flora seemed able to do?

In spite of her worries, Kailey kept driving. She was too close to turn back, and the more she thought about it, perhaps it was a good thing that Cassie knew she had driven out to spy on her. At least Cassie would know that Kailey was not giving up.

There had been something about the odd gaze that Cassie had given her at the cemetery. Not only did the glare indicate recognition, her eyes and slight smile were nothing less than sheer mockery. Taunting her. And then the woman flirted with Vincent's coworker right in front of her. Despicable. A woman, provided she was in fact human, could not be more disrespectful. A demon on the other hand ... There was no end to what games they might play for entertainment.

Perhaps Cassie's stare had been nothing more than a provocation. A dare. Cassie was too smug to consider that Kailey wasn't afraid of the challenge. The fact that Kailey had actually gone inside Nocturnal Trinity looking for answers was enough to prove she wasn't letting her brother's death go. Kailey suspected Vincent had not committed suicide, and Cassie somehow sensed her suspicion.

Kailey had hoped that she could talk to Cassie face to face at the funeral. At least, that had been her original plan. A person's eyes told a lot more about someone than her reactions and behavior.

She gasped.

Perhaps that was it? Cassie had only flirted with Frank and blown the situation out of proportion so she could leave the cemetery early to prevent Kailey from ever getting close enough to talk.

Maybe. But she still didn't accept that.

No.

Something more about Cassie troubled Kailey. A veil of darkness shrouded the woman. Kailey could only prove it by talking to her directly, which might be impossible now. If Cassie did have ties to Nocturnal Trinity, they had already informed her that Kailey was looking for her. Guilty parties tended to go into hiding or ... openly flaunt the success of their evil deeds as a means to terrorize others.

"Shit," Kailey whispered. She couldn't believe her eyes.

The silver limo was parked in the driveway near the house. Lighted candles flickered on the back patio. Cassie was associated with Nocturnal

Trinity. The Chosen vamps were paying her a visit, and Kailey didn't believe it was their respects for the loss of her husband. Perhaps congratulations were in order for her participation in his death?

Nervousness suddenly tightened Kailey's throat, making breathing difficult. Her heartbeat thudded harder.

Flora.

Kailey increased the car's speed and hoped Flora had not detected her presence. As she drove into another blanket of spiraling fog, she kept expecting that slight prick of sudden pain to stab into the back of her skull as Flora tried to regain control of her mind. It never came. She tightened her hands around the steering wheel to try to stop their shaking. A terrible thought had just occurred to her. If Flora took control of Kailey's mind while she was driving, she could have Kailey drive off a steep embankment to her death and it would look like an accident. No one except Flora would know the truth.

Kailey took several deep gulps of air, trying to calm herself. She needed away from there fast.

The winding road, the rolling fog, and a new wave of misty rain impeded her progress. Not a good time to challenge these creatures of the night. They held home court advantage. Besides she could only defend herself from physical assaults and attacks. She needed to learn more about the supernatural creatures and their weaknesses. She *needed* allies.

Kailey thought about what Raven had told her before disconnecting their conversation. Kailey needed to choose a deity. In a world of temples, churches, mosques, and synagogues, she held no interest in giving her allegiance to any of their doctrinal beliefs. She had witnessed more strife from those religions than peace and love. Hell, war torn countries were divided and living in poverty because of religions for centuries.

Since she had met the dark sinister forces that now opposed her, she was defenseless and held no power anywhere near equal to thwart their attacks. She understood she was vulnerable to their supernatural abilities and could be killed quickly should they ever decide they wanted her dead.

Kailey sighed. She kept driving, and slowly worked her way back toward her hotel. She thought about her conversation with Luna and Blaze and knew where she needed to seek help.

Micah.

According to the young couple, Micah seemed to be preparing for battle against those who owned Nocturnal Trinity. He had a personal vendetta. Quite possibly, Kailey did now, too. Once she gathered all the necessary facts, evidence, and pieced it together, she and Micah might do well to align together, if everything led straight to Nocturnal Trinity's front door. But she wouldn't know enough about that until later in the day after she talked to him. As long as he didn't come off as an overly charismatic man bent on adding more to his flock or he turned out to be some sort of a paranoid psycho, she might be willing to join his cause. Otherwise, she worked alone.

Her cellphone lit up and rang. Startled, she jerked back and almost screamed. Only Raven knew this number. She smiled and clicked on the speakerphone. But it wasn't Raven's voice that she heard.

She didn't know *what* it was.

CHAPTER 12

*S*tatic crackled over the cellphone. At first she thought it was just a bad connection, but soft words echoed, rattling a rhyme, a poem, and after a few moments, she recognized it to be a chant.

A spell?

"Who is this?" Kailey asked while watching the road.

The rambling mantra continued without any direct answer to her question. She took the phone in hand and glanced at the caller I.D. Her heart sank. It was Raven's number, but it was *not* her voice.

"Raven? Are you there?"

The chanting faded, replaced by dark laughter, the kind that bellows deep and long whenever evil triumphs. The call disconnected. The phone's light died.

Kailey shook with tremors. The air seemed suddenly colder even though she was combatting the condensation on the inside window with the defroster set on high. The heat didn't lessen the cold that chilled her to the core.

"Please be okay, Raven. Please be okay." She fought tears, but she didn't know what else she could do.

The clock on the dashboard informed her that 4 a.m. was almost upon her. She was only a few blocks from her hotel. She actually contemplated getting her belongings, checking out, and taking the first flight back to Boston. That seemed her best solution, but would leaving Seattle actually stop these attacks? By cowering or flinching at their power, would they simply stop bullying after they had won?

She doubted it. Besides, if she ran, she'd always be on the run, looking over her shoulder. The only way to deal with power-crazed individuals was to meet them head on and show no fear. When they lost their ability to terrorize, they lost a lot of their strength and set their attention on other timid individuals.

Driving into the hotel parking lot, she didn't see any activity. All was quiet. Apparently people had better sense than she did and had decided sleep was more important than searching for whatever roamed the night.

Kailey parked and turned off the engine. She stared through the windows, watching for movement. After a few minutes she became confident enough to open the door and step out. When her bare feet touched the cold wet pavement, she cringed. She really missed her shoes.

Running on the tips of her toes, she hurried to the front entrance of the hotel room. The desk clerk talked on the phone and ignored her entrance as Kailey made her way to the elevator.

When she exited onto her floor, fatigue and lack of sleep weighed upon her. She wanted to sleep but didn't know if she'd be able to. She only had a few hours before she was to meet Frank at the Langston Law Firm to see her brother's office. She might not find anything useful and only reap another dead end. She hoped not.

Kailey slid the keycard through the door's lock. The light flashed green. She turned the handle and stepped inside. She secured the door and looked around the room.

Exhausted, she sat on the edge of the bed, rubbing her feet against the carpet, trying to warm them. She typed in Raven's number, worried that she wouldn't answer or that something *else* did.

The phone rang constantly.

No answer.

No voicemail.

Kailey pulled back the thick bedspread, curled up against the headboard, and tucked the blanket around her. She wanted to get rid of the cold that clung to her, but she shivered more from her worries and fears. She hoped Raven was okay. She didn't know. She couldn't know.

What had come to their apartment? Whatever it was, she believed it was a result of the actions she had taken tonight. Raven was strong in the craft. Kailey didn't doubt that. Her friend's years of dedication proved to work in her favor. She believed Raven would find a way to thwart off any evil, but there was also the gnawing at the back of Kailey's mind that Raven might have been overpowered. She didn't have any way of knowing. She could only wait but patience was not one of her best virtues.

After a few minutes, her eyes closed and sleep claimed her. Dreams awaited, but not the pleasant ones. The nasty ones plagued her, the ones where something chased her but she never saw what was pursuing her. She only knew to run. Never stop. And the worst part was in not knowing that after she awakened in a few hours, her true nightmares were just beginning.

~

Kailey jolted awake with a gasp. Before she moved, her eyes searched the room. Although she didn't see anything, she couldn't shake the feeling of being watched.

According to the digital alarm clock, it was nearly eight o'clock.

Damn.

She had less than an hour to get ready to meet Frank. Groggy, she slung off the blanket, placed her feet on the carpet, and then she rubbed her eyes. A second later, she pressed Raven's phone number and let it ring while walking to the bathroom.

The phone rang out.

Damn, where are you, girl?

No answer, but at least Raven had not blocked this phone. Yet, Kailey worried that something bad had happened. That's what she hated about being so far away from home. She didn't have anyone else to call. Their closest friends had all headed back to their families after graduation. Some had taken trips to other places as self-reward for finally graduating.

Kailey set the phone on the bathroom sink and started the shower. While the water's temperature adjusted, she rummaged through her suitcase and picked out a comfortable blouse and blue jeans. She set out her running shoes that she wished she had worn the night before.

She hurried to the shower. Normally a long hot shower was the best thing to set her mood for the day, it eased her tight muscles, and helped her relax. She didn't have time this morning. Once she ran her errands and met Micah, she planned to get on the next plane back to Boston. She needed to know Raven was okay.

After the ten-minute shower, dressing, and dragging her baggage out of the room, she headed to the front desk to check out. She grabbed a Styrofoam cup of coffee from the complimentary breakfast bar and took a sip.

Bitter, but it would have to do. She grabbed an apple and a banana.

Out of the corner of her eyes, she kept attention for anyone that might be watching her. Few people stirred, but today she refused to let down her guard. She was on the offensive. One of the rules her martial arts trainers had taught her was to remain vigil and always show a badass attitude, even when one was afraid. It made potential attackers have second thoughts in their approach and often helped avoid fights. Physical attacks weren't her concern. It was the strange mind attacks and compulsion that worried her the most. She didn't know how to defend against those.

At the rental car, she put her bags and suitcase into the trunk. She gazed across the parking lot, looking for anyone standing around, and for people sitting in their cars, watching her.

Nothing.

"Good," she said.

On the road Kailey called the Langston Law Firm office. When the secretary answered, Kailey asked her to leave a message for Frank that she was running late, but should be there before ten.

She wanted to go by Vincent's grave and talk to him. She knew he wasn't there, but she still wanted to pay her respects one last time because after going through his office and meeting Micah, she needed to get home. She certainly didn't want to end up in the plot beside him.

There wasn't anything in Seattle for her except possible vengeance, provided the facts led to her suspicions. Revenge could come at a later date. Right now, Raven was more important.

At the cemetery, she parked close to where she had the day before. The skies were still an ashen gray. The morning breeze was soothing while she walked toward the graveside. Standing there, she felt nothing other than emptiness. She wanted to tell him so many things, but not like this. Not here. She knew the words were wasted because he could not hear them.

Kailey glanced down and noticed melted black wax. Strange footprints alongside bare footprints encircled Vincent's grave. She knelt to inspect the scene like they had taught her in forensic science class.

"Miss? Excuse me! Miss?"

She rose and turned to see a man approaching from a landscaping four-wheeler that had a small trailer hitched to it.

"Yes?" Kailey asked.

"I've already run a bunch of you off from here a few hours ago."

"I'm sorry?"

With a narrowed gaze he studied her. The elderly man pushed back his ball cap and scratched his brow. "You weren't with them, were you?"

"No. I just got here. This is my brother's grave."

"Oh, my apologies."

"*Who* was here?" she asked.

"Some weird folk. Doing some strange ... voodoo mumbo jumbo shit. Hell, I don't know what they were doing. I called the cops and told them, but I doubt they'll take it serious enough to send someone out. You know how that goes."

Kailey nodded. "What exactly did you see?"

"Most of them wore dark robes, had candles burning, and stood here chanting. Needless to say I told them to skedaddle because I had the cops coming out here. They left pretty darn quickly then."

"When were they here?"

"Before sunrise. But I don't know how long they had been at the grave."

"Thanks for making them leave."

The old man shook his head. "Hell, I'm just glad they left. That kind of shit is scary. Never seen anything like that before, and I've worked here over forty years."

Kailey reached into her purse and took out her business card that she had printed for job fairs. "Sir—"

"Burt," he replied. He started to offer his hand, but he looked at the grime on his palm and fingers. He put it into his pocket instead. "I'd shake your hand, but it's a bit dirty."

"That's okay. Here's my card. Should you see anyone else unusual at the grave, could you please call me and let me know?"

He nodded. "Sure. Of course."

"Thanks again."

"Don't mention it." He turned, heading back to the four-wheeler. "My condolences."

The man revved the engine and slowly pulled away, leaving her alone with her thoughts.

Kailey looked at the odd cloven footprints with long claws pressed into the mud, which she assumed had to be demon prints. What else could they belong to? Why hadn't the cemetery groundskeeper notice these creatures? Her guess was that the demons hid their true identities like Eva had mentioned.

She took the cheap phone and snapped a few pictures of the gravesite. Then she knelt and scooped up some of the black wax and odd ash. Before she stood, she whispered, "I miss you, Vincent. I have no idea what you were after, but I'm working on it. I won't give up. That's a promise."

Kailey stood. A sharp wind whistled through the trees. A warmth rose inside that seemed to indicate he was at peace. Her earlier emptiness faded. She felt a bit of comfort rise inside as she headed back to her car. Perhaps it was her vow in finding the truth more than anything else.

Within the past twenty-four hours she had discovered enough evidence to tie Cassie and Nocturnal Trinity to her brother's death. Cassie wasn't human. Quite possibly, she was a succubus that had seduced her brother and eventually drained him to death.

How did Kailey fight against a demon and win? And why did it seem that Nocturnal Trinity wanted to protect Cassie?

CHAPTER 13

$\mathcal{K}$ailey was almost back to the car when a police cruiser stopped alongside her on the narrow blacktop. She placed the candle wax and ash on the backseat of her rental car and closed the door.

The officer lowered his window. "I received a call about some strange activity near a grave. Have you seen the groundskeeper?" His deep voice was smooth, almost luring with charm.

Kailey glanced around, trying to find the man, but didn't see him. "He was here a few minutes ago."

"Any idea which grave it was?"

She nodded. "My brother's. It's over there."

The officer got out and gently closed his door. He wasn't quite six feet tall, but his muscular physique was evident through his tightly fitted uniform. Even through his long-sleeved shirt, his massive biceps bulged. Apparently he never missed a workout. His rugged and aggressive stern face was broken by deep smile wrinkles. His dark brown hair was cut in a close burr, which indicated that he might have served in the military at one time. He glanced toward the fresh grave where she pointed. "Recent?"

"Yes. Buried yesterday."

He faced her and his eyes softened. His lips tightened. "I'm sorry."

She shrugged.

"I'm Officer Jeff Brady," he said, extending his hand. "Most people call me Brady. If I'm not keeping you from anything, do you mind walking to the grave with me?"

Kailey wanted to tell him that she needed to leave, but seeing the interest that brimmed in his brown eyes, not so much for the case as for her, caught her attention. She knew the look. The instant interest people sometimes got when first meeting a new person that they found attractive. Her eyes probably revealed the same interest. His smile also teased of his nervousness, and she liked that. Sincerity.

She sensed he was strong, not just physically, but an odd vibe came from him that radiated self-confidence without arrogance. He probably chose to be a law enforcement officer because he truly believed, "To Protect and Serve."

Since he was an officer, she might be able to get some useful information to help her understand what had happened to her brother and perhaps Brady knew more about Nocturnal Trinity. The softness in his eyes, however, indicated that he hadn't been an officer long. He probably hadn't seen a lot of violence that calloused most people's hearts, making them cold and indifferent.

"There's no gravestone yet?" Brady asked.

"No."

"Name?"

"Vincent Yates."

Brady's eyes widened. "The attorney?"

She nodded.

"And your name?"

"Kailey."

"Beautiful name for a lovely young lady." He blushed as he stammered with the words.

"Thanks." She fought the blush but lost.

He flashed an interested smile at her and loosened his collar.

"What?" she asked.

"You're not from around here, are you?"

"No. I was in college but planned to move here."

"Where are you from?"

"I've lived in Boston for several years."

"Major?"

"Journalism. I want to work as an investigative reporter."

He smiled. "Good field."

"What do you know about my brother's death?"

"That was quick," he said with a grin. "Right to the questioning."

"I need to know. He was the only family I had left."

Brady cocked an eyebrow, studying her. "They never told you?"

"Not much in details but I was told that he killed himself. That's what the news reported, too."

"Well, it's also what the coroner wrote in his report."

"Is there any way I can get a copy of that?"

"Sure," he replied. "Just need to fill out the paperwork since you are immediate family."

"How exactly did he die?"

"He was found in the swimming pool." He hesitated to say more.

"It's okay. I need to know."

"When he was pulled from the pool, he still had a syringe in his arm."

Kailey frowned. "A syringe?"

"They really didn't tell you anything, did they?"

"No."

"I doubt they'll get the toxicology report back anytime soon. That can take weeks or months, depending upon how backed up the lab is."

Kailey took a deep breath, crossed her arms, and stared down at his grave. "What do they believe he overdosed on?"

"Heroin."

She shook her head. "No. He never did any drugs."

Brady looked away. "Sometimes those closest to us are the ones we know the least."

"No. My brother held too much self-respect to ever subject himself to any type of drug addiction, much less kill himself."

"When was the last time you talked to him?"

"It's been a while."

Brady sighed. He rubbed his eyes and then he rested his hands on his gun belt. His eyes searched the gravesite.

Kailey faced him and looked into his eyes. She read his troubled expression. "What are you *not* telling me?"

"The Langston Law Firm has been under a lot of scrutiny for a few months. Well, for the past year, actually."

"In what way?"

"Let's just say that they've made unscrupulous ties with some of the shadier members of Seattle's higher echelon. And the dealings haven't been exactly on the up and up."

"Nocturnal Trinity?"

His eyes suddenly widened. "How'd you hear of that?"

Kailey smiled. "I was there last night."

"They let you in?" he asked with curiosity.

"I was chosen to enter."

He frowned with a sly curious grin. "Why would you want to go there?"

"Because I believe they are the ones behind my brother's murder."

"Murder? How did you arrive at that conclusion?" he asked.

"I know my brother. Don't you think the circumstances around his death are a bit suspicious?"

Brady shrugged. "In what way?"

"He drowns *with* a syringe in his arm?"

He shrugged. "It happens. All the paraphernalia was on a small patio table near the pool. Drugs make people do strange things, especially after an overdose. They might struggle to walk or seek help. I've seen worse scenarios that sickened even the iciest officers. But, tell me why you think he was killed and how his death is somehow tied to Nocturnal Trinity."

"It's complicated." She glanced at her watch. "I'd talk longer, but I am actually running late for an appointment."

"How long will you be in Seattle?" he asked.

"Depends on what I find out today."

"About your brother's death."

She nodded. "Yes."

Brady reached into his shirt pocket and pulled out his card. "Here. You can reach me at this number. Please, before you leave the city, call me. I want to hear your reasons. Nocturnal Trinity has nothing good to offer Seattle. The owners are possibly responsible for a lot of crimes. So, whatever you think you know about the operation, or whatever you discover, I'm interested. I want the nightclub closed down, but I need proof."

Kailey smiled evenly. "So do I, and trust me, I will find it."

"Maybe later, after you're done with whatever you need to do, we can get together for coffee or dinner?"

With a nervous smile, she blushed again. "We'll see."

"Just to talk. Not like a date."

"We'll see. I can't make any promises because I really do have a lot of things to take care of."

"Oh, sure. I understand. Be careful."

"I will."

"Remember, I'm a phone call away. Don't forget that."

"Thanks."

His smile excited her. She turned quickly and swallowed hard. Staring much longer, she feared she'd never leave. Never before had someone caught her attention like he had. That frightened her, and she didn't quite understand why.

CHAPTER 14

While Kailey drove she had a gut instinct that her brother had left something for her at his office. She wondered what it was. Her gut feeling had never failed her, but such never prevented her from willingly walking right into danger, either. She had done so last night, but the rewarding knowledge had been worth the risk. Meeting Blaze and Luna had not been an accident. Their encounter almost seemed predestined.

Perhaps a deity was blessing her with allies in spite of her obvious distrust in higher powers. She chuckled and smiled. It took more than the simple coincidence of a series of events falling into place for her to find faith. Finding evidence that proved Cassie had killed her brother or a group associated with Nocturnal Trinity had in some way contributed to his death brought her closer to justice. In spite of finding the guilty party and exacting vengeance, she doubted she'd be any closer to holding allegiance toward any higher power. She needed enlightenment, and that had yet to come.

Kailey shifted her thoughts toward Brady and struggled to understand her immediate attraction to him. Due to the supernatural creatures she had met, she reserved an even greater sense of apprehension in trusting anyone at face value. Her investigative skepticism prevented her from believing what someone told her until she was able to back the statement with solid facts. Without visible tangible evidence, she couldn't believe in any ideology, which was why she didn't believe in any god or goddess. However, within the past twenty-four hours, she had met a vampire and a demon; a host of creatures she had never believed existed, which made her wonder what *else* might be out there? Still, that wasn't enough to sway her. Surely these immortal beings were flawed by some weaknesses and had ways to be killed. She was gambling her life to prove that was true. Staying in Seattle *after* Flora had tried to frighten her away let them know she was tougher than they had expected.

The downside, of course, was that their next encounter might be more vicious, painful, or deadly.

The way Brady had stared at her made her smile. She liked that he seemed interested in her, and his compliments weren't overly flirty. He had been helpful with information others had not given her about Vincent's death. Meeting for dinner later might not be a bad thing. She doubted it would be anything more simply because of how Raven might react.

Although she had intended to express her true feelings to Raven, Kailey couldn't completely yield to that desire until she knew for certain that fate hadn't deliberately thrown Brady into her path, either as a real love interest or an excuse *not* to tell Raven. Was it wrong to keep her options open? She was still young. Love could be such a fickle emotion.

You mean lust and infatuation, don't you?

She glanced at her reflection in the rearview mirror. "Stop being so shallow."

As Kailey neared her destination, it dawned upon her what Frank had told her the day before. Some of the police, attorneys, and judges were members at Nocturnal Trinity. Brady might be a member as well.

Closing her eyes, sighing, and shaking her head, she mentally chided herself.

Dammit!

She hated questioning everything and constantly assuming the worst about any situation or person, but what else could she do? By not being skeptical, she lowered her guard. No, she refused to ever do that again. So, for the time being, Brady was in the same category as everything else, and that pained her worse than she understood.

Kailey parked near the Langston Law Firm. She pressed quick dial and hoped Raven answered. She didn't.

She decided to make the inspection of her brother's office as fast as possible. Cassie had probably already scoured it, leaving little chance that anything of pertinent value had been left behind. Then she could meet with

Micah to see what more she could learn about Nocturnal Trinity and what his contention with the nightclub was. Between the two places she figured she'd find enough proof on whether she should stay in Seattle or head back to Boston.

Kailey entered the Langston Law Firm. The blonde receptionist greeted her with a broad smile. She was young, shapely, and probably used as eye candy to entice the men seeking an attorney. Her low cut sweater revealed enough cleavage that even Kailey found it difficult to maintain eye contact. Kailey didn't like the idea of any business using women in such a manner. She would never subject herself to such degradation, but she understood that most men hated waiting. These same men tended to ignore such impatience around an attractive woman while their delusional minds entertained the possibility of getting a girl's phone number or asking her for a date. Some men would turn down a drink of ice-cold water in the middle of a desert to placate a chance to bed women outside their league.

"Hi. Do you have an appointment?" the receptionist asked with wide eyes and a dumb smile. The lady's voice was annoyingly chipper for this early in the morning. Her eyes were brown, which meant she bleached her hair.

"I called earlier. Frank asked me to come in today."

The woman nodded. "Yes. Are you Kailey?"

"That's right."

"One sec." She picked up the phone, dialed an extension, and whispered. She set the phone back into its cradle. "Please, be seated. He'll be right down."

Kailey nodded and sat down on an antique leather chair. Staring at the front door, she tried to picture how Vincent had entered when coming in for work, dressed in his gray three-piece suit. She imagined the broad smile he wore, realizing he had achieved his successful dream. She had always admired his zeal.

While she faded into the daydream, Frank eased closer and stood beside her. "Kailey?"

His voice shook her slightly. He almost seemed to appear out of thin air. Had she drifted so far into the daydream? She hadn't slept enough, but generally she was more alert than that. She gazed up and smiled.

"Follow me, Kailey. Your brother's office is upstairs."

She grabbed her purse, stood, and followed him to the elevator.

"Have you ever been here before?" he asked.

"I did see his office a couple of years ago, but I think it was on this floor."

Frank nodded. "Probably. So how are you holding up?"

The elevator door opened. He nodded for her to step inside first, so she did.

"I'm doing okay. The shock is still wearing off."

"It's difficult to lose someone at such a young age. It's—"

"Unexpected."

"Yes," Frank said, nodding his head. "It is. No one likes the cliché, but it does gets better over time."

Nothing ever matched the ache of losing someone you loved. Nothing. Softening of the pain over the years did lessen, except on holidays and birthdays, and during the lonely times at night when thoughts about the person weighed heavily on the soul. The only thing that could remedy those times would be having the ability to call, to hear the voice again, but instead she'd only find the silence of death combined with the absence of hope. That's when regret and longing drove like a repressive dagger, ripping through the healing veil to open the wounds afresh.

After her parents had died, Vincent had taken their roles, making certain that Kailey was cared for and loved. Although six years separated she and her brother, their intuitions were linked mentally like twins. Their empathy for one another notified the other whenever problems arose, whenever they needed help. That's why she knew Cassie was the problem, the reason why his soul was being whittled away. She had felt it, sensed it. Yet there was nothing she could do. Cassie had held him spellbound. Blind love and obsession blocked out rationality and kept him in isolation.

Had she the ability to do it over, Kailey would have taken a leave during her last semester and flown to Seattle while he was still alive.

His death seemed untimely for a young man with such a bright future, but the timing of his murder was perfectly planned. He died just days before she'd come to Seattle. Now that she was here, someone or something had also attacked Raven. The thought caused anger to well inside her.

When the elevator doors finally opened, she stepped out and waited for Frank to lead the way. He offered a reassuring smile, but his eyes reflected his pain as well. Apparently he and Vincent had been fairly close, even though they had not spent much time outside the office like they once had during the past few months.

At the third door on the right, he stopped and opened it. "Here you go. If you need me, my office is two doors back."

"Thanks."

Kailey stepped into Vincent's office, tucking her purse under her arm.

The room's temperature was cold. On his desk was a picture of her. Another frame held a photo of them together at her high school graduation. Her throat tightened. Heat rushed up her face and tears welled in her eyes. There was an ache inside her chest that tears could never wash away.

The room looked untouched. According to Frank, Cassie had already been in the office, but she hadn't disturbed anything. At least it didn't *look* like she had on the surface.

His leather briefcase rested on the seat of his high-back leather swivel chair. She walked over to the chair. Each compartment in the satchel was unzipped. Someone had frantically rummaged through the files and folders inside.

What was she looking for?

Kailey grabbed the briefcase and hefted it onto the desk. She plopped down on the cushioned chair and pulled open the center drawer. Everything in the drawer was cluttered and in disarray. She couldn't help but think how upset her brother would have been to see this. He had been a neat freak. Some accused him of being OCD, which, of course, he had constantly denied.

She started to close the drawer when a sharp object pricked the back of her hand. The tiny hole filled with a thick crimson drop. She leaned down and carefully ran her hand along the underside of the desk until her finger peeled away a tiny rectangular manila envelope that was taped above the drawer.

Inside the envelope, she found a key with an engraved number: **612**. She wondered what it unlocked. The key looked like one that might open a safety deposit box, and if so, which bank? She slid the key into the side of her purse and carefully shut the drawer.

Although she couldn't prove it, she believed Cassie was probably the one that had gone through everything. What was she, or whoever was responsible for searching through his stuff, looking for? The key might unlock the answer, provided she figured out what it unlocked. She wondered what was hidden inside the box and if it held any relevance to his murder.

Kailey moved a notepad aside on the desk and noticed Vincent's appointment calendar. Just a few days before his death, he had circled a date.

The 17th.

Inside the date's square, he had written Jaclyn D. @ N.T. In addition to encircling the date, he had placed three asterisks. That meeting was highly important. The *N.T.* had to be Nocturnal Trinity. Who was Jaclyn?

While her mind sorted through this information, the pendant on her chest grew warmer. She placed her hand over it.

"Find something that interests you?"

Kailey glanced up and made direct eye contact with Cassie. She stood right inside the door. An instance of fright widened Kailey's eyes. Cassie's eyes narrowed and a devilish smile curled her lips. Her sister-in-law closed the door and leaned her back against it, never taking her eyes off Kailey.

Shit. Just the two of us ... alone.

Cassie had made her grand entrance and solemn threat without much action at all. The fact that she shut the door informed Kailey that this woman wasn't going to let her leave. Not easily, at least. Like those at Nocturnal Trinity, it was her turn to frighten Kailey.

Of course, Kailey could scream, for what good that might do. Although the woman was thin and small in stature, if she was indeed a succubus, Kailey didn't want to agitate her. She didn't know how much power such a demon possessed, but it was probably more than she was able to fend off.

"How'd you get in here?" Kailey asked.

Cassie stood in silence, her eyes looking Kailey up and down, possibly sizing her up. While she did, Kailey stood absolutely still, barely breathing, but never took her eyes off the woman.

Kailey could see how Vincent, or any man for that matter, would fall hard for this woman. Cassie's seductive nature was the right flavor to entice either sex. Every feature on this woman's alabaster face was perfect. No flaws at all. The delicate layer of makeup accentuated each detail of her perfect cheekbones, nose, and chin. She didn't need makeup at all. Her toned body in the form fitted dress was too sexy. She wasn't a grieving widow, and no man possessed a strong enough will to resist this vixen.

"I sensed you'd be here," Cassie said, pursing her lips. Her voice held a cute British accent when she spoke, something Kailey didn't expect and Vincent had not informed her. This certainly wasn't the same inflection she had used at the cemetery. "You're the sister, aren't you?"

"Yes," Kailey replied with a gasp.

Cassie strolled midway across the room, standing between Kailey and the door. Kailey thought about making a run toward the door, but didn't. It was too soon to underestimate Cassie's speed or her strength.

Cassie puckered her lips and drooped her eyebrows into a saddened expression. "I had hoped to talk with you at the cemetery, but ... well, *that* wasn't a good time, was it?"

"I believe Frank felt the same way."

Cassie's eyes widened and quickly narrowed with anger.

Kailey couldn't believe she had blurted out the words, but her inner rage still had not recovered over her sister-in-law's behavior immediately after Vincent had been lowered into the ground. Had Cassie shown the slightest tinge of remorse and loss, Kailey might have slacked off in her suspicions.

"Oh, you caught that, huh?"

Kailey felt her jaw tighten. She crossed her arms and nodded. "Yeah."

Cassie shrugged and then smirked. "A moment of weakness."

"Does that happen often?"

Cassie's eyebrows rose with surprise. "What?"

"Do you have countless moments of weakness by throwing yourself at the friends of your husband?"

Cassie rushed a few quick steps toward the desk, but suddenly backed away. Her eyes leveled on the silver pendant around Kailey's neck with a sense of alarm. Strangely, the pendant grew warmer, almost burning Kailey's skin. Apparently, Raven's blessing held a power that Cassie respected, perhaps even feared.

Cassie scoffed. "Vincent is dead. There's nothing more he can offer me. I hurt inside when I'm lonely."

"You have an odd way of showing it by trying to seduce a married man."

Cassie paced back and forth, her eyes hungry with anger, peering at Kailey like a caged predatory beast trying to figure out how to break past its barrier to attack. Her eyes burned crimson red momentarily. She gnashed her teeth.

"I know what you are," Kailey said.

Cassie cocked her head and stopped pacing. Her glare narrowed with fierce heat. "Oh? What *am* I?"

"You're a demon. A succubus."

Cassie howled with a high-pitched squeal of laughter. "Such an odd accusation. Tell me. What makes you believe that?"

"Everything."

Cassie shook her head. "That's a bit vague. Can't you narrow it down?"

"During the last few times when I talked to Vincent through Skype, he was being sapped of his soul essence. My friend kindly refers to you as a soul-leech."

"How endearing!"

Kailey smiled and shrugged. "You'd have to know her."

Cassie rested her hands on her hips with a defiant smirk on her face. "You were at Nocturnal Trinity last night, weren't you?"

Kailey took a deep breath, nodded. "Yes."

An amused smile spread across Cassie's lips. "You should be dead. They weren't supposed to let you out alive."

The statement shot an icy chill down her spine. Instead of responding to the baited information, she decided to remain on the offensive. "So you don't deny what you are?"

Again, Cassie attempted to approach her, hesitated. Her eyes darkened like crimson blood. Her pupils glinted with evil. Kailey's insistence seemed to be breaking through Cassie's veil.

"They should have killed you," she hissed.

Kailey smiled evenly. She slipped a card from her purse. "Actually, they've made me an honorary member. I carry it with pride."

"Oh, *do* go back. I *dare* you." Less of the dainty British accent and more raspy sounds like someone with a severe sore throat hinting on laryngitis.

Kailey ignored the taunt. It seemed the angrier she made Cassie, the more information she was getting. "You killed my brother, didn't you?"

"He served his purpose. Nothing more."

"You killed him?"

"Yes!" Cassie glared. She flashed a quick glimpse of her pointed fangs, still fighting to suppress her true nature. Her human cloak was weakening, withering. "What spell is this?"

"No spell. I know no magic." She instantly regretted making the statement. She had revealed a weakness.

"Then *how* are you commanding me?"

"I'm not. The truth is revealing you."

"No. It's more than that." Her eyes once again fixated on Kailey's neck, and she pointed. "That pendant! Who gave you that?"

"My friend. The one who said that you're a soul-leeching bitch. Well ... I added the *bitch* part, but you get the point. And she's a witch, so that's where the power comes from."

Cassie searched the room with her eyes, as if she was looking for someone else watching her. She paced back and forth again like a nervous trapped animal, and when she stopped, her eyes narrowed at Kailey. Long jagged black claws tore their way through Cassie's fingertips. They were weapons that could slice through flesh easily.

"You found something in here," Cassie said. "What is it?"

Kailey shrugged. "Come and see."

Cassie growled. By the look in her eyes, it was evident that she'd rip Kailey apart, if ever she came close enough, but the pendant stayed her attack. "Give me what you found, or I'll tear your throat out and drink your blood."

Kailey had been right when she had told Raven this woman was a bitch with a capital B. Hell, if looks could kill, Kailey should have died minutes ago.

"I know what you really are, Cassie. I will kill you for killing my brother."

Cassie's voice deepened. The beauty of her face vanished momentarily as the pointy edges of her demon face emerged. In a few seconds, she returned to the beautiful woman that Vincent had fallen in love with. "Give it your best attempt, but you will fail. You will *die* trying."

Kailey took the two small picture frames off Vincent's desk. Those memories were hers and his. Not the demon's. She refused to leave the pictures behind. She tucked them beneath her left arm. "These are all I came for, Cassie."

"You lie."

Kailey shrugged. "So sue me. There are plenty of attorneys in the building. Mr. Langston has a thing for creatures like you. Ask him if he has an opening. No telling what favors he'll ask of you in return though."

The demon's eyes narrowed as if the suggestion insulted her.

Cassie rushed to the closed door and pressed her back against it. For whatever reason she seemed to think Kailey wouldn't approach. Had Cassie not shown apprehension and fear of the pendant, Kailey probably wouldn't have considered coming any closer. Besides, being on the second floor, the door was the only safe way out of the office.

Kailey took the pendant between her right thumb and index finger and marched toward Cassie. Cassie pressed her back tightly against the door. Fear widened her eyes. Her facial components contorted.

Cassie's once elegant, perfect face faded. Her true demoness features surfaced again.

"Damn," Kailey said, shaking her head. "I can see why you wear the human mask. Your demon form is quite hideous. I take it Vincent never saw this side of you?"

"Get ... back. Don't ... come any closer."

Or what?

Kailey was probably ten feet away from the succubus. The warm silver pendant glowed brighter. She liked that she was inflicting pain upon this murdering demoness. The pendant gave Kailey bolder confidence than she'd ever felt before. She seemed to understand what it meant to feel high. Her adrenaline surged. She liked the feeling.

Cassie's eyes burned flaming red like molten metal. Her skin darkened near the shade of eggplant. Sharp fangs gnashed and she growled. Although Kailey had hurled insults about her appearance, in spite of all the demon features, the succubus was still intoxicatingly beautiful, but she'd never admit that to Cassie.

Good show.

"*Get back!*" The warning reeked of desperation.

Her human expressions rippled, vanished, and a demonic face with red violent eyes stared at Kailey. For a couple of seconds, broad thick horns protruded from and curled back around the top of her head. Her feet suddenly looked like cloven hooves. Three dark apparitions spiraled in a strange smoky mist around her strange feet.

Kailey smiled.

After another step, Cassie hissed and bared teeth.

Confidence was one thing. Arrogance and power flaunting made Kailey careless. She kept advancing, bringing the pendant closer, and watching Cassie curl back against the door, scrunching smaller. The demoness' eyes pleaded. The spiraling whirlwind of apparitions rose into a grayish-black curtain that seemed to be trying to pull Cassie through another portal or realm.

Cassie raised her hand with her palm outstretched toward Kailey. "I warned you! Get ... *back!*"

Seconds later, Cassie wailed and vanished in the circling cloud of smoke, which smelled remarkably of sulfur. No surprise there. But the thunderous explosion was something Kailey never expected. The eruption of the force sent a shockwave that propelled Kailey backwards, lifting her six feet off the floor. She plummeted on her back and skidded across the carpeted floor.

It was a fantastic curtain call to behold had Kailey remained conscious to see it, but instead her world faded to black.

CHAPTER 15

$\mathcal{K}$ailey awakened with several people kneeling around her. Her head throbbed. It hurt to open her eyes, and when she did, a paramedic shone a penlight into each one of them, making the pain even more unbearable.

Lesson One: Never piss off a succubus.

Kailey attempted to move.

"Stay still," the male paramedic said.

"I'm okay," she whispered.

"Let me decide that, Miss."

She blinked hard and tears rolled down the sides of her face. She tasted blood. She must have bitten her tongue during the fall. It felt swollen and bruised. From the corner of her vision, she noticed Frank standing, looking down at her. His pale face showed his concern. She looked at him until her focus cleared. "What the hell happened?"

"I was hoping you could tell me," he replied, nervously adjusting his tie. "Some kind of explosion, but nothing here seems damaged. Except you."

Kailey leaned forward, trying to sit up.

The paramedic shook his head. "Don't. Not until Sally finishes patching your arm."

Kailey glanced to her left, watched the woman pulling bloody slivers of glass from the inside of her biceps. She blinked several more times, wondering how her arm got cut up. Then she remembered holding the picture frames. They must have shattered when she was hurled into the air and dropped to the floor.

She shook her head slightly, groaned, and looked at the male paramedic. "How bad is it?"

"You're banged up pretty badly, but nothing's broken. You don't have a concussion. Luckily. But you will probably have a bad headache."

Have? She already thought her head was going to explode. Her heartbeat thudded like a battering ram against her skull.

He smiled and stood. "You might want to get some X-rays, just to make certain."

Kailey shook her head. "No. That's not necessary."

Sally placed another bandage over Kailey's left biceps, smiled, and patted her shoulder. "You're good to go."

Kailey frowned, pushed herself up, and weakly said, "Thanks."

The two paramedics helped her to her feet and sat her in the swivel chair. Mr. Langston stood at the door with a crude and slightly amused smile on his face. His dark blue eyes held no compassion or concern. His mannerism seemed every bit as cold and calloused as a rugged hit man. He straightened his tie, gazed at her for a few more seconds, and disappeared down the hallway without uttering a single word.

She found it odd that her brother's boss didn't seem to care.

Frank pulled a chair to the side of her swivel chair. He motioned the others in the room to go so they had some privacy. The last one out closed the door.

"Do you remember what happened?" he asked.

"Cassie is what happened."

Frank looked genuinely confused. "What?"

"Why the hell didn't you tell me Cassie was here?" Kailey asked with a harsh glare.

Taken back by the accusation, Frank shook his head. "She wasn't *supposed* to be here."

"You didn't tell her I was coming, did you?"

"No."

"She said that she knew I'd be here. She expected me to be here. *Today.* And she showed up just minutes after you left the room. Seems hardly a coincidence."

"Honest, Kailey. I never told her."

Kailey placed her hands to her temples, hoping to lessen the throbbing pain. After a few seconds, she opened her eyes and glared at him. "Well, she was here. In full demon force, too."

"Kailey, are you still going on with that?"

Kailey's jaw tightened. She was a second away from slapping the stupid right out of him. It probably wouldn't help if she did, but she'd feel better. "Look, I went to Nocturnal Trinity last night."

"Was Cassie there?" Frank asked.

"No. But your boss, Mr. Langston, was."

Frank shrugged. "So? He goes there a lot. He's old, eccentric, and likes to believe he's equivalent to Hugh Hefner."

"He's a member," Kailey said. "I saw him."

Frank nodded. "Yes, of course. He has a lot of money. The rich are given membership without much hassle."

"Well, he has a thing for she-devils."

"What?"

"The succubae. He had one hugging on each arm."

Frank squeezed her shoulder and offered a sympathetic smile. "Kailey, look. You've been through a *lot* of stress. You lost your brother and took a nasty blow to the head just minutes ago, but you need to understand Nocturnal Trinity has a lot of costume freaks. People that like to dress up in unusual costumes and display their unique talents. Some might even argue that it's Halloween there every night."

Was he in denial?

"And you're probably still waiting for the Great Pumpkin, aren't you?"

He looked thoroughly confused. "What?"

"Nothing."

Kailey was about to argue that it *wasn't* costumes she had seen, but then she looked into his eyes. They appeared oddly different, hollow. His story was quite altered from what it had been the day before. That worried her. Someone had gotten to him. If it wasn't Cassie, then the responsible person was possibly still in the building. From the strange look in Langston's eyes, it was possible he might have played a part in controlling Frank's recall.

Staring at Frank, Kailey realized there wasn't any use arguing with someone who had had his mind wiped clean and was implanted with replacement memories.

She felt sorry for him. He had seemed a man of good character the day before. A part of her believed that since he hadn't taken Cassie home by himself after the funeral, she might be the one that had done this to him.

Perhaps she was looking for her next victim to drain. That was possible. A succubus would do that, right?

The only thing Kailey was getting from Frank was red herrings. She decided she needed to leave one herself.

"I'm sorry, Frank." She stood and patted his shoulder. "You're right. I need to just go rest and clear my head. Get a plane ticket back to Boston. Nothing more for me in Seattle. Thanks for letting me get these pictures."

"Sure. No problem." His eyes indicated an emptiness to understand what was really going on, other than what someone wanted him to know. She hated to think that anyone or anything possessed such power. She needed to know how one possibly defended herself against it.

Kailey gently pulled the pictures from the broken frames and shattered glass. She grabbed her purse and carefully slung it over her shoulder, and then headed out the door. Instead of waiting for the elevator, she took the stairs. She didn't like the thought of being hemmed inside a tiny-boxed room; especially after discovering Cassie could *pop* up anywhere. At least she could run down the stairs, if necessary.

The way her head throbbed, she hoped she wouldn't be forced to run anytime soon.

Kailey decided not to leave Seattle until she killed the succubus or died trying. No higher power demanded that she do so, and even if one did, at this point, she'd ignore such a command. Foolishly she had thought the pendant was strong enough to destroy the demoness, which was almost a deadly mistake. She had greatly underestimated Cassie's power, but she had renewed respect for what this demon was capable of doing.

The magic radiating from the pendant had deterred Cassie and prevented her from stepping within a certain radius. However, that didn't stop Cassie's power or any distance spells within her arsenal from afflicting pain or worse. Kailey assumed the explosive exit was minor to what she could actually do. Yet, she couldn't help but wonder *why* the demon simply hadn't killed her.

Pain radiated down Kailey's spine. The feeling in her left arm had gradually returned, making the cuts burn like fire. Her throbbing headache pounded with an unrelenting rhythm that made her squint. While she drove, she was thankful for the thick overcast sky. Any brighter of light would probably immobilize her from functioning for several more hours.

The hour was fast approaching noon. Her stomach growled, but the nausea kept her from stopping at a drive-thru to get something to eat. Maybe the paramedic was wrong. Maybe she did have a concussion.

Kailey continued following the GPS directions to get to the Metaphysical Ritual Supply Shop. Euphemisms weren't what they used to be.

She tried Raven's cell number again.

Still no response.

This wasn't like Raven. She worried about what might have happened. The last they spoke Raven had heard noises outside their apartment. Raven had been concerned that the intruder was an evil spirit or a demon.

If it were anything like Cassie ...

Two days ago, Kailey would have thought her friend deranged about the suggestion of evil spirits, but now? Not so much. Not with the creatures she had seen at Nocturnal Trinity and certainly not after her recent encounter with Cassie.

She knew Raven was capable of taking care of herself. The magical power she had enchanted upon the pendant was proof of that. But this long silence, not answering her cellphone, or sending a quick text telling Kailey that she was all right, sent panic waves through her. Her already sick stomach tightened and churned with acid, making her almost hurl inside the car.

Kailey turned into the narrow alley where she had driven Luna and Blaze the night before. When she parked at the front of the mystic shop, she felt partway relieved. She wasn't certain why, but she guessed the reason was the thought of seeing a familiar face, provided Blaze and Luna were still here. The worst part of being in Seattle was the lack of close friends, but she hoped all that changed after she talked to Micah.

Opening the car door, she stood, and then quickly leaned against the side of the car until she gained better balance. She was dizzy. Her vision darkened. Shaking her head, she blinked several times, hoping the sudden blurriness went away. It didn't.

Bells chimed as the door of the magic shop swung open, and Luna excitedly ran out to meet her. Blaze wasn't far behind.

"Are you okay?" Luna asked, frowning with concern. Today her blonde hair was streaked with one purple strand and a bright red one. Her eyes and concerned expression indicated that she cared about Kailey, and in spite of her pain, Kailey was glad to see a caring face.

"You look rattled," Blaze said.

Kailey eased the car door shut, still propping against the car. "I've had better days."

"Did they come after you again?" Blaze asked with a tinge of fear in his eyes.

Kailey shook her head and immediately winced.

"Here." Blaze offered his arm to support her. Luna took her by the other arm. Together they helped her through the shop door. When the door closed behind them, a sheltered cozy feeling washed over her.

In the corner near the door was a small round table covered with a purple velvet tablecloth. A crystal ball was covered by a gray cloth and set in the center of the table. A long black curtain was pulled to one side. The corner looked to be where someone might occasionally read Tarot cards for customers.

A dark film coated the store windows, blocking out the majority of the sun's rays while keeping the area around the table darker. Cat statues lined the velvet throw blanket on the inset of the window. A pleasant blend of nag champa incense filled the air. The smell soothed her.

Luna helped Kailey sit at one of the two chairs, and Blaze headed toward the back of the shop. "Are you okay? Can I get you anything?"

Kailey raised a hand slightly and closed her eyes. "No. Thanks though."

Luna sat down across from her. Her wide eyes studied Kailey like a small child might a famous person.

Kailey sensed strong energy somewhere in the shop. This was far different than the dark energy that flowed through Nocturnal Trinity or around Cassie. This was a power that she welcomed and didn't fear.

The energy Kailey felt was moving toward her, growing stronger and stronger. For a moment, the overwhelming energy made her well up inside, as if a gentle hand had reached into her soul to remove all her pain and sorrow. She resisted the urge to cry, to dissolve into a shambled wreck and shielded herself behind her stubborn will. She needed her anger of loss. That was her drive to fight and her only hope to achieve vengeance. Without anger she felt vulnerable, weaker.

Blaze returned with a stocky man just under six feet in height, and he looked to be in his mid to late forties. He had brownish blonde hair with streaks of silver above his ears. His tanned face made his pale gray eyes look almost silver in color. His firm jaw and facial components made her believe he was Native American, but that was only a guess on her part.

Wrinkles tugged at the corners of his eyes and around his mouth. Short dark stubble covered his cheeks and chin. He wore a midnight blue robe that had small pale, triple goddess symbols patterned throughout. On his right hand he wore a silver ring with a large square ruby, and a turquoise ring on the left.

"Is this her?" he asked Blaze.

"Yes."

Kailey stared at the man. There was kindness in his eyes, but also weariness. This man obviously didn't sleep much. His warm gentle smile pushed aside any question of his sincerity. "Micah?"

He nodded and cocked a brow while studying her. The way he stared, she assumed he was trying to read her aura and get a sense of the type of person she was. Some of Raven's friends had done that when Kailey first met them.

She mentally shrugged. Let him look.

"I expected you to be taller," she said.

Micah shrugged and offered a soothing grin. He chuckled softly before leaning closer and peering into her eyes. "Are you okay? Tell me what happened."

Kailey propped her elbows on the table and rested her head in her hands. Her long wavy reddish-brown hair drooped downward like a curtain, blocking the view of her freckled face. "My head hurts so badly."

Micah looked at Luna. "Get her a cup of the herbal tea that I taught you to make."

"The healing tea?" she asked eagerly, rising from the chair.

He nodded. "After you drink some tea and relax, we can talk. Okay?"

"Sure. Provided this pain goes away."

Micah smiled. "It will."

CHAPTER 16

Fifteen minutes later, Kailey finished the hot minty tea and set the teacup on the saucer on the table. Micah sat across the table from her, smiling. The table, although near the front door, was nestled in the dark corner, allowing them privacy.

Several customers searched through the occult books and CDs on the other side of the shop. A gray-haired woman stood behind the counter near the cash register, talking to one of the patrons.

Micah stood and pulled a curtain to box them in, out of the customers' view. "You feel any better?"

"Yes. Remarkably. You sure that's *only* tea?"

He laughed in his soothing manner. Intoxicating power flowed from the gentleness in his mannerism, his eyes, and his rich voice. "Yes. *It's* tea. A special blend."

"No drugs?"

Luna looked appalled at the implication. "Of course not!"

Kailey flicked her gaze to Luna who rested her hands on her hips, and then Kailey glanced back at Micah with a teasing smile. "Seems I upset her."

"Luna has worked hard on learning the proper healing incantation she was reciting while making the tea for you. She's still a novice, but she learns quickly."

Kailey smiled at Luna. "You did great. No pain at all."

"Honest?" Luna asked.

Kailey nodded. "Honestly."

Luna's disappointed frown faded. She smiled, relieved, like a kid that had just learned to tie her shoe correctly for the first time. "Thanks."

Kailey was surprised the girl hadn't skipped away.

"Seems you've gained some enemies lately?" Micah asked.

Kailey nodded, slightly rolling her eyes, and immediately after doing so, she thought of Raven. "You could definitely say that."

"Blaze and Luna told me about how you were rushed by the Psi-vamps last night."

Had it been that recently? That seemed days ago. "Yeah, I didn't make any close friends at Nocturnal Trinity yesterday evening. Kind of had to make a quick exit instead."

"Why did you go there in the first place?"

"Did you read about the attorney that committed suicide? Vincent Yates?" she asked.

"Yes. Why?"

"That's my brother but he didn't kill himself. His wife, Cassie, killed him. She is a succubus."

Micah's eyes narrowed with interest. He gently folded his hands together on the table. "You can prove this?"

"You saw what kind of shape I was in when I ... when they helped me through the door?"

"I saw you were in a lot of pain, yes. Thus, the tea and Luna's healing spell."

"Cassie did that to me. She killed my brother. Now, she wants me dead."

"Interesting. I'm surprised you're alive."

"Why?" she asked.

"Full moon and her immense power. Most humans cannot withstand their attacks. What happened?"

"I provoked her."

"Something shielded you. Otherwise, there is no doubt that you'd be dead."

Kailey lifted the pendant from the inside of her shirt and let it rest on her chest. "She seemed to be repelled by this. When I came too close, she flung me into the air and then she vanished."

"She probably teleported to escape."

"I thought she had done something like that. So they can really do that?"

Micah nodded and smiled. "Nice amulet. Someone loves you quite a bit."

Kailey looked confused and offered a slight shrug.

"Whoever cast the protective spell on your necklace holds a great deal of love and affection for you."

"And you can tell this, *how?*"

"The pendant radiates power," he replied.

"If she is still alive."

Micah smiled. "Oh, she's alive."

"How do you know that?"

"Her power still flows from your medallion. If she were dead, the power of her magic for this spell would have faded. It wouldn't have protected you, either."

Kailey's eyes moistened with tears. She took a deep breath at the news, feeling a sense of hope and relief. "So a witch's power only lasts while she's alive?"

"At the intensity this is shielding you? Yes. It wouldn't be anywhere near that strong had she died. Curses, now, generally last for generations if done properly."

"I wonder why?" she asked.

"Grudges die hard."

"So does revenge," Kailey said evenly.

"True. Now why do you think this Cassie killed your brother?"

Kailey explained her last Skype conversations with Vincent, Raven's reading of his aura drain, and that even though her brother wasn't a drug user, he was found in the pool with a syringe stuck in his arm.

"I see. So he had never used drugs?"

Kailey shook her head. "Never."

Suddenly, the syringe made sense. With the succubus draining Vincent's life, his outer appearance somewhat resembled someone who was a junkie. Because of that resemblance, the paramedics and the coroner must have believed he was using, which prevented them from doing a more thorough report.

Of course, there should be drugs in his system whenever the toxicology report came back. Unless ... the coroner was also a member of Nocturnal Trinity.

Micah stared intently at her. "No way he might have been experimenting with them?"

"No."

"You're positive?"

"Cassie basically flat out told me that she killed him."

"She's taunting you."

Kailey frowned. "Why would she confess? I don't understand that kind of arrogance."

"Because she's protected."

"By whom?"

"Nocturnal Trinity's council."

"They have a council?"

Micah nodded. "Yes. The symbol tells anyone straight out what it consists of."

Kailey propped her chin on her hands and gave an endearing smile. "Perhaps you'll educate me then? Because other than the three factions coming together in unity, I have no idea."

"Okay." Micah motioned for Blaze to bring him a folder. Blaze brought it and set it on the table. Micah slid a drawing of the nightclub's emblem from the folder. "Most people give this crest a simple glance as they pass by. Nothing more. They see the 6-6-6 on the outer edge of the circle, but 666 is no longer frightening to most individuals. It's greatly downplayed by society and Hollywood, of course. And when people see the other symbols associated with the emblem they don't see any connection."

"What connection?"

With his finger, he traced what each symbol represented. "The council elders consist of six vampires, six demons, and six witches. By joining an alliance they have bound their powers together to become stronger while also protecting each of their factions."

Kailey nodded. "That much I know. Raven told me almost the same thing."

"Good. Then you know what the symbol represents."

"Pretty much."

Micah cupped his hands together. "Cassie taunts you because she is protected by eighteen powerfully elite individuals. Their power is equivalent to a small supernatural army. She has no fear of you and is daring you to try to stop her."

"Why?"

"So she can kill you."

Kailey thought about the impact of that information. She had been extremely foolish to approach Cassie the way that she had. But at that moment, she had never imagined the magnitude of power the succubus possessed. Of course, she had never thought Raven's spells ranked as highly as she did now. As Micah had mentioned, Kailey probably should be dead. Raven's spell had saved her life. She was thankful to be alive.

"I just don't understand why she killed my brother."

"You might never know."

Kailey sighed. "She had chosen him for some reason. She said that he had served his purpose, but then when I was in his office, she wanted to know what I had found."

"*Did* you find something?"

"I did." Kailey dug in her purse until she found the key. She slid it onto the table.

Micah picked up the key and examined it. He glanced from the key to her eyes. "612? We need to find out what it unlocks."

"I agree."

"Looks like it might open a safety deposit box. What do you think?"

"That was my first thought, too."

Micah stared deeply into her eyes and then smiled. "I'd like to help you."

"What's your interest in this?"

"I have my reasons."

Kailey shook her head. "I need to know *why* you're so interested in Nocturnal Trinity. You keep sending people like Luna and Blaze to get inside information for you. Why?"

"I have my reasons."

"I understand that, but I have no one in Seattle that I can fully trust because I don't know anyone. Blaze and Luna seem okay, but I only met them last night. You, just a half hour or so."

Micah gave a kind smile. "I realize that you're skeptical."

"No, this isn't skepticism. It's a fact. Last night when I was inside Nocturnal Trinity, I placed partial trust in the ones around me, and that didn't turn out so well."

"Okay, I'm not going to rush your decision or your trust. So before I'd ask you to join us, I'll certainly tell you my reasons. But first, please tell me something."

"If I can."

"Who invited you into the nightclub and who did they allow you to meet?"

"Flora is the one that chose me."

Micah nodded. "She's the female dominant vampire, the oldest of the three sisters. Nicodemus is the male dominant and the oldest male."

"No one ever mentioned Nicodemus, but she frightened the hell out of me."

"She should. You need to respect her power. She's ruthless and known to play cruel tricks on people."

"I have firsthand experience with that."

"You left Nocturnal Trinity unscathed. You're fortunate. Most that she has chosen have not been as fortunate."

His eyes grew heavy with grief.

"You speak from personal experience, don't you?"

Micah swallowed hard. "Unfortunately, I do."

"What happened?"

He looked away. "Perhaps at a later time, I can discuss it. But not now."

"Okay, sure. Sorry."

"Such is life. Occasional joy and loss. If one is lucky, it evens out in the end."

Kailey studied him. He was protective of his emotional pain and managed to hide it well. Kailey still battled hers until she started kickboxing and martial arts. Kicking a three hundred pound bag of sand was a great way to get the aggression out for a while. But after Cassie admitted she had killed Vincent, Kailey's rage had resurfaced. The problem was that she wasn't able to fight these creatures physically. She most likely would never get close enough to attempt to do so.

Kailey took the key and placed it inside her purse. She gazed at Micah. "What frightened me most about Flora was her mind controlling power. She took control of all the people on the dance floor and used them to encircle me. She tried to prevent me from leaving, using them as a barrier."

"That's one of the powers the elder vampires have."

"It's unthinkable what they can do with that kind of power."

Micah nodded. "It is. But this is what you need to understand. All three factions in Nocturnal Trinity need fresh blood to maintain their power and rule. Vampires and some of the demons need blood to feed. While other demons and dark witches need it for incantations. But with the mind control abilities that Flora and Nicodemus possess, getting blood is never a problem."

"They have desperate volunteers begging to get inside."

"I know. That's what makes it enticing."

"How?"

"By being overly selective and making it an exclusive membership, it builds the hype and interest. People need to know what's inside. Their lustful curiosity makes them willing to do anything to get inside. I mean *anything*. It's human nature. Whenever people are told they can't have or do something, that's when they want it the most."

"That makes sense. The demon told me that people flock there because they lack family security and want to belong to a group where they feel safe."

"While that's partly true, it's not just about belonging, or the desired need to see what's inside. A magical drawing flows from within Nocturnal Trinity, tugging and calling to people's subconsciouses that their lives are missing something. They believe that void can only be filled by discovering what's inside the nightclub."

Kailey said, "Hundreds were waiting more patiently than I'd expect a crowd to be. I assumed before the evening was finished that people might slug it out to get closer to the door."

Micah shook his head. "They wouldn't want to jeopardize any chance of being chosen. But overall, our society makes it worse."

"How?"

"When offered eternal life as an undead vampire, with the way Hollywood portrays vampires in this glamorous, glittery light, a lot of youth readily accept the turn, thinking about how cool being a vampire would be. Afterwards, there's buyers' remorse for a lot of them, once they fully understand the reality of the sacrifice they committed. There's no going back to a normal human life. Some go into a rage, killing a lot of innocent people. Unfortunately, the vampire that sire them ends up killing their own spawns."

"That's horrible."

"It is." Micah sipped his tea. "Luna told me that you were given an honorary membership for Nocturnal Trinity? But you're saying that Flora tried to keep you from leaving?"

"Yes. The membership was a gift after they revealed the cruel practical joke they had played on me."

"Ah, don't you see?"

"What?"

"Flora was flaunting her power to you. " Micah smiled. "But the card still allows you back inside."

"Not that I'd want to necessarily do that. I'm not too thrilled about ever returning."

Micah shrugged. "She was probably trying to frighten you off. She smacked your curiosity enough that should you return she might seek to turn you. They like people who lack fear."

Kailey's eyes widened. *Turn me?*

"If your intent is to destroy the succubus," he said, "you may have to return."

Kailey leaned back in the chair and crossed her arms. "To destroy Cassie, if that's what it takes, I'd go back to do that."

"About six months ago I sensed an evil powerful creature emerge in the city. Its arrival sent a ripple effect through our spiritual plane. Greatly disturbing. Nothing like this had existed prior. At least nothing of this magnitude had ever to Seattle during my lifetime."

"You think it is Cassie? That's about the time Vincent met her."

"It might be. I don't know for certain. My guess is that she could be the one, but not necessarily."

Luna brought more tea for Kailey and for Micah. Micah nodded his appreciation. "Now, Kailey, tell me more about your encounter with this succubus."

She blew steam off the tea and sipped it. "She definitely didn't like the magic on my pendant. Her demon features began to show, especially when I moved closer to her."

"Then you had angered her quite a bit."

Kailey laughed softly. "I have the bruises to prove it."

"Unfortunately, you've not seen the last of her."

"Yeah, in-laws, what can you do?" Kailey said with a forced smile.

Even though she wanted to laugh it off, his statement made her uneasy. Since Cassie had vanished, the demon could possibly appear anywhere when she least expected it, and that troubled her.

"Don't worry too much."

"How can I not?"

"You have us." A wave of energy flowed from him, brushed her skin, and then encircled her. He used magic, too. She held no doubts that he possessed a great deal of power. Contrary to her preconceived thoughts that he had used charisma to charm Luna and Blaze to gain their devotion, she felt his sincerity and for some unexplained reason, that made her want to help him as well.

Kailey took out her phone. She pulled up the pictures she had taken at the cemetery and slid the phone across the table. "I went to my brother's grave this morning. I found this."

Micah shook his head. "This isn't good."

"Why? What does it mean?"

"They were trying to conjure your brother's spirit."

"What?"

He offered a solemn nod.

"Séance?" she asked.

He shrugged. "Certainly not trying to call him up as a zombie or they'd have dug up his casket."

Kailey started to laugh at the suggestion, but Micah's eyes and facial expressions remained stern. "You're not teasing, are you?"

"Not at all. That's why I believe they were trying to call up his spirit."

"For what reason?"

"He apparently has information that they need. Perhaps it is the key that you found in his office. You need to find out where that box is."

Kailey nodded. Then she pointed at the strange footprints in the picture.

"Those are definitely demon prints. Cassie may have been one of the ones in that ritual circle. Who else did you meet in Nocturnal Trinity?"

"A male demon, Jinn. He's an incubus," she said.

"He's a charmer. The male representative of the demon circle."

"Eva was the witch."

Micah scratched at the stubble on his chin. "So they allowed you to meet three of the main inner circle. The leaders. On your first visit, too. Impressive."

"That's unusual?"

"Very."

Kailey sighed. "Why then did they choose me?"

"Perhaps they sensed why you were there."

"To find Cassie?"

He nodded. "That and they wanted to know what strengths you have, and more importantly, your weaknesses."

"They view me as a threat?" she asked.

"Possibly. Especially now."

"Why?"

"Because of your confrontation today with the succubus. You survived. That will increase their curiosity about you."

"Okay, so Jinn is a demon. Does that make Cassie his leader counterpart?"

Micah shook his head. "No. She's something far more powerful than he."

"There are other succubae there. I saw two of them escorting Mr. Langston."

"Some humans are so foolish."

"Are they like Cassie then? Their power, I mean?"

"No. She's a different strength and higher up their chain of command."

"I don't understand."

"Let's put it this way. If Cassie is the being that was summoned into our realm, she is bound and controlled by the eighteen council members, which by the way might be why you weren't allowed to die. Basically they reined her in. She's shackled to them. Our biggest problems arise should she ever break free of their control."

"What would happen then?"

"Pardon the pun, but all Hell will break loose."

"Then why the Hell did they bring her here?" Kailey asked.

"Apparently they want more power, as if they don't possess enough already."

"Damn."

CHAPTER 17

Micah glanced around the shop and then through the front door window. He checked the clock on the wall and glanced outside again. He seemed to be waiting for someone. "Which rooms did they allow you to see inside Nocturnal Trinity?"

"The first was the VIP room for the vampires. Then Eva took me to the witch VIP room."

"Good. They wanted to gain your confidence."

Kailey shook her head. "I don't think so. They set me up for their joke."

"Not necessarily."

"What do you mean?"

Micah rubbed his left palm. She noticed a thick scar that cut across his lifeline. "Did they give you any information that they probably shouldn't?"

"Well, Eva indicated there was a rift within their alliance."

Micah chuckled and shook his head.

"What?" she asked.

"That's great information. Useful actually."

"In what way?"

"Division causes distrust. Once that happens, things begin to fall apart, and people scramble to secure alliances."

Kailey frowned. "If they turn on each other, that's a good thing? So that could weaken their power?"

"Yes, it actually does. The only downside in that is if the succubus can break free of their hold. The good part is that she will attack them first."

"And then what?"

"Let's hope that it doesn't get to that stage. However, it would give us a window of opportunity. With her attention on attacking them, we might be able to destroy her."

"Why will she attack them?"

"Out of resentment for binding her. And the fact that they can send her back to the abyss."

"Eva mentioned something about that."

Micah gave a simple nod and folded his thick hands together where she could see dark symbols tattooed on the back of his wrists. "Yes. No demon wants to be sent back there. Once summoned out, should they go back—"

"They cannot come out again?"

"Technically, they probably can. Just not immediately. Essentially it's like they get sent to the end of the waiting line."

"Really? I figured it would be much worse."

"It can be," he replied. "Did you get to see all of the dance floors and bars?"

"Only the one with all the Goth dancers."

"And that's all?"

She nodded. "Yes. Not long after that was when Flora turned the crowd against me. Oh, and when the three came together to reveal the *surprise*, Flora did insinuate a warning for Eva to watch herself."

"Marvelous." He beamed an even smile and his dull gray eyes brightened.

"Okay, I've told you all of this, and yet, I'm still confused even though you seem excited about the information. Explain how we can possibly destroy Cassie when she is more powerful than Jinn and the other demons. If she is being controlled by all eighteen council members—"

"I never said that it would be easy. People will die. Probably some of their council members will die."

Kailey's eyes narrowed. "And you're comfortable with that?"

"When you understand the magnitude of their power and the dangers it represents for all of Seattle, you'll see why it is necessary. Remember, vampires are technically dead. They have no soul, and regardless of how they wish to personify themselves, they prey upon humans. You have no idea how much bloodshed those six vampires have spilled around the world. The murder rate in Seattle is much higher than other major cities, but it's not reported. If any of these vampires die, we're doing the city a favor."

"So you're talking war?"

Micah shrugged. "Maybe a large skirmish. War sounds a bit extreme."

"But you're insinuating the entire Seattle area."

"That's not an exaggeration, if they succeed. Already they have gained mind control over judges, police, and other pertinent residents in high places of power."

"Mr. Langston?"

Micah nodded. "Once they turn them into vampires or use their mind control, this entire city is theirs. They control the laws, enforce them ever how they see fit, and as you've seen, albeit on a much smaller scale, a group of people under their complete control is more dangerous than most imagine."

"That's true."

"Well, when you factor in witches and demons being influenced under mind control, stopping the council after that point will be impossible."

"The vampires can do that?" she asked.

"According to their truce, the elder vampires have sworn *not* to do that. But it doesn't mean that they won't eventually break the agreement. And with the division you mentioned occurring between them? The Founders have cracks in the foundation of their unity. A vampire's true nature is to never be equal or secondary to someone else. And besides that, if they continue turning voluntary humans into vampires, their numbers keep increasing, and giving them more power."

Kailey nodded. "What about the demons? How do they increase their numbers?"

Micah smiled. "That's the problem. They can't. Not unless the council agrees to summon more demons from the abyss. The agreement must be mutual, and it's highly unlikely that the witches and vampires want more demons to contend with."

"Then don't the vampires have the advantage over the other two factions?"

"In a way, they do, but they have to be careful."

"Why?"

"Someone has to protect them during the daylight hours. Piss off the other two groups, and one of them if not both will turn against the vampires and stake them while they are asleep."

"Is this the check and balance system that they told me about?"

Micah nodded. "Their mutual unity is actually in their best interest."

"But you're also suggesting that the vampires could actually compel the witches and demons?"

"Yes. Those six siblings are Old World vampires. They are unbelievably strong."

"Then why would the demons and witches allow the vampires to turn more humans, when that gives them a larger number?"

"But there are only six original vampires. They have the greatest power. Should one of the elders die, the other five become stronger, which is another reason the other two factions protect them. The demons and witches are still more powerful than newly turned vampires. But should the vampires use mind control over the witches and demons, that's where our greatest dangers lie."

"Why?"

"Their next move might be to take over state level operations. Think of what they could accomplish with a governor operating under their influence and jurisdiction."

An entire state functioning under the rule of eighteen individuals with their own sinister agenda was frightening. If such control eventually covered the whole state, the possibility that their lust for this type of corrupting power might spread like a virus into the neighboring states, and on and on.

Where did it end?

She shook her head, trying to grasp the potential threat that was rooted inside a small nightclub—Nocturnal Trinity. She had read the eagerness in the eyes of those standing in the line of hopefuls the night before. Micah spoke the truth. With their desperation as Flora had approached, had she offered entrance to anyone willing to become one of the vampires, the line would have turned into a chaotic scramble to see who got to be turned first.

Kailey believed the possible threat of Cassie and the council should not be ignored. Using preemptive tactics by destroying the succubus first was the best means they had to thwart what the council planned to do next. She couldn't help but wonder how Micah had such knowledge of the nightclub and the council members. Micah was hiding something. She wondered what the limits of his powers were and why he was so interested in recruiting her to ... his secretive organization. He had never said. Luna and Blaze didn't know enough to clarify, either, leaving her to picture their group to be a coven. She no longer believed it was a coven. She wasn't certain *what* he was in charge of. Whatever it was, at least he had a good storefront to conceal his operation.

For whatever he planned against Nocturnal Trinity, his reasons were personal, and according to the pain that surfaced in his eyes every now and then, he had lost someone dear to him.

Kailey found it interesting that she had no unusual powers like a witch, demon, or vampire. She was simply a person who loved journalism and investigation. She was also good at reading people through their manners, eye contact, and the way they carried themselves. However, all she read about Micah was his sorrow, but he was good at keeping it hidden. That common thread between them was enough for her to almost consider joining his cause. The more she learned, the more she was leaning in that direction.

"Knowing what you do about Nocturnal Trinity and how powerful the council is, why would you send someone as sweet and innocent as Luna in?" Kailey asked.

"She and Blaze volunteered."

"They could have easily been killed, you know?"

Micah replied, "Not easily, but the possibility does exist for any of us wanting to stop the Nocturnal Trinity circle. They all know the risks involved."

"Why not easily?"

"I have a couple of members already inside Nocturnal Trinity that have gain some trust of the outer council members. But they still cannot get into a lot of places, and sometimes, like with your situation last night, the council takes potential recruits into these private areas, hoping to entice them. Sadly some get turned into vampires. Some that are found untrustworthy ... disappear."

"Disappear?"

Micah nodded.

"Any idea what happens to them?"

"They could be mind slaves and compelled into being non-complaining blood banks. There are so many areas inside Nocturnal Trinity that are off limits to guests. For all we know, they might even have a dungeon."

Kailey cocked a brow. "Seriously?"

He shrugged and again he looked out the window; he pulled aside the curtain slightly and looked in the direction of the clock again.

"Are you expecting someone?" she asked.

He nodded. "Actually, I am."

"Who?"

Micah smiled. "It's a surprise."

Kailey didn't like the sound of that. She stiffened in the chair, ready to bolt past him to the door. She'd had enough surprises within the last twenty-four hours. She clutched the handle of her purse and stood.

"It's not a bad surprise, Kailey. I promise. Nothing like those you witnessed last night can enter my shop. Too many safeguards and spells are in place. Trust me. You're safe here."

She stared into his eyes for a few moments. He never flinched or attempted to break their gaze. There was gentleness in his eyes. She was certain serial killers probably possessed a similar friendliness in their mannerisms, too. How else did they lure so many people to their deaths? However, nothing indicated any sinister action on Micah's part, and he didn't seem to be using his charisma to persuade her. At least she didn't detect any power flow coming from him, like she had with Flora. All she could do was take him at face value. Slowly, she sat back down.

"Apparently you have some type of magical abilities," Kailey said. "Why don't you go into Nocturnal Trinity and snoop around yourself? Instead of putting these two in danger?"

"The council at the nightclub would sense my presence three blocks before I even got there."

"So if you cannot go inside, how do you intend to fight them?"

"Still exacting that plan."

Kailey sighed and rolled her eyes.

"Well, we can't go in with the possibility of being blindsided," Micah said. "I'm gathering information, and what you handed me today is more useful than anything I've gotten in months."

"How?"

"I'll explain that after my guests arrive." He reached into his robe pocket and retrieved his cellphone. He punched a single digit and put the phone to his ear. "Are you anywhere near? Okay. Good. Thanks."

Kailey frowned with curiosity as he put the phone away.

"They'll be here in less than five minutes." He stood. "Come. I'll show you where we're having the meeting. They'll come in around back."

Micah pushed aside the curtain and headed toward the back of the store. Luna smiled at her, and she waved her hand, encouraging Kailey to come. Kailey stood and followed. She wanted to believe that Micah was a trustworthy person. Perhaps he was. She liked mysteries, but at this point, she had her reservations. Her skepticism dug in its heels. Her survival instincts kicked in. She wondered what new surprises were in store for her now.

CHAPTER 18

In the backroom, a long oval mahogany table set in the center of the room. Matching bookcases lined the back wall. Like Luna had mentioned, the shelves were filled with all types of occultic and religious books. Old books. Books of this nature were subjects that often attracted Kailey's attention. In spite of holding no allegiance to any particular deity, her curiosity had led her to research a vast majority of religions, magic, and supernatural creatures. However, most of these creatures or *monsters*—like demons, vampires, and werewolves—she had believed were fictitious in nature, even though accounts of such beings were centuries old.

To concur with those that stated, "Seeing is believing," she was now a believer that such dark creatures did actually exist. She had seen them first-hand and some of them wanted her dead. But even after reading all the various books about these supernatural creatures, she didn't know if all the information was correct or a myth in how to destroy them.

Kailey walked to the closest bookshelf and ran her finger across several aged tomes. The bindings indicated some of these books were several centuries old but age had not tarnished them nor the knowledge contained inside. She was intrigued, like she often was when she and Raven had visited bookstores and magic shops in Salem. Kailey had gathered herself a small library of various spell books and religious texts that she kept, hoping some day she'd be more inclined like Raven to pursue the solitary path. That day was closer than she had ever anticipated, but she understood that to reach even Raven's modest level of magic took years of dedication. To be equal to Eva ... that must have taken decades or longer. Was Eva an immortal witch?

While her mind rummaged through the various book subjects, the back door opened and a gentle cold breeze from outside stirred through the room, but her interest in these books had overtaken her to the point that she didn't hear or sense that someone had crept up behind her.

"Kay?"

Kailey turned on her heels. Wide-eyed, she stared into Raven's eyes. "Oh, my ... God!"

Raven wrapped her arms around Kailey. "*Goddess!*"

Involuntary tears slid down Kailey's cheeks. Relief rushed through her and overwhelmed her. She embraced Raven tightly, fiercely, and she didn't want to let her go. "Oh, Raven. I've been worried sick about you."

"I love you, girl," Raven whispered in her ear. "I love you so much."

"I love you," Kailey whispered back without faltering.

Still embraced, they pulled back and looked one another in the eyes. Kailey read the want in Raven's eyes. Her heart melted. She watched Raven's eyes move to Kailey's lips. Excitement rushed through Kailey, and without hesitation she met Raven's kiss.

Raven's soft thick lips parted, gently closing on Kailey's. Raven's breath smelled of mint and the hot tip of her tongue tenderly ran across Kailey's lower lip. Kailey's lips loosened, allowing her to kiss Raven deeper. The sisterly feeling that Kailey had insisted for so long was no longer there. Not the slightest hint or inhibition. Passion burned instead. Never had she experienced the heat of a kiss that burned into her soul.

Raven's arms looped around Kailey's neck as they kissed. Kailey allowed herself to surrender. She found that she didn't want this kiss to end. She wanted more. Much more. Kailey slipped her hands under Raven's blouse and moved them upward.

Micah and a woman cleared their throats, startling her and Raven, causing them to open their eyes and peer to the side while continuing the kiss. The passion was so intense that Kailey had forgotten about everything else around her.

A large bald man wearing all leather stood behind Micah and the elderly woman. His hardened gaze and narrow eyes made him menacing. Tattoos covered his throat and sleeveless, muscled arms. He simply shook his head with a slight grin and headed into the other room. "Don't stop on my account."

She and Raven finally broke their kiss. Their chests rose and fell heavily as they fought to catch their breath. Raven had a sly hungry look in her eyes. Kailey smiled and licked her lips, still experiencing the warmness and excitement running through her body. She leaned back against the bookshelf, placing one hand to her head and the other over her heart. Her heart hammered in her chest. Her knees weakened, and she almost slid down to the floor. Closing her eyes, she took a deep breath and slowly exhaled.

When Kailey opened her eyes, she caught the gazes of Micah and the elderly woman. Micah grinned, but the woman gave a stern look as she studied Kailey and then looked at Raven. Luna stood with her arms crossed. She held a disappointed and somewhat jealous expression on her face. Uncertainty creased her brow. Blaze reached and took Luna's hand into his.

Raven smiled and grabbed Kailey's hand, intertwining their fingers together.

"This is her?" the woman asked.

Raven nodded. She smiled broadly. "Kailey, this is Skye. She's the leader of our coven."

Kailey smiled. "Nice to meet you."

Skye crossed her arms. Her aged wrinkled brow was level with a frown. "The feeling isn't mutual, my dear. At least not yet."

Kailey took a deep breath, uneasy at the woman's cold tone and harsh expression. She wondered what she had done to offend the woman since they had never met. This seemed to be a consistent theme for Kailey lately.

Micah waved his hand toward the table. "Please, be seated."

As they took their seats, Kailey looked at Raven. "Why are you here? I've tried to contact you over and over since last night. You never answered your phone."

"I left my phone in the apartment. There wasn't time for me to get it."

"Why not?"

"Because of what you sent after her," Skye said.

Kailey's brow furrowed and then rose in question. "What?"

"The demon," Skye said in an even tone.

Worried, Kailey glanced at Raven. "I never did any such thing."

"Skye ..." Raven whispered.

"Raven, don't deny that. It is because of her that the demon came."

Micah said, "Not directly."

Skye turned her gaze toward him. "Directly or indirectly doesn't matter. The end result is what concerns me."

"I would never do anything to harm Raven," Kailey said.

Skye remained solemn, expressionless. "There's a demon mark upon you, Kailey. Someone wants you and those you cherish *dead*."

Demon mark? Vampire mark? What the hell?

Kailey swallowed hard. The news disturbed her greatly. "Is this true?"

Raven nodded. "We ... our coven gathered, and we traced the demon as having been summoned from this area. Quite possibly this is due to the demon that drained your brother's energy."

With pleading eyes, Kailey looked at Skye. "I know no magic. And even if I did, I'd never put Raven into harm's way. She's my best friend."

Skye gave a weary shrug. "The magic used to summon the demon came from near here. Quite possibly, it still lingers in your apartment back in Boston."

Micah said, "Then perhaps we can agree on one thing here. This succubus demon needs to be destroyed before her power matures."

Skye frowned. "How do you propose we do that?"

"Others in my group should arrive at my estate within the hour. After they arrive we can drive out there and discuss it more. Meanwhile, let's allow these two to catch up while you and I get more acquainted."

Skye took a deep breath, frowned, and gave a single nod. "Very well."

~

Kailey sat beside Raven at the table. The others went into the shop, leaving them alone.

"Raven, I'm so glad you're okay. I ... I had nothing to do with the demon."

"I know, hon," Raven said, still holding Kailey's hand. "Skye overreacts."

"Well, maybe not completely."

"What do you mean?"

"Cassie *is* a succubus."

"You have no doubt?"

Kailey nodded. "This pendant that you blessed forced her to show her true self earlier today when I got too close to her."

Raven rolled her eyes. "Too close? What did I tell you?"

"I know. But she's the one who walked in on me. Not the other way around. But I saw her true form. She's a full-fledged demon with horns, a tail, and cloven feet. Because of this pendant, I'm lucky to be alive."

"That explains the demon then."

"Why?"

Raven smiled and leaned against Kailey's shoulder. "Skye mentioned the mark on you, right?"

Kailey nodded. "What does that mean? A mark? Blaze thinks I have a vampire mark, too."

Raven studied Kailey for a few moments. "One way to explain it is that they have you in their sights. On a deeper level, usually more intimately, they mark you to keep track of you. Not sure how to explain that. Perhaps your sister-in-law realized that you knew what she was, so by attacking or killing me, she'd get you to leave here."

"I don't think it's just her that wants me gone."

"Who else?"

Kailey sighed and shook her head. Having Raven close comforted her, and she felt so much peace flowing from her, knowing no harm had come to Raven. She didn't know what she'd have done if Raven had died. She explained the cruel trick the three council members had played on her. "Oh, Raven. I feel like I'm awake inside a horrid nightmare. Things I never believed existed are *real* and now they want me dead."

"It's okay. We're here. We'll protect you."

"How did you know to contact Micah?"

"That's was Skye's doing. She follows her intuition and never makes hasty decisions. She sought wisdom for our next action, and this magic shop was where she was directed. She called and talked to Micah."

"Why would she want to help me? She doesn't even know me."

Raven looked up into Kailey's eyes. "She knows *me*, and she's like a mother to me. Well, to the entire coven. Basically protecting you is protecting me."

"But vampires, demons, and werewolves, Raven?"

"They have werewolves in Seattle, too?"

Kailey shook her head. "I was told they weren't in the city but well south of here. Salem, Oregon."

"Another Salem. How quaint."

Kailey's fingers tightened around Raven's. She was at ease, thinking about their passionate kiss. Looking down at Raven's lips, she wanted to continue kissing her, but the time wasn't appropriate. She found that the only questions she had didn't revolve around her sudden desire to be solely Raven's but why she had fought these urges for so long, especially since she knew how much Raven loved her.

Perhaps her fear of loss was what had held her back. Losing parents before she became a teenager, and then losing her brother, the last of her family, she didn't want to lose anyone else. She needed love and a companion. Other than Vincent, Kailey didn't know anyone else better than she knew Raven. Four years together as roommates, they were practically a couple, and knew one another quite well. They were always together, and as she thought about it, they held similar interests.

"Have you changed your mind about us?" Raven asked.

Kailey smiled. "You have to ask?"

"I've heard excuses for so long."

Kailey squeezed Raven's hand. "I know. I'm sorry. I guess I was just sorting through my feelings."

"I've been patient. I know that love takes time."

"You're more patient than anyone I've ever known."

"Good things come to those who wait, right?"

Kailey smiled. "That's what they say."

Luna stepped into the backroom. She smiled at them. Raven smiled back. "Can you tell me where the restroom is?"

"Sure," Luna said. "Go through the door and there's a hall on the left. The restroom is at the end of the hall."

"Thanks," Raven said, almost crossing her legs. She glanced at Kailey. "After the ride here, I'm about to burst!"

Raven headed through the door.

"She's your witch friend from Boston, huh?" Luna asked.

Kailey nodded. "My best friend."

Luna sighed and looked to the floor.

"Something wrong?" Kailey asked.

"I didn't know she was your girlfriend, too. Well, you didn't seem to act like you had someone."

"She's been my roommate for four years."

"And your girlfriend for that long?"

"No. That's ... erm ... rather recent."

"Like today?" Luna asked.

"Yes."

"That's what I was afraid of."

"Why?"

Luna glanced nervously back at the door. "I probably shouldn't say anything."

"It's okay. What is it?"

"I think she's cast a love spell on you when she entered the shop."

The statement made Kailey flinch. "What makes you say that?"

"I sensed her power when she was near you."

"She's a witch."

Luna swallowed and forced herself to glance into Kailey's eyes. "That much is obvious. But she has a spell to charm you. It's a *strong* one."

The accusation made Kailey frown. "She'd never do that."

"She has."

"You're certain?"

"I'm fairly certain. You can ask Micah since I'm rather new at this, if you'd like. Maybe I'm wrong."

An uneasiness rose inside Kailey. Could it be true? Her infatuation toward Raven was beyond her resistance. *Dammit, another problem she needed to sort through.*

Luna gave a bleak smile. "I'm sorry. I probably shouldn't have told you."

Kailey's brow furrowed and she shook her head. "No, it's okay, Luna. I'm glad you did. I appreciate your concern. And friends should always warn friends whenever they believe the other is in trouble, right?" Kailey forced a smile.

"Right. Thanks. Be careful," Luna said, turning and heading out the door.

Raven came back into the room a few minutes later, almost skipping as she approached. She'd never held a broader smile on her face than at this particular moment. Raven embraced Kailey. "I love you so much."

Kailey hugged her back and looked toward the door where Luna had stood moments before. Raven's hair smelled of strawberries. Kailey breathed in the scent and closed her eyes. The warmth in Raven's embrace and touch was soothing, holding every comfort of security a frightened person hoped for. Just a half hour earlier, she had thought that Raven might be dead, and now, here she stood.

Without releasing Kailey, Raven asked, "Is something wrong?"

Kailey realized she had not answered. "No, Raven. I'm just so tired."

"But it's still hard for you to say it?" Hurt showed in her eyes.

"No, it's not. I do love you. The past few days have been exhausting."

Micah stepped into the room with Skye and Blaze. "It won't get any easier tonight."

Kailey and Raven turned toward them. Kailey frowned. "Why not?"

Micah's face was grim. "I received word a few minutes ago. Dale, one of the ones I have on the inside, is dead."

Luna rushed into the room, crying. She ran to Blaze, and he wrapped his arms around her. She obviously knew Dale.

"Dead?" Kailey asked.

Micah nodded.

"What happened?" Raven asked.

"We'll discuss it at my estate. Most of my group is already out there. The rest of them are on their way. This shop is too close to Nocturnal Trinity, if they're probing an eavesdrop spell."

"I can ward off such a spell," Skye said.

Micah gave an acquiescing nod. "I imagine you can, but the use of your magic will only alert them that we have new witches in the city."

Raven glanced at Skye.

Skye nodded. "That's true."

"We all need to maintain a low profile until we can figure out the best way to get inside the nightclub and banish the succubus and her powers."

"And you believe by being at your home that we're better out of their reach?" Kailey asked.

"Yes."

"Why?"

Micah smiled. "You'll see."

CHAPTER 19

*W*hile Kailey rode in the backseat of Micah's Camry, she held Raven's hand. Kailey leaned her head against the cold passenger side window and stared out, taking in the beauty of a foggy Seattle. Where the sun fought to penetrate the fog, vibrant orange, red, and yellow pastel shades colored the clouds. This spectacular sight would soon be engulfed in darkness, replacing what momentarily presented itself as hope against a never-ending chaotic storm attempting to decimate Seattle. When darkness fell, that's when the monsters of the night emerged and that was also when they were strongest.

She still found it strange to unearth the knowledge that dark creatures like vampires, demons, and werewolves existed. For a reporter that was the story of a lifetime, but something she could never report. Such a news article immediately buried her career before it even got started. One professor had warned her class that writing about bizarre phenomena had killed many professional careers over the years, not just reporters but also police officers and government officials whenever they announced *proof* of Bigfoot or aliens from outer space. Reporting such things made a reporter appear unhinged, even though most people wanted to believe.

Even concrete evidence didn't work in her favor for the citizens of Seattle. Most had already been charmed and compelled by the vampires, demons, and witches that ruled Nocturnal Trinity. And if what Micah predicted was their goal, Seattle might well become an army to carry out the Unity's deepest desires. No one could stop them, once they reached the height of such power.

Raven rested her head on Kailey's shoulder. The slight raspy sound of her breathing let Kailey know that she was sleeping. She was probably as tired as Kailey. But Kailey had too many things on her mind that prevented her from seeking sleep. She doubted she could relax enough to doze.

Kailey thought about what Luna had said. She didn't think that Raven would ever use magic to charm Kailey into loving her as more than a friend. Kailey didn't sense the slightest tinge of magic. Her feelings when she turned and saw Raven had been a genuine rush of love and great relief. Weren't they? The second she had met Raven's eyes, Kailey could no longer contain her emotions. She released all inhibitions, but it had not been due to any magical charm. *Or had* it? She simply wanted to allow herself to open her heart like she should have done a couple of years earlier.

Kailey knew her heart. She loved Raven, and Raven had been patient enough to allow Kailey to date other college men and women even though hurt had shown in her friend's eyes. But there never had been any bitterness from Raven. No reason to harbor reprisal. Just an undying patience.

Raven had told her that Kailey needed to see what else the world of possible love interests had to offer, and that perhaps eventually Kailey would realize where her true love abided. And Kailey had. Today.

Kailey loosened her hold on Raven's hand. Gently, she massaged her thumb against Raven's palm. Raven gasped slightly and nuzzled against Kailey. Raven's other hand moved and softly rested on Kailey's stomach.

Kailey smiled at having someone who was her dearest friend become even closer. She liked the tenderness of Raven's touch and wondered where their new relationship might lead. They knew so much about one another. She shook her head and sighed.

All this time, you were right here. So close and yet I kept you out of reach.

The heavy cloud-cover hung over the massive Elliot Bay. Nightfall was settling. The reflection off the water made the clouds look twice as thick as they actually were. The ominous sky whispered unknown dangers to come.

Had it not been for Cassie admitting she had killed Vincent, Kailey would happily head back to Boston with Raven. But knowing ... *knowing* that Cassie had murdered him, she refused to let that go. She also didn't want the people who worked with him and those he had represented in court to think he had deliberately overdosed on drugs to kill himself. His reputation needed to be restored.

She slid the key out of her purse and studied it.

What does this open?

Micah drove to the end of the highway and waited for the cars ahead to drive onto the ferry. She tucked the key back into a side pocket of her purse. Watching the cars pull into the open-mouthed ferry that greatly resembled a metal whale with its mouth fully opened was daunting. She thought about how trapped they were. She wasn't claustrophobic, nor did she fear water, but for some reason crossing that lake on a ferry isolated them and prevented any quick escape should anyone from Nocturnal Trinity be following them. That made her uncomfortable.

Once Micah pulled onto the ferry and parked where an attendant directed as their designated spot, Micah shut off the engine. He caught Kailey's gaze in the rearview mirror. "Feel free to get out. It takes about a half hour to cross the bay. The upper deck has places where you can watch the bay while we cross and there are vending machines and a snack bar."

She nudged Raven.

Raven opened her heavy eyelids, yawned, and glanced at Kailey. "Where are we?"

"On a ferry."

"Cool!"

Kailey took her excitement as a signal to open the car door. They got out and stretched. Micah opened his door, closed it, and leaned back against the car door. He crossed his arms and scanned the cars parked all around his. He wore sunglasses even though he hadn't inside the car, nor did he actually need them now.

His facial expressions were partially weighted by sorrow and disdain. She believed the sadness she had seen in his eyes overshadowed his true inner desires. His modest exterior seemed a front to cover his darker side, which possibly thrived on rage and bloodlust. Human time bombs often kept those around them clueless and uninformed to their true natures until after it was too late. Without warning they snapped, killing a large number of people, some of which had trusted them the most.

She didn't have powers, but she sensed whatever he hid was possibly as dangerous as the information they hoped to retrieve about Nocturnal Trinity. He had mentioned that he'd disclose more information once they arrived at his estate, and she wondered what significance that held for her.

Dale had been killed. To her the information wasn't shocking, as she didn't actually know the man. However, he seemed an important member of their group. Luna's reaction to his death had proven that much.

Raven took Kailey's hand and led her to a narrow set of stairs. Kailey glanced back toward Micah. A tall muscular man, a couple inches over six feet in height, approached Micah. The man had long wavy blonde hair. His broad shoulders, thick arms, and narrow waist showed that he was physically fit and probably worked out a lot. For a moment, she feared Micah might be under attack, but when the man reached Micah, the two shook hands and embraced. From the other side of Micah's car, a slender brunette approached and the two men pulled her in for a tight embrace. She figured once they reached Micah's house, she'd be introduced.

She and Raven climbed the stairs and found a small table near a window where they could look out while the ferry crossed Elliott Bay. They stopped at vending machines to get bottles of Pepsi. Kailey needed something caffeinated to kick her butt into gear since she was extremely tired from enduring the stress of the past couple of days.

The Seattle Skyline was lighting up as darkness swallowed the city.

"Almost reminiscent of New York at night," Raven said.

Kailey shrugged. "A bit. But I find this view more soothing."

"Why?" Raven asked, furrowing her brow.

Kailey sighed. "I'm not certain. For the past two days, I have liked these overcast skies. I feel sheltered."

"I have days like that."

"Have you seen Skye?"

"She rode in the car with Blaze and Luna. She is probably around somewhere."

Kailey glanced around the tables and back at the bay. "I wonder if we all got on this ferry."

Raven shrugged. "I don't know. I sorta went to sleep."

"Yeah ... and you snored, too."

Raven feigned a shocked expression. "Did I?"

Kailey nodded.

"That might complicate our sleeping arrangement when we return to our apartment."

While biting her lower lip, Kailey looked into Raven's eyes. She didn't sense any treachery that Raven might have placed a love spell on her. But would she actually know? Could she be charmed into not recognizing the spell's power?

"What's wrong, love?" Raven asked. "Hey, if you're not comfortable sleeping together yet, I get that."

Kailey shook her head and refocused her eyes, like she's been jarred from sleep. "No. That's not it. I'm sorry."

"Don't be. I know you've been through a lot. But I don't want you to be uncomfortable. Never do something that doesn't feel right to you."

Kailey placed her hand atop Raven's and squeezed. "Raven, honest. My mind drifted. I actually look forward to returning to Boston with you."

"No apartment hunting? Now, *I'm* disappointed."

"That's not out of the question, yet. Let's see what we find out at Micah's place."

"Okay. So what else is troubling you?"

"It's about Vincent's death."

Raven wrapped her hands around Kailey's. "Tell me."

"I told you that they said it was suicide."

Raven nodded.

"Well, earlier this morning I went to the cemetery and the landscaper told me that he had run off a group of people from his gravesite." She pulled up the picture on her phone and slid it to Raven.

"Damn," Raven said. "These clawed footprints? Never actually seen any prints like this except in research books. Demons?"

Kailey nodded. "That's what Micah thinks. But that's not the disturbing part."

"What is?"

"An officer came to the cemetery because the landscaper had called and reported it. He told me that Vincent was found in the swimming pool with a needle stuck in his arm from an apparent overdose."

Raven shook her head. "Oh, Kailey—"

"He didn't overdose. I know it."

"I believe you, hon. I really do. But don't stress yourself out like this."

"I'm not going to just let it rest."

"You shouldn't have to."

Kailey sighed and shook her head. "But you remember how he looked?"

Raven nodded.

"I think someone killed him, possibly Cassie finished draining him, and then they put the needle into his arm after he died or was near death. His face during the last time we talked did resemble someone on drugs."

"That's true. Are you insinuating a cover up?" Raven asked.

"Wouldn't it fit? For them to do that?"

"Of course. Throws police off of a possible motive."

"Or they simply wouldn't look any further into an investigation. People love open and shut cases, which seldom actually drop into their laps as easily as this one. Or some of the police department are linked to it."

Raven shook her head.

"What?" Kailey asked. "You don't believe me?"

"No, Kay, it's not that. Your mind scrambles for every possible answer. Constantly."

"So?"

"That's not a bad thing. It simply means that you chose the right major in college and will be excellent in your career. I'm not implying anything negative. I meant it as a compliment."

"Oh?" Kailey forced a perplexed smile. "Well, there's more."

"Do tell," Raven said. She leaned forward on the table and beamed interest in her eyes.

"Raven, don't patronize me."

"I'm not. Tell me. I'm giving you my undivided attention."

Kailey leaned back against her seat. Her jaw tightened.

"Do you want my interest or not, love?" Raven asked.

"Don't mock me."

"I'm not. I swear, Kay."

Kailey licked her lips and searched Raven's eyes. Raven's eyebrows rose implying that she was genuinely waiting. "Okay. Well, the limo that I saw at Nocturnal Trinity that dropped off the vampires was at Vincent's house later last night."

"Damn, seriously? You drove out there?"

Kailey nodded. "I know they are all somehow tied to his murder."

"Why would they want him dead?" Raven asked.

"That's what I keep trying to figure out." She glanced around the tables again, looking to see if anyone was watching them. No one was, as far as she could tell. She slid the key out of the side pocket of her purse. "I found this in Vincent's office. Micah believes the group was probably at the cemetery hoping to conjure Vincent's spirit to get information. This key might be what they want."

Kailey slid the key back into the purse quickly.

"Wonder what it goes to?"

"That's something I plan to find out. But whatever it is cost my brother his life, so finding out will be dangerous."

Raven peered into Kailey's eyes. "I'm in this with you until the end. I always have been."

"I know and I greatly appreciate that. But you don't need to risk your life over this."

"Nor do you."

"I have to know that I made it right. My brother should be alive. I'm not letting that succubus bitch get away with this."

Raven shook her head and rolled her eyes. "Again, you definitely picked the right career choice."

"Why's that?"

"You're aggressive like a bulldog. When you bite down on something, you don't let go. I don't know that investigative reporters have this much zeal. Of course, you're much prettier than a bulldog." Raven winked.

"Hey!" Kailey crinkled her nose and shook her head.

"I only hope that you're a lot more cuddly. But if you *do* bite me, be gentle. *Very* gentle." She grinned and wiggled her eyebrows up and down and then winked again.

Kailey felt her face redden and heat rose from around her neck up into her cheeks. She looked out the window at the whitecap waves the evening breeze churned, trying to suppress her growing embarrassed smile. She twisted off the cap of her Pepsi and took a sip.

Raven must have sensed Kailey's uneasiness and quickly changed the subject. "What do you think about Micah?"

"I wanted to ask you the same thing," Kailey replied.

"You've talked to him longer. Does he seem to be on the level to you?"

"The best that I can tell? Yes. He's not told me everything though, and I believe he's suffered a painful loss. He told me that he would tell me more later."

"Perhaps after we get to his house and meet with his friends."

Kailey shrugged. "Some members of his group are on the ferry with us."

"Really? Other than that menacing man that was at his shop? The biker wannabe."

"Yes. Right as we started up the stairs, I saw him greet a man and woman at his car. Both appeared in top shape. Almost like MMA fighters."

She knew the reference would get under Raven's skin, but she teased anyway.

"Please, dear, let the MMA dream go."

"Why?"

"Don't want my woman having cauliflower ears."

Kailey laughed at the gross expression on Raven's face when she made the statement. "I suppose that could be a downside."

"Hell, yeah."

Kailey took a couple of deep breaths to calm down. Laughing actually felt good. A sense of relief washed through her. She was happy Raven had come to Seattle. Once her inner giddiness settled, she spoke in a more serious tone. "Micah's team, other than Blaze and Luna, might be militant types."

"You really think so?"

Kailey nodded.

Raven hand combed her hair from her eyes. "That's not necessarily a bad thing, based upon what you experienced at Nocturnal Trinity."

"I know. What does Skye think about the situation, other than blaming me?"

"She wants to find out why the three factions have unified themselves into one group. Magic is never to be used for evil purposes, which is why she seemed so angry earlier. Her anger isn't really directed at you though. She knows someone here summoned the demon to attack me to get to you. The problem is that the responsible people probably didn't realize that I'm a witch."

"That's true, but why did you call, screaming at me?"

"What?"

Kailey nodded.

"That wasn't me."

"It *sounded* like you."

"I told you that I left my phone."

Kailey shuddered. "You think the demon called me on your phone?"

"Quite possibly."

"How could it mimic you so well?"

"Probably heard me talking to you before I had to disconnect the call."

Micah and his two friends came up the stairs and stopped beside Kailey and Raven's table. He smiled and said, "Kailey, Raven ...This is Ashley and Jacob. Jacob is Dale's brother."

Kailey fought tears. "So sorry for you loss."

"Me, too," Raven said.

"Appreciate that, ladies," Jacob replied. There was harshness in his voice but no trace of sadness could be seen in his eyes. Anger and the need for vengeance buried any other emotion, and for a moment, she wondered if that was how others witnessed her eyes. He didn't mask his emotions, and his intimidating stare would make most hardened men flinch. "The guilty ones involved in his death will pay."

Kailey found it impossible to hold the man's angered gaze. She glanced toward Micah instead. "So where is this ferry taking us?"

"Bainbridge Island. My home is on this side of the island."

"Smart," Raven said.

"Why?" Kailey asked.

"His home is surrounded by water, making it more difficult for those practicing evil magic to trace us with a locator spell." Raven looked toward the island.

"Really?" Kailey asked, still looking at Micah.

Micah nodded. "That's exactly why I chose to live out here. The spectacular night view of Seattle's skyline is, of course, an added bonus."

Kailey glanced toward Raven. "How does water prevent them from finding us?"

"Water is cleansing and for purification. Being surrounded by water can act as a buffer or barrier against those seeking to do evil. This island is the ideal place," Raven said. "Unless, of course, the evil ones are also reside there."

Ashley stood with her lean, muscular arms crossed. Her tight jaw was firm. Her large brown eyes were beautiful but fierce and intimidating. Her thick muscular legs filled out her leather pants, making them snug and tight. The woman seemed to have no body fat at all.

Some women would kill to look like that.

No emotion showed on her face, which actually made her even more unapproachable. Kailey doubted many men had enough courage to ever ask this woman out. Only a foolishly brave soul would ever attempt to come near her.

Micah glanced at his watch. "We should arrive at the dock in less than fifteen minutes, but unloading the cars might take a bit longer at this time of the day. People are heading home after work. So, enjoy the view a bit longer, and come back down to the car once we reach the dock."

Kailey nodded. "Sure."

He started to walk away, stopped, and glanced over his shoulder. "Oh, by the way, a couple of my friends have fired up the grill and food should be ready to eat when we get there."

Raven smiled.

"Great," Kailey said. The thought of food suddenly made her hungrier. She barely remembered breakfast and after her horrid head injury, she hadn't wanted anything to eat. As much as she enjoyed watching the swelling waves lapping the surface of the lake, she now wished the ferry could travel faster.

CHAPTER 20

About an hour later Micah drove his car onto the paved side driveway. Kailey and Raven stepped out of the car. Across the dark lake the Seattle Skyline glowed vibrant colors that mirrored on the water's surface. In many ways the mixtures of colors reminded her of Christmas wonder. The Space Needle also caught her eye.

"So much for New York," Raven said, taking Kailey's hand into hers. "That's one breathtaking view."

"I agree."

Micah headed off the side of the paved drive and motioned them to follow. The side path was gravel and crunched beneath their feet as they walked between rows of towering evergreen shrubs. Another car parked in the drive, followed by another. Skye, Blaze, and Luna got out of one car and walked down the path after Kailey and Raven.

The savory smell of grilled steaks, chicken, and hamburger drifted with the swirling evening breeze. The rain had slacked but the overcast sky hovered slightly over the tops of the skyscrapers across the bay. Faint splinters of moonlight occasionally stabbed their way through thinner clouds.

A small pavilion set near the lakeshore. Beneath the roof six tall men sat on the short rock wall around the pavilion perimeter. Three women sat at a table, eyeing Kailey and Raven while they finished their beers. Empty beer bottles set on the table and the concrete floor. Cigarette butts were crushed in a large marble ashtray.

"Food's ready." The cook was a burly man with gray hair and a thick beard.

The men seated on the rock wall pushed off and hurried for the plates of food. Their thin spandex shirts looked more like body paint. Kailey was beginning to think Micah had invited a physical fitness group to his house.

Kailey reluctantly looked at the plates and then at Raven. Raven shrugged.

"Go help yourselves," Micah said. "Don't mean to rush you, but we need to set up for the meeting. There, you'll be introduced after we discuss Dale's murder."

Raven, who was always bolder at social functions, tugged Kailey by the hand and together they stood in line behind the muscled men.

"Looks like a Chippendales lineup," Kailey whispered. "I've never seen so many buffed men in one place."

"Not something that interests *me*, but drop a twenty and see if the shirts start to fly."

Kailey chuckled and shook her head. "No thanks."

"Fine, then let's eat, unless you'd rather gawk at the men?" Raven said coldly.

Kailey chose one of the steaks that was well done. Most of the others were too pink or nearly rare.

She worried about Raven's quick jealousy over such an innocent observation. Kailey worked out in several different gyms in Boston with men and women, so it was natural for her to notice people who trained hard to stay in top shape. She hadn't even expressed interest in the guys, only made a simple joke. The day wasn't even over, and Kailey had only decided to give their relationship a chance a few hours ago. Why the sudden jealous hostility?

After everyone had finished eating, several of the men started a large fire in the center of a circular concrete slab in the backyard near the beach. As the flames rose, the members stood in a semicircle with their backs to the flames. Micah faced them.

From behind him, two men approached, walking in single file. They hoisted and balanced a black plastic bag over their right shoulders. Micah stepped aside, and the men carefully set the bag on the pebbled beach.

A body bag?

One of the men caught her gaze, nodded, and gave a charming smile.

Kailey took a sharp breath. The air coming off the lake seemed strangely colder. A chill shot down her spine.

It was Brady, the officer from the cemetery. He was associated with this group?

Brady and the other man joined the others around the fire. Skye silently slipped up beside Kailey and Raven. The fire danced in her eyes as she watched with concern.

Micah cleared his throat. "I've asked all of you here tonight because we lost Dale today."

All of the onlookers bowed their heads slightly. Several sniffled and wiped their eyes, but a couple emitted what sounded like low guttural growls of anger.

Micah dropped to one knee beside the body bag. He grabbed the zipper tab and pulled it down the top of the bag. After unzipping the bag, he parted it, revealing the Dale's dead stiff body inside. When he lifted Dale's right arm, the corpse's wrist was bruised and black.

"Damn," Micah said.

Jacob left the semicircle and stood beside his brother's body. Rage gleamed in his eyes. "What did they do to him?"

Others approached and helped lift Dale's nude body from the bag and set him on the smooth gravel. His left wrist was identical to the right. Both ankles were scarred with two puncture marks surrounded by dark bruises and on his neck was another bite mark.

Kailey felt sick. She looked away. Raven embraced her. Luna had turned her back and nestled her head against Blaze's chest.

Looking over Raven's shoulder, Brady stared into Kailey's eyes. His brow was furrowed and tears brimmed. He wiped away one tear, grimaced, but never broke their gaze. For some unknown reason, she knew he was on her side. They were somehow partners in finding her brother's killer as well as Dale's.

Micah stood and shook his head. "He's been drained by five vampires, which is one less than the vampire inner circle of Nocturnal Trinity."

Skye stepped closer to the body. "Have you checked his back?"

Jacob and Micah rolled Dale over. In the center of Dale's back was an odd bite that looked totally different than the other marks.

Skye took a step back and chanted strange words.

Micah gave her an odd look. "What are you sensing?"

"That's a demon bite."

"Was it the succubus?" Kailey asked, looking toward Skye.

Skye shrugged. "Not certain, but if it is, she bit him three times. There are six demon fang marks."

The others turned toward her with narrowed gazes. Jacob came toward Kailey. His hands were balled into tight fists and his dark gaze was murderous. Spittle formed at the sides of his mouth. "What do you know of this?"

"Nothing. It was just a question." She held her hands up in surrender.

Raven moved between Jacob and Kailey. Although taller and thinner than Kailey, Raven's defensive action made her look even bigger. But Jacob wasn't impressed or even slightly taken off guard. Kailey believed he could simply toss Raven aside with little effort at all.

"Jacob!" Micah said.

Jacob turned and Micah shook his head.

"She knows something," Jacob said.

"Her brother was killed by the inner circle of Nocturnal Trinity, too," Micah replied. "That's why she's here."

Jacob glanced back at Kailey. His eyes softened. "Is that true?"

Kailey nodded, her eyes fresh with tears.

"My apologies and condolences," Jacob said.

"Thank you," Kailey said softly with a meek smile.

One of the women standing near Dale's body asked, "How did they discover his identity?"

"We may not find the answer to that," Micah replied.

Jacob's jaw tightened. His voice held a gravelly beast growl. "I'm going in there and ripping them apart."

"Hastiness will get you killed and expose the rest of us," Micah said. "We need to use effective strategy."

Skye approached Micah. "You need to tell me exactly what is going on with the Unity within Nocturnal Trinity. They didn't simply drain him. They performed a blood ritual. Five of the six vampires partook of his blood, but the remainder was used for something else."

"What do you mean?" Raven asked. "You've mentioned the existence of vampires to our coven, but you've never implied that you have personally dealt with them."

"I've had my encounters over the years, Raven. But this ... you have dark magic being used under the guidance of master vampires, the witches' spells, and whatever evil the demons can attach to it. Something more is going on. I need to know what you know."

"In time," Micah said.

Skye frowned. "No. If you want my help, I need the truth of what's going on here."

Micah held a finger toward her, nodded, and then he turned his attention to the men and women standing around the fire and Dale's body. "Luke, Jill, Madison, and Brady—zip Dale back into the body bag and take him to the cellar."

They nodded in response and began their task.

"The cellar?" Kailey asked. "Aren't you going to call the police?"

"How do you think he got here?" Brady asked with a grin.

His gaze and smile flattered Kailey. Standing beside Raven, she quickly looked away. Raven glared at Brady and then at her.

"What the fuck is this?" Raven whispered harshly. "You *know* him?"

"He's the officer I talked to at the cemetery."

Raven crossed her arms. "I see."

"So no police?" Skye asked.

Micah shook his head. "We take care of our own matters. Too many police are sided with the Circle of Unity inside Nocturnal Trinity. Well, except for Brady here. Should they do a thorough autopsy and check his blood, there's always the possibility that someone will discover more than they need to know. And the last thing we need is for the wrong people to be sticking their noses into our business."

"What are you going to do with his body?" Kailey asked.

"He's our family. He'll be treated with the greatest respect."

"We either talk," Skye said, "or the three of us are heading back to Boston tonight."

Kailey liked that Skye had included her in their number, but she wasn't ready to leave Seattle yet. She felt a bit more at ease with the elderly coven leader. Skye's eyes reflected of a woman with great wisdom, understanding, and mysticism. Kailey wished to know more about her.

"Give me five minutes," Micah said. He looked at Jacob. "Take them to my study. I have several things to discuss with my folks here, and I'll be right inside. I promise."

Skye gave a slight nod of acceptance. She, Raven, and Kailey followed Jacob toward the two-story rock house. Raven deliberately walked two steps ahead of Kailey, still crossing her arms. Raven's eyes stared coldly ahead, almost void of consciousness and seemed trancelike. Kailey had known her long enough to know when Raven was mad, but why was she this angry? Was she actually *jealous* of the police officer?

Did Kailey think Brady was cute? Of course. He was quite handsome and a bit meeker than most police officers she had met. No chip on his shoulder. He seemed charismatic and caring, which were qualities that she loved in a man or a woman.

Perhaps Raven's jealousy stemmed from knowing that Kailey was attracted to men and women. She wondered if Raven viewed that diversity as a threat of possible promiscuity. This jealous display was also a caution flag that Kailey needed to watch, and a reason she had chosen *not* having a relationship with Raven in the first place. She'd rather keep her friendship without ever being lovers than for jealous resentment driving them apart forever.

She sighed and tried to think about something else.

Micah's house was beautiful. Polished rock walls enclosed the large bay windows, which reflected the glow of the Seattle Skyline and the flickering fire that the misty wind struggled to weaken. Two upper decks led out of sliding glass bedroom doors. Like most of the other houses she had seen on Bainbridge Island, the fronts facing the bay were mostly large windows that offered the owners gorgeous panoramic views of the bay and the skyline. She wished she were on the island for better reasons so she could enjoy her surroundings.

Large evergreen spruces sporadically filled in the landscape, offering shadows that made her take second glances, giving her the sensation that someone might be watching the activities on Micah's property.

Kailey didn't understand these people, or Skye, and periodically, she didn't understand Raven or herself, either. Everyone seemed to be keeping secrets. No one wanted to divulge information for the greater good, even though many lives were at risk. She didn't view them as a team because they weren't trying to work together. At least they weren't yet. She, Skye, and Raven were still standing on the outside of this circle. That had to change. Tonight. Otherwise more of Micah's group would be dead, or perhaps she or Raven might wind up in that number as well.

The more of Micah's people she met, the more she wanted to know what bond connected them together. They were more than just friends. Perhaps not blood related, but something at the core of their group entwined them into a family-like tribe. Micah had seemed to hint at something when he mentioned that a thorough autopsy might draw the attention of others. But to what exactly?

With all Kailey had learned about supernatural beings during the past forty-eight hours, she was ready to accept that a pack of werewolves was actually in Seattle except for ... the full moon. None of these people were changing into wolves, nor were any acting like animals.

So ... scratch that.

There was anger and rage stirring inside of them, but she carried those traits, too, knowing that her brother had been murdered. The aggressive need for revenge was a common thread between their group and hers. And no one was sprouting fur and fangs, which greatly relieved her.

Nocturnal Trinity was a greater threat than most club seekers and vampire wannabes ever imagined. With the police and judges on the side of the nightclub owners, murdering undesirables or people that opposed them went without any threat of punishment. Her brother and Dale were prime examples, which led Kailey to wonder how many others might have died in a similar fashion.

With Micah insistent that they deal with Dale's body and not let the proper authorities take charge, this meant that Dale ceased to exist in society and would essentially vanish without a trace. The idea made her uneasy.

Damn.

Was Nocturnal Trinity doing the same thing? If so, hundreds of people could be dead and missing with families actively trying to find them.

Dale had been drained of his blood by five vampires. According to Micah and Skye, there were *six* vampires in the inner circle. Had the other been the overseer to the ritual? What purpose did the demons' participation play in Dale's torturous bloodletting and death?

They had also intentionally left Dale's body for them to find. What was their purpose for doing that? A warning? A threat?

From what she knew, Vincent had not died violently. Of course, she never saw her brother's body, either. She needed to talk to Brady and get a copy of the autopsy report. She hoped the coroner wasn't affiliated with Nocturnal Trinity. The more people that Nocturnal Trinity pulled into their mind controlled web, the stronger the club became. Resistance decreased greatly because all any investigator had to say to a filed complaint was that they were looking into the situation. Often that was enough to keep the pressure off for a while.

Kailey definitely saw Micah's point. As Nocturnal Trinity ascended their control through the political ranks and over government officials, their power and authority could eventually spread like a wildfire, taking town after town and city after city under their influence. Once they dominated a state, then what? Congress? The Presidency? With an attractive candidate capable of charm and vast mind control, there was no end to their control.

Nocturnal Trinity was ground zero.

Kill the root. Kill the tree.

Jacob led them through the glass patio door into a dark paneled dining room with a large rectangular oak table. He passed through into a windowless room where bookshelves lined three walls. A dozen plush chairs formed a semicircle. A tall lamp in the corner lit the small library, casting ambient shadows across the room.

Native American artifacts were in glass topped end tables and the oval centerpiece table. Carved wooden statues of wolves set on top of the tables.

Jacob motioned with his hand. "Please be seated."

Kailey sat on the left hand side of the room in the chair closest to the door. Raven took the seat right beside her but kept her hands folded together on her lap. Skye sat opposite Kailey on the right hand side. Jacob stood just inside the door with his arms crossed.

Jacob remained quiet. His eyes flicked to each of them for long moments as if he were evaluating or trying to read them. He didn't seem a hostile threat to any of them, but his anger from the loss of his brother lingered in his eyes. His jaw muscles tightened as he ground his teeth.

Kailey turned to face Raven. Raven huffed.

"What's your problem?" Kailey asked.

Raven glared at her and started to reply.

Micah entered the room, followed by the female they had seen on the ferry. Ashley gave each of them a slight nod, walked past, and sat farther back in the room. Brady entered and stepped to the side of Jacob. His gaze went to Kailey and then to Raven, who openly looked scorned.

Brady's eyebrows rose in question at Kailey. She offered a slight shrug.

"Okay," Micah said. "You need answers. I know. So ask your questions."

"Any question at all?" Kailey asked.

"Sure. Within reason."

"Even the darker things?" Skye asked with a skeptical frown.

Micah shrugged. "Ask, and we'll see where it takes us."

Skye smiled. "Then let's get started."

CHAPTER 21

Kailey shifted slightly in the chair and faced Micah. "Eva told me last night that Flora and her siblings are from Croatia and have lived in Seattle for nearly two centuries. Is that correct?"

"Sounds accurate to me," Micah replied. "The age part at least. When they arrived in Seattle is something I don't rightly know."

Skye stared into Micah's eyes. "How old do you estimate that they are?"

"Probably two to three hundred years old."

"Still children at play," Skye said, laughing softly.

Micah smiled. Curiosity gleamed in his dark eyes. "You know more mature vampires?"

Skye grinned and offered a single nod. "In the New England states there exists a clan of quite reserved and dignified vampires. Unlike these spoiled vamp-brats at Nocturnal Trinity, they are not ones to play games. Seldom are they seen or spoken about, but if ever they appear, they come out to correct the wrongs others in society have made."

"Why didn't you ever tell me about them?" Raven asked.

"They don't concern you or our coven, dear."

Micah grabbed a chair from the kitchen and returned. He sat facing them. "Anything else?"

"What are you?" Kailey asked.

"I'm afraid I don't understand what you mean," Micah replied with an odd smile.

"I sense something different about you and your friends. It's not magic like Eva or Skye. Somewhat mystical maybe. But I want to say canine, like perhaps a werewolf because you and your friends act like a pack, but then we are under the full moon tonight and no one has changed."

Brady grinned. Jacob's eyes widened, and he glanced at Micah.

Skye's eyes also widened at the remark, and she stared at Kailey with a bit of admiration. "I thought the same too! And the moon, yes." Skye smiled at Raven and winked, as if signaling her approval of Raven's choice. Raven stared at the floor.

"What makes the two of you think that?" Micah asked.

Kailey replied, "What you said about the autopsy and why you didn't want the authorities to take Dale's body. Something they might discover? What were you implying?"

"I didn't mean to imply anything. Poor choice of words."

Kailey shook her head. "No. You meant the words but probably didn't think to catch yourself until after you had spoken. So, what are you?"

Micah scratched the stubble on his chin. "It's difficult to explain."

"You said that you'd answer any question," Kailey said.

"I know, but—"

"I need to know," Skye said. "If you want my help."

Kailey smiled. She liked having backup, especially from someone who was powerful in magic. Skye's abilities were a leverage to get answers in exchange for help.

Micah waved his hands in surrender. "You're right. It's just … okay. I was … we were werewolves."

"Still are," Jacob said with his deep, gravelly voice. His crossed thick muscled arms flexed and veins thick like cords swelled. His brow furrowed defensively. Anger possessed him and his voice. "Don't denounce what we truly are. My brother died *because* of what we are, and he was helpless to defend himself."

Ashley slid to the edge of her seat. Her eyes suddenly resembled a wolf and her jaw tightened. Brady crossed his arms but seemed indifferent by the statement. For a moment, Kailey thought Jacob and Ashley might actually rush at Micah for his statement. Brady appeared amused by their sudden anger.

Contention within the group?

Never a good sign.

Jacob was taller and heavier with more muscle than Micah, but the dominant stare in Micah's fierce gaze caused Jacob to swallow hard and take a couple of steps back. Height and size didn't matter should the two come to blows. Micah was the Alpha. No questioning that.

"He's right," Micah said. "We are still werewolves, but due to my magical abilities, I've been able to prevent our transformation during the full moon."

"You prevent yourselves from changing?" Kailey asked.

He nodded.

"How?"

Skye gave a shrewd glare at Micah. "Magic?"

"Yes, I'm a shaman."

Kailey frowned. "So why hide that you're all werewolves?"

"It's the only way we can remain in Seattle without Nicodemus detecting our presence."

"Which may have ended with the death of Dale," Jacob said.

Micah sighed. "That's true. I fear that, too. I'm sorry that we lost him."

Jacob's eyes brimmed with tears. "I appreciate that, Micah, but Dale believed in your cause and willingly died doing his duty. As would I on any given day."

"That's what pack brothers and sisters do," Micah said softly.

Jacob and Ashley nodded.

Micah said, "The demon and the vampires that fed on Dale probably know what he was, which limits the amount of time we have to act."

"I'd say that your time for hiding has run out," Kailey said.

"Why do you believe that?" Micah asked.

"They left Dale's body for you to find. Since he's a wolf, too, they are apparently trying to draw you out or into battle."

Jacob's eyes narrowed. "She might be right."

Micah nodded. "Probably so."

"Since he was a werewolf, what happened to the vampires that fed upon him?" Raven asked.

"I'm not certain. Usually, vampires go into a frenzy of violence or it can sicken them. The witches, no doubt, could have offered them healing. However, at the age these vampires are, I doubt they'd get sick. But feeding off his blood, they'd know that he was a werewolf and not an ordinary human. And the demons ... who knows?"

"How'd the demons get here?" Kailey asked.

"In Seattle?" Micah asked.

She nodded. "Yes. Why are they here and what does it benefit for them to unify with the vampires and witches?"

"To understand that, you have to know the history of Seattle. The Great

Seattle Fire in the late 1800s destroyed over thirty city blocks and opened a portal for the demons to come through. That portal is beneath Nocturnal Trinity." Micah folded his hands together. "While reports from that time period indicate a reason how the fire was *accidentally* started, what they didn't know was that it was actually intentionally set."

"By whom?" Kailey asked.

"My guess is Nicodemus did it, but finding actual proof now is impossible. Since he and his siblings are the ones who'd benefit the most, it fits."

"Why would he cause so much damage?"

"He needed a distraction to open the portal to summon demons to Seattle. The heat from the engulfing flames also helped conceal the molten portal summoning circle. Without that raging fire, the open portal would have caught the attention of commoners in the downtown district."

"How?"

"The smell of burnt sulfur. But due the massive city fire, people were too busy scrambling to find their loved ones, gather valuables, and for some, trying to put out the fire."

Skye smiled and nodded. "Camouflaged. Quite brilliant actually."

Micah shrugged. "Indeed it was."

"And the fire didn't consume him or the others?" Kailey asked.

"The witches placed a protective heat shield around the summoning circle. They had to. Blood sacrifices were made to entice the stronger demons to surface, and once Nicodemus released six of the strongest demons through the portal to align with them, they offered their alliance to the vampires and the witch coven that day for freeing them. A unity that the three factions have kept for over a hundred years."

Raven frowned and cleared her throat. "How is it that you know so much about Nicodemus and the inner circle of power that Nocturnal Trinity possesses?"

Sadness filled Micah's eyes. He stood and shook his head, grabbed his chair, and headed back into the other room.

"Wait!" Kailey said, rising to her feet.

Jacob quickly stood and stepped between her and the door.

"What?" she asked with narrowed eyes. "He promised he'd answer our questions."

Jacob shook his head. "Your question is too painful for him to deal with right now."

"How is that painful? There has to be a reason behind his knowledge of the nightclub and its founders. That information isn't something one can get off Wikipedia or at the library."

Jacob glared at Kailey. "He's done with this for now."

"But—"

Ashley crept up behind her. Her wolf-like eyes glowed in the lamplight. "Let it be, girl," she said in a gruff, almost animalistic voice. Her eyes and tone were meant to intimidate Kailey. She succeeded.

Kailey pressed her chin to her chest and lowered her head. She didn't want to look directly into Ashley's eyes for fear that the woman might view her gaze as a challenge. Although Kailey was confident with her own fighting skills, she didn't think she held much chance of winning a fight against a woman that was half wolf.

Jacob and Ashley left the study, leaving the three women alone with Brady. The backdoor opened and slammed shut.

"What did I ask that was wrong?" Kailey asked Brady.

"Be patient," Brady said, following after his pack. "In time, he'll tell you."

The door opened and shut again. Brady was gone.

"I don't have that kind of time. Can you believe this?" Kailey asked.

Skye shrugged. "I suppose the Q&A is over, my dears. Let's head back to Boston."

"I can't," Kailey said softly.

"You'd like to know more about Brady, wouldn't you?" Raven asked.

Kailey frowned and stared at Raven. "What the hell is wrong with you, Raven? I never knew you to be the type to become sorely jealous."

"I saw the interest in his eyes for you. You didn't exactly hide yours, either. You know how you're unable to hide your feelings."

"Hell, Raven. I barely talked to him at the cemetery."

"But you—"

"Girls!" Skye scolded. Her eyes narrowed. "This is the last thing you need. Division and ill feelings breaks one's focus. Raven, you know this quite well. How effective is your magic when anger and jealousy control you?"

Sadness overshadowed Raven's eyes. Being chided, she stared at the floor and crossed her arms like an angry child. "Not very good at all. You're right, Skye. I'm sorry."

Kailey turned and shook with sobs.

"We should return to Boston," Raven said.

"No, I *can't*."

Raven slipped up behind Kailey and wrapped her arms around Kailey's waist. "I'm sorry, Kailey. Honey, there's nothing more we can do here. Unless we want to end up like Dale."

Kailey gently took Raven's hands into hers. "It's not over for me. You two can go back. I won't rest until I get the answers I need and know who is responsible for Vincent's death."

Skye smiled at Raven. "You said that she was stubborn. She's a bit mule headed; I have to agree. But, as much as I hate to admit she's right, what she says is the truth. It's the only way to uncover what's really going on."

"You mean *stay?*" Raven asked.

Skye nodded. "We need to know who or what sent that demon."

Raven glanced at Kailey. "I suppose we have to look for an apartment tomorrow then?"

"I suppose so."

Skye said, "I think it best that we find our way back to the main part of the city away from this island and let the undercover wolves do whatever ritual they must do for their dear departed friend."

Kailey headed for the back door. "Any idea what happens to them for cloaking their true selves?"

"I'd say the only thing that is altered is their appearances," Skye replied. "Whatever strengths they have probably haven't changed. In fact, they may have enhanced their human senses by containing their wolf nature inside. I don't know much about werewolves though. I wish I knew even less about vampires."

CHAPTER 22

Kailey stood at the door as Skye and Raven left the house. Kailey pulled the door closed. Near the bonfire that was now half its former blazing glory, several of the men and women stood talking.

Gravel crunched underfoot as the three of them headed down the narrow path toward the driveway. Raven grabbed Kailey by the hand and smiled at her. Kailey returned the smile.

"Kailey!" Micah said, sprinting from the beach toward them. "Wait!"

Kailey turned. Her spindled reddish brown hair was damp from the cold mist. She pulled her hair back over her shoulder.

"Where are you going?"

Skye shook her head. "We're headed back to the Seattle."

"Look, I'm sorry. Please stay. Besides there aren't any more ferries going back until tomorrow morning."

"What?" Skye asked. Her eyes narrowed. "You have us trapped out here?"

"No. I have a boat, if you absolutely need transported back. But please stay. What I need to tell you in order to answer your last question is difficult for me to discuss. It's very painful, but it's also why I need to break the Circle of Unity that's the backbone of Nocturnal Trinity's power. If we allow their group to continue to grow in power, there's no stopping them. To do that, I'll need your help."

Brady joined them.

Kailey looked at Brady. "He brought us out here at a time when we can't ferry back to Seattle?"

Brady frowned, staring at her and then gazing toward Micah. He gave an odd smile. "You really told them that? Why?"

Micah said, "I just hoped it would give me time to explain my reluctance in answering the question." He looked at Kailey. "There is one last ferry back, but if you intend on using it, you'd best be leaving in about a half hour."

"We'll stay and listen provided you plan to actually tell us everything," Kailey said.

"They will probably not reach the ferry in time," Brady said.

"If they miss it, we can use my boat," Micah said. "Please, give me a few more minutes of your time."

The sincerity in Micah's eyes and voice was genuine. Pain was evident behind those mysterious eyes, much like in her own. She couldn't walk away without at least hearing what he planned to do. Kailey glanced to Skye for guidance.

"It's your decision," Skye said.

Kailey nodded. "We'll hear you out. But why do you know so much about the inner circle of Nocturnal Trinity?"

"I will explain that in a few minutes. But it does no good to tell you if you we can't agree on an attack plan."

"What are you proposing exactly?" Skye asked.

Micah motioned the three of them to sit on the large rocks that lined the edge of his driveway. "Kailey, you have the membership badge, so as a member you can take someone inside. You could take Raven."

Skye gave him a stern glance.

"Hear me out." He held both palms toward in a peaceful manner. "Your membership may be the necessary key for us to finally break their alliance."

"How do you plan to protect us once we're inside?" Kailey asked. "That's their playing field. They call the shots in there. With power like they possess, whomever else you have on the inside could die like Dale did. It could be us as well."

Micah smiled bleakly. "The risks are great. I understand that. But all we need to do is break their unity and the succubus will attack their council."

"Then why don't you enter with us?"

"Kailey, they'd sense me or my pack members four blocks away, especially now that they've killed Dale."

She frowned. "Because you are werewolves? I thought your spell masked that from them?"

Micah smiled. "To a certain degree it does, but we cannot completely hide our scent that permeates in our sweat."

"Then why didn't they detect Dale before now?" Kailey asked.

"I made a concoction that cloaked his scent. Apparently, it had worn off, or the witches did a seeking spell and exposed him. I'm not certain. But the concoction only works on one pack member at a time. For our full number, or even for half of us, there's no way to mask our overpowering pheromones. We'd be detected quickly. So you need to understand the urgency of the situation, too."

"What's that?" Skye asked.

"Dale's death was more than just draining him of his blood."

Kailey crossed her arms. "What do you mean?"

"Only five of the vampires fed on him with the demon, which means one of the vampires partook in something else," Micah replied. "Probably something very dark and dangerous."

Skye's eyes widened. She nodded. "A blood ritual."

"That'd be my guess."

Skye stared into Micah's eyes. Her voice became stern. "You wish to put these girls into the heart of that nightclub? That's too dangerous. Raven can use magic, but only to a limited degree. She's not a novice, but she still has years of learning ahead of her. Still she's not powerful enough to go against whatever dark magic they used in their blood ritual. And Kailey, she's helpless in such matters. This is too much for you to ask them to risk."

"I can go with them," Brady said.

Kailey glanced at him with uncertainty.

"Not a bad idea," Micah replied.

"How can he enter if he's a werewolf and you cannot?" Kailey asked.

Brady smiled. "I have a badge."

"Do they know you're a werewolf?"

"No. But now I can use the concoction," Brady said. "And since it will be fresh when I take it, I shouldn't have any worries about it wearing off. Besides, a lot of police officers that are members know me. It won't seem too far out of the ordinary for me to call one and ask to tag along since a member can only bring one guest each night."

"Not a bad idea," Micah said.

Kailey rubbed her eyes. "To whom will your fellow officers place the most loyalty? The badge or Nocturnal Trinity."

"I hope my badge."

Kailey said, "That would be my hope, too. But since so many people lust for power and success, they might opt to side with the Unity."

"It's a chance I'll have to take," Brady said.

"No, it's a chance we'll all be taking," Kailey replied. She glanced at Micah. "So why don't you use the potion to mask your scent and do the dirty work yourself?"

Micah replied, "They know I'm an Alpha."

"I see."

"What's a blood ritual?" Raven asked Skye.

"Something we never do," Skye said evenly. Fierceness narrowed her eyes. Anger tightened her jaw. "And since the demons probably participated, we have no idea what kind of incantation they used but if done properly you might face an enemy unlike anything I've ever encountered. To send them in ... even with Brady, it's suicide."

"I understand there are great dangers." Micah shoved his hands into his pockets.

"Trust me, I'll keep a close eye on them," Brady said.

"I'm afraid you don't fully understand what I'm saying," Skye said.

"It's complicated, but I've fought against them before," Micah said. "I was younger then, but in aging, I've grown stronger and smarter. I'd never deliberately place these girls into harm's way. I'm one of the good guys."

"I'm not arguing your virtue," Skye said. "I just don't understand why you're willing to put everyone else's lives at risk and not your own. Do you plan for them to battle the Circle of Unity for you?"

Micah shook his head. "Of course not."

Kailey nodded. "She's right, you know. Flora has enough mind-control power to turn forty to fifty dancers into mindless zombies that obey whatever she commands them to do. She might possibly be able to control even more than that number. She got into my mind when she tapped me as her guest and then tried again when I was attempting to leave, just to show me that she could. That's a tremendous amount of power."

"I know," Micah said.

Kailey gave an exasperated sigh. "And you said that Nicodemus is worse?"

"Yes. He is." Micah's eyes darkened with anger. His voice lowered and his jaw tightened. "Out of all of those in their Circle of Unity, he's the one I'd see dead."

"So this is personal."

"Yes."

"And why you know so much about Nicodemus?"

"He's part of why I know what I do about them."

Skye studied him with extreme scrutiny. "Then what do you plan to contribute in order to stop him?"

"Once they are on the inside, I plan to enter with the rest of the pack to kill Nicodemus."

"Then explain the reasons behind his crimes and why you wish him dead," Skye said.

Micah nodded. "It's more than I care to rehash right yet."

Kailey could see an internal battle raging inside Micah's eyes. Each time he seemed ready to explain why he knew, another part of himself fought to keep the information concealed. What was going on inside him?

She shook her head. "No. If it's that personal, we have a right to know. No one wants to risk their lives over a blind cause."

"Trust me, it's not a blind cause."

"I do trust you, to an extent, even though I barely know you," Kailey said. "That's why we need to know more. Don't ask me to place my life or theirs on the line for your personal vendetta. I will happily help provided I believe your reasons are justifiable. Believe me, I have a personal grudge, too. My brother's death won't be in vain."

Micah stared at the lake. The moon broke free of the clouds momentarily to reflect its glow off the mirror surface. His face looked longingly into its light, as if he yearned to change, to become what he was supposed to be on this night. The moonlight beams washed over him. Tears came to his eyes and glistened. Others in his pack came to stand beside him.

Ashley placed her hands to his back and gently rubbed him, nuzzling her face against the center of his back like a wolf might show affection toward another wolf.

Jacob whispered in a low, rough tone, "Jacob, turn us back into what we are meant to be."

Skye slipped up to Kailey and grabbed her hand and Raven's. Slowly she led them a few yards away.

"Yes," Ashley hissed next to Micah's ear, and then she bit at the air. "Please."

More tears flowed from Micah's eyes. He shook uncontrollably. "You know I cannot."

Jacob snarled. His nose creased, and he bared his teeth. Although human, a glimpse of his inner wolf surfaced. Whatever spell hung over him, snapped the wolf back inside. "I sense your desire to lead us, to run free through the night into the dense forests, to hunt, to kill. Don't deny us that."

"We can't. Not yet. The time isn't right."

"It's never right," Jacob said. "Even though we all ache for it!"

The others near the smoldering fire lined themselves along the edge of the lake water, staring at the moon. Their longing faces tightened. They appeared to be trying to let their wolves break through the restraining spell, but they were unsuccessful. Micah's power was too great, and their resentment toward him was increasing.

Jacob placed his muscled hand on Micah's shoulder and turned Micah to face him. Micah met Jacob's angry gaze with a gentleness. Jacob clenched his teeth. His voice deepened. "The only reason I don't rip your throat out right now is I'd be trapped like this forever."

"That's your wolf talking."

"No, it's *me*. I want the damn spell removed. All of us do!"

"You agreed when I offered."

Jacob pushed Micah back. "I did but I never knew these strong urges to change into the wolf would be more painful than actually turning itself."

"It will pass."

Jacob gnashed his teeth and pointed to the men and women along the edge of the lake. They had dropped to all fours and were beating the graveled beach with their fists, growling, and some releasing howls. "Look at them. Haven't we suffered enough? Release us!"

"I can't. Fight the yearnings. You'll become stronger. And when the time is right for me to reverse the spell, your liberation will create the strongest pack the world has ever seen. You'll have power unlike you ever imagined."

Brady reached up and clasped Jacob's shoulder, squeezing. "Come, brother. Let it rest. We agreed."

"No, this is killing us!" Jacob snapped at Brady.

"Brother, come. I believe we shall be released shortly," Brady said with a level stare at Micah. "Two years is sufficient time, Micah. Rethink your ideology and let us act as we're meant to be. We have the strength to take down Nicodemus tonight, provided you allow it."

"The time isn't right," Micah replied.

"The time is *now*," Brady said. His eyes turned fierce brown like a wolf's.

"Your doubt keeps us all prisoners," Jacob said. "Reconsider or we take a vote."

"Please," Micah reached his hands out toward Jacob to embrace him, like a father to a son. Jacob snarled and turned away. He joined the others on the beach. Dropping to the ground, he pounded his hands into the gravels and sand until he bruised and bloodied them.

"While the moon is still full," Brady said, "I encourage you to release us. I respect you as our Alpha and who you are as a person. However, for the greater good of the pack, I will join them in opposing you if it becomes necessary."

Micah opened his mouth to speak, but Brady turned and left him to join the others along the shoreline.

Ashley continued nuzzling Micah, whimpering softly like a sad pup. He turned toward her and embraced her. Pressing her face into his chest, she wept. He ran his hand through her hair, combing it, and petting her.

Micah whispered while rubbing her hair, "It will be okay. Everything will be okay."

Ashley's fingers spread wider. Veins popped up on the back of her hands. She grabbed the sleeves of Micah's robe and gripped the material tightly. It looked like she might have been trying to allow her wolf to begin its transforming process. Then she bit into his shoulder. Micah showed no pain and let her lick at his wound, which after a few seconds, seemed to calm her. Once she relaxed, she wrapped her arms around his waist and stood on tiptoe to kiss him, but Micah turned his head.

Sadness and disappointment claimed her eyes. She whimpered with pouty lips. Her aggressive nature was gone. She rubbed the tip of her nose beneath his chin and gently licked and kissed his neck. He ran his hand down her hair, caressing her.

Raven watched the pack's crazed behavior and glanced toward Kailey with wide concerned eyes. She shook her head with a disgusted expression on her face. "He has them trapped."

Kailey nodded. "I see that, too."

"The suppression will drive them all insane," Skye said. "There is a reason lunacy is what it is."

"Micah!" Kailey shouted. Anger loomed in her eyes. Although she didn't know the full reasoning behind the werewolves' suppression, the thought of Micah abusing his shaman power angered her. She wasn't certain that what she was seeing was a different form of bullying or not, but it seemed like it to her. He had them under his control against most of their wishes.

Micah whispered into Ashley's ear, kissed her cheek, and watched her go join the rest of the pack. She looked longingly over her shoulder at Micah while she walked away. Micah walked to them. Blood leaked from the bite on his shoulder. "Sorry, but as their leader I have to attend to their needs."

"We understand that," Kailey said. "How long have you suppressed their inner beasts?"

Micah's eyes searched for several moments. "About two years."

"Two years?" Skye asked. "You're driving them insane."

Micah shook his head. "No. As werewolves we recover quickly."

"Their resentment toward you is frightening," Kailey said. "They will turn on you if you don't release them."

"They know they'll be trapped forever if they do."

"Are they?" Skye asked with an odd glint in her eyes. Her boldness was as great as Kailey's but in a different manner. She possessed magical abilities to back her words. "Killing you kills the spell, does it not?"

Micah shrugged. "It may, but it very well may not. A shaman's spell can be altered into a curse with the proper placement of words, and I always place a protective clause in my incantations. Helps eliminate the cutthroats that get obsessed with power."

"That may be a chance they're willing to take by the looks of it," Skye replied with a grim smile.

"They haven't yet."

Skye smiled. "Emphasis on the 'yet.' Perhaps you should give them what they request. In return, we'll help you bring down Nocturnal Trinity."

"I thought that was the purpose of this meeting?" he asked, staring from one to the other.

"Initially, that's what you implied, but you've done almost everything except volunteer the information most vital to us," Kailey said.

Again, he gave a nonchalant shrug.

"Ashley holds a lot of affection for you," Kailey said. "Why did you reject her?"

Micah turned his gaze and sighed. "I cannot be intimate with her just yet."

"Why not?"

"Enough with the questions!" he shouted.

"But you promised," Kailey said.

"So ... I ... did." Breathing became difficult for Micah. His face reddened. His took heaving breaths but seemed labored, breathing through his open mouth, and fighting to keep his balance as he battled the inner wolf that was trying to overtake his humanity.

Kailey folded her arms as she watched him. "You keep averting direct questions that would give us answers that we need."

Veins swelled on his forehead and in his neck. His jaw tightened.

Kailey opened her mouth to speak.

"No," Skye said, looking directly at Kailey. "Don't. You need to get away from him. *Now.*"

Raven nodded. "Kay, come here."

"He promised!" Kailey said with a furious gaze. The anger in her voice echoed, causing those along the shoreline to turn and direct their attention at her.

"Let it be," Skye said. "We best get ourselves to the airport and head home. This matter apparently isn't important enough for him to truly want our assistance. You need him more than he needs us."

Micah gritted his teeth.

Kailey faced Skye with hurt in her eyes. "I thought—"

"Sometimes a good bluff calls their hand," Skye whispered.

Kailey smiled for a moment and then turned to face Micah. Anger and obvious disappointment was in her gaze. "She's right, Micah. Our part is done here. Since you're not willing to give us any better insight, we're leaving. For good."

CHAPTER 23

The expression on the shaman's face was frightening. His face reddened to the point that he looked like he might explode from his rage and rip into a murderous frenzy. His inner wolf or beast, or whatever the hell it was, lingered just inside his gaze and his flesh. Like a trapped animal ready to lunge at its aggressors, Micah stood posed and ready to kill. She had never seen such viciousness in a person's eyes. She half expected to become a victim instead of a potential team member.

Brady rushed between Micah and the women. He placed his hands against Micah's chest. "Micah, I'll take them across the bay in your boat." He glanced at Kailey. "Get your things. I'll get you out of here."

"No," Micah said. "They're *not* leaving."

Micah's voice rumbled with a deep, frightening growl. His eyes blazed and changed momentarily to that of a hungry, angry wolf.

Kailey understood that she should be frightened, and she shook inside, but somehow she kept her external expressions bold and tucked her fear deeper.

"Oh, we're definitely leaving," Kailey said. "You didn't keep your end of the deal. No answers. No help."

Skye stepped between Micah and Kailey. She raised her hand toward Micah and her eyes narrowed. Even though Kailey didn't really know the woman or how she cast spells, she thought Skye was readying something defensive.

"Answers?" Micah snarled. "That's what you want, right?"

"Yeah, ten minutes ago," Kailey replied.

"Don't provoke him," Brady said to Kailey. He was still pressing his hands against Micah's chest. "Give him some space."

"Gladly," Kailey replied. She motioned to Raven and Skye. "Let's go."

Micah's eyes narrowed and darkened. The animalistic fierceness in his gaze and the guttural growl that emitted from deep inside his throat showed why he was the Alpha. All the gentleness and hospitality he had shown since they had met him was gone. There was a low rumbling sound in his voice as he spoke. "You want the reason for *why* I want Nicodemus dead? He killed my wife. Is that *not* a bad enough offense?"

The words flowed with gruff hatred. The air around them grew strangely silent for a moment. The quiet before the unexpected storm.

Kailey stopped in midstride, swallowed hard, and a rush of fear tapped into her mind. Chill bumps pimpled her arms, her neck, and down her back. She shuddered, as did Raven and even Skye. Kailey read the alarm in Skye's eyes, making Kailey realize that she might have pushed Micah too far, but in a way, she didn't regret doing so if Micah revealed information that would help them break the binding power of the Circle of Unity.

The magic of Micah's spell was losing its control and his anger was nearly forcing his transformation to occur anyway. She couldn't imagine how violent the beast side of him could actually become, especially since his own spell was having difficulty reining him in. Should he break past that magical barrier, what wrath became unleashed along with his wolf? Would his beast direct his hostility toward them?

Kailey looked into Micah's eyes. No words came to her. What could she possibly say? The rage burning in the shaman's eyes could never be soothed. Not by mere words and it probably would never lessen until he had exacted his revenge by killing Nicodemus. What she viewed in his troubled gaze was the equivalent to the power of a fiery bolt of lightning gathering its force from nature to cast exceeding damage to anything within its path.

Everything around them seemed far away like they were locked inside an invisible bubble. All the elements paused, waiting to see what Micah was about to do. Was he about to use his shaman power to draw upon the energy of nature to destroy them?

Kailey bravely, or foolishly, took a step forward and extended her palms upward, bringing them together in a prayer like manner. She dropped to her knees. She offered a respectful bow of her head and leaned forward.

That was something her sensei had taught her. She wasn't making a challenge. Instead, she was displaying her respect and humility.

She rose to her feet. "I'm sorry. I can't imagine your loss, but I do understand how this ordeal upsets you so much. Truly I do. I wouldn't have pressed you for answers except that for us to destroy what Nocturnal Trinity seeks to do, we must work together. That means no secrets."

"I'm sorry that my rage is consuming me. I cannot venture back to that night in my mind without my wolf trying to surface. I loved her more than anything else in this world, and he took her from me."

"No, that's understandable. Some people cope by blocking out the bad memories."

"I've held it in too long. I've denied my wolf his right to revenge, and selfishly, I've done the same to the rest of my pack."

"What happened to your wife?" Kailey asked softly.

Micah gritted his teeth. "Jeannine and I were set up."

"How?"

"She and I had moved into Seattle to set up our shop, eventually planning to have the rest of our pack in Vancouver move here. At the time, I didn't try to hide what we were with magic, but we never actively announced that we were werewolves, either. And although we had heard about Nocturnal Trinity, we never expressed any interest in checking it out."

Micah stared at the clouds, looking for the moon, and continued, "One day, we had a visitor in our shop that extended an invitation sent by Nicodemus for us to come before evening hours to meet him."

"Why?" Kailey asked.

Micah shook his head and sighed. His anger was waning, or perhaps he was reining it in, but his eyes remained fierce. "He was entertaining the idea of joining our wolf faction with the Trinity, and having four groups in their unity to make them even more powerful."

"Really?" Skye asked. "He invited you to merge with them?"

"In words only. The reality was far different."

"What happened?" Kailey asked.

Micah closed his eyes. His expression was a mixture of anger and immense sadness.

"I know that it's difficult," she said. "But perhaps telling us can help us figure out a solution."

"To be honest," Micah said. "One of the reasons I had formulated the spell to contain our wolves was to keep me from leading the pack into Nocturnal Trinity."

"Why?"

"Because when I do, it will be a messy bloodbath. The only one that I want to see killed is Nicodemus, but he is highly protected because he is at the top of their hierarchy. To get to him, dozens of others will die. There's no question about that."

Brady nodded. "He's right."

"There's no way to single him out?" Skye asked.

"No. His siblings are always with him or within calling distance."

Skye wrung her aged hands together. "So it's a safe assumption that he is the one who controls the Unity?"

"Yes, he does. And those that worship the undead and long to earn their approval would willingly sacrifice themselves to keep him alive. People are so foolish and blind."

"I don't mean to cause you any further mental pain, Micah," Kailey said softly. "But can you tell us what happened to your wife."

The wind shifted over the bay and a fine mist sprayed across their faces. He wiped the moisture from his face with the sleeve of his robe. "She was deceived. As was I."

"In what way?" Skye asked.

"Foolishly we thought that the invitation was for us to join their Circle of Unity. But instead, Nicodemus sacrificed her by bleeding her out on the summoning circle in some strange attempt to increase his power. I never got to tell Jeannine goodbye and how much I loved her. I never even knew she had gone into the other room. I thought she was still seated beside me."

"They compelled you?" Raven asked.

Micah nodded. "Yes."

"How?" Skye asked. "With your magical power and being a werewolf, I'd think you'd have felt their attempt."

"We were under the new moon when our power was at its weakest," Micah replied.

Skye winced. "And the sacrifice? Did Nicodemus succeed in gaining more power?"

"No. Thankfully. Well, nothing permanent anyway. But he did offer to resurrect her as one of the undead."

"But she was a wolf?"

"Yes."

Kailey looked at Raven. "Can that be done?"

Raven shrugged.

"Rarely," Skye said. "I know of only two in North America. That doesn't mean there aren't more."

"You've met them?" Raven asked. The sudden interest in her eyes indicated that there was far more about werewolves and vampires that she didn't know.

"No," Skye replied. "And I have no intentions of doing so either. Their power ... let's just say, I doubt they have any equals apart from one another."

Kailey looked at Micah. "I don't see why you haven't already gone in to kill Nicodemus."

Micah took a deep breath and stepped away from Brady. "Because I am a shaman. I was a shaman before I ever became a wolf. Shamans heal others. That's why I bound my wolf inside my human form, hoping that by doing so, I can continue doing what a shaman does."

"But your wrath is killing you," Skye said. "Even if you're able to suppress the beast, you are fractured within, which lessens your effectiveness as a healer."

"That is true. I have realized this for a long time. More so over the past six months, which is why I keep sending in people to scout out the nightclub, hoping to find a pattern of when Nicodemus makes his presence known. He is rarely seen."

"I saw him," Kailey said.

Micah frowned. "You never told me this."

"Well ... I don't know which one he was. All six of them emerged from the limo and went through the Founders' door."

"I see. It's rare that he leaves Nocturnal Trinity. From my understanding, that's where their caskets are."

"I saw those too."

"The caskets?"

"Yes."

Micah nodded. "Yes, you told me that you entered the vampire VIP room. Do you remember how you got inside there?"

"Unfortunately, no. They compelled me, and we surfaced in a dark soundproof hallway."

"How about the way you exited? Would you remember how to get to that door?"

Kailey's brow creased as she thought. She drew a blank and shook her head. "No, but we'll figure it out. What about Jeannine? If you were compelled, when did you realize she was gone?"

"Her scream," Micah replied. His eyes went vacant as his mind carried him back, and he stared at the waves gently washing along the shoreline. "I heard her scream."

Brady carefully reached toward Micah and placed a hand upon Micah's shoulder and squeezed. Brady closed his eyes. Tears leaked down his cheeks.

"I followed the echo down a winding metal staircase. I found her lying on her back in the center of their summoning circle in a pool of her own blood. Nicodemus was kneeling over her, his fangs dripping with blood and it was running down his chin."

"What about the other vampires?" Skye asked.

"None. Just he and her. I saw her blood. So much blood. I never thought a person could bleed so much. My first impulse was to kill him. I tried. Believe me I did. I rushed him, even though I knew vampires were strong. But I have also learned that vampires that feed upon an Alpha wolf increase their strength even more. My attack was nothing. He flung me across the room and against the wall. The impact would've killed me if I were only human.

"I came to my feet and rushed again. Had I been in wolf form, I probably could have hurt him, and he knew that, which is why he had extended the invitation at our weakest time of the month. The second time I hit the wall, everything spun. He picked Jeannine up, cradled her in his arms, and offered to turn her if I agreed. I refused."

"Why?" Kailey asked.

"Because that wasn't something that she'd ever want."

"Nicodemus left the room with her. I lost consciousness."

"You never saw her again?" Skye asked.

Brady placed both hands on Micah's shoulders and squeezed. Ashley came over and embraced him. They offered their comfort to ease his pain. Brady's body shook with intense anger and sorrow. "I awoke with her in my arms in an alley dumpster on the other side of town. She was dead."

Kailey felt horrible for insisting that Micah expose the deepest pain in his life, and she hated herself for doing so. However, she hated Nicodemus even more, and this gave her more than enough incentive and motivation to go back to Nocturnal Trinity to destroy Cassie and Nicodemus. Apparently, Cassie probably wouldn't be in Seattle if not for Nicodemus and the summoning circle.

"I'm so sorry," Kailey said, wiping tears from her eyes. "I'm willing to go back to Nocturnal Trinity and do whatever I can."

Raven nodded. "Me, too."

"I appreciate it," Micah said. He looked at Skye. "Could you help me cast a spell over these two young ladies?"

Skye glanced at Raven and Kailey. "What kind of spell?"

"Concealment. I don't want those at Nocturnal Trinity to recognize Kailey when she returns. She has a membership badge, and if they don't recognize her, the two of them will have a better chance at finding possible access doors to the vampire VIP lounge. Luna can help them find more suitable club clothes."

Brady shook his head. "There's no time for that. Not if you wish to catch the ferry."

"You're right. Tell everyone to get back to the cars. Skye we can do the incantation at my shop. Luna has clothes there that Raven and Kailey can wear." He glanced at his watch. "Or they have time to buy new clothes."

Raven looked at Kailey with wide eyes.

Brady shook his head. "Micah, have you ever taken a girl shopping? Since time is a factor ..."

"What are you trying to say?" Kailey asked, crossing her arms.

Brady flashed a teasing smile. "Nothing all men don't already know."

Micah replied, "Perhaps you two can save the shopping for another day."

Raven moaned a disappointed, "Aww."

Brady rushed to those still standing along the shoreline.

"While he gets them, we'll ride in my car," Micah said.

CHAPTER 24

An hour later they were all gathered inside the back of the magic shop. Micah lit incense and a few spell candles. Soft meditation music played on an old CD player. He then sat at the head of the table while the rest of the pack each took a seat. Kailey stood, waiting to hear what Micah planned to announce.

Luna beamed at Kailey and Raven. "Come on, you two! I have some really cool clothes you can wear. We have a changing room back here."

Raven gave Kailey an odd side-glance with her brows raised as Luna skipped out of the room. Raven whispered, "What? Is she five years old?"

"Behave," Kailey whispered, nudging Raven with her elbow. They left Skye at the table and followed Luna.

Raven shrugged.

"Be nice," Kailey said.

Raven crinkled her nose. "She kind of brings it on herself."

"She's a good kid."

"She's *our* age, for crying out loud."

Kailey shook her head. "Okay, so she's a bit ..."

"Ditsy?"

"*Immature.*"

Raven shook her head and rolled her eyes. "At least my life won't be in her hands. I can only pray to the Goddess that the girl has a decent taste in clothing."

Kailey sighed. "I'm not one to admire drab colors and pale makeup."

"I have my days—"

"I guess we all have our moods."

Raven grinned. "You're just now picking that up about me after four years of living together?"

Kailey laughed softly. "I've kept quiet about a lot of things."

"That tends to be the best quality in a partner."

"I may not be as silent as before," Kailey said.

"You've proven tonight that you're quite stubborn and won't let up until you get an answer."

"What else was I supposed to do? He wasn't answering the questions."

Raven rolled her eyes, a bit more dramatically. "I wasn't complaining. I actually admired your backbone."

"Really?"

She nodded. "Yep. But I was getting concerned that Micah might just yank your spine right out of your body though. He was rather pissed."

"I worried about what he might do, too."

Luna peered out from a closet. "Hurry up!"

"Mommy, can we have a sleepover tonight?" Raven whispered in a high-pitched whiny tone while clasping her hands together and pulling them to her chest. "And play dress up?"

Kailey frowned. "*Raven!*"

"Sorry," Raven said. "But she's annoying the crap out of me."

"I thought you always insisted that people be more tolerant?"

"When it comes to religion, sure."

"She wants to be friends," Kailey said. "Other than Blaze and Micah, I don't know that she has many."

"No surprise there."

"She's also studying witchcraft."

Raven turned with wide eyes and started to speak.

"No. Don't you *dare* say a word. The last thing she needs is criticism. She's a good person. Even you needed a mentor."

"Yes, but I never acted like *that.*"

"And we don't know her upbringing, either."

Raven bit her lower lip, giving consideration to the suggestion. She nodded. "That's true."

"You should at least try to be supportive."

"Okay, I'll try."

On the hanger rack made from PVC pipes hung several black vinyl miniskirts with various designs. Chrome crosses, buckles, and oddly placed zippers were sewn to them. One pink vinyl miniskirt hung along with the black and screamed its difference. Raven slid the pink one partway out. Her nose crinkled her distaste. She shook her head and shoved it out of sight.

Luna nodded. "Yeah ... pink's not to my liking either. Sorry that I don't have any leather ones. I've always wanted leather, but it's a bit pricey."

"Well, we don't want to overdo it," Kailey said.

Raven rolled her eyes. "No, *we don't.*"

Kailey frowned at her and then cocked one brow. "What you have are nice, Luna."

Raven pulled a vinyl bustier from the rack and held it up. A white Gothic cross accentuated the front center. "I do like this one."

Luna smiled. "It's one of my favorites, too."

Kailey leaned close to Raven and whispered, "See? You two *do* have something in common."

"I just hope it doesn't chafe my nipples," Raven replied, sticking out her tongue.

"Go try it on," Luna said with a great deal of optimism in her voice. "Let's see how it looks on you."

Kailey tried to remember how the other young women were dressed when she stood in the line of hopefuls outside Nocturnal Trinity. None of Luna's clothes were out of the ordinary, so her attire wasn't why she was never chosen. Based upon clothing alone, Kailey's dress should have been an immediate ignore by most of the dedicated Goth and Emo crowd. Of course, Flora had also hinted that picking Kailey was more for entertainment purposes than anything else. At least, when she returned this time, she didn't need to hope to be chosen because she held membership and could easily go inside without question.

Raven emerged from the small dressing room, wearing only the top and her black panties. The bustier pushed her ample breasts upward, making them budge and nearly spill out over the cups. Raven stared at herself in a vertical mirror fastened to the wall. "It seems a little tight."

Luna's eyes widened. "Wow! You certainly are larger than I imagined. Gosh, I'd have never guessed."

Raven smiled at Luna's envious tone. "Maybe I should pick another one."

"No," Luna said. "That's ... perfect. You'll definitely catch the attention of every man in the room."

"Then I should *definitely* pick another one," Raven said, winking at Kailey.

"Nonsense," Kailey said. "We're going in for only one purpose and that's to see if we can find the door that leads to the vampires' VIP room. It might be helpful for men to think you're interested in them."

"Eww!" Raven said, crinkling her nose and sticking out her tongue.

"No, really, Raven. There are three dance floors. I've only been on one of them. Guys tend to like to impress women, which can help us if they're willing to give us a tour of the ground floor."

"I'm afraid I'm not that good of an actress," she replied.

"Not even for one night?"

"Oh, you will do fine," Luna said. "The secret of keeping a man's interest is in—"

"What's below the waist?" Raven asked.

"No ... well, maybe that is what they check out first. But the way this top shows off your breasts, they may actually fight over you."

Raven grinned at the thought.

"Once they check out your body," Luna said, "and look into your eyes, that's how you keep them."

"Really?" Raven said. "Few men can keep eye contact. So ... do tell."

"Flirt at them with your eyes. Wink."

Raven glanced at Kailey in the mirror. "I tried that for four years with a certain someone and it never worked."

"I'm not a man," Kailey said.

"Thankfully," Raven replied.

Raven kept the bustier, picked out a black mini-skirt that had more buckles than crosses. She seemed more turned off by crosses than a vampire. After she dressed, she sat down and Luna began applying a near smoky black eye shadow.

"That dark? Really?" Raven asked.

Luna nodded. "Yes."

"Looks like Kailey gave me the beating of a lifetime. Two black eyes, and our relationship has just started."

Kailey shook her head. "If I had given you two black eyes, you'd have excessive puffiness and swelling to go along with it. Possibly a broken nose."

"And eventually, cauliflower ears."

The snide remark angered Kailey. She took the clothes she had chosen and walked into the changing room. She yanked the curtain closed. As much as she loved Raven, she didn't know if it were possible to go beyond their friendship into a relationship as she had thought she could earlier in the afternoon.

Raven was always sarcastic, but in a much politer way. She had not ever made Kailey the direct target of such cynicism, except when she talked about Kailey's MMA goal. Never had Raven spoken with such bitterness and tried to find fault with all of those around her, either. But since Kailey had decided to chance having an intimate relationship with Raven, Raven had become mean and possessed with jealousy that Kailey had never seen in her roommate before.

She didn't want to deal with Raven's attitude right now. Doing so was a distraction to what they planned to accomplish. They needed to support one another and watch each other's backs. If Raven continued with her verbal belittlements, their conversation after they left Nocturnal Trinity would be a heartbreaker for each of them.

Kailey refused to be bullied by anyone, and that included Raven.

Lovers should never put down the other's dreams and ambitions. They are supposed to cheer one another with kindness and encouragement, but Raven was nowhere near in the vicinity of what a healthy relationship should be. How did Raven keep her spiteful attributes hidden for four years? Or had Kailey simply ignored them?

"You about finished?" Raven asked.

"Almost."

"Hurry then. I want to see my girl."

Kailey slid the curtain open and stepped out. The black miniskirt stopped a couple inches below the curve of her firm buttocks. The net stockings hugged into her muscular thighs that were a bit too tan to pull off Emo, but inside the dance floors beneath the flashing lights, it really wouldn't matter how tan her legs were. She wore knee-high boots with numerous zippers instead of laces.

The dark gray tube top hugged her modest breasts, and she wore a short vinyl top that didn't button, exposing her flat stomach and back.

Raven ran her tongue across her upper lip and gave a little cat growl. "I could see you dressed like that all the time. Of course, we'd never leave the apartment."

"Thanks, I guess."

"How does Raven's makeup look?" Luna asked.

"A bit darker than normal, but you did a great job."

Raven looked at herself in the mirror. "Not a fan of the black lipstick."

"It's the norm," Kailey replied.

"Seriously?"

Luna and Kailey nodded.

"Damn. I'd be depressed all the time, too."

"It's not a permanent change," Kailey said. "This is so we blend in with the crowd."

Raven got up from the table in front of the mirror so Kailey could sit and let Luna do her makeup and hair. Raven picked out a pair of scuffed boots and sat on a stool to put them on.

"Once I finish your makeup I have some cool henna tattoos we can put on you," Luna said.

"That would be great since I don't have any tattoos at all," Kailey replied.

"They're pretty dark images," Luna said. "If you don't mind that?"

"That's fine. I don't need many."

"You have any Wiccan ones?" Raven asked.

"Oh, definitely." Luna pointed toward a small box on the corner storage shelf. "Look in that box and get what you'd like."

Raven looked through box and sorted through various tattoos.

Luna sorted through different dark shades of eye shadow. "How do you feel about eggplant? It's a dark, purplish black."

"Sure."

Luna beamed and seemed to glow with happiness even in the dim lighting outside the small dressing area of the shop. "I want to make the two of you look different. Seldom will you find two people that are nearly identical. I tend to change my appearance each time I go out. It's a lot more fun."

Kailey opened her eyes after Luna applied the eye shadow. Luna took an eyeliner pencil and drew several stars from the corner of Kailey's right eye to her ear. "Those are cute."

Luna smiled.

"You ever think about being a makeup artist on a professional level?" Kailey asked.

"No, not really."

"You should look into that."

"Thanks."

Kailey glanced into the mirror and noticed Raven in the background. Her face held a soured expression, almost a disgusted look. When Raven caught Kailey's glance, Raven rolled her eyes and shook her head, quickly averting eye contact.

Kailey wondered what was wrong with Raven and why she was acting like a high school bully. She had never seen this side of Raven before. Of course they had enrolled into two completely different majors, so they never took classes together. They had breakfast together, and usually only saw each other late in the evening at their apartment, but each devoted their time to their studies in separate rooms. And then they slept. Even with that little time spent together during the weekdays, surely Kailey should have caught this side of Raven, but she had missed it. Or, Raven was really that good at hiding it.

Now that they had officially become a couple, Raven's true personality had emerged. Raven now had what she had desired for four years and simply let her guard down. And if this was her true nature, Kailey knew the relationship was doomed before it blossomed into anything fruitful and long lasting.

Luna scrunched Kailey's reddish brown hair and used various colors of hairspray to give it a wilder look. When she finished, she said, "There! What do you think?"

Kailey looked at her ashen gray face with the dark purplish circles around her eyes. She resembled some of those that dressed up for Mardi Gras that she had seen in pictures. Death relishers.

"Much better than anything I could have ever done," Kailey replied.

"Now let me apply some tattoos on you two."

CHAPTER 25

*A*fter Luna applied several tattoos of dark fairies and what appeared to be dead dolls, the three of them returned to the table where Micah and the wolf pack were sitting.

Brady turned and looked at Kailey. He nodded his head approvingly of her attire and makeup, and then he smiled. Kailey smiled back, despite Raven's low groan.

Skye sat on the opposite end of the table from Micah. He had set several types of weapons on the table. Sharp wooden stakes, vials of holy water, and a small crossbow that could easily be concealed beneath a trench coat were within a hand's reach of Micah.

"So when should we bless the young ladies with the concealment spell?" Skye asked.

Micah noticed Raven and Kailey standing with Luna. He smiled at them. "Looks like they are ready to travel to Nocturnal Trinity, so now will be the best time. Good work making them up, Luna."

"Thanks." Luna lowered her gaze and blushed.

Micah pointed to the tall shelf against the far wall. "Feel free to use whatever ingredients you deem necessary in formulating your incantation."

Skye rose from her chair and walked to the shelf. After a few minutes of studying the items, she plucked two apache tear stones from a basket. The glossy black stones glimmered slightly by her touch. She returned to the table and set them down.

"I need only Micah, Raven, and Kailey in the room with me," she said softly. Her gaze was stern. The rest of the pack along with Luna and Blaze stood and headed out the back door. "I need three candles. One black, one gray, and one silver."

"Give me a minute," Micah said. He left the back room and headed out into the store.

"What kind of spell is this?" Raven asked.

"Once enchanted, the black stones will protect the two of you from psychic attacks. Since Flora is capable of reaching into your minds to control or compel you, this will thwart any direct mental attack that she might attempt. That will be the last resort of protection they offer. The use of the candles while I cast the spell will bind a spell of concealment that enables you to blend in to your surroundings with others inside Nocturnal Trinity. Quite useful in keeping attention drawn away from you."

"We've never done a spell like this," Raven said.

"We never had a reason to."

Micah returned with three tall candles and crystal candleholders. He brought them to Skye. "Are these the proper size?"

She nodded. "They'll do just fine. Do you understand the significance of the colors and stones I've chosen?"

"Of course. It's not a basic spell, which makes it even more powerful," he replied. "Won't it require several people to work it?"

"The four of us should suffice," Skye replied.

"I don't know magic or how to ... " Kailey said.

"I'll give you a step-by-step of what is required of you."

Skye eyed the wooden stakes and other weapons on the opposite side of the table. "If you would?"

Micah scooped up the stakes. He placed them into a basket beside the door. He then took the holy water and crossbow and set them on a shelf.

Skye slipped her wand from a hidden woven sheath inside her left sleeve. The glossy ebony wood was worn by age and constant use. In her elderly delicate fingers the wand suddenly seemed like an extension of her, and in many ways it was. Kailey didn't understand how she felt this, but the power from nature and the Goddess that Raven kept insisting upon, radiated around Skye's fingers and the wand. Chills flowed down Kailey's back, and she found herself in sudden awe. Her hand slipped to the pendant on her necklace, which was now warmer than a few seconds before.

Kailey had watched Raven do mediation and healing spells, but never had she watched an enchantment ritual. When Raven blessed the pendant, she had done so privately, and Kailey understood why. Kailey's doubts might have prevented the blessing from ever occurring. But after the attack at Nocturnal Trinity, she held no doubts about magic at all. Raven could work magic, even as a novice. And Kailey sensed the power flowing into this room, and even Raven's eyes were filled with wonder.

"Before we begin," Skye said, "you must understand that each of you need to keep a stone on you the entire time you are inside Nocturnal Trinity for the blessing to keep you concealed. Also note that you will *not* be invisible. You will blend into the background like a chameleon does in nature. But that doesn't mean that you can't deliberately make yourself known to those around you by foolish actions. Foolishness can get you killed. Do you understand?"

Kailey and Raven nodded.

Skye instructed each of the other three where they should stand on each side of the table. Raven slid her wand from her purse and glanced to Skye. Skye gave an approving nod and smiled.

Skye said, "Each of you need to take a few moments to clear your mind from any outside distractions. Close your eyes, take a deep breath, and exhale slowly. Do this several times. Picture a place that you find peaceful and safe. Go there in your mind. Float. Relax."

Kailey's mind drifted to the only place she could recall where she never felt threatened in any manner. When she was young and her parents were still alive, the forest behind her home in Tennessee was the most serene place she had ever seen. Even years later, she had yet to find a place with such solace.

The narrow foot worn path that cut through the leafy trees stopped at a gentle meandering stream that trickled and bubbled into small swirling pools. Thick pads of plush moss deflated as she stepped barefoot to the edge of the water. She'd slipped her feet into the water during the hot summer months while mocking birds sang from the edges of the forest front.

Deeper in the trees, squirrels darted up and around thick oak trunks, watching her with grave interest, almost curiously fearful that she might come closer. Often she sat there with her eyes closed and at peace.

Due to the loss of her parents and the busyness of her college studies, she had somehow forgotten the tranquility of how soothing nature could be. And now, thinking back on the place, she realized the energy of nature that had been surrounding her, but she had been blind to it. Chills shot through her and the sense of new enlightenment made her feel light inside.

"As I pray to the Goddess for her blessings on the stones, focus your attention on them," Skye said in a voice that seemed miles away, echoing slightly on the wind.

Kailey nodded but did not open her eyes. The peace that flowed through her almost pulled her into slumber. Now she understood why her sensei insisted on deep meditation for relaxation before training and afterwards, but never had she entered this type of zone where she actually shut out the whirl-winding problems of the world.

Skye began her humble prayer. The modest words were softly spoken as if whispered to a lifelong friend. A flow of power whipped around Kailey. She nearly opened her eyes, wondering if the others in the circle felt the same sensation, but she kept them closed because she didn't want to lose the connection of magical power.

When Skye repeated the prayer the second time, Raven joined in. On the third repetition, Kailey and Micah joined in. Energy radiated beneath her feet, slowly moving up her legs. Although this was a sensation she had never experienced before, she didn't fear the power. She welcomed the warmth. As this force permeated upward, she was met with equal force from both sides. Magic from Skye and Micah swayed into her, undulating into her fingers, her hands, and moved slowly up her arms. She was now part of the magical conduit.

Kailey's skin pimpled with large chill bumps. Her eyelids fluttered. All she saw around the edges of her eyes was a pure white light glow around her vision. No images. Only light.

Her mind focused on the two black stones on the table. With her eyes closed, she pictured them, felt and somehow watched the magical energy surging from their hands and tunneling in ribbon-like tendrils through the air and entering the black stones.

After several minutes the power surge finally ended. Skye immediately started a new chant, one that held specific blessings for protection of Raven and Kailey. A feathery touch, soft as silk, flowed from the top of Kailey's head down to her feet, which felt, in many ways, like soft breath brushing across one's skin. She smiled because the sensation tickled.

When Skye finished speaking, Kailey opened her eyes. Sweat droplets beaded her face and Raven's. Skye and Micah, however, were drenched in sweat. There was a strong glow in their eyes.

Kailey stood in awe as the magical energy continued pulsing through and around her body. Surprise also possessed Raven's facial expressions.

Skye lowered her arms. She tucked her wand back into its sheath, and then she pointed. "Each of you take a stone. From the moment you pick it up, keep it on your person. Don't lose or set it down. Otherwise the power bound between you and stone vanishes. The spell will be broken."

Kailey took the stone closest to her. She almost expected to be jolted by an electrical shock from the magic-like static electricity, but all she felt was the fading warmth of energy. She tucked the stone inside a small zipper pocket on her miniskirt and then watched as Raven did the same with the one she had taken.

Micah seated himself, rested his elbows on the table, and rubbed his tired eyes with the palms of his hands. When he stopped, he waited for his eyes to adjust. He looked weary. "Remember when you get to Nocturnal Trinity that you are only there to search for the door to the vampires' VIP room. Nothing more. Understood?"

Kailey and Raven nodded.

"Do not engage with Flora or Nicodemus," Micah said. "Or the succubus."

Skye returned to her seat. "At the first sign of trouble get out of there. Kailey, you know when Flora is attempting to tap into your mind. So, provided she has the power to get past our protection spell on those stones and you feel the slightest prick of energy from her, get Raven's attention and leave immediately."

The urgency in Skye's voice brought nervousness to Kailey and by the look in Raven's eyes she was alarmed as well. Their uneasiness reflected when they gazed at one another.

"The best thing for you two is to find a place on the floor and dance together," Micah said in a soothing, reassuring voice. "We've blessed you with magic so you can blend in. Now, physically do that as well."

The door opened and Brady stepped inside. "I contacted a buddy of mine on the force. Richard said that he can take me into Nocturnal Trinity as his guest tonight."

"Good," Micah said.

"Time to find some chaffing leather," Brady said with a grin.

Micah looked at Skye. "If you don't mind, can you drive Raven and Kailey to Nocturnal Trinity?"

Skye appeared uncertain.

"You can drive my rental," Kailey said.

Skye frowned. "I thought Brady was offering to come along to help watch over them."

"He is, but I have some business our pack needs to discuss before Brady can head in that direction."

"I don't know—"

"You can park a couple of blocks away," Kailey said.

"Yes," Micah said. "Do that and wait until Brady gets there. He can park nearby and discreetly, so his friend doesn't suspect our intentions."

"But you will be there?" Skye asked Brady directly.

"Yes, ma'am."

"Good. Girls, let's go," Skye said, rising from her chair.

Brady stood and headed to the door, opening it for them. After Skye and Raven exited, he gently grabbed Kailey's arm. She looked at him with uncertainty when he handed her his phone. "Put your number in for me. I'll call you when I'm finished here."

She nodded and put in her number. The heat of a blush crept up her cheeks.

"Thanks. Don't start without me, okay?" he asked.

"Okay."

After she caught up with Raven, Brady gathered together the other pack members and told them to come inside.

Once Kailey got to the car she gave Skye the keys. "Why don't you drive until we park?"

"The less we move in and out of the car, the better it will be to keep others from paying a lot of attention to us," Kailey replied.

Skye took the keys with a bit of uneasiness. "Okay. But you'll have to give me the directions as we go."

Kailey smiled. "GPS will do that. Trust me, it won't be that bad."

CHAPTER 26

*K*ailey and Raven rode in the backseat while Skye drove. After a few blocks, Skye seemed a bit more relaxed about driving in a new city and liked how the GPS gave her the directions ahead of time.

Nightfall made this part of the Seattle streets seem eerier. The constant mist that had settled over the area for the evening made the roads slick. Areas of pavement shimmered beneath the streetlights. Wisps of fog flowed like puffs of smoke with snakelike tendrils. Along the sidewalks, the closer they came to Nocturnal Trinity, the more people they saw walking dressed in their dark party outfits.

Nocturnal Trinity was a fiery pit drawing these dazed moths into its seductive dangerous flame.

After last night's incidents at Nocturnal Trinity, Kailey didn't ever expect that she'd come back so soon to a place where she had had the hell scared out of her. She had no way to explain why she was actually looking forward to returning when she knew it was in her best interests to stay away.

Perhaps her eagerness stemmed from having the blessed stone and a veil of protection around her. Or, maybe she was thankful to have Raven with her this time, and entering with a friend lessened the worry of constantly looking over her shoulder, wondering from where the next possible attack might approach.

Even though Kailey was unhappy with Raven's behavior, she knew

Raven would watch her back while she watched Raven's. The downside was that Raven didn't have any idea what Flora or Cassie actually looked like, which left Kailey as the one to be more cautious. And if Cassie was in her succubus form, Kailey had only caught glimpses of what her demon form looked like before she had attacked and disappeared.

Kailey wondered if she'd recognize Cassie but that probably didn't matter since Cassie would most likely flaunt her presence to Kailey. True to a demon's nature, Cassie wasn't about to allow Kailey's wound to mend. Instead, she'd rip it open and try to infect it, making it fester and stay raw.

Raven tried to slide closer to Kailey, but Kailey placed her purse between them. She believed they needed to be more focused on what might happen inside Nocturnal Trinity rather than being playful or getting cozy. Besides she also wanted to have a serious talk before they continued down the path for a romantic relationship. She was partially shocked at Raven's rude dominating behavior, and unless Raven was willing to see that, Kailey was ending the romance before it ever escalated any further.

"Something wrong?" Raven asked.

"We can talk later."

"What is it?"

Kailey faced Raven and smiled. "Raven, let's keep our heads clear and focus like Micah told us to."

"You're mad at me, aren't you?" Raven whispered.

"No. I wouldn't say that I'm mad. It's just that we have things to discuss later this evening *after* we leave the nightclub."

"Okay."

Kailey leaned toward Raven and whispered, "Regardless of whatever happens between us, I hope that we can always have our friendship."

Sadness tugged at Raven's eyes. Her thick beautiful lips puckered. "So you are thinking about breaking up when we've only started?"

Kailey shook her head with frustration and sighed. "That's *not* what I'm saying. But things do happen."

Raven's eyes brimmed with tears momentarily. She took a deep breath and her jaw tightened. She turned and stared straight ahead.

Heated tears formed in Kailey's eyes, but she took a tissue from her purse and dabbed at them so her makeup didn't run. Not that tear-streaked mascara made any difference amongst all the partiers inside Nocturnal Trinity. Some deliberately painted sad faces with fake teary black streaks to advertise their solemn gloom. She didn't want to be in that group with real or fake tears.

Confrontations in the fighting ring were one thing Kailey readied faced, but emotional clashes with someone she loved hurt worse than the physical bouts and inevitable bruises, which was why she generally kept her mouth shut to spare the feelings of the other. But, no longer. She had lost too many loved ones in her life, leaving her devastated and miserable. Life was too short for her to live in misery with someone that continually berated or tried to press her down.

"Now isn't the time, Raven," Kailey whispered.

"For us?"

"No, for us to discuss anything outside of what we're going to do inside Nocturnal Trinity. One misstep on our part will get one or both of us killed. When I said that I love you, I meant it. Okay?"

"Okay."

"Don't over read my need to talk to you as more than what it is. Talk."

Skye glanced into the rearview mirror. "We are only a few blocks from Nocturnal Trinity. Should I find a place to park?"

Kailey nodded. "Any spot along the sidewalk is fine."

Skye pulled into a parking spot. The windshield wipers swiped a half circle of the fine mist off the glass.

Kailey dug through her purse until she found some change. She got out and fed the parking meter. Quickly she hopped back into the rear seat.

"How long do you think it will be before Brady comes along?" Skye askcd.

"No idea."

More hoodie wearing Goths walked along the sidewalks on both streets. Alice Cooper, Rob Zombie, and Marilyn Manson would be proud. Although tonight's crowd was not as many as the night before, there was still a large group of dedicated hopefuls.

Kailey ran her fingers across her membership badge. Without immediate entrance she knew that she'd have never tried to enter Nocturnal Trinity again. She refused to stand in that line like a desperate soul that didn't have a life. Besides, she had been inside, and nothing except her rightful revenge gave her any reason to ever want to return.

Kailey's phone lit up. She read the text. "Brady said that he's on his way."

"What?" Raven asked. Her eyes sharply glared at her. "You gave *him* your number?"

Kailey shrugged and nodded. "Yes. Why shouldn't I have? He needed to let us know when he was coming."

"When did you give it to him?"

"Right as we left the magic shop."

"I see. You sure it wasn't when you first met him earlier in the day?"

Kailey frowned. "No, it wasn't." Although he had given her, *his*, but she wasn't about to mention that.

Raven shook her head. "I could tell that you're interested in him. You can't hide it, and now he has your number? Wow."

"*This*, Raven. *This* is what we need to talk about. Your damn jealousy. Regardless of how you might try to convince me otherwise, you're insanely jealous of me. Maybe even obsessed. That's something *you're* unable to hide."

Raven's eyebrows rose. She opened her mouth to speak.

"No," Kailey said. "I won't tolerate that kind of behavior. I don't have to put up with it."

Skye remained silent. She placed her hands on the steering wheel and watched the street.

Anger stirred in Raven's eyes. She looked away. She didn't seem to have any remorse for her attitude.

"Look, Raven. Are you capable of keeping your focus when we get inside Nocturnal Trinity? Be honest. Because if you can't, I will go in by myself."

Skye glanced into the rearview mirror. "That's not a good idea."

Kailey met her gaze. "I know that it isn't, but what else can I do? Raven is obviously distracted."

"As are you," Skye replied.

Kailey released a frustrated sigh. "You're right, Skye. I am, but at least I have been trying *not* to be."

"Raven," Skye said. "Whatever hang ups you're having, you best set them aside for the next few hours, or I'm driving both of you back to Micah and tell him we can't do this tonight. Is that clear?"

Kailey nodded.

"Raven?" Skye asked.

"Yes, ma'am."

"Kailey's right. You need to focus. You can get past the relationship problems later. And if you want a mediator, I'll be happy to counsel with you."

CHAPTER 27

Ten minutes passed before Brady pulled into the parking spot behind Kailey's rental. He emerged from his vehicle wearing what she thought looked like a biker outfight. Leather jacket, leather pants, and black biker boots. When he reached the side window, she noticed that Luna had applied a blazing skull tattoo to his neck.

Kailey glanced at Raven. "We leave our purses in the car with Skye. That will save some time since they will insist on looking through them."

Raven nodded and handed her purse over the seat to Skye.

She stepped out of the car.

He smiled. "What do you think?"

Kailey laughed. "A bit rugged but no worse than any of the others I've seen."

Raven emerged from the other side of the vehicle, slammed the door, viciously eyed Brady, and then she started down the sidewalk. "Let's go."

Brady gave Kailey an odd glance.

"She's jealous."

"Of me?" he asked.

Kailey nodded. "Of everyone that speaks to me, apparently."

"You two are in a relationship?"

She shrugged.

"For how long?" he asked.

"Today, when she and Skye arrived at the magic shop. She's been my roommate for four years, but I had never committed to her, even after the countless times she asked."

"What made you change your mind then?"

Kailey took a deep breath. "Got tired of being lonely. Since we knew one another for so long, and I do love her and have feelings for her, I thought we should give it an attempt to see where it went. However, I think it was over before it really even started."

"Ah, I see."

Disappointment showed in his eyes, which meant that he had been interested when they had talked at the cemetery. This also meant that Raven was right in her assumption that he might be attracted to Kailey.

"I guess we need to catch up to her," Kailey said.

She and Brady sped up to a near jog. Raven walked with her arms crossed. Her soured expression was nothing less than mild irritation. Ahead of them a young man wore a black hoodie jacket with the white-lettered slogan, "*Only freaks come out at night*," stenciled on it.

Raven shook her head. "Ain't that the truth?"

Brady chuckled. "I suppose we all get placed into that category tonight."

Raven didn't respond. She just walked faster, leaving Brady with Kailey.

Kailey slowed her pace.

"Is she mad because of me?" Brady asked.

"She's mad about a lot of things. But jealousy is her worst enemy."

"Maybe it will settle."

"I hope so. Where's your partner?" she asked.

"I'm currently looking for one," he replied with a teasing grin.

Kailey smiled back. "I meant the officer you were meeting here?"

"Richard said that he'd meet me at the door, so I'll wait outside until he shows."

Raven stopped across the street from Nocturnal Trinity. The evening air was crisp, and small frosty clouds drifted from her mouth. Kailey couldn't help but to think how the cold air matched Raven's recent conduct. Despite Raven agreeing to Skye's advice about setting things aside, Raven had not let the issue go.

Seeing Raven like this was sad and disheartening.

Who is the true bulldog?

Kailey finally began to realize that the one person she held as her dearest friend, the one she had thought she could always rely on through thick and thin and who had sworn would always be there, turned out to be quite the opposite. The betrayal cut deeply and felt like a rusty serrated dagger stabbed into her soul.

"So Richard doesn't know what you are?" Kailey asked.

"No," he said, shaking his head.

"Why does he frequent Nocturnal Trinity?"

"A lot of the police officers do. Memberships are given to some quid pro quo."

Kailey frowned. "Meaning?"

"Those who accept the memberships obligate themselves to keep an eye out for anyone that might be trying to hold up the place or somehow sneak weapons past the bouncers to kill a vampire. Or, they are expected to turn a blind eye if one of the inner circle severely maims or accidentally kills someone."

"Seriously?" she asked. "People come here to kill vampires?"

"Kailey, there are vampire hunters, Demon-hunters, and sorcerers who practice dark magic that thrive on the opportunity to lessen the numbers of those they consider enemies."

"Who pays them?"

"Most aren't looking for a bounty. They simply want the recognition and reputation for what they are. For some, that's a badge of honor."

"Have anyone ever actually tried to kill Nocturnal Trinity members?"

Brady nodded. "Yes. None have succeeded. Yet. And unfortunately a lot of murders in this area go unreported or never investigated."

"Really?"

"Really. We have boxes of cold cases that could be solved if the investigator would simply write 'now a vampire.' But there's that unwritten loyalty a few officers hold toward Nocturnal Trinity."

"Why would anyone even attempt to publicly kill a vampire?"

"Revenge is the main motivator. If one's spouse or significant other is turned into a vampire, the victim might live forever, but he or she is no longer the person they had once been. That brings about a different type of insanity. The lover seeks to kill the vampire responsible, but often dies before getting close enough to complete the goal."

Kailey shook her head in disbelief.

"What?" he asked.

"It's just ... how could I have not known about all this?"

"The vast majority of society is blind to it, but now that you know, you're never going to forget it."

"No doubt about that. Especially not after last night."

Brady smiled. "Tonight's a new night. Who knows what surprises might unfold?"

Kailey's chest tightened. "Please don't make me any more nervous than I already am. Has Nocturnal Trinity ever offered you membership?"

Brady shook his head. "No."

"Any particular reason why they haven't?"

"None that I know of. But if they offered, I'd accept only for Micah's benefit. Nothing particularly grabs my interest here, other than protecting you or others like you from becoming victims."

Kailey blushed, seeing the concern in his eyes and the warmth of his smile that curved his lips. "Does Seattle have a fairly good size vampire population?"

"Currently there's not any way to know their exact numbers because they are still too secretive to emerge publicly."

"Do you believe they ever will?"

Brady shrugged. "No laws are on the books to protect them, which is partly why they stay underground."

"So killing them wouldn't be a crime in the eyes of the law?"

"Probably not since they are undead."

"You haven't had any cases of vampire attacks?" she asked.

"Have you *heard* of any?"

She shook her head. "No. I didn't know they existed until last night."

"Trust me, if such an attack happened in public and the media got hold of it, you'd have heard about it. That's why Nocturnal Trinity wishes to gain the loyalty of law enforcement officers, attorneys, and judges."

"That makes sense," Kailey replied. "But, due to an outright panic, it's possible the police department would cover it up to prevent hysteria."

"I'm not saying that it hasn't happened. It does happen. Other officers have done that, but I don't have any knowledge of how often it occurs. I'm only informing you that I've seen cases where I suspect the deaths and disappearances are vampire related. I'm betting it is more commonplace."

Kailey glanced toward the long line of hopefuls. "And what about here? How many vampires do you think come to Nocturnal Trinity?"

Brady shrugged. "Inside members might be fifty or more. It's hard to say."

"You really think they'd have that many?"

"With nearly four million people in Seattle? That would be a very low percentage. The true number is probably a *lot* higher. And it will continue to escalate."

"What makes you think that?" she asked.

He nodded toward the line of waiters. "Over a hundred already lining up to get inside tonight. My guess is around ninety percent of those would probably allow themselves to be turned without a second thought if offered the chance."

"That's kind of frightening."

"It is, but it's also due to their misconceptions."

"I suppose," Kailey said.

"Everyone fears death. No one wants to die. Even the most miserable people who kill themselves only do so because they feel like there's no alternative. Ever wonder why all these people come here, dressed like they are?"

Kailey smiled. "I've thought of reasons why."

"And why do you think they do?"

"Some have always felt like society rejects and probably want to frighten others away so people don't bother them."

"Possibly. My guess is that a lot of them hope they can scare Death away or at least delay his arrival. That's also why most would readily accept vampirism because it grants them life eternal or living death, whichever way you wish to view it. They believe such a life is glamorous, but they don't understand the true darkness until after they've already been deceived."

"You sound like you knew someone that had become a vampire," Kailey said.

Brady nodded. "I did. Her fate did not come as she might have hoped."

"What happened?"

"After Diana turned, her violence outweighed her rationality. No amount of coaxing could persuade her that I only wished to help and not hurt her." Sadness filled his eyes. "Her hunger for blood blinded her to who I was. She was like a rabid animal and would have killed me just to feast on my blood."

"Was she your girlfriend?" Kailey asked.

"No. She was my partner. We worked homicide cases together."

"Oh. So you had to kill her?"

Brady shook his head and tucked his thumbs behind his belt. "No. She's still alive ... if you can call it living."

Kailey looked confused. She stared into his eyes, seeking more information.

"Diana told me that she was going to Nocturnal Trinity to talk to a client. She didn't return to work the next day. I kept trying to contact her by phone, but she never answered. I stopped by her apartment several times, but her place was vacant. After two days, I returned to her place during the daylight hours, picked her lock, and searched her apartment. I found her and other surprises as well."

"What did you find?"

Brady cleared his throat. "A coffin. Two dead bodies. They were probably street drug addicts that she had drained during her feeding frenzy. I swear if it had been nighttime when I entered her apartment, I'd be dead."

"Why?"

"Like a fool, I opened the coffin because I feared she had to be the one inside. She was. Her eyes opened in an instant, but before she rose, I slammed the coffin lid shut and ran for the door. I flung open the door several seconds before her icy cold fingers gripped my arm. Sunlight scorched her fingers, making her screech and release me. I ran."

"Where is she now?"

"In the coffin."

"How do you know?" Kailey asked.

"I returned at noon the next day with thick silver chains. I wrapped them around the coffin and locked it together with heavy-duty padlocks, trapping her inside. Micah, Ashley, and Jacob helped me move the coffin to a storage unit."

"Why didn't you kill her?"

"I should have, but it's hard to kill a friend, regardless of whether she's a monster or not. Would you kill me because I am a werewolf?" Brady asked.

"No. Of course not," she replied.

"See? And we're not even close friends. You hardly know me." His endearing smile returned.

Kailey understood what he meant. The decision to kill someone, even if they've changed into something that's no longer human ... could she ever do that? If Vincent had become a vampire or something worse ... no, she didn't believe she could have killed him.

"I thought silver was something that harmed werewolves," Kailey said.

"I wore gloves. Thick ones. However, small bits of silver, like your necklace, don't hurt us. But any silver that enters us like a blade, a bullet, or an injection of silver nitrate will kill us. Those items aren't something people can readily buy. Someone whose goal is to hunt werewolves have to find a person capable of making a silver knife or bullet."

"So you're fairly safe from that type of attack?"

Brady nodded.

"Do you think Diana willingly became a vampire?" Kailey asked.

His smile faded and pain returned to his eyes. "No. Diana loved living too much. She was a beautiful woman, full of ambition and fight. She'd never willingly become a vampire. I believe she was compelled."

"I'm sorry."

Tears moistened his eyes and he looked away.

Kailey didn't like seeing his agony, so she changed the subject. "What did Micah need from you before he sent you to watch over us?"

Clearing his throat, he said, "I cannot reveal that right yet, but trust me, it was a good thing."

"It's sad about Micah's wife," Kailey said, finally standing beside Raven again. They stood directly across the street from Nocturnal Trinity. "His anger and pain weigh him down."

Brady gave a grim smile. "Had I been a werewolf when Jeannine was attacked, I'd have done everything possible to kill Nicodemus. She and Micah would not have entered Nocturnal Trinity without backup. I'd have made certain of that."

Gazing into his eyes, she saw the depth of a man she'd love to know more about. His sincerity and passion to do whatever was necessary to help others was something she rarely found in people. She stared at his lips a bit too long, swallowed hard, and took a deep breath. "You weren't part of his pack?"

He shook his head. "No. That came later. I'm the youngest in the pack. Barely two and a half years old by human years. Or fourteen in wolf years."

"So you're a bratty teenager?" Raven asked with a smug look on her face.

He smiled but she turned away, not entertaining one of her own or giving him a chance to reply.

"And you volunteered to suppress the change?" Kailey asked.

"Sure. Since I've not been a werewolf very long, it actually isn't as bad for me as it is for Jacob or most of the others. Plus it helps since I'm in law enforcement. Less aggression. No cop brutality."

"Nice to know," Raven said, rolling her eyes and walking away.

"Seems like all of you work out," Kailey said. "You're all in great shape."

Brady smiled. "There's no such thing as a fat werewolf."

"Really?" Kailey asked, smiling and waiting for the punch line.

"Oh, Goddess." Raven sighed.

"Honest. There aren't any because our metabolisms are extraordinarily high."

"I see."

"Might use that for a recruitment slogan," Raven said.

Brady ignored the comment as he stared toward the parking garage. "There's Richard. I'll go meet with him. It's been nice talking to you."

Kailey smiled but noticed the frown coming from Raven. "You, too."

"You two go on inside. Remember to keep a low profile and be safe," he said.

Kailey nodded and watched him hurry down the sidewalk. Richard, his friend and partner, looked more evil than cop. He was thin, about five foot ten, with dark slicked back hair and a very pale complexion. Like Brady, he had chosen to wear leather, and Kailey believed it didn't matter what the man wore, he'd still pass for a classic anemic vampire.

"Glad to see him leave," Raven said with a sigh. "Sayonara."

Brady shook hands with Richard, firm and quick, and bumped shoulders like old buddies sometimes do. While there was a smile on Brady's face, no hint of warmth or friendship came in response from Richard. Richard's gaze was cold, harsh, and made Kailey uncomfortable. Was he actually a vampire?

Raven took a step off the sidewalk onto the street between two parked cars. "You ready or do you want us to wait for your boyfriend?"

Kailey grabbed Raven's hand and turned her sharply toward her. "Would you please stop it with all of your snide comments? Or are you deliberately trying to push me away?"

Raven shrugged. "I figure you're as good as gone anyway."

"You're certainly trying to drive me away and doing a hell of a good job, too."

"From our earlier conversation, it seemed like you're ready to break it off."

"If this side of you is dominant, yes. It's over. Definitely over. I've never known you to act this way. Ever. I—" Kailey's voice crackled as she fought tears. "I missed you so badly when I arrived here without you. When I lost touch with you and feared you ... might be dead ... I honestly thought my world was over. Then you surprised me. When I saw that you were safe and *here*, I wanted us to be partners, and for some damned reason, you've been a selfish bitch ever since." Angered that she had to fight tears, she stepped past Raven. "Come on. Let's get this the hell over with."

"Kay, wait," Raven said softly. "I'm sorry."

Kailey stopped and turned with surprise.

Tears glistened in Raven's eyes. "You said that you want a heart-to-heart?"

Kailey nodded.

Raven leaned back against the hood of the car. She wiped tears from her eyes. Like a small child frightened in a thunderstorm, her eyes reflected fear. "I don't like being here."

"At Nocturnal Trinity?"

Raven nodded. "Here and in Seattle in general. I'm out of my element. I want us to go back to Boston and get away from all this."

"We will."

"I'm sorry for my behavior. It's my defense mechanism, my way of coping with my fears. I'm out of my comfort zone, I hate being so far from home, and I'm nowhere nearly as brave as you."

"Actually, I'm quite frightened. I didn't want to come back, but I need to know what really happened to my brother. For closure. For justice. And I certainly wouldn't be here if we didn't have Brady as backup."

"I'm more afraid of going in there. After seeing that demon outside our apartment, Kailey, I've been afraid of every moving shadow. Its scaly skin and green eyes haunt me. And now we're going into a club where demons are members. Do you realize how crazy that sounds?"

"I know."

"So to deal with that, I've verbally attacked almost everything about everybody. None of them deserve it, especially not you."

Kailey pulled Raven close and hugged her tightly. She whispered into her ear, "We're going to be okay. We just stick together, look around, and we get out of there. Okay?"

"Okay."

"I love you, Raven."

"I love you, too."

The sincerity in Raven's voice helped ease the growing tension Kailey had about continuing her relationship with Raven, but it didn't resolve Kailey's uncertainties. She still wasn't convinced that what they had intimately started could be redeemed or that after what they had to do tonight could totally save their friendship. She was willing to consider it, but what she didn't want to do was go inside the nightclub with any type of division between them. She needed to have no doubts that Raven had her back.

Kailey glanced up to the roof of Nocturnal Trinity. The two Psi-vamps stood guard, as they had the night before. She tilted her head downward to make it appear like she was looking at the street. A part of her worried that these beasts might leap and rush her, but unless they had some kind of telepathy, they didn't know her and probably wouldn't recognize her since she was dressed completely different than she had been the night before.

But with everything that had occurred one night earlier, she was more apt to believe Flora had instructed them to pursue her, maybe not to kill her, but to certainly scare the hell out of her. If that was all they were required to do, they had been successful with that task.

For a moment, Kailey was short of breath. Tightness squeezed her chest. At least she had not been the one that flung the holy water on them, and she believed what Blaze had said afterwards about him not being able to return. He was probably right. They undoubtedly were watching and waiting, ever hopeful that he did return so they could exact their revenge.

"Something wrong?" Raven asked.

"Don't make an obvious look," Kailey said, "but those vampires that tried to attack me last night are upon the roof."

Raven pulled Kailey close into an embrace again. Raven's gaze was directed toward the nightclub. "I see them. How many are there?"

"I saw two last night, but there might have been more than that."

"I see three individuals up there," Raven whispered, pulling away from Kailey. "But one of them is a victim."

Kailey turned to see the two Psi-vamps biting into a woman's throat. She wasn't fighting, so she had been obviously compelled or charmed.

Kailey tugged Raven's hand. "Let's get inside. For some reason, I'd feel safer inside than out here."

"Me, too."

As they crossed the street, she noticed Brady and Richard talking to two sultry vamp wannabes. Although she'd never admit it to Raven, she felt a bit of jealousy rising in her chest. Her stomach tensed. She knew it was selfish of her to think it, but she was hoping Brady's conversation with those women didn't lead to anything else, other than information about the ones responsible for Vincent's and Dale's murders.

Before Kailey turned her attention away from Brady and toward the line at the main entrance, she berated herself. *You can't have it both ways.*

Her intuition was right. Tonight, she had decisions to make. The final outcome of those decisions would be determined by what happened inside Nocturnal Trinity. She was uneasy about what she might choose.

CHAPTER 28

Kailey presented her badge to the large black bouncer at the main entrance door. His nametag displayed his name with photo identification.

Titus.

The name seemed something he had been destined to grow into. He weighed approximately three hundred pounds with huge shoulders that almost met his ears. Wearing a skintight black t-shirt, the outline of his chiseled chest and abs were prominently presented. Best she could tell, he had no body fat, and in the world of bodybuilders, he probably made those around him envious of his massive steroid growth.

Titus glanced at her badge, looked into her eyes without blinking, and in a deep voice said, "She's your guest?"

Kailey looked at Raven and back at the man. "Yes."

His bald head creased as he peered around each of them. "No purses or bags, ladies?"

Kailey nervously shook her head.

He frowned. "You sure now, ladies? Girls gotta have their purses."

"Honest."

His stern rocklike face broke into a broad smile as he opened the door. "All right babies, you two enjoy your night."

His sudden change made Raven and Kailey turn to one another with their eyebrows raised. Raven smiled, took Kailey's hand, and together they entered Nocturnal Trinity.

Immediately the blasting music cascaded around them in a near deafening wave. Computerized controlled strobe lights, lasers, and wash lights kept pace with the DJ's music. Sweet smoke and fog drifted through the crowd.

"Is that marijuana?" Raven asked.

Kailey nodded. "Yep."

"Sweet," she said in her throaty voice. "Breathe it in."

Kailey gave her an odd side-glance, laughed, and then shook her head.

Raven shrugged.

Dancers waved their hands in the air. Glowing neon bracelets of various colors wrapped around most of their wrists. Others swung glow sticks that made weird illusions as they sliced through the air. The swell of the crowd was intimidating, and for a few minutes, Kailey and Raven stepped to the side of the door and simply watched.

"Nothing quite like this back in Boston," Raven said, leaning close to Kailey's ear.

"I know!"

"So they're pretty liberal here? Pot smoking. Half nudes."

"Anything goes," an older man standing behind them said. He was shirtless and flashed a perverted wink at them. Sweat dampened his grayish chest hair. Wrinkles covered his drawn face. Bits of drool leaked at the sides of his leering smile as he stared at Raven's short skirt and then to Kailey's. He licked the drool from his lips and made a smacking sound that sickened Kailey.

She grabbed Raven's hand and pulled her toward the dance floor. The stranger cackled as they hurried away.

"Let's go. He's a bit too creepy."

Raven laughed. "You caught that, too? Eeww."

"Would you like to dance?" Kailey asked.

Raven smiled. "I'd rather get something to drink first."

"Sure. Let's make our way to the bar then. Far from the wrinkled perv against the wall."

"I'm all for that."

Kailey kept a careful watch for Flora or Eva while she and Raven took a shortcut to the bar by directly avoiding the dance floor. Remembering Flora's power, Kailey wished to avoid being in the center of a crowd again. She kept an occasional glance toward the main door, just in case she and

Raven needed to exit quickly. Of course, she understood that she'd probably feel Flora well before she ever saw her.

Kailey gently placed her hand over the black gemstone, closed her eyes, and hoped. She thought of the ritual, the massive power flow that had encapsulated around her, and tried to recall the sensations she had felt for reassurance. It was times, like now, when she really wished she believed a higher power existed. Someone or something to pray to would be nice. She didn't know if her doubts could ever be quashed.

The main door opened, allowing three more visitors to walk inside the club. The bouncer's huge muscled arm pulled the door closed again.

Perhaps there was no quick retreat with the massive bouncer at the door. He had not been on duty the night before. Getting to the door was one thing. Getting past his muscular wall of flesh was not something she wished to attempt in a hurry. Generally, it didn't matter what function one was at, but a person running from an event tended to look guilty of something. Security guards or bouncers were quick at stopping their exit to find out more.

Kailey slid her hand into Raven's and they interlocked fingers. Raven offered no resistance. When the bar was within sight, Kailey stared at the glowing fiery red and orange pentagram that hung and shimmered upon the far wall. An ominous feeling swept over her. Upon closer examination she noticed windows were set within the symbol. Horned beings sat behind the glass, washed in the lava-like glow of the pentagram. This wasn't the dance hall she had visited the night before. From her observation, this must be the demon section of Nocturnal Trinity and they were watching the activities on the dance floor from their VIP room.

She wondered if Jinn was up there or possibly somewhere else on the dance floor, trying to find himself a gullible sex slave. Of course, since he could alter his outward appearance, he might be in any of the other dance halls. Uneasily she let her eyes trace across all the dancers.

The darkness lingering over this floor was thick. The music thundered loud oppressively violent sounds and lyrics. The dancers moved with undulating perfection, matching the intense rhythm. Their glassy eyes were frightening to behold. They seemed lulled into hypnosis or possession. Either way, they didn't have control over their actions, which disturbed Kailey. They were essentially mindless individuals that simply needed a prompt to do whatever they were programmed to do. With demons, she imagined either mischievous or evil deeds were the results.

Kailey had witnessed Flora's mind controlling power. As a victim, she had felt it. How much worse could demons control those that willingly chose to serve darkness? These were individuals who'd offer their souls to be granted wealth, power, and control. This dangerous crowd seemed willing to blindly follow horrible masters.

She wondered if Flora would even dare set foot into this section of Nocturnal Trinity. Perhaps the factions maintained strict control over their own mobs. Did they each have a written agreement to respect the boundaries of the others' territories?

Flora had mentioned the distasteful pranks that were causing a rift between their groups. Maybe they were infringing on one another by violating proper zones within Nocturnal Trinity? Kailey didn't know, but for some reason she believed she wouldn't see Flora in this part of the club.

While most of the dancers were dressed in similar Goth and Emo attire like the patrons she had seen the previous night, these individuals wore much darker makeup with evil tattooed symbols and jewelry. Pentagrams. A *lot* of pentagrams were visible in various tattoos, jewelry, and makeup adorned the people. None of the patrons feared being shunned for their loyalty, as this was one of the few places where one held the freedom of belonging with prejudice.

Raven stood at the bar impatiently waiting for Kailey.

The female bartender glanced at them as she wiped down the bar. She had the left half of her head shaved, revealing the tattoo of a coffin ablaze in a fiery pit. The right half was spiked in various directions and colors. Her nose was pierced with a broad brass ring. A chain ran from the side of her nose to her left ear. Her stretched earlobes were plugged with two-inch obsidian plugs. The woman's ears and lips were studded with various stones.

When she noticed Kailey rudely staring at her, she bared her fanged teeth. Kailey looked away. She took the hint. Not a friendly crowd here. Certainly, the woman was most likely a demon, and Nocturnal Trinity wasn't a place to gawk at them like people did at a freak show. This was the demon territory, and Kailey admitted to herself that staring was rude.

This woman was *not* human. She didn't think the woman was a succubus because the ones she had seen preferred to adorn themselves with irresistible beauty. This woman was probably a demon or a half demon if they could cross with humans.

Damn. I need a field guide to know who is what.

"Order something or get away from my bar," the barkeep snapped.

"A shot of whiskey," Raven said.

Kailey stared at her in shock. "You never drink whiskey."

Raven shrugged and grinned. "Always a first time, and tonight's the night."

"You?" the demon asked.

"What do you suggest?"

The female demon smiled. With the jagged teeth and fangs, Kailey couldn't tell if it was a good or bad smile. "Give me a minute."

She turned and grabbed a couple of bottles from the rack behind her. She mixed different tonics together and poured them over a glass of ice before finally setting it on the bar in front of Kailey.

"Screaming Demon," she said.

Raven winked at Kailey. "Seems appropriate, doesn't it?"

"Shh!" Kailey placed her finger to her lips.

The bartending demon cackled in an eerily deep laugh. Her eyes flamed orange for a brief second before dying back down to cold obsidian. "I don't recall you two in this part of Nocturnal Trinity before. You expanding your curiosities?"

Kailey shrugged and sipped the drink. The liquor hit the back of her throat like liquid fire, burning up to the back of her nose. Her eyes watered, and she gasped. In a harsh gargled reply, she said, "You might say that."

The barkeep laughed. "Doesn't look too promising if you can't handle *that* drink."

Kailey's hand went to her throat. She coughed. "You're probably right."

"Don't be so quick to agree." She extended her scaly hand to Kailey. "My name's Meg."

"Kailey," she said, accepting the handshake. Meg's hand felt rougher than snakeskin. "This is Raven."

Meg shook Raven's hand.

"Hit me with another shot," Raven said.

"Raven!" Kailey said.

Meg chuckled. "A bit overly protective, aren't you? She seems to be handling hers better than you." She filled Raven's shot glass.

Raven placed the shot to her lips and quickly tipped her head back, downing in one quick gulp. "Another!"

Kailey didn't say anything but her perplexed glance was enough.

Raven waved her off. "I'm fine, Kay."

Meg refilled the glass. Raven downed it.

Kailey leaned closer to Raven. "We need to keep our senses keen."

Raven nodded. "No more. I promise. I just need to get the edge off my nerves, okay?"

Kailey placed her hand on Raven's and squeezed. "Okay, if you're working on completely *numb*."

Meg brought two beers to the men on the other end of the bar.

"You ever think about what Brady was telling you?" Raven asked.

"What?" Kailey replied.

"Living forever."

"As a vampire?"

Raven nodded.

"Hell no. Have you?"

"Would it really be that bad?"

"God ..."

"Goddess," Raven said with her brow firming.

"Imagine what you'd give up."

Raven turned on her stool and faced Kailey. Propping her elbow on the bar, she rested her chin atop her fist. The dazed look in her eyes showed the alcohol was quickly affecting her. "What exactly would I be giving up, dearie?"

"No sunlight."

"I'm a night person anyway, so eh. Besides I'm dark skinned, so I have no need to tan."

Strike one.

"But it's more than just not being in the sunlight, Raven. Think about the beauty of life that you'd be missing? Colors are much more different during the day than at night."

"Maybe. But for eternal life? That is an easy compromise. As a practicing witch, imagine what my power could be in a hundred years? Two hundred?"

Kailey thought for a moment, trying to counter her friend's argument. "You love to eat. From the lore at least, you won't be able to eat the foods you love. No spaghetti, lasagna, or pizza."

Raven winced. Those foods were her greatest weaknesses.

Point for me.

"You'd have to drink blood, too," Kailey said. "Didn't you nearly faint when we helped that lady from the car wreck a year ago? Her head had struck the side window, and she was covered in blood. Remember all the blood?"

Raven expressed a look of disgust. "Okay, I think you've made your point. Welcome to the anti-recruiting campaign."

Meg stood before them. Neither had seen her move or approach. "That might be a downside, but you're missing the overall benefits."

Kailey couldn't tell if Meg was being sarcastic or truthful, but since she was a demon, sarcasm was most likely her intention. "And what would that be?"

"Vampires aren't susceptible to disease like humans."

"What about demons?" Kailey asked.

"Not to human diseases. Then again, some of my kin are able to inflict plagues of our own invention at times." She looked at Raven. "What ever would *possess* you to want to be a vampire?"

"I wasn't being serious," Raven replied.

Meg laughed wildly in an annoying high-pitched tone. "Lie to a demon? Now, seriously. Witches should know better."

Raven's eyes widened for a moment, and then she glanced toward Kailey uneasy that Meg knew Raven was a witch. Kailey shrugged. Raven shifted uncomfortably in her stool. Due to the amount of whisky she had drunk, Raven probably didn't remember mentioning her witchcraft powers. That was one damning effect of too much alcohol.

"Don't be alarmed, sweetie," Meg said. "It's not like I'm reading your thoughts. Demons manipulate others through lies, so we're quick to detect when others lie to us. I know you're a witch because I sense the magic in your aura, and I work around witches in the club all the time. Your tattoo is also a big clue. Not to mention, you did bring it up a few seconds ago."

Meg flicked her gaze toward Kailey. "You? Hmm, you're a bit harder to read. You dedicate yourself to no deity. You're conflicted about your relationships ..."

Raven jerked toward Kailey with unspoken accusations burning in her gaze. Raven had already suspected Kailey had a secret attraction to Brady. Did Meg somehow read that? No. Surely not.

"You should take those talents to a fair, Meg" Kailey said.

Meg's eyes narrowed. A spark of orange blazed around her tiny pupils. "Careful."

"I didn't mean anything disrespectful. I only meant that you'd probably make more money doing that than tips gathered from such a young crowd. Most, I assume are unemployed college students."

Meg grinned, revealing her jagged rows of teeth. "You're probably correct, but I enjoy what I do there. Pathetic people tip better than you can imagine, and I've never been under tipped. You know why?"

Kailey shook her head.

"Because who'd shortchange a demon? Knowing what we're capable of, most tip more generously than less."

"Even if they're drunk?" Raven asked.

"I won't allow people get drunk here. If that's what they want to do, they can go elsewhere."

"You gave Raven *three* shots!" Kailey said.

"She's not drunk. Lightly buzzed, but I won't serve her another, and if you two choose to head to one of the other bars, I simply alert them with your membership badge number, and they won't serve you either."

"Okay, that's good to know," Kailey said, taking a deep breath. "Tell me something though."

"Sure," Meg replied.

"Why do you support telling others about the benefits of becoming a vampire? Doesn't that increase their numbers over demons?" Kailey asked.

Meg shrugged. "Doesn't make a difference to me how many vampires there are. Demons cannot make more of our race. We can cross species with humans, but we can't turn them into demons."

"Then what real benefit do you have here?"

"On your plane?"

Kailey nodded. "Yes."

"We have the powers to manipulate. Humans always seek us out for various favors, and if they are willing to pay our price, we often give them the lusts of their hearts."

"Like what?"

"Greed has many faces, dear," Meg said. "A lot lust for wealth, fame, and personal energy."

"What's personal energy?" Kailey asked.

"Charisma, magnetism. Used properly, people can influence others to place them into prominent employment places or political offices. Rich people give them luxurious gifts without truly understanding why. Or they can possess a hypnotic attractiveness that makes people sexually desire them. Ever wondered why some beautiful women sleep with dog ugly people?"

Raven nodded. "All the time."

"Well, there you go. That's why. Their charismatic magnetism enables them to energize physical chemistry with the people around them. They've been touched by a demon."

What the hell was this? Meg seemed to be throwing out sales pitches for demons and vampires. She could picture the slogan on a business card: "If you're not content with your present dismal life, let *us* solve your problems."

Damn.

No wonder so many were being suckered into waiting in a line that never seemed to shorten. Ever hopeful. Ever wanting. Once someone finally picked them, they were so desperate to become a part of the club that they allow themselves to be initiated into one of the factions without thinking through such a radical life-changing decision.

"And what does it cost them to gain such power?"

"Their souls," Meg replied with a cold tone. Nothing hinted she was joking. She was serious, and Kailey believed her.

The price was steep. More than she'd ever offer. But how many had already done so? For people who didn't have much in life, they often were the eager ones that did stupid things without thinking or weighing the consequences. Being society rejects, many didn't have family or friends to offer helpful advice. Some wanted revenge on those who had hurt them and didn't care what the price for power was.

"Skeptical, are you Kailey?" Meg asked.

Sitting on the stool, Kailey crossed her arms. She understood such a gesture was a defensive mechanism, but she was fine with that. She wanted Meg to back off. Now.

Before Kailey spoke, Brady came to the far edge of the bar and sat on a stool. Richard wasn't with him, which somewhat relieved Kailey. She was careful with her glance not to acknowledge that she knew him.

Without breaking eye contact with Meg, Kailey said, "No. I believe that's possible. I've met people like that. They also turn me off. But I never imagined they received that type of charm from demons. What good are their souls to you?"

Meg laughed low and evenly. Her menacing eyes flickered. "Such things are never revealed, except to those who offer them up. Care to place yours into my possession? Then I'll gladly tell you." She winked.

Kailey placed her hands onto the bar. Seconds later, her hands formed tight fists. Raven reached for her hand, but Kailey pushed it away. Meg noticed the tension in Kailey's hands, so she didn't take her eyes off Kailey.

"What kind of power do you possess?"

Meg didn't seem to like the question.

"Kailey," Raven said, shaking her head. The look in Raven's eyes indicated that she knew Kailey was getting agitated. Raven's pleading voice wanted to prevent a fight from starting. "Let's just go. We don't *need* this."

"In a minute, Raven. Tell me, Meg."

The fire returned to Meg's dark eyes. Anger flickered in her gaze. Her jaw tightened. She took a towel and began rigorously wiping the bar. Kailey expected a sudden violent attack, but that didn't happen. She guessed that demons didn't like demands. Begging, perhaps, but never demands. But somehow Meg maintained control and refused to lash out.

"I'm here to serve," Meg replied softly. Her eyes smoldered from her anger. "To serve and direct. That's all. Nothing more. I've been a guide for many to find their ways into the darkness."

Kailey wondered what suppressed Meg's anger. How much did it take to set her off? Kailey tended to get better answers from people whenever she got under someone's skin. But that was with people, *not* demons.

Then Kailey thought about the demons in the VIP, looking out their hidden windows. Were they watching and was that why Meg subjugated her temper?

"So you're a guide leading them into darkness? Is that how you get your kicks?" Kailey asked. "I guess demons are as evil as what people say. You prey upon people's low self-esteem to proselyte them."

Meg flashed her teeth and emitted a low hiss. "It's best you that pay your tab and move on. My tolerance and hospitality ended sixty seconds ago."

There's the lioness she was looking for.

Looking into Meg's intense gaze, Kailey suddenly recalled how Cassie had nearly killed her. It was foolish to provoke an unpredictable beast, especially when the beast was a demon with powers unknown.

Take a few steps back, Kailey.

Kailey nodded to her inner voice and handed her credit card to Meg. Kailey shook her head and waved her hands in kind surrender. "I'm sorry, Meg. Truly. I've misjudged your intensions and I shouldn't have done that."

Meg swiped the card through the reader and handed it back to her. "Just go."

"I'm sorry," she said softly. And in a way she really was. Confrontations were the best way for investigative reporters to get their information, but sometimes they, like she, crossed lines too quickly, not only striking nerves, but also insulting potential allies. Burning bridges was not always the best strategy, unless it was in full retreat.

Kailey extended her hand to Raven and helped her down from the stool.

"Here you keep telling *me* to keep a low profile," Raven said as she walked away. "And you just start mouthing off at a demon of all things."

"I'm sorry. I know. You're right."

"Let's find a restroom," Raven said. "I think I'm going to be sick."

CHAPTER 29

*R*aven stooped over a toilet and violently hurled up most of the whiskey she had drunk. Kailey cringed. Already suffering a nervous stomach from foolishly aggravating Meg, the sound of Raven vomiting further nauseated her. Kailey figured she was only seconds away from executing a follow up performance of her own.

Kailey wet a thick wad of paper towels with cool water and pressed them to her face, trying to think of anything other than the whiskey revisited theme song Raven kept belting out. She wondered how long someone could puke, but then she realized Raven was merely dry heaving now.

Kailey eased into the stall, waved her hand over the sensor, and waited for the commode to flush. Once the water swirled downward, she placed her hand against Raven's back.

"I think you're done," Kailey said. "Let me help you to the sink."

Raven nodded without speaking.

Kailey took her hand and helped Raven stand. At the sink, Kailey ran cold water and soaked fresh towels, handing them to Raven. Raven wiped her mouth and leaned against the counter top.

"No more whiskey," Raven said. "*Ever.*"

"That bad?"

"Worse."

Kailey rubbed Raven's shoulder. "I'm sorry."

"Nothing ventured," she replied. A second later, she held her mouth to the running water to swish. She spat into the bowl and wiped her mouth with the wet towels.

"Let's find the dance floor beneath the vampire VIP lounge, so we can get out of here."

"I'm for that," Raven replied.

Right as they turned to head for the restroom door, the hinges whined. In stepped Cassie in her human form. Her eyes widened when she saw Kailey, and she made a quick retreat.

How did Cassie recognize me?

The stone should have kept them invisible to anyone else. Of course, the shock of recognition in Kailey's eyes was probably what Cassie had read first, which was why she'd fled.

"That was her," Kailey said.

"Who?"

"It's Cassie."

"You're sure?"

Kailey nodded. "Of course I'm sure."

Raven ran toward the door.

"No, Raven. Don't."

Raven was out the door before Kailey could grab her hand to stop her.

"Raven, wait!"

Kailey sprinted through the door as it began to close. Brady stood a few feet away.

"What's wrong?" he asked.

"Cassie. Raven went after her."

"The succubus?"

Kailey nodded.

"Shit," Brady said under his breath. "Don't lose sight of Raven. We have to stop her and get the hell out of here. Tonight's not the night for any confrontations. We're greatly outnumbered. And without cellphones we have no way to contact Micah if we're detained."

"I'll try to catch her."

Kailey hurried through the narrow corridor that led into the next dance room inside Nocturnal Trinity. Raven's head bobbed above some of the dancers as she ran after Cassie. But Cassie was no longer in human form. She had abandoned her human charade and turned into her seductively beautiful demoness form. She was far more dangerous as a demon, too. But if Cassie chose to take a different human form altogether, Kailey and Raven could never identify her.

"Why the hell are you chasing her?" Kailey growled in frustration.

If it's to prove your loyalty to our relationship, this isn't necessary.

Brady stopped beside her. "Keep following Raven. If you can grab her, do so. Stop her. I'm going to head toward the far wall beneath the vampire cross and see if I can cut her off."

Kailey nodded.

"Don't lose sight of her," he said sternly. "Her life may depend upon us stopping her before she gets to the succubus."

"You think Cassie would kill her in a public place?"

Brady shrugged. "The law would be in Cassie's favor if she did. No one here will be an eyewitness. Hell, Raven could disappear forever and no one except us would be the wiser. Without a body, usually you don't have a murder trial. It's damn near impossible to prove in court."

The words chilled Kailey. Her stomach sickened.

Brady cut through the dancing mob.

Which meant the Founders of Nocturnal Trinity could kill Kailey and Brady as well. No one on the outside of the nightclub would be any wiser.

To Kailey's immediate left was another bar. Directly in the center left was where the DJ and her equipment were set upon a raised stage platform. The stage towered a good six feet above the dance floor. Two massive bouncers stood with their thick muscular arms crossed, watching the crowd.

Suspended in the air were tattooed ladies dancing in barred cages. They wore G-strings and were topless. With their extreme artsy tattoos, however, tops weren't necessary because they didn't appear nude at all. Another cage held a seductively dressed succubus with leathery bat wings. Her skin was an ashen gray. She sat on the floor of her cage with her legs crossed rather inappropriately for what little she wore. Her crimson eyes glowed. She snarled, spat, and thrashed her tail at onlookers whenever anyone stared too long.

To Kailey's right was a lounge with dim lighting. Several female succubae flirted with humans by wrapping their scaly tails around the men's necks while giving lap dances.

The performances seemed too creepy, so Kailey turned away.

She stood on tiptoe at the edge of the dance floor until she located Raven again. Raven continued chasing Cassie.

Kailey shook her head and rushed into the crowd. The pulsating music and blinding lights messed with Kailey's equilibrium. She stumbled forward while hurrying after Raven, but soon found that the moving crowd had swallowed Raven and the succubus, enclosing a human wall around them.

Suffering mild vertigo as it were, the swaying crowd made the sensation even worse. Dancers pressed against her, acting as a barrier of swinging arms that she dodged and pivoted through while trying not to be knocked down or rendered unconscious. The way some of these horrid, wild dancers moved ... what might be considered a swinging arm movement could accidentally knock someone out cold.

"Shit!" Kailey said, feeling the heat of the pressing crowd. "Not this again."

She had never been claustrophobic, but after nearly getting pinned by the hypnotized mob the night before, she found it difficult to breathe or to think straight. She feared that Flora might suddenly appear and turn this crowd against her as she had done with the other one.

Pressing through the crowd, Kailey tried to look over the dancers, still occasionally seeing Raven fighting her way toward Cassie. The crimson glow of the succubus' eyes narrowed. Cassie hissed like a cat at Raven before she dodged farther into the mob.

Every few seconds, Cassie stopped and turned, waiting for Raven to get closer, and then she'd dart forward. Then it dawned upon Kailey.

"Damn."

Cassie was deliberately leading Raven bit by bit, just staying slightly ahead of her, out of reach, and coaxing her to pursue. She was baiting her. And Raven kept foolishly following.

It was a trap.

She wanted to yell a warning to Raven, but she couldn't without drawing direct attention to herself. Of course, with the blaring music, Raven could never hear her. And because she, Brady, and Raven were running across the dance floor, someone in the VIP lounge overhead was probably observing them. But what else could she do? She had to stop Raven before her roommate became the succubus' next victim.

Raven, for whatever reason, had chosen to run after Cassie. Perhaps due to jealousy, loyalty, vengeance? A combination of the three? Hell, Kailey didn't know, but she suspected the answer was somewhere in between.

Soft laughter rolled on the fringes of Kailey's mind. No deeper. Just on the edge, like a gentle laugh whispering in her ear.

Flora!

"Shit!" she said, pushing through the crowd, trying to get Raven, but also keeping an inadvertent watchful eye for the mind leech.

Ducking, shifting sideways, and gently pushing arms out of her way, Kailey worked her way through the dancers. None seemed to impede her progress. So far. Cassie exited the crowd on the far side of the room. Instead of running elsewhere, the succubus waited for Raven.

Raven stepped from the dancers and rushed toward Cassie.

"*No!*" Kailey said. There was no sense not shouting anymore. Flora knew they were there. How? With the blessed stones, their presence shouldn't have been revealed so easily to the powerful vampire. Of course, Cassie had recognized her in the restroom, so it was quite possible the succubus used telepathy or another demonic means to let Flora know that they were inside Nocturnal Trinity. And Cassie had run directly into the vampire section of the nightclub and not into the demon's unit where she probably had better protection amongst her kin.

This was a deliberate setup to pull Kailey into whatever scheme the succubus and the vampires had established. There was a reason why they had wanted Vincent dead and his hidden key, which thankfully she had left in the vehicle with Skye. Keeping the key hidden might be the only way they would get out of Nocturnal Trinity alive.

Brady ran toward the succubus from the far left edge of the dance floor. Cassie turned toward him as he approached. He moved with greater speed than she had ever seen a man run before. He was frighteningly fast, almost a blur.

Raven stood about six feet away from Cassie with her fists raised. She paced slowly toward the succubus with less fear than she should have had. Perhaps the lingering effects of the whiskey had given Raven added braveness. From what Raven had told her outside Nocturnal Trinity, she had been terrified when she had seen the demon at their apartment. Why did she fear it, and not Cassie?

Kailey wondered what the other demon had looked like. What kind was it?

Flora's haughty voice whispered, "Didn't you learn your lesson last night, little one? Why have you come back? Enjoy the show."

Kailey turned and looked all around her, trying to find Flora. The voice wasn't inside her head like before. She had whispered while standing beside her, but she *wasn't* there.

Kailey tapped the membership badge hanging around her neck. "This is why I'm here. You gave me this."

Laughter roared right outside her ears again, trying to mesmerize her, and the sound of the loud music seemed to lower drastically. Flora's laughs brought chills down Kailey's back. She knew the vampire was close by, but why did she continue to keep herself hidden?

Flora had yet to penetrate into Kailey's mind to establish control. An invisible barrier seemed to have thwarted her stabbing mental touch. The enchanted stone was working, or at least hers *seemed* to be.

Cassie's long tail swayed back and forth. The pointy tip reached behind her, pulling open a glass-faced door that reflected all the dancing array of laser lights, which prevented anyone from seeing exactly what lay on the other side. When the door opened, a set of stairs descended into an even darker room. Above the door a small sign stated: Underground Patio.

Kailey didn't want to let the demon retreat down those stairs. She wasn't certain where the lower level led or how many other demons, vampires, or witches might be down there waiting. She needed Cassie to remain on the main floor.

Kailey locked eyes with Cassie and her jaw tightened. Kailey fought to get around the last half dozen or so dancers that stood between them. Even though she realized how close the demon had come to killing her, Kailey pushed people out of her way, determined to reach the succubus before she exited.

Cassie pointed her long finger at Kailey. "I warned you yesterday. Stay away from me!"

Raven advanced toward Cassie.

Kailey made her way around the row of dancers. "Raven. Come here. Get away from her!"

Brady slowed, trying to wrap his arms around Raven, but the demon's long tail whipped forward, stabbing into his left shoulder. He winced and grabbed her tail with both hands. He tried to yank her off balance, but instead, she pulled him straight to her. Brady stood face to face with Cassie. Her gaze into his eyes suddenly relaxed him. The sternness of his face weakened. His shoulders slumped.

Cassie smiled, licked her lips, and a second later, Brady leaned forward, hungrily kissing her. His eyes closed. He was locked in ecstasy. Her hand reached to the obvious bulge in his pants. She vigorously rubbed him. He groaned, still kissing her, lost within her seductive power. His hands went to her breasts, squeezing gently, carefully. His arousal increased, despite the hundred or so people around them, and oblivious that this demon was their enemy, a murderer.

Blood trickled from where she had stabbed his shoulder, but he wasn't in any pain. His hands worked to unlace the front of her corset, letting the fullness of her ample breasts spill partway out.

Her hand rubbed the back of his head while she continued kissing him. Brady pressed his body against her.

Raven stared back at Kailey, her stunned surprise evident. "What the hell?"

"She's spellbound him." Kailey felt sick, seeing how easily Cassie beguiled him by stirring his lusts.

Cassie kept kissing Brady and stroking him. Blood trickled down the sides of his mouth, where her fangs had apparently sliced into his lips during their kiss. Brady didn't flinch from pain, nor did he seem to notice the cuts.

He was held prisoner by her seductive spell, unable to get enough of her, and unless they had a way to break him away from her, Brady would have sex with her right where they stood.

Raven fanned her face. "No shit. I hate to say it, but it's getting heated in here."

"What? This is turning you on?"

Raven shrugged and signed with her index finger and thumb. "A little bit."

"We have to get both of you away from her."

Flora laughed.

Kailey stepped toward Cassie with her fists raised. But the demon's tail swept around, striking Kailey near the back of her knees, knocking her legs out from under her and sending her hard against the floor. She fought to remain conscious as pain shot through her entire body. She hurt too much to even try to raise herself.

Cassie's tail looped around and grabbed Brady around his waist and lifted him off his feet. He desperately reached for her. She smiled, licking blood off her lips and then flung him into the crowd of dancers.

With the loud music, no one heard the outburst and scuffling. No one seemed to be paying attention to the succubus at all. Only when Brady landed slightly dazed, knocking down several people, did any of the dancers deviate from what they were doing. They hadn't witnessed any of the sexual tension Brady and the succubus had performed. Instead of adding to the commotion, they tried to help him up. Once Brady climbed to his feet and shook his head, trying to get his bearings, he headed back toward Kailey and Raven, averting his gaze from the succubus.

He looked embarrassed that he had lost control and given in to his lust.

Kailey winced. The room spun around her. The fall had rattled her. Cassie wasn't even using her demon strength and hit harder than any fighter Kailey had previously sparred against.

Brady stood over her, offered his hand. "Let me help you up."

Kailey took his hand, stood, and leaned against him to keep her balance. She opened and closed her eyes several times, hoping the fuzziness would fade and that she could see clearer. When her focus cleared somewhat, she located Raven.

Raven took a step toward Cassie, raising her hands in what Kailey expected to be the beginnings of a spell. Before Raven or Kailey even noticed, the demon's tail shot forward, wrapped around Raven's throat, and the succubus pulled a startled Raven into her arms.

Long black nails extended on Cassie's fingers. She pressed the razor tip of one fingernail to Raven's throat.

"Back away," Cassie said in a hissing tone, "or I slit her throat right here."

Flora's laughter echoed again.

Kailey swallowed hard. "Let ... her ... go."

"Girl," Flora said, "do you really think you have any bargaining chips here?"

Show yourself, bitch.

"And what?" Flora whispered. "Are you challenging me?"

For Raven, I will kill you.

Laughter. Endless laughter. "I'm already dead. Undead."

Then I will turn you to ashes and scatter you into the wind.

"You have bark. Let's see how well you bite."

Kailey gnashed her teeth and pulled free of Brady's support, but he remained beside her, ready to catch her if necessary.

Cassie backed toward the door, pulling Raven with her. Raven's eyes widened with fear. Tears spilled from her eyes. She held fast to Cassie's arms, but she didn't fight. The razor tip of the fingernail pressed against the side of Raven's throat, indenting her pale skin. A thin crimson ribbon trickled down the side of her neck.

"You're hurting her. Please, let her go," Kailey said.

Cassie shook her head.

Brady stepped toward Cassie. The succubus hissed, crinkled her nose, and showed her fangs. She pointed a finger. "Uh, uh, uh."

"Give me what I want," Flora said.

What exactly do you want?

"The key. You bring that to me within the next twenty-four hours, and your friend is free to leave. If you do not, she is as good as … well, let's just say … undead."

Kailey felt her stomach tighten and twist with pain.

How do I know that you're not lying to me?

Flora laughed again. "You don't."

Kailey began to wonder if living for centuries caused a person to go insane, or was Flora already there *before* she was turned?

Why do you want the key?

"Because your brother had stolen property that belongs to us."

My brother was not a thief.

"Then you didn't know him as well as you thought."

If he stole something, he must have had a good reason.

"The business was between us and he. You don't have a role in this battle, unless you don't bring me the key. Look at your frightened little friend. Wouldn't it be so terrible if something *horrible* happened to your girlfriend? Believe me, there are far worse things in this world than death."

Kailey tried to swallow the lump in her throat, but she couldn't. Her mouth was dry. Her twisting stomach brought a sour taste to the back of her mouth. Flora's presence faded. Kailey's attention turned toward Raven and the succubus.

Cassie pulled the door open with the tip of her tail, holding Raven tightly, and backed through the threshold.

"Help me," Raven said softly, desperately. Tears brimmed at the edges of her eyes and spilled down her cheeks.

Brady took a step forward, but Kailey grabbed the bend of his right arm and tugged. She shook her head.

"What?" he asked, looking into Kailey's eyes. "We can overpower her and get Raven."

"No. We can't go after her."

"Why not?"

"Kailey!" Raven pleaded. "Help me."

Kailey wiped tears from her eyes. She looked from Raven to Brady. "Flora spoke to me. She wants the key or she's going to turn Raven into a vampire or do something possibly worse."

"What? A vampire?"

"Yes."

"No, she won't. Not if we get her back."

"We can't. Trust me. Flora is intent on carrying out this threat. She's watching us. Hell, probably all of them are watching us by now."

"So?" he said, his hands balling into tight fists.

"Like you said earlier, we are outnumbered. Even if we could grab Raven, there's no telling how many more will come after us and corner us. Then we have no guarantee that any of us will get out of here alive."

Brady weighed the information and nodded. "You're right."

"I have to give her the key, and only then will she let Raven go."

"What key? The one you showed Micah?"

She nodded.

"How does she even know you have it?" he asked.

"Assumption mainly, but most likely Flora now knows for certain by either reading my thoughts or listening to what we're saying. But now, I'm certain she knows."

He frowned. "She really has that kind of power?"

Flora's taunting laughter whispered around Kailey.

"Yes. Trust me. She does."

Brady went to the glass door, grabbed the handle, and pulled it open. "I'm not exactly certain that she can stop us that quickly."

Raven shrieked, just beyond the descending stairs. Only their shadows were visible. Raven's breaths were little gasps, like she was being choked.

"Brady, please," Kailey said softly. "We won't be allowed to take Raven out of here."

"But I can get her. I see them."

Had he already forgotten how Cassie had thrown him fifteen feet across the room with such little effort? Or was it his bruised male ego that made him seek to get revenge for being bested?

"You'd never reach Raven before the demon kills her. Cassie will slit her throat with her fingernail. Raven is already bleeding."

"I know. That's why—"

"Brady, no!"

Kailey stepped beside him at the open door. She was ready to fight him if necessary. He was blind to their immediate danger.

Cassie's red eyes blazed in the shadows as she sneered from the dim hall at the foot of the stairs. Smoke billowed around Cassie and Raven. Within that misty swirling smoke, little evil faces encircled them. An instant later, she and Raven vanished.

Brady let the door close. "Damn."

He turned and looked down at Kailey.

She placed her hands on his right forearm and let them slide down until she held his hand in both of hers. "I don't want to leave Raven in Nocturnal Trinity. I don't. You know that and it pains me more than I can say. But we need to get out of here. We might not have a lot of time left."

"Where's the key?" Brady asked.

"In a safe place," she replied, fighting not to visualize in her mind where the key was since Flora could read her thoughts and probably was at that moment.

Kailey faced Brady. Sticky blood coated his lips. She reached up and wiped the blood away with her thumb and then showed him.

"What the hell? That's mine?" His left hand instinctively reached up and rubbed his lips. He winced, suddenly realizing the cuts and feeling the pain.

She nodded.

"Is that from ... kissing her?" He took a handkerchief from his pocket and wiped the blood off her thumb and then his lips.

She smiled. "Yeah. You got a bit carried away."

Brady's face reddened. His eyes looked foggy, like someone who had drank too much or had been drugged. He looked away, shaking his head, and tucking the handkerchief into his back pocket. "I ... I can't believe she enticed me so easily."

"Few could resist such beauty and power."

"I'd think I should be able to."

"Because you're a werewolf?" she grinned.

He nodded. "Actually, yes."

"Don't forget the full moon. You're hormones are out of whack." She smiled. For some reason, she had always wanted to say that to a man. Women heard it too much.

Kailey noticed his frustration and that he seemed to be mentally beating himself down for giving into temptation. But the lure of the succubus made her demon features more attractive than frightening, capitalizing upon her uniqueness as something to be coveted and not disdained. Add that to Cassie's well-endowed, perfect *Penthouse* body proportions and even the most dedicated religious fanatics cast away their inhibitions, allowing them to be enslaved to lust and sexual gratification.

She smiled at him. "Brady, few people could push her away, male or female."

Brady frowned and shook his head. "But there was more than just her appearance. Something more pulled me to her."

"Mental hypnosis?"

He shook his head. "No. Nothing like that. It was more like a sweet scent. Like smelling your favorite dessert or candy you've not had in a long time when you're on a diet. Your mouth waters, you lose your mental discipline, and suddenly find that you've gorged yourself in spite of the calories. You can't stop eating. That's a stupid comparison, I suppose."

Kailey held back her laughter. She didn't want to make him feel worse. But it wasn't a bad comparison at all. Because for men, the two best ways for a woman to keep a man around seemed to be great food and unforgettable sexual pleasure. It wasn't necessarily a huge secret, but something that most men seemed unable to notice. By successfully providing one or both, women often kept their men from wandering. Not always, but the odds were in their favor if they satisfied a man with either.

"Not at all. Scents are part of what our senses pick up and trigger, reminding of us comforting memories."

Brady acted like he didn't hear her. His mind seemed to be racing, trying to find rationality. "Pheromones perhaps?"

"Perhaps. Or some type of spell power."

Still holding his hand, Kailey stepped closer and rose on her tiptoes. With her free hand, she pulled aside the bloody tear of his jacket. "How's your shoulder?"

His eyebrows rose. "My shoulder?"

Standing on tiptoes, she examined the place where the pointy tip of Cassie's tail had stabbed him. It had stopped bleeding and didn't appear to be deep. Probably only a warning when Cassie tapped him.

Kailey patted his arm. "You'll live."

Brady smiled.

Kailey lost her balance on the tip of the odd boots and fell against Brady. To most, the act probably looked deliberate, but the cumbersome boots were to blame. Her face pressed to the center of his chest, and his arms immediately wrapped around her, keeping her from falling.

Cradled in his arms, feeling the warmth of his body against hers, and smelling the fragrance of his cologne and sweat, she wished they were anywhere else except inside Nocturnal Trinity. She deeply inhaled his fragrance, feeling a wash of desire seep through her body and into areas she didn't expect to have aroused during a time she should be thinking of other things. Her nipples hardened. Her heart raced. She struggled and fought the urge to wrap her arms around his waist because, for so many reasons, it wasn't appropriate. She wanted to playfully nip at his chest and ...

Dammit! What the hell was happening?

Raven.

Think about Raven!

Kailey placed her hands against his muscled chest and pushed herself back, but his arms remained around her. His hands rubbed her lower back. She looked into his eyes, and everything Raven had said about him being attracted to Kailey was true. There was no denying the hunger in his gaze, the gentle curl of his smile, and his strong, firm arousal that pressed against her.

"Let me go, Brady," she whispered.

He did so without hesitation or argument.

Flustered, she pulled away and placed her hand against the wall, steadying herself. A wave of emotions rushed through her. Her heartbeat escalated and breathing became more difficult. Heat radiated from her flushed face, so she fanned her face with her hands, attempting to cool down. She became lightheaded and closed her eyes, trying to focus on staying conscious. What the hell was happening?

Wait.

Her mind raced.

The succubus. Pheromones. That had to be it. Both she and Brady were under the lingering effects of her seduction. Perhaps her enticing scent was still on Brady.

"Are you okay?" he asked.

Kailey nodded. "I'll be fine."

"You're not mad?"

She faced him with a smile. "God, no. Why would I be mad?"

Brady shrugged. "You just look ... uncomfortable."

"I think we were under the succubus' influence that she had over you earlier."

"Are you sure that was all it was?" he asked, winking. "Because I don't—"

She blushed, biting her lower lip to prevent herself from smiling, but a sly smile found its way to her lips anyway.

Flora's voice came in a whisper, "You have three minutes to get out of Nocturnal Trinity. Only three. Do not return without the key."

Kailey gasped and reached for Brady's muscled hand. His calloused palm and fingers joined with her delicate hand. Their fingers interlocked. She squeezed and pulled him to follow her. "We have to go. Now. Flora said that we only have three minutes."

He frowned. "You heard that, too?"

She looked surprised. "Yes. You?"

Nodding, he replied, "Yes. This time I did."

"Well, now I don't feel so special," Kailey said.

"I guess we've worn out our welcome. What happens if we refused to leave?" he asked.

"I don't want stick around to find out. Whatever it is, it *won't* be pleasant."

CHAPTER 30

Kailey and Brady walked with brisk steps around the perimeter of the vampire dance floor. She found wearing Luna's boots even more awkward when she was walking at a rapid pace. At least the dancers had not turned into the mindless zombies under Flora's malicious control like the previous night.

Brady interlocked his fingers with hers but the awkward attraction that had burned between them at the entrance of the Underground Patio was gone. She liked the warmth of his touch, and the added security that if someone rushed toward them, it was less likely they'd be immediately separated.

Kailey wanted to head back to the Underground Patio to find and rescue Raven. She really did. She liked holding Brady's hand, but at the same time, she felt guilty knowing how furious and jealous Raven would become, if Raven saw them. In a sense she believed she was betraying Raven in two ways. One, she had no choice but to abandon Raven. The second reason was that she was holding hands with the man Raven had already accused Kailey of having a crush on. Although she could argue that their handholding was, in a way, strictly innocent, Raven would never believe Kailey if she saw them walking hand in hand. And minute-by-minute Kailey was finding it even more difficult to convince herself that she viewed Brady as only a friend and nothing more. Deep inside she knew differently. She knew she wanted to learn more about him.

She found herself torn in what she really wanted in a relationship, but this wasn't the time for her to sort through her desires.

Recalling Raven's terrified expression broke Kailey's heart. She'd never seen Raven so vulnerable, so tiny and helpless. To defy Flora's command and try to find Raven was not an option. At least, not at this moment. Besides, Cassie had not simply dragged Raven away. She had disappeared with her. Kailey didn't have any idea where the succubus might have taken her or even where to start looking. The main floor of Nocturnal Trinity consisted of three dance floors with separate DJ booths, lounges, bars, and kitchens. She had only seen two of the sections, but what more was on the lower level? For all she knew, the lower level could be a labyrinth where the stronger, darker creatures resided.

After all, Kailey was new to discover the existence of vampires, were-wolves, demons, and powerful witches. What else might be caged below? Zombies, ghouls, what?

Fear pricked at her mind because she barely knew what to do to destroy vampires. She knew what most considered common lore, but was that based upon actual fact? Perhaps the stories and legends in fiction were developed from real accounts. She almost hated that she had partway mocked Luna and Blaze for their devotion to Micah because now she knew she'd have to become a dedicated disciple as well. It wasn't the first time that she had been forced to eat her own words. Besides, knowledge was survival.

What else was on the upper floor between the VIP areas? Flora had led her through a dark corridor from the main entrance. No, that wasn't exactly the case because Flora had taken control of Kailey's mind. The vampire might have taken her through various corridors while Kailey was under Flora's control. If so, there was no way to know what else was on the upper floor.

The vampire coffins were inside the VIP room, which meant that they would not make it easy for people to find that room. An invitation into that room was a privilege that few ever received. She couldn't recall where she had exited, no matter how much she concentrated. Had Flora wiped that from her mind, too?

Probably.

When Flora had chosen Kailey outside Nocturnal Trinity, the vampire hadn't picked her as a potential recruit. She had chosen her because she was Vincent's sister. Flora only wanted the mysterious key that Kailey possessed. So much so that the vampire had taken Raven hostage until she received what she wanted. Blackmail, ransom, either or both fit the situation. How Flora had known Kailey could get the key was something Kailey didn't understand. Perhaps because Cassie had failed finding it at Vincent's house or office, Flora might have thought that Vincent had mailed it to her?

What had Vincent taken that was so essential to Flora and the Circle of Unity? Apparently it was valuable enough to kill him over.

Thinking back to her brother's burial, Cassie had thrown herself at Frank, but that might have only been to seduce him to find out if Vincent had given him the key, which he hadn't. They desperately wanted that key. Why? What *had* he stolen? Her curiosity as to what it opened burned inside her mind.

The irony was that he had hidden it right under their noses. Of course, none of them expected him to do so, which made them look everywhere except the most obvious place. Cassie had been close to finding it.

But Flora knew Kailey had the key. Her insistence for the key meant she knew Kailey had it. Although Kailey hadn't fully disclosed she'd found it, she had inadvertently affirmed she did when Flora offered an exchange of Raven for the key. With Flora lingering near Kailey's mind, Kailey forced herself to think of anything except the key and where she had stashed it. That was for her benefit and for Skye's safety since she had left it in the car.

She had expected Cassie wanted the key, so she didn't bring it or her purse inside. She didn't like the fact that Flora had gone through her personal items the last time, and she refused to allow that to happen again. But Cassie wasn't the only one interested in the key. Flora seemed even more determined to possess it.

When Flora had used her mind control the previous night, Kailey held no doubt that the vampire must have read into her thoughts and discovered whom Kailey held the dearest.

Raven.

No one else. At least not at that particular moment.

And in spite of their obvious differences and near split as girlfriends, Kailey couldn't abandon Raven. Raven was her friend. She couldn't allow Flora to hurt her. Flora banked on that, knowing Kailey would either give the key willingly or die trying to rescue Raven. However, without having the key on her person, it was less likely Flora would kill her.

That didn't guarantee Flora would *not* inflict unrelenting pain or a debilitating curse upon her. The vampire flaunted that she liked to torture;

whether physically or mentally, it apparently didn't matter. Thinking about that troubled Kailey even more. Flora had openly stated that she'd subject Raven to things *worse than death.*

Severe merciless pain was often enough to make people do anything to escape the torture. There's only so much the mind withstood before the bargaining began. Death was often much more favorable than constant suffering.

Brady's hand tightened around hers. "Stay alert."

She nodded and swallowed hard. "You're expecting something to happen, too?"

"Yep."

The dancers continued swaying and moving to the music. None seemed controlled by anything other than their reckless dance moves. But Kailey knew Flora wouldn't let her and Brady leave without exhibiting some sort of lesson. Since Flora wanted the key, Kailey expected the vampire to exact her power, showing them that she was always in charge.

Kailey suddenly thought about the huge bouncer at the door. Titus was at least twice the size of Brady, possibly more so in bodyweight. Although he had an intimidating stare and a menacing attitude when he had checked her membership badge at the door, he mellowed and seemed to have an endearing personality, which possibly could be nothing less than a teddy bear most women liked to cuddle. She figured he used his size and muscle to make people second guess his true nature, which possibly made most patrons who thought themselves to be bad-asses to rethink their behavior. Although Kailey pictured him as a gentle giant ... under Flora's mind control, the vampire could use him as a human tank against Kailey and Brady.

As far as Kailey knew, there was only one visible way in and out of Nocturnal Trinity. For security reasons it might be a good thing. In the case of a fire? Not a good decision at all. Hundreds of people might die trying to get out.

Scanning the walls, she didn't see any fire exit signs, which directly violated the fire codes. She didn't have to guess how they got past those laws.

These mind parasites were able to get whatever they needed or wanted without any opposition from city officials at all. However, she believed there had to be other exits, maybe hidden or disguised, but other doors had to lead outside.

Hidden panels?

Trap doors behind the bars and DJ stands?

Perhaps.

Richard approached Brady near the narrow hallway that led out of the vampire dance floor into the neighboring demon hall. He stepped in front of Brady with a leering smile as he looked at Kailey holding Brady's hand. "That was quick."

"What?" Brady asked.

Richard looked at his wristwatch. "We haven't been here long at all, and you've already found yourself a pleasant night companion." He peered around and stared at Kailey's ass, shaking his head and letting a whistle escape his lips. "Damn. Nice. You're a better charmer than I thought."

Brady shook his head. "It's not like that at all."

"Oh?" Richard's eyes darkened and narrowed, making his pale face brighter in the dim corridor. No white remained in his eyes. Evil possessed him. His glance made chills go down her back. He licked his lips, still staring at Kailey. "Guess even cops have to *pay* for ... some services now."

"Hey!" Kailey took a step forward. Brady gently pulled her behind him, stepping between her and Richard.

"Easy," Richard said. "We're both cops. You're not going to be arrested, dear. Take care of his needs, and then mine—"

"What's gotten into you, Richard? That was really uncalled for," Brady said, shoving his free hand against Richard's chest. His voice deepened and his other hand tightened around Kailey's. "Apologize to her."

"You'd defend her?"

"You bet I will."

"Really?" Richard said with an odd smile.

"Bank on it." Brady's voice deepened, even more, like a growl. His eyes narrowed, strangely *like* a wolf's.

Richard didn't react with any intimidation. He stood his ground, almost expecting a fight, maybe even wanting a fight.

Kailey pulled Brady's hand. "Let's go. We don't have time for this."

Brady stared at Richard a moment longer. "Looks like you've gotten yourself drunk a lot quicker than normal."

Brady turned to leave with Kailey. Richard grabbed Brady's arm. Before Brady reacted, Kailey planted the tip of her boot into Richard's groin with a harsh swift kick. Richard toppled backwards, fell clutching himself, and groaned in pain.

Nothing was more embarrassing for a man to be taken down by a woman while others watched.

Flora laughed.

Dammit! I should've known. You're enjoying this, aren't you? Kailey seethed.

"Immensely," she replied.

Shit.

Like a whisper of wind fluttering from a soft falling feather, Flora's voice spoke right outside Kailey's ear. "Just getting started."

"Run!" Kailey said. "This is Flora's doing. She's apparently controlling your friend.

"Trust me. That *isn't* his normal behavior."

Brady tore into a sprint down the corridor. Kailey ran twice as hard to try to keep up with him.

"I sorta guessed," she replied, catching up to him. "But with everything else going on, I don't have the confidence to assume anything isn't what it is, until the facts present themselves."

"So she told you?"

Kailey nodded. "Yes, with the loudest whisper I've ever heard."

Entering the demon dance sector of Nocturnal Trinity, Kailey noticed Jinn talking to two young girls. Each of the girls kept her eyes focused upon his. One touched and rubbed his muscular forearm while he bore a wide grin. They were mesmerized by him.

Still gushing the charm factor, are we?

As she and Brady rushed past, Jinn made eye contact with her. His eyes widened with instant surprise. His stunned expression caused Kailey to flash her cutest dimpled smile. Apparently, he hadn't expected her to return, even with the membership card. Of course a few hours earlier, she had never imagined she'd have ever returned either. Boston was a much better alternative, but she had no choice but to stay in Seattle until this was all settled.

Kailey glanced over her shoulder. No one pursued. Not Richard. Not the dancers. No one. Jinn looked concerned, but instead of heading toward her, he returned his attention to the two young ladies fawning over him.

Good demon. Incubus to the core.

Kailey grabbed Brady's arm, slowing him.

"What is it?" he asked.

"If Flora's planning to attack us, I don't think it will be in here."

"Outside?"

Kailey returned to a normal walk. She shrugged. "Maybe, or the bouncer. You remember Titus, the mountain of a man?"

Brady nodded, but he didn't seem concerned. Of course, she'd never actually seen a werewolf fight so ...

Jinn's surprise in seeing her indicated that he didn't know anything about Cassie taking Raven as her hostage. His lack of knowledge and concern about the situation was something she found extremely interesting. What did Flora stand to gain over the others in their Circle of Unity by obtaining whatever the key held secret?

If Kailey uncovered that, she might discover enough leverage to turn the demons and witches into her allies, instead of having them as her enemies. Then again, they might kill her to get whatever Vincent had taken. She wouldn't know until she found it.

Flora had been the one to mention the growing rift within the three alliances. But why would she reveal such a weakness to a total stranger? For Flora to build a false friendship with Kailey gave the vampires no added benefits. If anything, it proved that Kailey could capitalize upon the fissure and widen the gap within the unity.

Flora was smarter than that. She had to have some other ulterior motive because she'd never have survived two hundred plus years otherwise. So what was it?

Kailey and Brady neared the entrance. A long line of members pressed their way past the bouncer as he hurriedly checked each badge. She and Brady stood patiently waiting for a pause in the linear traffic, so they could exit. Nervously, she inserted her hand into his. Brady smiled.

When they finally approached the door, the large man eyed them suspiciously.

Kailey's stomach tightened, and she took a deep breath, expecting to have to defend herself.

"Quite a short visit, young lady," Titus said. "You not find the place to your liking?"

Kailey forced a smile. "It's okay."

He glanced beyond her and Brady. "And your friend? Where is she?"

"She decided to stick around a bit longer," Kailey said, sighing.

He laughed heartily. "As pretty as she is, she'll have no problem getting hooked up with someone." He glanced at Brady. "Looks like you're not leaving alone, though. Something good came from being here."

Kailey playfully placed her other hand over Brady's and smiled. "Definitely."

She squeezed around the bouncer and Brady edged along with her. Her heart hammered in her chest. She feared Flora would take control of him at any second, but he wasn't the one she needed to worry about. As she increased her speed down the steps and toward the street, her badge swayed back and forth on her lanyard.

Young men and women standing in the line of hopefuls pleaded for her to choose them. She ignored them. She didn't have time to debate with any of them, nor did she intend to reenter Nocturnal Trinity until she talked to Micah and Skye about the key. Until they decided the safest way to rescue Raven, they didn't have any other options.

The most foolish thing she could do was get the key out of her purse and march back in to get Raven. There wasn't any guarantee that Flora or Cassie would even let Raven go. Hell, she had no assurance that she and Raven would be allowed to live.

Two extremely pale young women in black skirts and corsets whistled and waved at Kailey, trying to get her to stop, to talk, but Kailey stared at the asphalt, sloshing through the thin layer of rain water that flowed over the roadway in sheets, building into a stronger current alongside the side-walk's edge.

"What would it take for these people to realize how much danger they'd placed themselves into if they did go inside?" Kailey whispered.

"Some people only learn by their mistakes. And some never do even after failing miserably time after time."

"Life can't be that boring, can it?"

Brady shrugged. "I can't see how. Seems being around you is turning into one big adventure after the other though."

She cocked a brow and gave him a harsh side-glance. "Gee, thanks."

He grinned, squeezed her hand, and pulled her close to his side.

Midway across the street, Kailey kept her eyes focused on her rental car. Skye sat behind the wheel. When she looked in their direction, Kailey gently pulled her hand free of Brady's. The last thing she needed was to have to explain holding Brady's hand and Raven's absence. Of course, there wasn't any way to avoid the questions about Raven's whereabouts.

Several screams came from the line behind them. Kailey turned to see the two Psi-vamps leap off the roof, landing on the edge of the sidewalk and missing the line of people by inches.

They rushed toward her and Brady with such speed that she didn't have time to start running. One lunged forward with both clawed hands aimed for her throat. She ducked. His hands clumsily came together swooshing through the air and missing their intended mark.

Since he was over a foot taller than Kailey, she lunged forward, ramming into his abdomen with her shoulder, and pushed him upward, sending the vampire into a somersault. To be so tall, he was remarkably light. He flipped over her and his back thudded hard on the pavement. She turned to prepare for his counterattack. Looking at his shriveled face, she noticed the blistered scars where Blaze had flung the holy water across the vampire's face. The water had left a nasty scar.

The vampire gnashed his teeth, showing his fangs, and hissed. He turned over and onto his side to push up, but before he could stand, Brady slammed the other vampire on top of it. Before either managed to move, Brady reached inside his leather jacket and pulled out a wooden stake.

Kailey's eyes widened. "How'd—?"

Brady pressed a knee into his attacker's stomach. A second later, he drove the stake through the vampire's chest. Ribs crackled. A harsh shriek echoed momentarily as the beast helplessly gripped at the stake with both hands, trying to yank it out. Brady held the end of the stake and pushed his weight down onto it, preventing the vampire from removing it.

The vampire's eyes widened in horror as death paralyzed it. His skin shriveled—dry and leathery—and quickly decayed into a fine dusty powder that crumbled away from its skeleton, revealing bright white bones.

The soft falling rain tapped consistently against the brittle bones, dissolving them into another layer of dust. The sheets of rain that washed across the pavement carried the powdery residue away.

Some of the people in the line stood stunned, horrified, but continued watching instead of fleeing.

The bouncer shouted, "Hey!" His eyes widened as he pointed and frowned at where the vampire's body had dissolved. The giant's voice rose in a near falsetto. "What the hell, man?"

Did he not *know* that he worked for vampires?

Brady prepared for the second vampire's attack. Without time to retrieve the stake, he stood in a defensive pose. Kailey set her feet at the proper width to maintain the best balance and huddled her stance forward should the vampire rush at her again.

The Psi-vamp rose to his feet, glancing back and forth between Brady and Kailey, not knowing whom to attack first. He waited longer than she expected. Perhaps his hesitation resided in the fact that most people had enough sense to run away from vampires, not *at* them. He didn't seem to know how to deal with people who took an offensive stance.

His gaze turned to the dust particles of his partner floating away with the water.

Kailey glanced to Brady, and he shrugged.

The vampire hissed, revealing his large fangs. He rushed straight at Kailey, perhaps thinking she was the weaker of the two. A couple of girls in the line screamed. Others cheered like all of this was part of some type of outside performance. Several shouted in favor of the vampire. Kailey rolled her eyes and shook her head.

She caught the vampire's right wrist, twisted, and swung him over her shoulder. He crashed hard on the pavement, his eyes wide with surprise. He was up in a second with some of the bystanders cheering. He held his wrist. His face crumpled from pain. Angered, he charged again.

Kailey grabbed the vampire's wrist again, clutched his elbow, and sharply bent his arm backwards. Bones snapped. The vampire winced, snarled, but he was unable to attack. To prevent having his arm ripped off, he flipped in the direction that Kailey twisted and shoved, tossing him upward and then he crashed onto his back.

Strange gutturally sounds rumbled in his throat. Intense pain and anger showed on his contorted face. His eyes instantly filled black, and he flashed fangs. Even with his right arm totally useless, he pushed himself to his feet. Apparently he didn't understand when to give up and admit defeat.

Kailey spun a swift roundhouse kick, catching him in the abdomen. The impact pushed inward and then upward into his ribs. An audible cracking sound made some of the crowd grimace and groan.

The vampire grabbed his ribcage with his good hand, whirled around from the momentum, and dropped face first onto the wet pavement.

Titus stood at the edge of the sidewalk, still stunned by what was going on. He genuinely seemed startled about what these Psi-vamps were in spite of his huge size.

She hurled the vampire's broken body into the line of people. "Is this what you're here for? Do you want to be a creature like this?"

Most screamed and scattered. Others helped the vampire to his feet, begging him to feed, to turn them. Although injured, he obliged, yanking the closest hopeful and tearing into her neck. Instead of the act being plea-surable, as the victim must have expected, she screamed in intense agony, struggling to pull away. Blood spilled from the deep gash, and she strug-gled to pull free. The vampire showed no mercy as he ripped and tore into her shredded neck, drinking her blood. The other wannabes screamed and ran.

"Kailey!" Brady yelled. "Let's get the hell out of here!"

She turned toward him, nodded, and sprinted toward the car where Skye sat. She glanced over her shoulder. Titus was running toward the vampire. She guessed he was attempting to save the young woman, but with the amount of blood pouring from the gaping hole, an ambulance could never arrive in time to save her. The best Titus could hope for was to stop the vampire from attacking anyone else.

Kailey opened the rear door of the car and got inside, slamming the door shut. Brady stepped to the side of the driver's door.

He opened the door and said, "Slide across. Let me drive."

"Where's Raven?" Skye asked, scooting across to the other side.

"They have her. Let's get out of here, Brady," Kailey said.

"Not without her," Skye replied.

"I'm afraid we don't have any choice," Brady said, starting the car.

Tears filled Skye's eyes as she faced Kailey. "No. We *don't* leave her here. You made her a promise. We all did."

"We don't know where they took her," Kailey said with sorrow filling her voice. "And if we try to find her, Flora said that she will turn her into a vampire."

Skye shook with anger.

Brady turned the car in the street to head the opposite direction and take them back to where Micah and the others were waiting. Skye grabbed at the steering wheel. He placed a gentle hand upon hers. "We're coming back for her. We will need help though. It will take more than the three of us to find Raven."

"That girl is like a daughter to me. If anything happens to her—" The mixture of sorrow, anger, and betrayal formed in her eyes and facial features.

Kailey was too ashamed to hold Skye's gaze, so instead she looked away, and glanced through the back glass of the car. Titus desperately pulled at the vampire, trying to pry the young lady free from the vampire's hungered mouth. As huge and muscular as he was, he was unable to free the woman. Flora stepped through the door and walked down the steps toward the frightened people that had stepped out of the line and were huddled in small circles around where the vicious vampire tore at the dying girl.

"Shit!" Kailey said.

"What?" Brady asked, glancing into the rearview mirror.

"Flora's outside. Drive faster," she replied, watching the street behind her.

The onlookers that were crying and filled with fear suddenly became relaxed. Flora raised her hands toward them and was apparently talking to them. One by one, they headed toward her, unafraid, and then marched past her toward the door. Once she had them under her control, her face revealed her fury. She headed to the street, grabbed the wooden stake, and stiffened as she watched Kailey through the back glass of the car. If you could hear anger, Kailey would have become deaf.

Flora stormed across the pavement to where Titus was trying to restrain the Psi-vamp. She shoved Titus aside without much effort and drove the stake through the vampire's heart, making him dissolve into ash. None of those that had stood in line noticed, and after a direct gaze into Titus' eyes, he fell under her control. He leaned down, picked up the dead woman, and turned to follow the others inside Nocturnal Trinity.

"Oh, God," Kailey whispered.

"What?"

"She's bringing them all inside. Why would she do that?"

Brady sighed and sped up. "Damage control."

"What?"

"The last thing she'll want is for anyone who witnessed the vampire killing that woman to report the incident to the newspapers or the local television news."

"What will she do?" Kailey asked.

"Wipe their minds. Make them forget. Some of them will probably disappear entirely. She won't risk having any witnesses escape."

"Damn," Kailey whispered.

Skye faced Kailey. "How did Flora get Raven? Those stones were blessed to keep you unnoticed."

"Flora wasn't the one who took her," Kailey replied. "Cassie did."

"The succubus?"

Kailey nodded. Skye turned away.

Skye wrung her aged hands together, mumbling words in a low whisper, and rocked back and forth in her seat. Her eyes closed and her tears shimmered even under the faint wash of the streetlights as they rode beneath them.

Seeing Flora come outside Nocturnal Trinity troubled Kailey. Fear crept inside her. She expected at any moment for Flora to reach forward with her mind and seize control of Kailey, but she didn't. Perhaps keeping control of the crowd prevented the vampire from reaching her, or maybe the stone still offered its protection. All she felt coming from Flora was immense anger and searing hatred. There was no mocking laughter, nor any verbal threat. The absence of those indicated Flora no longer wished to play her taunting games. The worst of what Flora truly was had come to the surface and nothing was going to suppress her monster.

Kailey now feared what Flora would do to Raven.

CHAPTER 31

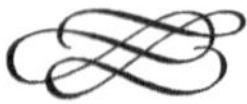

Skye wiped away tears and turned to face Kailey. "Why did the succubus take Raven?"

"Raven and I were in the restroom and Cassie stepped inside. When she recognized me, she fled. Raven ran after her. I tried to stop her, but she—"

"We both tried to stop her," Brady said.

"But *why* would she take her? What reason?"

"I'm certain Flora instructed Cassie to do it."

"But why?" Skye's eyes narrowed. She expected a direct answer to the question and wasn't going to stop pressing until she got it.

"Because Flora wants something that I have."

"What?" Skye asked.

"A key that unlocks a box."

Skye frowned. "What box?"

Kailey shrugged. "I really don't know. I've been trying to figure it out."

"Where's the key?"

"I have it hidden in my purse."

"You *have* it with you?" Skye's voice was a harsh gasp.

Kailey nodded.

"Then give it here. We go back and get Raven."

"I considered that as Brady and I were making our way outside. We have no guarantee that Flora will release Raven or not turn her, especially now, after what happened outside the nightclub."

"We must try."

Brady shook his head. "No. Kailey's right. We need to find out what the key unlocks. We don't know what's in the box. Blindly handing them the key might give them something that makes them even more powerful than they already are."

"So they know where the box is?" Skye asked.

"Apparently so," Kailey replied. "Late last night I went by my brother's house and the vampires' limo was parked there. So they are working with Cassie to find the key. They desperately want whatever it unlocks. According to Flora, my brother stole something from the Circle of Unity, and that's what they want back. They apparently killed him for it."

Brady frowned, staring into the rearview mirror. "Really? She told you that?"

"Yes," Kailey replied.

"Then we cannot give it to them."

"Why not?" Skye asked.

"There's a strong chance that whatever it is will make them even more powerful," Brady replied. "This is something we need to discuss with Micah."

Kailey leaned forward and looked at Skye. "I believe they took Raven because she's important to me."

"Even more so to me, dear," Skye said, trying to gain control of her emotions. "I don't think they understand the battle they've started by taking her. I knew going inside Nocturnal Trinity was a bad idea in the first place. No amount of warning or persuasion will deter young stubborn minds."

"They're holding her because she assumes I will give her the key."

Skye peered into Kailey's eyes. "You do intend to give her the key in exchange for Raven, right?"

"We'll get Raven back, Skye," Brady said.

"You cannot guarantee that," she replied softly.

"Perhaps not, but the pack has come together and are awaiting us at Micah's estate."

"With all the disunity in your pack," Skye said, "I hold little faith they will be of much help."

"How can we get to Micah's estate at this hour? The ferries don't transport at this hour, do they? I thought the last one—" Kailey said.

"We have a few boats on this side of the bay at a marina. Jacob is waiting for us."

Skye shook her head. "I don't wish to cross the water. Is there any way that I can stay at the shop tonight? I need to be alone for the night on this side of the water barrier."

Brady shrugged. "I don't think Micah will mind if you stay there."

"Thanks. I need a place to meditate and clear my thoughts, maybe work on a few spells. I will even try to connect with Raven's spirit to make certain that she's okay."

"I can have you there in a few minutes."

"I appreciate it." Skye forced a slight smile. The light from a streetlamp washed over her saddened face, making her looked feeble and much older than earlier.

Brady drove through the quiet streets, his mind suddenly swallowed in thought. Skye stared out the side window, watching the buildings and the occasional pedestrian. Kailey welcomed the silence but much preferred talking. The silence was when worry took its opportunity to pry inside her mind and make her picture so many bad outcomes for Raven. And not knowing the true intentions for Raven's capture, many scenarios played out in her mind.

None of these were good.

Seeing the hurt in Skye's eyes, Kailey didn't want to be near her. Skye was a great woman, and seemed much like a grandmotherly type, but the present underlying tension between them, not quite blame, but awfully close, made Kailey even more uncomfortable. She understood why Skye wished to be alone. Just being near Kailey could probably stir up more negativity and grief, which affected Skye's concentration, rendering her magic less effective.

Raven meditated a lot, and Kailey understood why. Other religions did so, too. Even in Kailey's martial arts training, meditation was what they did before they warmed up in order to cleanse the mind, the soul, and shut out any negative thoughts. That made a person fresh and free to concentrate on the task at hand. Kailey often did the same a half-hour before an exam. She found a quiet spot, closed her eyes, and focused on that class and test. She didn't worry about the next class or the assignment due next week, the rent, or what she needed to eat for lunch. She honed in specifically to the test and what questions might be asked. Everything else was unnecessary information at that particular time.

Learning to focus in such a way prevented the ever-thoughtful mind from assailing her with distractions. And right now, she was such a distraction to Skye, a bad reminder for why Raven had not come out of Nocturnal

Trinity with her and Brady. She needed to put some distance between her and Skye, so Skye could regain control of her concentration.

Brady turned onto the narrow alleyway. The headlights cut through the thick sheet of blackness, sending scooting shadows fleeing and vanishing. Skye sobbed and sniffled. Her body quivered.

Filled with remorse, Kailey placed a hand on Skye's shoulder. "I'm so sorry."

Skye's withered hand covered Kailey's and squeezed softly.

Brady parked the car, got out, and headed toward the side door with the keys.

Kailey leaned up against the back of the seat and wrapped her arms around Skye's shoulders, giving her a firm hug. She kissed the elderly woman's cheek.

Skye turned with moist eyes but kept a tired smile on her face. "I don't blame you, Kailey. I know Raven. She's a curious spirit, and she loves you. She ran into direct danger tonight trying to prove her love for you without weighing the risks or consequences. I've known her so long that I have no doubt that's what she'd do. But, I see that you have taken a sudden affection for this young man, haven't you?"

Kailey relaxed her embrace. Taking a deep breath, she opened her mouth to speak, but Skye shook her head and placed a gentle finger against Kailey's lips.

"Kailey, love's an odd emotion. Often we mistake affection and friendship for love, but you must search deep inside yourself. If you cannot fully give yourself wholly to Raven, then it is best that you tell her sooner than later."

Kailey leaned back and wiped away tears. "I know. What happened earlier today, when she and I kissed, was—"

"Dear, you needn't explain your relationship with me. I offer no judgment either way you choose. I understand that Raven can be ... more than difficult in her own right. She's a stubborn one, the most stubborn lady in my coven. Since she was born an Aries, one can expect nothing less than how she behaves. She went after Cassie to prove her love and devotion to you. She'd die for you."

Kailey smiled, fighting against tears. "She would. I know."

"But what she sees with you isn't true love."

"How do you know?"

Skye turned and faced Kailey. "I see her behavior. I saw how she acted toward you today. She doesn't seek a romantic relationship where the two of you share equally in all things. She wants to possess and own you. Something a witch should never do. She knows better."

"You sensed that too?"

Skye nodded. "For over two years, I've seen how she frets about you. Her yearning for you has overtaken her. Despite my advice she pursued her own intentions. She's occasionally questioned if love spells work. I think she's tried to find a love spell to draw you to her."

"Was that what had happened earlier?"

"You tell me."

Kailey thought for a few moments and finally shook her head. "No. Maybe? My reaction was more for how I felt. I feared that she was dead since I couldn't reach her by phone. I was torn up about that. I constantly pictured the emptiness of my life without her and kept wondering what if I had made a big mistake by not giving myself the chance to see if we could be a couple. When I saw her and knew that she was alive, my relief was so overwhelming that I couldn't help but kiss her. Don't get me wrong. I *do* love her."

"I know you do. I understand. There are many levels of love."

Kailey remained silent for a moment. Not having her mother during those awkward teen years had left a void because she never really had anyone she could ask advice about dating and romance. She could never have talked to her brother about such things. That would have been ... too uncomfortable. Instead of struggling to figure out what love was, Kailey dedicated herself to marital arts and schoolwork, but even then, she was still plagued by questions about dating and finding a suitable companion. It was nice talking to Skye who seemed open to listening and offering her insight. Her soothing voice and gentle mannerisms showed that she cared.

"Luna said that she sensed a love spell," Kailey said.

"She did?"

Kailey nodded.

Skye sighed. "I had thought so, too, but I hoped she hadn't gone against my advice."

"But, I also rushed my actions because of my emotions, and after we started kissing ... this is so embarrassing, I wanted to do more than just kiss her. That's why I reconsidered having a relationship with her after four years of turning down her advances."

"I understand. Arousal can be confusing. Intense passion can strip your rationality and misguide you. We can be blinded by desire. But few relationships last beyond that once the fire of lust fades."

Kailey sighed. "Not even an hour had passed after I decided to take a chance of having a steady relationship with Raven before her jealousy surfaced unlike anything I'd ever seen from her before."

"True love is free of jealousy. It's free of fear. Love is giving and trusting. Never selfish."

"I'm still torn, Skye, about Raven. I really am. Before we entered Nocturnal Trinity, I had pretty much decided to break up with her after we left."

"Did you tell her that?" Skye asked.

"Not directly. I did tell her that her jealous behavior was something I wouldn't tolerate and if she continued, we were done."

Skye smiled. "Good. That was something she needed to hear."

"Maybe. But now I feel so guilty."

"Why?"

"Because now, Raven's gone again, and possibly in more danger than she ever was in Boston."

"It's an unfortunate, worrisome situation, but this isn't your fault. You should never fear speaking from your heart in a relationship. If you're afraid to talk to the one you love, you're not in a healthy relationship."

Brady stood outside the open door of the magic shop. He stared toward the car, shielding his eyes against the bright headlights.

Skye opened the car door. "I have some things I need to take care of in private. You find out what you can about that key when you meet with Micah and the others."

"I will. I just worry that you'll hold this against me."

Skye turned and shook her head. "Child, a true witch holds no grudges. 'Do No Harm' is what we must live by."

"Then why do others, like Eva who bends that rule, not live by it? How can we fight against them if we are to do no harm?"

"Nothing prevents us from fighting to protect a friend or loved one. That is one of the strongest instincts you'll ever find in nature. To put your life on the line or make the ultimate sacrifice to save another, there isn't a greater love."

"Thanks, Skye."

Skye smiled. "See you tomorrow morning. Until then, Blessed Be."

Skye closed the door and headed toward Brady. She entered the shop without hesitation, and Brady closed and locked the door behind her. Mist blew and gathered on the windshield. The wipers did a quick swipe, clearing the glass. Brady sprinted to the driver's side door and opened it.

"Please, ride up front with me," he said, smiling. Excitement rose in his voice.

Kailey got out and sat in the front seat. Although it was getting late, his energy levels were high, and he was wide awake.

He backed the car and turned, heading back to the main road. "Micah has released us from the animal binding spell."

Kailey leaned forward in her seat. "He did? When?"

Brady nodded. "He was working on the ritual when we left to go to Nocturnal Trinity."

"Oh. How do you feel about that?" she asked. "Does it make you feel differently?"

"My senses seemed more alert. I have revived energy. I hunger for things. Food. Nightfall."

"Why did Micah change his mind?"

Brady grinned. "I don't think he wanted a mutiny on his hands. Besides, we've endured the lack of our transformations long enough. For some reason he believes that by not changing for so long that we will be more in tune with our wolves' senses and the pack will be stronger."

"Do you believe that?" Kailey asked.

Brady shrugged. He kept both hands on the wheel and his attention was more on the road than her. "I don't know, really. It's too soon to tell, I suppose, at least when it comes to our physical and mental strength."

He seemed much more hyper.

"So how do you know if it's taken effect?" she asked.

"Energy is rushing through me. Everything seems different. My senses are keener. Smell, sight, hearing. It's incredible."

Kailey smiled. She couldn't help it. She now realized that when she had fallen into Brady's arms she wasn't under the influence of Cassie's pheromones. She was actually strongly attracted to him. "So I take it that this change happened very recently. Like maybe in the past fifteen minutes or so?"

Brady laughed. "Something like that, Kailey. I know I haven't done any drugs, but it would be easier to explain this sudden euphoria if I had." He lowered the side window and let the cool air flow through. Inhaling deeply, he released a long sigh.

"You're not going to ... change into a werewolf, are you?"

Brady glanced at her and smiled. "That urge hasn't coming over me, which is probably a good thing."

"Uh, yeah," she replied, scooting her back against the car door.

Brady laughed. "Believe me, I know when my wolf-side wishes to emerge. Hell, you saw everyone earlier at the shoreline."

Kailey nodded. "Yes, and I wonder what we're going to be seeing once we get there. I'm pretty sure people in that community are going to be calling animal control if a bunch of wolves start howling at the moon."

"I think they'll keep themselves in check. At least for a while."

"I hope Raven's okay."

"Me, too," Brady replied. "I really would have taken a chance at fighting that demon to rescue her."

"I know. But she would have killed Raven well before you got to her."

Brady's hands tightened on the steering wheel as he looked at her. "Yeah, that's the only reason I didn't rush her. I wish I could have done more, Kailey. She's your friend and I failed you and her."

"No, you didn't. I don't blame you. There's nothing we could have done to change the circumstances."

"I promise you though, I'm not finished fighting."

The sincerity in his voice matched the warmth in his eyes. His words were spoken with confidence and determination. She believed he was a man that backed what he said with his actions. Time would tell.

CHAPTER 32

When they arrived at the marina, Jacob and Ashley were waiting near the boats under the metal awning. Brady parked the truck in the adjacent parking lot.

"Tell me something," Kailey said.

"Anything," Brady replied.

"How did you get that wooden stake inside Nocturnal Trinity?"

He grinned. "Richard told the bouncer that I was an officer."

"So he didn't even check?"

"No. Besides Richard is a regular, so he's pretty trustworthy."

Before they got out of the car, Kailey said, "Is Richard a vampire?"

Brady turned sharply toward Kailey, as though the question caught him completely off guard. "No. Why?"

Kailey half chuckled. "Poor man then."

He held an inquisitive grin. "What?"

"He just looks like all the stereotype vampires from the old B movies, that's all."

Brady laughed. "Now that you mention it, I suppose he does."

"You've never noticed that?"

"No."

"Odd, and here I thought you had all that insight to the world around you, being a cop and all."

"So I'm not exactly keen on his particular fashion statement, but he's outside during the daylight almost every day so I know he's not a vampire." He stared into her eyes a bit too long and then he focused on her lips. "But perhaps tonight my interests lie elsewhere."

Kailey bit her lower lip and looked away. Heat flushed her face. A nervous smile came to her lips.

A small flashlight beam shone from the boat dock, flashing on and off three times in their direction.

Brady opened his door. "That's our cue."

Damn!

How she wished they had had five more minutes alone together. An hour would be even better. Reluctantly she opened her door and stepped out into the light misty breeze. The night air was colder here than the street outside Nocturnal Trinity, perhaps from the frigid air that hovered over the bay. She crossed her arms and leaned forward, trying to make herself a smaller target against the whipping wind.

Brady walked close beside her, passing cars with empty boat trailers. Few people fished after nightfall on the bay during the winter months, but some were foolish enough to attempt the task. Die hard fishing enthusiasts.

Kailey wanted to hold his hand but that action was too premature in her mind, even though his attraction toward her was as strong as hers for him. She liked his boldness in how he let her know where his interests were. And although she'd love nothing more than to see where it led, they had business to attend first. She'd never forgive herself if something happened to Raven while she pursued intimacy with Brady. Her guilt would kill both relationships. The last thing she needed was to suffer even more loss.

Jacob clasped hands with Brady in a brotherly handshake. Jacob nodded toward Kailey. "Where's your friend?"

"They retained her at Nocturnal Trinity," Brady said.

"What? Why?" His voice echoed his inner anger. Even though he didn't know Raven or Kailey, he held some kind of loyalty toward their cause. She didn't understand it, but she was thankful to have new friends determined to help her.

"We'll explain on the way across the bay," Brady replied. "Things might get pretty bad when we go to get her back."

Jacob gave an even smile. "Then I suppose Micah removing the spell was perfect timing."

Ashley grinned at Kailey in an unsettling way, which was more a hint of the pack having her back than a threat and how much Ashley looked forward to shedding blood. "Don't worry. They won't keep her long." She leaned into Kailey and wrapped her with a fierce hug.

"Come on," Jacob said, untying the boat. "Micah will want to know what you've found out. Did you find the door to the vampires' lair?"

Brady shook his head. "No."

"What?" Jacob asked with a concerned expression. "That's something we needed to know."

"We never had a chance to even look," Kailey said. "The succubus took Raven. The rest of our time was spent getting out of there."

Jacob sighed. "I guess I'd have to have been there. Sorry that they took Raven. But our pack will do everything we can. You have my word."

He spoke with true authority like he was the Alpha.

Jacob glanced toward Brady. "Feels good to finally be free of Micah's containment spell. A shame you weren't there, brother. But he can release you once we get to the island."

Brady smiled. "I think he already has."

Ashley's eyebrows rose. "Really?"

Brady nodded.

She looked impressed. "Micah's far more powerful than we imagined, Jacob. He was able to free Brady from that great a distance."

Jacob held a soured expression on his face. Kailey guessed it was because he had underestimated Micah's magical power. If he had any intent to challenge Micah's authority, he'd rethink doing so now.

"That's why he's the pack leader," Brady said.

Jacob grunted but didn't voice his slight resentment toward the comment.

Ashley stepped across the side of the boat and seated herself.

Jacob extended his hand toward Kailey to help her step over into the boat. He looked back toward the parking lot. "Where's the witch?"

"She asked that we drop her off at the magic shop," Kailey replied.

"Why?" Jacob asked suspiciously.

Kailey sat down on one of the side seats in the boat and tucked her purse close beside her. "To have some time to meditate and gather herself. Raven's like a daughter to her. She's worried sick about her."

Jacob nodded. "Fair enough."

Brady climbed into the boat and sat beside Kailey.

After everyone settled into the boat, Jacob started the motor. He drove slowly from the marina and once they were a few hundred yards from the shoreline, he increased the engine's speed. The front of the boat lifted from the sudden velocity and bounced slightly, crashing against the frothy crests. The cold breeze splashed the fine mist across them.

The boat rocked hard and as Jacob turned sharply toward the left, Kailey found herself huddled against Brady's chest, suddenly craving his warmth while trying to avoid the water spray that soaked her hair and caused her makeup to run. She shivered. He enveloped her with his arms.

Kailey didn't know which was worse, the constant gray sky and rain, or the heavy snows that were falling in Boston. She supposed the cold rain was easier than the ice and snow, but the chill of either was equally cold.

When she glanced to the other side of the boat, Ashley smiled almost teasingly. The she-wolf shook her head. Kailey was glad it was dark and the only light was the side amber panel lights because her face heated to a hot red. She felt like she was in high school again where the other girls teased one another about crushes.

However, she was colder than she was embarrassed, so she didn't slide from Brady's embrace. She placed her hand across his hard abs and closed her eyes. Somehow, she wished all the things about Nocturnal Trinity was one big nightmare that she'd eventually awakened from, but if it were a nightmare, she didn't want to awaken without Brady.

Jacob tilted his head back and let the misty breeze wash over his face. Lifting his hands, he roared with laughter and excitement. "So much energy flowing through me. I've not felt this good in a *long* time."

"Yeah," Brady said, rubbing Kailey's back. "Me, either. I figured you would be out in the woods somewhere running and enjoying the night."

"Would have loved to, but Micah's asked that we don't just yet."

"And that doesn't bother you?"

Jacob shrugged. "At first I thought it would, but I'm really feeling good inside. I guess the sudden release from the spell has helped ease my tension and aggravation."

"I can see that."

Jacob took the wheel again and sat on the damp seat. "So tell me what happened back there."

"Well," Brady said. "If Nicodemus is the strongest of the vampires, we will find ourselves in a great deal of trouble."

"Why's that?"

"Because Flora has power unlike anything I've seen. She can speak into your mind from wherever she's hiding."

"Really?"

Brady nodded.

"You never saw her?"

Kailey opened her eyes. "She came outside the nightclub after Brady killed one vampire."

Jacob turned with an impressed look upon his face. "I imagine you got her attention doing that. Returning to rescue Raven will be a battle now."

Brady gave a single nod, acknowledging the truth in the statement. "I realize that, but I wasn't given any choice. It was kill or die. I don't have time for death right now."

Jacob grinned and then bellowed a laugh. "Nor do any of us."

"Micah says that she's the second strongest," Brady said, "but Nicodemus has yet to surface."

"Odd."

"I know," Brady replied. "Not sure what that means."

"Maybe he's out of town?"

"Could be. Or he's simply not interested in what Flora's up to."

Kailey closed her eyes again and pressed her ear against Brady's chest. Drained from fatigue and stress, she wanted to fall asleep, but she fought to remain alert. Eventually, she'd lose that battle.

"What worries me," Kailey said, "is what will become of those Flora hypnotized to enter the nightclub."

Brady looked down at her and combed her wet hair from her face with his fingers. "It won't be good for some of them. I imagine a few of them will be killed, some will be turned, and others might wake up tomorrow and not remember a damned thing that happened tonight."

Jacob gnashed his teeth. Anger stirred in his facial expressions. "The blessed stones the witch made for them didn't work?"

"To a degree, I suppose they did," Brady replied. "The demon somehow saw past the magical veil. She recognized Kailey and fled. Raven ran after her."

"Niiice," Ashley said. "What was she thinking?"

"Apparently she wasn't," Brady said. "No offense, Kailey."

"No, she's impulsive sometimes and always stubborn." Kailey opened her eyes. The Seattle Skyline was lit up, stabbing its brilliant colors against the black cloud ceiling as if trying to pry apart the dismal night sky to let the bright moonlight shine through. Even during the lights' magnificent attempt, the shroud denied the colors their access, much like hope tried to override Kailey's miserable losses. Both failed.

The boat tipped sharply to the left as Jacob guided it along the shoreline toward Micah's estate. Kailey sat up. Remnants of the bonfire flickered near the beach. Shadows of people indicated that many of them were still gathered around the warmth of the smoldering logs. The heat thwarted the cold misty rain but was slowly losing the battle.

Jacob cut the engine and eased the boat to the sandy bar. Several of the pack ran from the fire to the boat. Jacob flung a long nylon rope out to one of the bearded men. The man grabbed the rope and tethered it to a wooden post. Jacob dropped the anchor to prevent the bottom of the fiberglass boat from scraping the pebbles and sand on the shore.

Kailey tried to stand but the rocking waves and whipping wind made it nearly impossible to keep her balance. A rough wave struck the side of the boat and knocked her backwards into her seat. Brady extended his hand to her, helped her back to her feet, and steadied her by wrapping an arm around her waist.

Ashley stepped off the side of the boat and stood knee deep in the water. The expression on her face indicated the water was icy cold. She shivered. "Brrr!"

Kailey was already chilled to the bone. The last thing she wanted was to get wetter and colder. Ashley turned her back to Kailey. "Climb on."

"Seriously?" Kailey asked.

"Sure. The beach isn't but a few feet away. No sense in you getting soaked, too. Besides, my metabolism allows me to warm faster than yours."

"Thanks."

Ashley shrugged. "Don't mention it."

Brady helped Kailey balance until she slid her legs over Ashley's shoulders and Ashley held Kailey's knees firmly. Once in piggyback posture, Ashley sloshed her way to the pebbled beach. Kailey clutched her purse tightly. Brady stepped off the boat, making a heavy splash in the lapping waves.

Once they were near the bonfire, Micah approached. He smiled, but his eyes looked much different than before. Although there was gentleness in his smile, his eyes were fierce like the wolf that resided inside of him. She found it difficult to hold his gaze.

"Welcome back," he said. "Where's the rest of your group?"

Fighting tears, she replied, "Cassie took Raven. Skye is staying the night at your magic shop."

Micah frowned. "Why did they take Raven?"

"Because of the key that I have. Flora has given me twenty-four hours to give it to her."

"Then we need to find out what it opens quickly."

She nodded.

"Come on," Micah said. "Let's go into my house and get out of the weather."

 icah sat at the head of the long rectangular dining room table. Ashley was seated to his left and Jacob to his right. Kailey sat with a heavy plush towel wrapped around her, sipping hot tea. Her insides felt like ice, and she couldn't control her shivering.

Brady was seated right beside her with an open bottle of Corona. He seemed unfazed by the cold, perhaps due to his metabolism. Jacob and Ashley were also at ease.

The steamy tea helped heat her inner core, but her uncertainly chilled her. She was seated at a table with a pack of werewolves that had been recently released from their magical suppression. These were the same people who, a few hours earlier, had been raging to change beneath the full moon overhead, and yet, now, they sat calmly with those urges gone. She couldn't help but wonder what might trigger their need to change again, and should that happen, she didn't like being surrounded by them since she was the only human in the dining room. They would most likely be unpredictable and attack or kill her. At worst, she'd be dead. At second worst, she'd be turned into one of them. Since neither of these options fit into her five-year future plans, she didn't like either outcome.

Kailey had so many questions about their nature, but the timing seemed inappropriate to ask. Without realizing it, she had slid her chair almost against Brady's. His radiating body heat flowed over her cool skin, slightly warming her. She felt safer with him beside her and believed he'd protect her should any of the others alter into their wilder beast forms. But nothing guaranteed that he would or could. After such a transformation, did they retain their human rationalities or were they like ravenous creatures that killed anything in their path or sight.

Since she'd never seen a werewolf, she was quite certain she'd freeze in terror if one of these people transformed right in front of her. She'd be too terrified to run or try to defend herself. She would become vulnerable prey, much like a hypnotized mouse staring into the cunning gaze of a snake before the snake squeezed the rodent to death and ate it.

The adjoining kitchen gleamed in a glossy white. Beneath the dim lighting, the counter, cabinets, and walls almost glowed. The dining room walls were more windows than wood, giving a perfect panoramic view of the Seattle Skyline on the other side of the bay.

The key set in the center of the table. Micah picked it up and studied it. Puzzled, he shook his head. "What makes this so important to Flora?"

No one answered the rhetorical question, but each of them focused upon the key like the great mystery it was. Any answer they offered was simply a guess. Nothing more. This was deductive reasoning at its best, which often took days to unravel in order to find the actual truth. They didn't have that kind of time. Less than twenty-four hours was what Flora had given, and the clock was ticking.

"That's what we need to find out," Micah said, finally answering his own question. "Kailey, have you told me everything?"

"About what?"

"Where did you get the key?"

"From my brother's office."

"And Cassie first confronted you there?"

She nodded.

"She wanted this?"

"Yes. She had been in his office the day before and apparently had searched for it. The contents in his desk drawer were strewn. I haven't a clue as to why she wants it though. She nearly killed me."

Micah set the key back on the table. His eyes narrowed and with his newfound Alpha voice, he said, "Think about the things in your brother's office. Surely there are other hints that will help us. Concentrate. Tell me what you see."

Kailey closed her eyes and tried to retrace her every step when she had entered Vincent's office. Then she remembered as she had sat in his chair she saw his calendar schedule. Jaclyn's name was written on the seventeenth day of the month with N.T. circled scribbled beside it. She told them about that.

"We don't know that your brother met this person at Nocturnal Trinity for certain," Micah said.

"No. I have no idea who she is, either. He never mentioned her to me whenever we talked."

Micah glanced toward Brady. "We have to find her. See what she knows."

Brady nodded. "I'll see what I can do at the police station. But with only a first name, we don't have much to go on. If we had somewhat of a description of her appearance that would be best."

"We have less than twenty-four hours though," Kailey said.

"I know," Brady replied. "That's not much time."

Kailey pulled her cellphone from her purse. "What's the number to your shop, Micah?"

He called out the numbers while she typed them in. "Why?"

Kailey shrugged and put the phone to her ear. After the third ring, Skye picked up. "It's Kailey. I was afraid you wouldn't answer."

"I almost didn't, dear, but Luna and Blaze insisted that it was probably you. What do you need?"

Kailey sighed. Propping an elbow on top of the table and resting her forehead against her hand, she stared at the table. "This key is important to Flora for some reason."

"You've already established that."

"I know. Sorry for bothering you, but I just remembered that my brother had scheduled a meeting with a woman named Jaclyn on the seventeenth. From what he scribbled beside it on his calendar, there's the chance that he met with her at Nocturnal Trinity. Is there any way you can perform a spell that might give us a clue as to who this Jaclyn is?"

"Not offhand. You cannot track her physically?"

"No. I don't have a last name."

"What does she look like?"

Frustrated, Kailey shook her head. "We have no idea."

"How do you expect me to find someone without any more information than that?"

"I was being hopeful."

Skye chuckled over the phone. "I'm a witch, not a psychic."

"Let's say that whatever the key unlocks holds something that is detrimental to severing the Circle of Unity in Nocturnal Trinity. What would they fear the most?"

"A great number of things actually. Any magic that might reverse recent protection spells that their witches have used. Or perhaps something that can gain control over them. Since Flora is capable of mind control, imagine the damage someone could inflict if she took control of a witch."

Chills pimpled Kailey's arms. Indeed such power wrought unforeseen consequences, not just for Nocturnal Trinity, but also for those residing throughout Seattle.

Skye said, "I'm sorry that I cannot be of more help to you."

"It's okay. Sorry that I interrupted whatever you're working on."

"Get some sleep, Kailey. You need to be alert for when we confront Flora and the others at Nocturnal Trinity tomorrow. I'm old, but I'm going to do everything I possibly can to get Raven back safely. Be ready."

Before Kailey could reply, Skye hung up the phone. Kailey set her phone down on the table. Micah's inquisitive gaze didn't require any further prying.

"Nothing she can do with what little information we have, either," Kailey said.

Micah shrugged. "I figured as much. Otherwise I could have found something by now."

Kailey's face reddened.

Brady reached his hand beneath the table and rubbed her leg, trying to comfort her. "The best we can do is go to the police station in the morning. If nothing else we might be able to get a warrant for Nocturnal Trinity's surveillance tapes on the seventeenth."

Micah stood. "There's not much more we can do tonight. I suggest you all get some sleep. We rise early tomorrow. Ashley, show Kailey to one of the guest bedrooms upstairs."

Ashley nodded, rose, and stepped around the side of the table, motioning for Kailey. "Come on. You probably want to get all that extra makeup off."

She nodded. "A shower would be nice without the fear of looking like a raccoon afterwards."

Ashley led her to the long curved set of stairs. The walls were dark walnut paneling with elegantly carved patterns. The carpeted stairs sunk beneath her feet while she walked.

"Brady has taken to you quite fondly," Ashley said.

"You think so?"

Ashley gave Kailey a sly stare. "Don't tell me you haven't noticed."

Kailey grinned and blushed. "I have."

"I thought you had a thing for Raven."

"I wanted to give it a chance," Kailey replied. "But she had something different in mind than I did as to what a relationship consists of."

"So you're not a lesbian then?"

"I'm bi."

"Ah, okay. That's cool."

They turned to the left at the top of the stairs, passing a half dozen bedroom doors before stopping at the end of the long hallway.

"What about you?" Kailey asked.

"What do you mean?"

"I see how you look at Micah."

Ashley sighed deeply. "Perhaps one day, but not before he avenges his wife."

"But you want to be with him?"

She nodded. "More than anything."

Ashley opened the heavy four-paneled door.

Kailey's eyes widened with surprise. The large bedroom was unbelievable. She had never seen anything quite as lavish. The antique four-poster bed had twisted pencil posts that supported a curtained canopy. A nightstand was on each side of the bed with earth tone feather table lamps. All the furniture was antique and hand carved.

Ashley flipped on the light switch and pointed. "The bathroom is over there. There's a shower and tub, whichever you prefer."

Kailey smiled. "A shower's fine tonight. Thanks."

"Don't mention it. When Micah says that we rise early, he means it. Usually before five a.m."

"Okay."

Ashley pulled the door closed. Kailey sat on the edge of the bed and unfastened the boots. She peeled away the socks and let her tired achy feet sink into the plush carpet. Sighing, she rose and headed to the bathroom.

The motion sensor lights brightened when she stepped into the bathroom. The tile floor was cold, but after having her feet encased in those hot tight boots, she welcomed the coolness.

Kailey turned the shower on and undressed in front of the mirror. She noticed another door on the other side of the bath closet where the towels were stored. Timidly she approached, twisted the knob, and pushed the door outward. Another bedroom almost identical to the one she was in. The lamp was set to dim, but no one seemed to be in the room, which was a relief to her.

She pulled the door closed, but she didn't find any way to lock it.

Steam rose in the shower, so she slipped inside, allowing the hot water to soak over her stiff hair. She washed her face with soap under the water, wiping away the dark makeup. Along with the makeup and hairspray, she washed away the lingering cold that had chilled her after crossing the bay. She scrubbed at the tattoos but accomplished only making them fainter.

Fifteen minutes later, she shut off the water, grabbed a towel, and dried off. Not knowing who might sleep in the adjoining room, she searched through the dresser drawers for something to wear. Finding a man's white T-shirt, she pulled it over her head. The shirt covered her to her knees, but with her clothes still in the car across the bay, she didn't have any clean panties. Even with the shirt, she felt exposed.

Kailey walked to the bed and pulled back the bedspread and blankets. Someone rapped softly upon the door. She gasped, wondering whom it was. Her heartbeat increased. She pulled the blanket around her.

"Kailey," Ashley said, pushing the door open. She held a small bag in her hands. "These are new, if you'd like to have them. I didn't think about you not having anything to wear."

Kailey lowered the blanket and walked toward Ashley. She peered into the Victoria's Secret bag to find new panties. "Thanks. I found this shirt in the dresser. Not sure who it belongs to."

"Don't worry about it. If you need anything else, please let me know. I'm three doors down the hallway."

"Okay, thanks."

Ashley returned to the hall and pulled the door closed. Kailey locked the door behind her. She returned to the bed, took the tags off the pink G-string, and slipped them on. She felt a bit better, not as exposed, but really wished she had her suitcase and her own clothes.

Tapping the lamp on the nightstand, she set the light at its dimmest level. She pulled the blankets tightly over herself and stared at the brilliant canopy cloth above her, reflecting on everything that had happened since her arrival to Seattle.

The silence around Kailey was haunting. She found herself worrying about Raven. No matter how hard she tried, she couldn't get Raven's frightened facial expression erased from her mind. It was almost like Raven was standing directly in front of her. The helplessness in her roommate's eyes troubled her deeply. Sleeping might be the most difficult thing for Kailey to do, but she'd welcome it if slumbering could numb her mind.

Tears burned at the edge of Kailey's eyes, but she refused to let them fully emerge. Sadness weakened her. She needed anger and determination if she wanted to truly help Raven.

"I'm sorry, Raven," she whispered.

Kailey grabbed one of the extra fluffy pillows and wrapped her arms tightly around it in a fierce hug. After twenty minutes, she drifted off the sleep.

CHAPTER 34

Kailey was startled awake by the nightmare. Sweat dampened the sheets beneath her. Her thin T-shirt was soaked, clinging to her as she sat up at the edge of the bed. Rubbing her eyes, she took a quick breath. Her heart thudded against her chest.

Raven, in the dream, had appeared before Kailey. Bite mark scars were healing on Raven's throat. Her eyes suddenly filled with blackness, revealing the evil that now possessed her. Prominent sharp fangs protruded from her upper teeth. She hissed and pointed her finger at Kailey. "See what you did to me? I am hideous. Cursed."

"No," Kailey said, shaking her head. "I wanted to save you."

"You left me behind to be with Brady. You betrayed me and our love to be with him."

Tears streamed from Kailey's eyes. She vehemently shook her head. "No. I wanted you safe. Flora ... Flora lied. She lied and turned you."

"You will pay."

Raven's form in the dream rushed, leapt, and defied gravity as she flew across the room toward Kailey. Kailey jerked awake before Raven reached her. And yet, while awake, she felt eyes watching her.

Kailey set her feet on the carpet and slowly stood. She made her way to the bathroom, the lights flipped on, and she looked at her reflection in the mirror. She looked paler without the Goth makeup that Luna had applied earlier. Could fright actually do that?

The nightmare held some unknown truth to it. Kailey believed the dream was a revelation, and not the wicked imagination that dreams often plagued upon people. She had the feeling that Flora had already turned Raven out of spite. Key or no key, Raven was now a vampire.

Tears filled her eyes. She turned on the water and sobbed. She leaned down and washed cold water over her face. When she turned the water off, grabbed a hand towel and wiped away the water, she caught Brady's reflection in the mirror. She jerked around and almost screamed. He stood just inside the adjoining bathroom door.

He stood wearing only his boxers. True to what he had said, apparently werewolves were never fat. He was chiseled. Each muscle of his abs and chest were perfectly outlined. On his chest, she noticed the pale scars where a wolf or some other animal had clawed him long ago. She wanted to run her fingers over them, to touch him.

"Are you okay? I heard you scream," he said, softly.

Had she screamed before she awakened? As frightening as the dream was, she probably had. She occasionally had nightmares, but nothing as extreme as this one. She never recalled screaming from one before.

Kailey turned to face him. The sweat dampened shirt clung to her skin, making her firm breasts and hard nipples visible through the thin material. She took a sharp breath and her body shuddered. She swallowed hard and closed her eyes. "It was a bad dream. I dreamt that Raven was turned into a vampire."

When she opened her eyes, he stood only a few feet from her. He stepped closer, placed a gentle hand to her chin, and lifted until her sad worried eyes met his. "It's going to be okay. We'll get her back."

"What if the dream is true?"

"I doubt it is, but we'll deal with it when the time comes. Worrying only keeps us unfocused."

"I know, but I'm scared something bad has happened to her."

Kailey looked into his eyes. He directed his gaze to her lips. Nervous excitement went through her. When he leaned in to kiss her, she didn't back away. Instead, she moved toward him.

His warm lips parted as he kissed her gently the first time. She rose on the tip of her toes, wrapping her arms around his neck, and she kissed him harder. She pressed against him. His hands pulled her shirt above her waist and then he cupped her bare buttocks, lifting her upward. She wrapped her legs around his waist and immediately she felt his firmness pressed against her. She flushed wet in an instant.

She lowered her feet to the floor as need and desire pulsed through her.

His thumbs looped around the narrow elastic waistband of her G-string, quickly sliding them down her muscular thighs. He squeezed her buttocks and lifted her so she was face to face with him. Nervously, she sought his eyes and saw the sexual hunger in his eyes.

Brady set her upon the bathroom counter, kissed her several more seconds, and then he pulled back long enough to pull her shirt over her head. When their lips met again, his hands gently squeezed her breasts and then he teased her nipples even harder by softly pinching them. She broke their kiss and tugged at his boxers until they dropped to the floor. As he stepped out of the shorts, she glanced down, and her eyebrows rose. For a man of average height, he was much larger than she had expected.

He pressed against her, grabbed her knees, and spread her legs wider. Swallowing hard, she leaned back, arching her back, halfway expecting pain as he pressed against her opening. Instead he slipped deep inside her without any resistance. She was relieved and quite surprised because she had never gotten so turned on and dripping wet before.

"Oh God," she moaned.

She gasped, pressed her face against his chest, and dug her fingernails into his shoulders with his first few thrusts. She had no control over the groans escaping her mouth as he drove deeper and deeper with each thrust.

Brady pulled back, nearly all the way out, and paused, making her anxious and wanting. When her eyes pleaded, he acquiesced, plunging deep inside again. God, she didn't want him to stop.

She leaned forward to kiss him. She couldn't stop. She wanted more.

"Harder," she panted.

Brady cupped her buttocks and pulled her tightly against him, driving his fullness farther inside. Kailey moaned and bit his lower lip.

"Ye-s-s-s," she groaned in an anguished sigh. "Oh, yes ..."

When she opened her eyes, she read the hunger in his. He kissed her passionately again, but he didn't release his firm grip on her butt and continued pushing deeper. She slid to the edge of the counter to allow him to fully enter her, all the way inside. The warmth of him within her brought her to ecstasy.

She leaned back, her head against the mirror, and he increased his momentum. Her breaths were soft and jerky. She was caught somewhere between pleasure and pain, but she didn't want him to stop. Nothing she'd ever experienced felt this intense and satisfying.

She whispered, "Love my fears away. Please."

Brady leaned down and kissed her softly. He lifted her off the countertop and turned toward the door that led to his room, carrying her. Kailey wrapped her legs tightly around him, holding him firmly inside her. He carried her to the bed and eased her down while remaining over her, holding himself slightly above her.

She smiled, leaning up to meet his lips. Gently, she bit his lower lip and tugged. He grinned, placing his hands over hers, then he gave her a deep, long kiss before burying himself inside her again. She jerked, arching her back. He released her hands and she placed hers against his thick chest.

Her body quivered involuntarily. A soft moan gasped from her mouth. She closed her eyes, surrendering every bit of her to him. She was lost in him, his touch, his scent, and his desires. She ran her hands down his sides, sighing softly with each push he made, her body rocking with his rhythm.

Sweat pooled between her modest breasts, meandering into the muscled grooves of her abdominals. Beads of sweat covered him.

His eyes peered into hers. Hiding right behind his gaze, she glimpsed the wolf inside, its hunger, its desire, and seeing the beauty of this marvelous beast made her no longer fear the moment she'd eventually see Brady in his wolf form. He was her lover and her protector. Gently, her fingers traced the scars on his chest. Seconds later, she kissed them while he continued loving her.

A half hour later, Brady arched back and groaned with one last vigorous thrust. He held himself firmly inside her. Warmth flooded her and she panted, licking her lips. He closed his eyes and moaned with great relief, slowly lowering himself over her. She kissed his chest and squeezed his waist.

He trembled slightly, his thickness softening. Slowly he pulled out and fell beside her. She turned to her side to face him. Taking his hand, she placed his palm between her breasts. Her heart raced. She smiled at him. Panting, he returned the smile.

His heavy eyes closed a few minutes later as he lay beside her on the bed. A few more minutes and he was snoring softly. Kailey placed her head to his chest, listening to his heartbeat, while his left arm draped over her. In the dim light that spilled from the restroom, she teased his chest hair. She kissed his chest and sighed, running her fingers across his scars.

Why was it that most men dropped into a coma-like slumber after sex, and she was suddenly wide-awake, full of thoughts?

Kailey still felt the warmth inside her from where he had been. The lingering euphoria cascaded through her, washed away her stress, and made her feel somewhat hopeful. She knew that she didn't have to stand alone against the rising tide of turmoil. She never wanted the fulfilling sensations to end, but eventually all good things ended.

Having sex with Brady wasn't about love or lust. For Kailey, it was more about trust. And after he had stood beside her and helped her escape Nocturnal Trinity, she knew he was someone she trusted. With everything. Before she'd ever have sex with someone, she needed to know that she could completely trust the person. After several embarrassing mistakes, that was the one condition she placed upon herself whenever she met a potential lover. Several times she had mistaken trust for another's lust and discovered she had been used. From then on, she carefully reevaluated her approach toward possible relationships and kept herself at arm's length.

But from her first encounter with Brady at the cemetery, his demeanor displayed the type of man he was. He didn't display arrogance and his actions to help or defend others was greater than pursuing his own wants and needs. He was willing to risk his life in order to rescue Raven, in spite of her obvious scorn toward him.

Having lost so much in her life, and now contending with the possibility that Raven was lost forever, Kailey didn't have much left.

Strangely, Kailey didn't believe she had betrayed Raven by having sex with Brady. She held no questions about whether she and Raven would ever be a couple. She knew they could never be due to the possessive nature Raven had exhibited, and casting the love spell to make her love Raven went beyond any rationality. As Skye had pointed out, that wasn't a loving rela-tionship. Besides, Kailey had already predetermined that their relationship was over before they even entered Nocturnal Trinity, but she did feel responsible for placing Raven's life into danger.

But Raven's impulsive attitude was what had gotten her into trouble. Had she kept a low profile like they had been instructed, Raven might not be held captive inside the nightclub.

Kailey watched Brady sleep. Easing closer, she pulled the blanket over them and snuggled against him. His muscled arm tightened around her, and she felt safer. Minutes later, sleep captured her again.

CHAPTER 35

A female sternly clearing her throat awakened Kailey. When she opened her eyes and the room came into focus, she noticed Ashley standing at the edge of the room with her arms crossed and a sly grin spread across her face.

Kailey eased up and slid her back against the headboard, carefully keeping her blanket pulled to her chin. Glancing to her left, she discovered Brady was gone.

Before she could ask, Ashley said, "Brady's outside with the rest of the pack. I told you that we rise early."

"That you did," Kailey said, nodding her head.

"When I didn't find you in the *other* bedroom ... I assumed you'd be here."

"Things sort of happened."

Ashley laughed softly. "Aren't you the lucky one?"

Kailey blushed. Her face heated.

"Come," she said, shaking her head and laughing softly. "Perhaps I should have chosen a better choice of words. Follow me."

Kailey's face reddened even more, but she didn't bother with a verbal reply. The expression on her face probably revealed more than words could ever express.

"I have some clothes that should fit you. After you dress, we'll start making breakfast. The guys are actually trying to catch a few salmon."

"That sounds great."

"Yeah, if they catch any."

Kailey scooted toward the edge of the bed and found that she was rather tender and raw. It was amazing how much pleasure had overridden the pain of their intense sex, but her sudden smile indicated she had no regrets.

"Perhaps I can take a quick shower?" Kailey asked.

"Sure. I'll go get some clothes."

"Thanks."

Ashley left the room, and Kailey hurried to the bathroom. She looked at herself in the mirror, seeing something about her that she had never seen before. Her face beamed with satisfaction. While she wasn't about to openly admit she and Brady were a couple, she was pleased at where things between them had escalated.

She turned on the hot water and stepped into the shower, adjusting the temperature. Steam rose inside the glassed-in shower. She lathered a bar of soap and scrubbed. Her mind raced toward Raven, the nightmare, and for a moment, she thought she heard Raven cry. The pendant around her neck went cold, almost icy, in spite of the hot water cascading over her.

"Raven?" Kailey asked, stepping back from the water spray. Her hand went to the pendant. The silver was so cold it felt hot. She released it. When the pendant touched the skin between her breasts, it burnt like fire.

"Kailey?" Raven's voice whispered around her over and over and over.

Kailey kept brushing at the pendant, trying to keep it from touching her skin. Finally she had no choice but to yank the chain off. It hit the shower floor, turning instantly into a tarnished black. Raven's voice faded to be heard no more.

"Shit!" Kailey said, reaching for the chain. She picked it up and examined the pendant. It looked charred as if it had been burning for hours. What had happened?

The nightmare replayed before her eyes. Raven, a vampire, stood across the room from her. The nightmare was a warning. A premonition. Nothing else that anyone told her could ever convince her otherwise. Her roommate was no longer human. To believe anything else set Kailey up for disaster.

Flora was evil to the core. Kailey should not have trusted the vampire to keep her word. She had already turned Raven, and probably would use her mind control to make Raven appear human, so she could get close enough to Kailey to kill her.

The magic pendant Raven had made for her gave the only warning

Raven could offer. The last of her binding magic was gone. The black tarnished look indicated the lack of Raven's soul, now captive to wherever vampire souls were contained. Raven was a vampire.

Kailey grieved. She should have fought to get Raven out, instead of believing Flora would make such a trade. Whatever Vincent had that belonged to Nocturnal Trinity was something she intended to find and use. It must be something that could destroy the Circle of Unity, and if it could kill Flora, Kailey would use it.

Angered, Kailey slid the shower door open and flung the necklace toward the sink. Weeping, she pushed her face under the shower. She didn't want to cry, but she couldn't stop the sudden sobbing, so she tucked her chin to her chest to prevent inhaling the water as she gasped for air. With her head beneath the hot water, she placed her hands and forehead against the tile wall. Her hands slowly balled into tight fists.

Who was this Jaclyn? She needed to know. Immediately.

To release the anger, she punched the tile wall. Hard. Then again.

The skin on her knuckles split, but she hit again and again, feeling no pain. "Why? Why? *Why?*"

"Kailey!" A muscled hand reached around, gently grabbed her shoulder, and turned her toward him.

Brady.

He pulled her out of the water spray and against him. He embraced her, resting his chin atop her head. "What's wrong, Kailey?"

Kailey couldn't form the words to speak. She pressed her face to his flannel shirt and sobbed. Her body slumped against his. His arms wrapped around her, keeping her from collapsing. Blood leaked from her battered hands, dripping to the floor with the remnants of the showering mist and swirling in a pool, slowly disappearing down the drain.

Brady's calloused hands held her cheeks and turned her face up toward his. "What's going on?"

Tears spilled from her eyes. "Raven."

"What about her?"

"She's a vampire. I know it."

"That was just a nightmare."

"No, Brady, I'm not talking about the dream." She pulled from his hold, stepped out of the shower, and found the necklace on the floor.

Brady grabbed a towel and wrapped it around her.

"See?" she said, holding the pendant up to him.

He took the necklace and shook his head. "What happened to it?"

"It became extremely cold and started burning me. I had to yank it off."

"And this somehow means that Raven's now a vampire?" he asked.

"The nightmare seemed too real."

"Some dreams are that way."

Kailey shook her head. "No. Not this one. Before this pendant changed, I heard Raven's voice. She was crying for help. Don't you *dare* say that it was my imagination."

"I'm not patronizing you. I'd never do that. Here, let me look at your hands."

Brady gently took her hands into his and examined her knuckles under the light. They were busted open, leaking blood. "These look bad. They'll be bruised later."

"I've had worse in fights. I'll be fine."

"All the same, let's get some bandages over them." He opened a drawer and found a box of Band-Aids and Neosporin. While he carefully applied them to her bleeding knuckles, her towel dropped to the floor. "Let me get that for you."

"No," she replied. "I'm okay."

"It is a bit distracting," he said.

"Oh, is it now?"

"Yes."

"Why is that?"

Brady smiled and his face reddened. "Because you're the most beautiful woman I've ever seen."

The sudden bluntness of his statement made Kailey blush. She bit her lower lip. She never expected such a flattering compliment. In fact, a man had never said such a thing to her before.

Most of the guys she had been around, who dared to even ask her out, were others that trained at her gym. Those were the men she had mistakenly thought had wanted to date her for more than just sex.

Raven had complimented Kailey far *too* often, which became more annoying than believable and was another reason she had kept Raven at a distance. The excessive praise was a major turnoff.

He placed the last bandage on her hand. "As much as I'd like to stay in bed with you all day, we have a lot to accomplish this morning so we can get Raven back."

"It may be too late for that," she replied softly.

"Perhaps not."

"You don't believe in premonitions?"

He shrugged.

"How would you explain the pendant and my hearing Raven's voice?" she asked.

"Don't forget that one third of the Circle of Unity are witches. Powerful witches. There's the chance that one of them might have done this to get you to let down your guard. Make certain that you don't lose your focus. Remember everything they taught you about investigating criminals at college. You need that frame of mind if we're going to find out what your brother hid."

Kailey nodded. "And if Raven is a vampire?"

Brady pulled her nude body against him. "We'll deal with that then. But right now, don't entertain the thought of what she *might* have become until we know for certain. You said that you wanted the facts first, didn't you?"

"Yes," she replied, nodding. "How many vampires have you killed?"

"Counting tonight's?"

She nodded.

"Half a dozen."

"And you didn't think that was information that I needed to know?" she asked.

"Vampire slayings are on the down low," Brady replied. "We don't file police reports for them."

"Really?"

He chuckled. "Would you?"

"I guess not."

"Not much evidence left. Body's gone, and explaining the circumstances would simply have the officer sent for a mental evaluation. Get one of those on your record and your credibility goes downhill quite quickly."

"The same with reporting news to the media."

"Exactly."

Kailey examined the bandages. The feeling was coming back into her hands. Her knuckles throbbed. "So why did you kill them?"

"The vampires?"

"Who else?" Her eyebrows rose with suspicion and playful accusation.

Brady grinned. "No one else. The vamps ... well, each case was different. These were turned without, I'm assuming, the top vampires inside Nocturnal Trinity knowing lesser vampires had turned them. They left the nightclub and later killed others in a feeding frenzy. Separate cases spaced apart."

"How do you explain the murders to the reporters?" she asked.

"Often we don't. We can't exactly have residents believing a wild animal roams the streets either. Panic does crazy things to normally rational people. They start packing guns and killing innocent people because they aren't properly trained in how to use a gun. Or they get hero complexes and stupidly kill someone they believe is up to no good."

Brady cupped her hands over his and inspected his bandage work.

"I'll be okay. Really," Kailey said.

He leaned toward her and kissed her lips.

The bedroom door creaked open. A few seconds later, Ashley stood outside the bathroom door and shook her head. "Perhaps I should start knocking. Here, some clothes, girl. Otherwise you'll never be able to get him to keep his hands off you."

Kailey laughed, grabbed the clothes, and pulled them to her, covering her breasts.

"What the hell happened to your hands?" Ashley asked.

Brady replied, "She thought beating up the shower wall was a good idea."

Ashley's frowned and crossed her muscular arms. "I have to admit. It helps sometimes. But save your energy for the real battle. Micah told me that he needs to see us all ASAP."

"About?" Brady asked.

She shrugged. "I guess we have to go see. He's not partial to revealing secrets until we're all together, even to me." Her face saddened at the last part of her remark.

"Let me get dressed, and I'll be right down," Kailey said.

Ashley grabbed Brady's hand and tugged.

"What?" he asked as he was yanked toward the bedroom.

"If you don't let her get dressed, we'll all be waiting for another hour," Ashley said. "At least."

"What, you don't trust me to behave myself?" he asked.

"With her body?" Ashley said. "Hell, I'm not bi, but she's hot enough to make me question *my* sexuality."

After they left the bedroom, Kailey dressed, attempted to fix her damp hair but gave up, and noticed that she was still blushing. She had never been one to get embarrassed so easily or to blush, but around Brady, she found herself doing it far too often, which frightened her somewhat. She was taken by him and knew it. The fact that being near him flustered her was the clearest sign she liked him and could possibly find herself falling in love with him.

So why did it make her so damn uncomfortable?

Because everything she had loved in life had been rudely and prematurely taken from her. Her parents and her brother were gone, and quite possibly now Raven had been snatched from those she treasured the most dear to her heart. And should she open her heart completely to Brady, she had even more to risk losing. Did she dare make such a gamble again?

CHAPTER 36

ailey picked up the cold, blackened pendant and tried to wash away the sooty color, but the water didn't remove any of it. For her, the pendant meant the end of Raven the witch, and the beginning of Raven's undead life as a vampire. She liked Brady's optimism that another witch within the Circle of Unity might have destroyed the pendant, but she didn't share his enthusiasm. Although she'd love to be the type of person who accepted the brighter side of life, she'd yet to experience it enough to chance taking that type of faith. Well, *any* kind of faith. There were more reasons for her to disbelieve in a god's existence than surrender herself to one because everyone else insisted she should. Fate was harsh enough. Did a deity lessen loss? Often divinity gave the sufferer something to blame whenever prayer didn't readily solve the situation.

She tucked the pendant into the pocket of her borrowed blue jeans and rushed downstairs to find the wolf pack sitting at the table. Bacon fried in the kitchen where Ashley and two other women stood at the stove while a man peeled potatoes over a bowl in the sink. She headed toward the kitchen but Micah pointed toward the empty chair at the table beside Brady.

"Please, sit," Micah said.

The huge bald man she had seen at the magic shop stood behind Micah, solemn and menacing. His throat tattoo was a symbol she didn't recognize and was as great a mystery as the man himself.

"But—" she said, nodding toward the kitchen. Ashley was looking at Micah with saddened eyes.

"More than enough cooks in the kitchen," Micah said. "Besides, you and Brady have a lot to accomplish in a short amount of time."

Kailey glanced around at the others seated. Some of the bearded men she didn't recognize from the previous night, but it had been dark and most had stood in the shadows. The wrinkles around two of the men's eyes led her to believe they were probably in their early fifties, but their physiques were well toned. The other three men she guessed were in their late twenties, and the two young ladies looked to be about her age.

In another place she'd have thought she was in a biker gang house. Leather jackets, long hair and beards, and a lot of tattoos caught her attention. A few chewed on unlit cigars. She guessed smoking in the house was not acceptable, for which she was thankful. But this was not a group she'd ever want to be on the bad side of.

Nervously, she sat down. Brady's hand reached beneath the table and found hers. She held his hand in between hers. She felt a bit easier, but she never liked being in a roomful of strangers and he was the only one she fully trusted. She realized the other pack members were studying her. The setting was almost like a group interview, and she supposed in a way it was so they could find out more about her.

"No reason to be afraid of us," Micah said. "Although you're not a werewolf, we consider you a friend of the pack. There's not one person within our family that won't come to your aid should you ever need us."

"I appreciate that." She smiled and made eye contact with each person seated at the long table. Their kind eyes regarded her, and each gave a slight nod.

Family.

She liked that thought because it was the security she lacked in her life.

"The reason I wanted to talk to you and Brady before you took the ferry across the bay was that Isaac, our contact on the inside of Nocturnal Trinity, relayed some information to me early this morning that will be beneficial to us."

"He found the door to the vampire VIP lounge?" Brady asked.

"No. Something else, which gives us even more cause for concern. I do believe it has to do with the succubus Kailey's brother married."

"What?" Kailey asked.

"Beneath the dance floors, there is another room."

Kailey nodded. "We know that. The succubus took Raven through the door into—"

"No. A floor beneath wherever that hallway is."

"Oh," Kailey glanced toward Brady with uncertainty.

Micah said, "The lower floor might be where the succubus took Raven."

"Why do you think that?" Brady asked.

"On the floor is a magic summoning circle," Micah said, "which is identical to the symbol above their outside door. That's probably where they summoned Cassie. That's how she came to our realm from the abyss. The succubus is so powerful that it takes all eighteen of the council to keep her bound to them."

Damn.

She wondered how she had survived Cassie's attack.

"Isaac actually saw the circle?" Brady asked.

Micah nodded and slid his phone across to Brady. The image on the phone sent shivers down Kailey's spine. The slab of rock that the design was carved into appeared to have layers of bloodstains.

"Is this the circle where your wife was killed?" Kailey asked.

The pupils in Micah's eyes widened, making his eyes nearly black. The others seated around the table clenched their hands into fists. She scooted closer to Brady, and Brady's hand tightened around hers. The question had aroused Micah's thirst for revenge. The other pack members sensed his kill instinct and responded in kind.

After a few seconds, Micah shook his head, pulling his rage back into check. "Yes, but I didn't know where it was exactly."

"They compelled you to forget its location?" she asked.

Micah nodded. "But now that we know and the pack is free of the restraining spell, we are going there ... tonight."

A loud crackle from the kitchen caught their attention. The woman cooking the bacon was rubbing her arm, and wincing. Bacon grease.

The smell of the cooking food drifted from the kitchen into the dining room. Kailey's stomach growled. Although not a fan of bacon, she was hungry. Another scent caught her attention. Fish. Had they caught salmon? She glanced toward the kitchen.

Ashley stood at the stove but was looking over her shoulder with a pining expression. Kailey felt sorry for her, but she understood why Micah wished to keep romance at a distance. Until last night, she had agreed with him, but now she was thankful that she had become intimate with Brady. In ways she couldn't understand, she felt stronger. Having someone she could share her interests, disappointments, and dreams with was something she never really had before. With the help of a partner to offer needful advice and support during the worst times kept a person from rushing headfirst into a horrible disaster.

Kailey looked at Brady and then back to Micah. "We need to find Jaclyn and find out what it is that my brother had or knew first."

Micah folded his hands together. In a solemn tone, he said, "That's probably the only way that we will be able to find where they are holding Raven. At least we can have some leverage. But even without what he had, we will go after them."

"It may be too late for Raven though," Kailey replied.

"What do you mean?"

She stood long enough to fish the pendant and chain out of her pocket. When she sat back down, she placed the pendant on the table near Micah's hand.

Micah lifted the pendant by the chain. "When did this happen?"

"While I was showering."

"On its own?"

Kailey halfway rolled her eyes, but quickly stopped herself, thinking of Raven. She pointed a firm finger. "Like I have the means to do *that*. I don't know magic. I certainly didn't set it on fire."

Micah frowned at her angry sarcasm but didn't address it by chiding her in front of the others. "What do you make of this then?"

"I think Flora turned Raven into a vampire."

Micah lowered the pendant and let the chain encircle it on the tabletop. "She gave you her word that she wouldn't, didn't she?"

"Do you trust her to keep their word?" Kailey asked, crossing her arms. An unnecessary question she knew she didn't have to ask, but only did because he seemed to be acting somewhat hypocritical in his views about the vampires.

Micah shook his head. "No. I don't. I know firsthand that you cannot trust them. But this pendant—"

"*That*," Kailey said, "was what Raven blessed to protect me. It had saved my life once when Cassie turned into her demon form and attacked me. Now, it's cold. Useless."

"I sense that the magic's gone," Micah said in a soothing tone. "What more makes you believe that she's a vampire?"

Brady cleared his throat. "She had a nightmare about Raven being a vampire."

"Are you prone to psychic phenomena?" Micah asked with his eyes focused upon Kailey. He asked in a serious tone and wasn't mocking her.

"No."

Micah studied her eyes for several long moments, but Kailey never looked away. "Then why do you believe this with so much urgency?"

"Because I heard her crying my name out just seconds before this pendant became so cold that I had to yank it off."

"Cold?"

Kailey nodded.

"And yet, it looks burnt."

"I know," Kailey said, shrugging. "But that's what happened. I swear."

"I'm not doubting your account. It's just odd to have such opposing forces working against one another through an object."

"What do you mean?" Brady asked.

"Well, the magic Raven had used was to protect Kailey, which it apparently did a second time."

Kailey frowned. "I don't understand."

Brady grinned. "So you think one of the witch elders of Nocturnal Trinity destroyed Raven's spell?"

Micah shook his head. "I'm not saying that is necessarily the truth, either. But something was trying to burn through the pendant. Maybe the succubus? Instead of the metal searing into your flesh, Kailey, the magic absorbed the heat by over-chilling it."

"Which still burned like hell," she replied.

"I imagine so," Micah said. "The magic spells cancelled one another, but unfortunately the opposing magic destroyed your protective amulet. I suppose you could compare it to a fuse shorting out."

"If it is the demon trying to attack me, what do you make of that?" Kailey asked.

"She's under the control of the Circle of Unity. If she's the one that set the attack, it merely means now she has unarmed you of one weapon that kept her at a distance. Now, she has no reason to avoid coming into close contact with you."

Kailey closed her eyes. Brady grabbed her hand under the table and intertwined his fingers with hers. She fought tears of frustration. "Okay. What do we need to do to find this Jaclyn?"

Brady shook his head. "You come with me to police headquarters. I will get in touch with Richard and see what he knows. We can ask other officers that frequent there, too."

"I have a suggestion," Micah said.

"What's that?"

"Kailey, besides Flora, who else gave you problems the first night you were there?"

"Eva and Jinn were the two others I talked to, but neither really harassed me. Jinn even scolded Flora for carrying their *joke* too far."

Micah nodded. "Eva was the witch. Jinn, the demon?"

"Yes."

"Brady, after we eat breakfast, you take Kailey to the police station. Several of the others will accompany me to the magic shop, so I can catch Skye up on our situation and see what she might have discovered overnight."

"What do you have in mind?" Brady asked.

"I will get back in touch with Isaac and ask him what he knows about the witch and demon. Should he know something, I will immediately contact you."

"Okay. Good."

Micah smiled. "I want the two of you to stay far away from the rest of us on the ferry. Just in case Nocturnal Trinity has spies on the ferry, we don't need to let them know you're associated with me in any way. In fact all of the pack needs to board the ferry as far apart from one another as possible."

"You believe it's that serious?" Kailey asked.

"A lot of people have died because of what your brother possessed, so yes, they will be watching for us. Maybe not on the ferry, but let's not take that chance."

Brady nodded.

Micah sighed. "Besides, the vampires won't be a threat toward us until after nightfall. That's when we need to have everything in place. Find what your brother hid. It might be all the hope we have to save Raven."

If she can be saved ...

CHAPTER 37

The ferry crossed the bay. She stood looking over the upper railing at the smaller fishing boats setting sail. Her hands gripped the rail. A fishy smell drifted with the wind. Fewer clouds were in the sky this morning, and she wanted to mock nature for *finally* giving her a glimpse of the sun but the sunrise was still a half hour or more away.

Brady slipped up behind her and put his arms around her waist, setting his hands carefully atop hers. She gasped like a silly schoolgirl at his unexpected advance. Her face reddened when she felt him hardened against her backside.

"Does it *ever* rest?" she said, teasing and glancing up over her shoulder.

"Not if I had my choice. However, that wasn't my intention."

"So like all other men, yours does have a mind of its own, too?"

"At the moment, yes. I really don't need that distraction, but I thought if we were cozy with one another, it would give us a more subtle way of keeping an eye out for anyone that might be watching us. We're the ones they will be looking for more than Micah and the others."

"Since we were at the nightclub last night?"

Brady nodded. "Yes, they want what your brother has hidden, so if Flora could have one of her loyal mind controlled zealots intercept it, she doesn't have to honor her word."

"If she hasn't already broken it."

"You're insistent that she has already turned Raven."

"Because I'm certain she has."

Brady leaned his cheek against her, both of them faced the water, and he whispered, "I hope that eventually you have more optimism than you presently do." He kissed her cheek lightly and started to pull away.

Kailey tightened her hands around his forearms and kept him from slipping out of his embrace. She winced, realizing her bruised knuckles were tender and swollen. "Brady, too many bad things have already happened in my short life. Raven has been my friend for four years. She's been too obsessive with her love for me, but what happened this morning with the pendant was nothing less than her warning me—"

"That she had been turned?"

Kailey nodded.

"So if Raven is now a vampire, we don't need to return to Nocturnal Trinity, whether we find what the key goes to or not."

Kailey shook her head. Her voice became colder than the morning breeze. "No, if Raven is now a vampire, I have even more reason to return."

"Why?"

"For the same reason Micah does."

"Revenge?"

"Oh, hell yeah."

"You realize the danger you're setting yourself up for?" he asked.

"I do, but I don't care. My brother is dead, and if Raven is a vampire, I might as well consider her dead, too."

"You keep reminding everyone that you don't have any special abilities like magic. How do you plan to defend yourself? I will be happy to fight by your side because your losses are now mine, but even the whole pack cannot necessarily keep you alive."

"I don't expect them to."

"I want you safe."

Kailey smiled and glanced back at him. She eased her grip on his arms and turned to face him, still in his embrace. "I can defend myself."

"I know you have trained for physical combat, but this is something far more difficult. Vampires have superior strength that you've never encountered before."

"I'm not so certain about that. Cassie nearly killed me."

"Vampires can move faster than your eyes can follow, Kailey. I'm not trying to frighten you, and I know you're stubborn enough not to back down even if you were afraid. But, understand, Flora can cross a room in an instant and snap your neck before you blink once."

Kailey swallowed hard. She nodded. Flora had moved like that at Nocturnal Trinity. Chill bumps rose on her arms. Each time that Flora had whispered into her ear or laughed had made Kailey wonder if Flora had actually been beside her and moved away before Kailey realized Flora had stood beside her.

No. Flora possessed the ability to enter minds. Kailey knew the ugliness of the vampire's mental violation, the strange loss of time, and the skin-crawling fear of wondering exactly what had happened. Not remembering what transpired during the absence was the worst aspect of the ordeal.

"I know how dangerous she is," Kailey said.

"She's yet to show you how powerful she is."

Brady's cell phone rang. He slipped it from his back pocket and looked at the screen. "It's Micah."

Kailey slipped from his embrace and scanned the seated passengers on the upper deck.

"You're sure?" Brady said into the phone. "Thanks."

After he disconnected the call, she asked, "Is something wrong?"

"We have a couple of people who are watching us." Brady remained facing the water.

"Where?" Kailey causally rescanned the seats.

"Micah said that they are seated near the stairs by the vending machines. We have no choice but to walk past them."

Kailey looked at two pale individuals seated right where Micah had indicated they were. Both wore tan trench coats. Their faces were thin and tinted slightly blue. They resembled the emaciated Psi-vamps. The evil glint in their eyes was disturbing.

"How are they in the sunlight?" Kailey asked.

Still not looking around, he said, "You think they are vampires?"

"Yes."

Brady causally turned, took her hand, and walked toward a table where they could sit and see the two men without making obvious glances.

As they sat, Brady said, "Yep. You're right. They are."

"How?"

"The sunlight?"

She nodded.

"Not sure. Diana was burned the instant sunlight touched her skin."

"Can you answer something for me?" Kailey asked.

"Depends upon the question."

"Why did you spare Diana when you know she is a threat to any person she comes into contact with?"

Brady looked away. Remorse took control of his facial expressions. "Could you kill Raven if she has been turned into a vampire like you suspect she has?"

Kailey took a sharp breath. Fair question. She struggled for an answer.

Brady took her hand. "Not so easy to answer, is it?"

"No, it isn't."

"I know I should probably stake her but deep down I hope there's a way to reverse it. But not even the strongest witches I've solicited can find a spell that will ever make her human again."

"So there's no hope?" Kailey asked.

"None yet."

"But you still let her live trapped in a coffin? Do you think that is fair to her?"

Brady's jaw tightened, as did his hand. She winced.

"I'm sorry, Brady. This isn't the time to discuss that. Of course, no time is appropriate and that's your business. I shouldn't put my nose into it."

"You're fine. It is something I need to sort through, but after we take care of Flora and Raven."

"What do you suggest we do about those two watching us?" she asked.

"When we reach port, we see if they head down or wait for us to leave first. My guess is since we don't have whatever they are looking for, they will follow us to see where we're going."

"Unless they want the key."

Brady shrugged. "True, but why would they want to do all the dirty work of searching for what that key opens. Flora's smarter than that. She will use these two as spies until we find what she needs. Then they will make their attack."

As the ferry came closer to the port, two of the older pack members approached the vending machine. While they talked and pointed at different items in the machine, Kailey noticed that they were inadvertently keeping a close view on the two vampires.

The one pack member with long silvery hair leaned back against a table while his friend clicked a handful of coins into a snack machine. Both wore black leather jackets and with their long hair and thick beards, most passengers would never dare a glance into their eyes for fear they were gang members. She supposed that was a good thing because people questioned them less and possibly avoided them, fearing brutality.

The two vampires paid no attention to them or even acknowledged the werewolves were near them. The vamps' attention was more focused on Kailey.

"I thought vampires could smell werewolves," Kailey whispered.

"Are you saying we stink?" Brady asked with a wry grin.

Kailey huffed. "No. Pheromones. Sweat. At least that was the impression Micah had given me."

"No. He meant his magical power. After Jeannine was killed, they expect him to eventually return, which is why he doesn't want you to be seen with him. The less they know about your connection, the better off we'll be when we strike."

"I see."

"And it's good that Joseph and Taggart are where they are," Brady said.

"Why?"

"Because once we go down the stairs to get off the ferry, the vamps will follow us, and Joe and Tag will ... let's just say, will get them off our trail."

The ferry's horn sounded and a recording came over the loud speaker informing passengers to make certain they had all their belongings and for the drivers to get to their cars.

Walk-ons descended the stairwells and exited separately. Several were already making their way past the vending area and toward the stairs.

"Let's go while we have a group of people walking with us," Brady said, taking Kailey's hand. "Flora won't want witnesses and since she's not nearby, she has less chance of mind controlling the mob like she did last night."

Kailey glanced toward the two vampires as she and Brady walked past. Their eyes were narrow, full black with no white in them at all. Their translucence skin was pale blue. No fat was in their cheeks or necks. She didn't know how to discern the age of a vampire, but on appearance alone, these two men looked like breathing corpses. Of course, they *were*.

"Why don't other people notice that they look like dead people?" she asked.

Brady turned at the top of the next set of descending steps and smiled. "Because the majority of people are blind to their existence like you had been until just recently."

"But wouldn't they see their horrible complexions and realize they suffer from a disease or something? I mean, look at them. They look contagious," she said, walking alongside him down the steps.

"No. As vampires they have the ability to mask their physical flaws by glamouring. Most people who see those two will view ordinary people in perfect health. How else do you explain why anyone with rational thinking would ever allow himself to be attracted to a vile emaciated person? People tend to run from hideous creatures or avoid those will abnormal handicaps."

"Okay, so for clarity's sake, you're saying that vampires really look diseased and not as beautiful as Flora appeared to me?"

Brady nodded. "Once turned, a person's body remains the age they were physically. However, to maintain beauty and attractiveness, they mask their outward appearances from decay. Of course, feeding on humans greatly slows the withering of flesh, keeping their skin elastic and youthful. And as you've seen for yourself, Nocturnal Trinity has no shortage of naïve volunteers."

Kailey glanced over her shoulder. The two vampires were at the top of the stairs, following from a modest distance. "They are behind us."

Brady grinned. "Tag and Joe probably aren't too far behind them."

"I hope so."

He pulled open the left side of his jacket and showed her three smoothly polished stakes.

"At least you're prepared. What about me?"

"If we need them, I'll hand you one. But Taggart will be disappointed if he doesn't claim one for himself."

"What about ol' Joe?" Kailey pulled reddish-brown strands from her eyes as the wind funneled around them.

Brady smiled. "Joe might look much older than the rest of us, but he's actually faster than any of us, which is why you won't need a stake. Tonight, however, you're going to need weapons. I know you are good with your hands and feet, but how about knives?"

"I've thrown them at targets, but never at anything moving. We also use fake ones for defensive training in case we're ever attacked on the street."

Brady held the railing as they descended. "Unless you've practiced over-hand knife training, using a stake might prove awkward since you hold it opposite than how you would a knife. I can show you some basic move-ments later this evening when we meet with Micah and the pack."

"If this is your idea of a first date, I'll be keeping my options open." Kailey smiled and winked.

Brady shook his head and grinned.

Once they reached the bottom of the stairs, Brady gently took Kailey's hand and sped up his pace, hurrying around others standing in line to get to the parking lot where Kailey's rental car was parked.

"How are your hands?" he asked.

"Stiff and achy."

"If we have to fight?"

"Adrenaline tends to override pain. Honestly, I've sparred with worse. Broken ribs hurt like a bitch, but I've had to exercise and practice round-house kicks with them. You learn to shut out the pain."

"Okay."

Both he and Kailey glanced over their shoulders. The two vampires also hurried, but they weren't too panicked about catching up to Brady or Kailey. Otherwise, they'd be shoving people out of their way. They nonchalantly walked with the flow of pedestrians that headed toward the parking lot and the sidewalks.

"I don't see Taggart or Joe," Kailey said.

"Me, either."

Kailey dug inside her purse for the keys to the car. Nearing the black rental car, she pushed the button on the key to unlock the doors. Lights flashed as the doors unlocked. She wondered where the two members of the pack were since Brady had believed they'd not be too far behind as backup.

The two trailing vampires headed straight toward them, not swiftly, but their attention remained directly upon Brady and Kailey. Kailey didn't say anything but she shook from the nervousness welling within her.

"Remember, they'd be foolish to attack us out in the open," Brady said.

"Why? Because Flora's nowhere near?"

Brady nodded.

"I don't feel anymore comfortable with that information. There's always the chance that they'd ignore her commands."

"Disintegrating vampires would draw far more attention than Nocturnal Trinity is willing to risk. This area is too congested with people. Oh, shit!"

Right as Kailey reached the passenger door, she noticed two women leaning against another vehicle parked near hers. Their eyes and complexions were identical to the two men behind them. They crossed their arms and then revealed their fangs.

"Trade you the car keys for one of those stakes," Kailey said in a low voice. She made a side-glance but kept the two female vamps in her peripheral vision.

"Let's hope we don't need them, but I'll gladly take the keys."

Kailey tossed him the keys. "How are they outside in the sunlight?"

Brady shook his head. "I don't know. The sun isn't visible yet. They really shouldn't be able to take direct light even during sunrise. Most readily flee into places heavily shadowed by now."

Before Kailey pulled the door handle to open it, growls came from behind them. She and Brady turned. Taggart and Joe rushed forward from the lines of exiting people. Their growls startled the two male vampires. A couple of women screamed and ran toward their cars. Others hurried toward the ferry from the parking lot.

When Kailey turned back toward the two female vampires, they had vanished. She scanned the parking lot, hoping to see what vehicle they might have retreated to, but they might have hurried and blended into the walking traffic on the sidewalks.

"Get in!" Brady yelled.

Kailey didn't hesitate. She got into the vehicle, locked her door, and strapped on her seatbelt. It didn't dawn on her until seconds afterwards that she had actually confined herself as an easy target should any vampire decide to rush against her door, smash her window, and attack her. It was nearly impossible to defend oneself while being strapped to a seat.

"We need to get my patrol car," Brady said, starting the car and backing up. "I can have someone drop this off for you at the rental place."

"Okay," she said, placing her hands against the dashboard to steady herself.

Brady sped past the two male vampires. Taggart and Joe had pinned the vamps against a car and their daggers pressed over their hearts. She watched from the side view mirror. The pack members pressed the tips of their daggers into the vamps' hearts. The vampires shriveled and crumpled to the pavement in dust.

Taggart and Joe turned, dusting off their hands and blue jeans, and then causally waved as Brady reached the end of the parking lot and turned onto the street.

CHAPTER 38

Taggart and Joe walked away from the car and headed back toward the ferry loading dock. Kailey guessed to meet up with Micah and the others.

In disbelief, she stared at Brady. "They turned those vamps to dust."

Brady shrugged.

"I thought you said that we didn't need to risk people seeing ... "

"Flora doesn't need that kind of attention, but from what I could tell, no one even noticed the confrontation, so we're okay. Besides, Taggart had a quota to meet."

"Micah gives quotas to the pack?"

"No," Brady said, shaking his head. "Taggart sets his own. He's often a lone wolf. Even before Micah granted us back our transformations, Taggart roamed the alleys late at night looking for any vampire strays that might have ventured out of Nocturnal Trinity hunting for blood meals."

"They do that?"

"Sometimes. Although the founding six vampires within Nocturnal Trinity are selective about whom they turn, often the blood orgies get out of hand and the younger vampires accidentally turn wannabes that leave the nightclub unattended."

"How could they not know that they've turned someone?" Kailey asked.

"From my understanding there's a point when young vampires drink too much blood and become somewhat intoxicated with euphoria. They get giddy or pass out. When that happens, victims believed to have been drained awaken and wander outside. It's rare, but it does happen."

Kailey's cellphone buzzed. She looked and didn't recognize the number but it had a Seattle area code, so she answered. "Yes?"

"Kailey? It's Flora."

Kailey took a sharp breath. His chest tightened. She almost asked how Flora got the number, but she realized Flora had taken her phone at Nocturnal Trinity.

"What?" Kailey replied.

"Do you have what I requested?"

"No, and our twenty-four hours *isn't* up."

Brady glanced at Kailey with concern. He mouthed, "Flora?"

She nodded.

Flora said, "Maybe not, but time is precious and fleets so rapidly ... for some of us. I wanted to *encourage* you to be diligent and remember what's at stake."

Kailey's jaw tensed. "Speaking of *stakes*—"

"Careful, dear. Threats are never a good way to conduct business."

"Business? Don't you mean blackmail and ransom?"

"That's a bit harsh. I'd rather think of it as unyielding motivation."

Kailey seethed, "You've already turned Raven into a vampire you sick twisted bitch ..."

"There, there. You again with such a vicious attitude, making hasty accusations without the slightest bit of proof. No trust comes from this younger generation."

Flora's condescending tone angered Kailey even more. She fumed. "Why should I trust you? You took Raven, and you're protecting a demon that killed my brother. I have no reason to believe you. Let me talk to Raven."

"What good would that do?"

"It would give me some peace of mind."

"Would it, now?"

Brady shook his head. He whispered, "Hang up."

Kailey frowned at him and replied to Flora, "Yes, it would."

Flora cackled a high-pitched whinny laugh, which seemed far more theatrical than genuine. "No, it wouldn't. You'd simply accuse me of using mind control to get her to tell you what you'd like to hear, so it's a no win situation. You have to trust me."

"You've turned her into a vampire. I sense it."

"You're a psychic now?"

"No." Kailey formed a tight fist in spite of the pain it caused her.

"You have my word that I haven't turned her. Again, I only called to let you know that time is fading. Punctuality is key."

"I have a clock, so I don't *need* ..."

Flora disconnected the call.

Kailey trembled inside, partly due to anger, and partly due to how helpless she felt in rescuing Raven. Regardless of what Flora had told her, Kailey still believed Raven was a vampire. She had almost told her that they had killed her two vampire spies, but that would have given away too much information. The last thing she needed was for Flora to be on the alert for an upcoming attack, which Kailey was actually beginning to look forward to.

She figured it was okay to let Flora know that she was pissed because that's how most people would react. Showing backbone instead of pleading and begging might not have been the best approach, but Flora had read her mind before, so the vampire knew what to expect from Kailey.

Brady reached his hand toward her balled fist. Blood leaked around the edges of the bandages. Pain radiated from her knuckles and past her wrist. He gently offered his hand. She held his fingers slightly while fighting tears.

After a few minutes of silence, Brady parked the car outside the police station. They headed up the steps and entered through the glass door. Once he reached his office, he sat at his desk and awakened his computer. He rolled another chair up beside him and motioned for Kailey to have a seat.

"We really don't have a lot to go on," Brady said.

"I know."

"It'd be a miracle if we figure out who Jaclyn is."

He picked up his phone and dialed an extension number. "Wanda, I need you to do me a favor, okay? Please contact the coroner and have her fax me a report of Vincent Yates autopsy? Thanks."

"What?" Kailey asked, feeling herself pale.

"You asked for a copy. Don't you want to know?"

She nodded. She did and she didn't. Reading it, whether it was genuine or faked, seemed so final.

"Did they give you a card for the car rental place? I want to call them so they will know to pick up the car here."

Kailey grabbed her wallet from the purse and slid the business card from its holder. She handed him the card and waited while he gave the clerk details about where to pick up the car.

The fax machine emitted strange sounds. A few seconds later, it printed out a couple of forms. Kailey's heart raced. The palms of her hands moistened with sweat.

After Brady hung up the phone, he leaned back and grabbed the autopsy paper, and handed it to her.

"That was fast," she said.

"Wanda's pretty quick at getting results."

Kailey scanned the autopsy report. "Anemic. Cause of death: Drowned. Syringe mark in left arm where syringe was removed. No drugs in his system?"

"The syringe was probably inserted after he died. My guess is someone drown him after they didn't get the key or information that would produce the key."

Kailey's jaw tightened. She folded the paper and tucked it into her purse.

When her saddened eyes met his, he said, "I'm sorry, Kailey."

"I told you he was murdered," she said. "He wasn't a drug user either."

He leaned toward her and she fell into his arms. She pressed her face against his chest, and he squeezed her tightly. "You did. You were right about him."

"We have to find Jaclyn," Kailey said.

"I know. I have a database, but we haven't a last name, fingerprints, address or anything. Like I said, that's not much to go on."

"Then we have nothing except the key."

"Which looks like a security deposit box key."

"I don't know which bank he used," Kailey said.

"That probably wouldn't matter anyway."

"Why?"

Brady smiled. "Your brother was smart. He wouldn't have used his own bank because Cassie would check there first."

"True. But he hid the key and for some reason she knew he had it."

"We need a locksmith. Although they will probably only be able to tell us what we already know. Nothing on the key indicates which branch of bank or credit union that might house the box it unlocks."

"Shit. Who'd think this would be so frustrating."

"And people wonder why police are high strung."

"What do we do?" she asked.

"Let's go get my patrol car. We can get some coffee and brainstorm."

"Don't you have coffee here?"

Brady cringed. "Phht. That's what they call it, but they cannot prove that's what it is. Besides, Seattle is the coffee capital of the world, or haven't you heard?"

"That's really true?"

"More coffee shops per capita than anywhere else. Come on."

Kailey grabbed her purse and cellphone. "What kind of coffee do you like?"

"Varies day to day."

"Like the weather?"

"No. Like whatever the special is."

Kailey rolled her eyes. "Seriously?"

Brady laughed and opened the door for her. "It's the cheapest way to try new flavors."

She grinned. "So never black."

He winced. "God, no."

For some reason that reply immediately made her think of Raven. *Goddess.* She wanted to smile and cry at the same time, but she knew it was necessary to remain strong. Even if her premonition that Raven had been turned, Kailey needed to remain strong.

Could I kill her if she has been turned?

Kailey took a deep breath and released it slowly as they headed down the back steps to the parking lot where Brady's patrol car was parked. She didn't want to dwell on that question. She was depressed enough.

"You okay?" he asked.

"Yeah, I'm fine. Lots of things for my mind to process."

"Am I one of those things?" He opened the front passenger door of the squad car.

Kailey stared into his warm eyes. She didn't flinch or look away. "No. I have no questions about you. Or us."

"That's good to know."

"Well, I have questions of things I want to know about you, but I don't question *us*."

He grinned. "So after all this blows over, some good ol' Q&A for both of us? I have access to a polygraph, too, you know?"

"This isn't truth or dare," she replied. "I'm talking about things like your childhood, school, etc."

He kept the broad smile and shook his head.

His smile made her want to kiss him. After last night, she didn't question what burned between them. It definitely answered what she needed to tell Raven, provided Raven was still human.

Kailey sat in the front seat. He shut the door and hurried around to the other side. She stared at all of the computerized devices on the dashboard. The dash camera, radar, and two-way radio were an intimidating set of gadgets for an untrained eye. She marveled at the technology.

No sooner had Brady driven out of the parking lot than her phone rang. She picked it up, didn't recognize the number, but due to all the strange circumstances, she answered.

"It's Burt from the cemetery."

"Hi, Burt."

"You asked me that if anyone was at your brother's grave to call, right?"

Kailey swallowed hard. "Yes. Why?"

"There's someone at it right now."

"Another group?"

Burt cleared his throat. "No. Just one person."

"Thanks."

"You want me to run the person off?"

"No. I'm with an officer now. We're on our way." She disconnected the call.

"What wrong?" Brady asked.

"Someone is at Vincent's grave."

He faced her and an odd smile crossed his lips. "So you want lights on to investigate?"

"If that gets us there any faster."

"Usually, it does. Want to do the honors?"

Kailey shrugged.

"That button there. Flip it."

She did. Brady sped up and the drivers ahead of them pulled aside. She was happy to have a quick escort to the cemetery, but she wondered exactly what they were about to come face to face with.

CHAPTER 39

Brady turned off the red and blue lights about a half block from the cemetery. Instead of making a full circle around the cemetery, he drove in through the exit road, which allowed him to reach the grave quicker. Within a minute he parked near Vincent's grave.

A small slender figure stood at the graveside wearing a black robe and hood. Kailey guessed by the stature, *this* visitor was a woman.

Before Brady put the car into park, Kailey was out the passenger side door crossing the narrow blacktop, marching toward the grave. She thought Brady had said something to her right before she shut the car door, but she was tired of people snooping around her brother's grave. The more she thought about Nocturnal Trinity and the harassment they had thrust her direction after the murder of her brother, the angrier she became. If she and Micah's pack didn't act soon to destroy the Circle of Unity, she feared the amount of carnage that would be unleashed on the unsuspecting guests that visited the nightclub. The possibility existed that they might try to increase their numbers greatly to form a small defensive army.

Although the sun was out, the cold biting air reminded her that it was winter, but the temperature didn't deter Kailey. The brisk wind swirled through the surrounding trees, making Kailey shiver but her boiling anger pressed her to confront this person.

"Who are you?" Kailey asked. She crossed her arms and narrowed her gaze but she was ready to attack in a moment's notice if necessary.

The woman turned sharply, audibly gasping. Startled, she pulled the front of the robe tighter. Sadness and brief fear claimed her facial expressions. She didn't appear to be a threat of any sort. Of course Kailey had learned over the past couple of days that looks often didn't reveal how dangerous someone could be. Cassie was a prime example. To the unsuspecting eye, the succubus lured men in by her seductive beauty, only to later go for the kill. Something Kailey wished Vincent had known well ahead of his demise.

"Why are you here?" Kailey asked. Brady eased up beside Kailey with his hand resting on his gun in its holster.

The nervous woman looked from Kailey to Brady's gun. She wiped tears from her eyes. "I'm Jaclyn. I came to pay my respects to Vincent. He's dead because of me." Guilt hung in her tone and curved her lips.

Kailey was stunned and glanced at Brady. "Jaclyn?"

"Yes," she replied, nodding nervously.

"I'm Kailey, Vincent's sister, and this is Officer Brady. We were trying to find out who you were," Kailey said.

"Why?" Her nervous gaze narrowed with concern.

"Because of this." Kailey took the key from her purse.

Jaclyn looked relieved. "Oh, thank goodness you have it."

"Why? Do you know what it unlocks?"

Jaclyn lowered the hood. Her black hair was graying near her scalp, but her smooth face was edged with few wrinkles. Stress tugged slightly beneath her eyes. And although tearful, her dark eyes hinted of mystical power, strength, and determination. "I know exactly what it unlocks."

"What?" Kailey asked.

"A safety deposit box."

"Where?" Brady asked.

"At JHT Credit Union," she replied.

"Why is this key so important that they'd kill my brother for it?"

"I will be glad to explain that to you, but it's best that we leave quickly," Jaclyn replied.

Kailey frowned. "Why?"

Jaclyn nodded toward the entrance of the cemetery. The silver limo Kailey had seen at her brother's estate and outside Nocturnal Trinity was headed around the center blacktop.

The vampires had arrived in broad daylight?

"They know you're here?" Kailey asked.

"Not yet, but they will if you don't get me out of here."

"You didn't drive?" Brady asked.

Jaclyn shook her head.

"Hurry, get in the back of my patrol car. We'll get you out of here."

Jaclyn followed Kailey and Brady to the car. Due to her high heel platform boots and the soggy ground, walking quickly was difficult and clumsy. Kailey guessed Jaclyn stood right at five foot tall, possibly a few inches under, without the boots. Kailey considered herself short, but she'd never sacrifice balance to *look* taller.

Brady opened the rear driver side door for her. "How'd you get here?"

"Cab."

"Why are they here?" Kailey asked, nodding toward the limo.

"I'm not certain. Perhaps they are planning to perform some sort of ritual to see if they can get an answer to where the key is," Jaclyn replied.

"Oh, shit!" Kailey said.

"What is it?" Brady asked, putting the car into reverse and gunning backwards to a narrow concrete slab where he could turn the car around without damaging or sinking into the grass.

"I totally forgot all about this picture. I had meant to show it to Skye."

"What picture?" Brady asked.

Kailey pulled out her cellphone, brought up her photos, and flipped through her pictures. About a minute later, after Brady had reached the blacktop, Kailey found the picture of the footprints around her brother's fresh grave. She turned in the seat and showed the picture through the protective glass. "This! The groundskeeper told me that he had run off a group of people there the other day. Micah told me that he thought whoever had left these footprints were probably trying to do some type of summoning ritual. Do you think they were trying to do that?"

"Yes. They were probably trying to summon his spirit to get information."

"So people can really do that?"

Jaclyn smiled. "They can try. It's doubtful he'd willingly give them any answers even if they were able to summon him."

Brady typed in a GPS search for the credit union address.

Kailey looked at Jaclyn. "My brother had never mentioned you to me, but I noticed that he had your first name circled on his desk calendar with the initials N.T. I assume that stands for Nocturnal Trinity?"

Jaclyn nodded.

"Why would he meet you there?"

"We didn't meet at Nocturnal Trinity. He met with me because I had information he needed about his wife Cassie and her ties *with* Nocturnal Trinity, more importantly, to the Circle of Unity. He didn't look well though. She's a—"

"A succubus," Kailey said, finishing Jaclyn's sentence.

"You know?"

Kailey nodded. "Yes. My college roommate's a witch and she's the one that first drew that conclusion. She thought that his aura and his blood were being drained."

"I think so, too."

"Are you saying that my brother knew that she was a succubus?"

Jaclyn shook her head. "Not when he first married her, but once he discovered the truth about her, he didn't live too much longer afterwards. She had been draining his blood and energy for weeks."

"She wasn't the only culprit," Kailey said.

"I know. She is controlled by those who run Nocturnal Trinity."

"So what did they want from him?"

"I gave him a Grimoire that could release him from Cassie's control, and once he destroyed her craving for his blood, we could have worked together to break the unity of power inside that nightclub."

Kailey frowned. "How do you know so much about them?"

"Eva's my mother."

"*What?*"

Brady looked into the mirror. A deep inquisitive frown formed on his face as he stared at Jaclyn. His eyes turned darker brown with a hazel glow.

Uneasily, Jaclyn waved her hands and shook her head. "Before you both get all defensive or worried, I'm *not* in allegiance with her or any of them. And although I'm the daughter of a witch from an ancient lineage of witches, my path is far different from hers, which is why I wanted out of the cemetery with you when they arrived. Those vampires and demons want me dead, too."

"Why would they want you dead?" Kailey asked.

"Because of the deathblow the Grimoire can deal to the Founders of Nocturnal Trinity. And because I practice a much darker magic than they do."

"So if your intention is to bring down the nightclub leaders, why haven't you done so?"

"I have powerful magic, Kailey, but I'm not foolish enough to think I can go against seventeen ancient beings with the types of incredible strengths they possess individually. It was never my intention for Vincent to use the

Grimoire to attack Nocturnal Trinity. I only gave it to him so he could research how to block Cassie's power from draining him."

"But my brother didn't practice magic. So giving the book to him only placed his life into danger."

Jaclyn shook her head. "No, he didn't practice magic, but he needed to read through the book. The knowledge was beneficial to him because it detailed for him the symptoms of what he was experiencing. Most people don't willingly accept what sounds ridiculous."

"I suppose so."

"Also, he needed the information since the majority of the Circle of Unity had been trying to find me to get the Grimoire and kill me for taking it. Had they found me and taken back the book, he was even more defenseless."

Kailey studied Jaclyn's eyes closely, looking for any brief moment of deception, but Jaclyn never broke eye contact. She seemed to be on the up and up. "He died anyway, even with the information."

Tears welled in Jaclyn's eyes. "I know. I feel so horrible about it. I told him that if he'd allow me, I could work a spell from the book, but he wanted to read about the possible consequences Cassie would suffer if I did. He really loved and held affection for her."

"She had him spellbound," Kailey said sternly and coldly.

"At first, I thought the same thing."

"You don't think that she did?"

Jaclyn sighed. "Although most victims can fall under that kind of control, it wasn't the case between him and Cassie. He really loved her."

"How can you be so certain she didn't have him mesmerized by her power or charm?" Kailey asked.

"With his permission, I cast a detection spell to see whether she controlled him by a lustful spell or not. She hadn't used one, which is unusual. I think she loved him, too."

"Really?" Brady asked.

Jaclyn nodded.

"I can't believe that," Kailey said, shaking her head. "I'm sorry."

"Your loss is still fresh and raw."

"If she loved him, why did Cassie keep feeding upon him?" Kailey asked. "If their bond was truly based on love, why did she drain him to the point that he became anemic? I read his autopsy report. Those results ..."

With a sad expression, Jaclyn replied, "I don't know why she went to that extreme, Kailey. That's why I offered to let him borrow the book, provided he kept it in a safe place where Cassie never found it, and hopefully he'd be able to find a way to thwart her feedings on him. He told me where he'd hide the book, but before I ever had another chance to talk to him again in person, he was dead. Somehow they found out that he had the book."

"Why would they kill him without having the key or knowing where he had hidden the book?" she asked.

"Perhaps she accidentally killed him?"

"I suppose." Kailey sighed. "Flora mentioned that there's a rift within the Circle of Unity, and she seemed somewhat miffed at your mother."

Jaclyn nodded. "I'm certain they blame her since originally the book belonged to my mother."

"You stole it from her?"

"I'm rather fond of the word, *borrowed*."

Kailey smiled. "I'm certain your mother or the other members of Nocturnal Trinity don't view it that way."

"Not at all, but really, I don't care. What those vampires and demons have done to innocent souls over the centuries is damning. They need the witches' magic to boost their power so they can perform most of their evil deeds. Without their link to witches' magic, the unity would dissolve. My mother and several of the other witches tried to break free of them years ago, but Nicodemus and the demons refused to let the witches leave the pact."

Kailey frowned. "So basically they were bound by blood to the circle no matter what?"

"Yes. Blood and magic."

"With their magic, why would the witches fear leaving? They could fight the others, couldn't they?"

Jaclyn's voice dropped to a near whisper. "You'd be surprised what demons are capable of doing when they are provoked. They threatened to possess any witch that left the Circle of Unity."

"How did you escape from Nocturnal Trinity?" Kailey asked.

"I am not a part of their circle. Since I'm a Voodoo priestess, the demons fear being near me because I can do them great harm, much worse than sending them to the abyss, and they know it. That's a reason why the vampires fear me and want me dead."

Kailey frowned. "Why do the vampires fear you?"

"Because I'm a necromancer. I can raise the dead. And if they had caught me at your brother's grave, they might have tried to force me to raise him. I wouldn't have, of course, but things would have gotten … bloody."

Chill bumps rose on Kailey's arms.

Jaclyn continued, "There's something about that level of magic that frightens most demons. I don't understand the reason why, but my ability was enough for Jinn and the other demons to convince the Circle of Unity to ban me from the nightclub. However, the other five witches with my mother within that circle take the demons' threat of possession quite seriously. But a lot of this is misconception by the witches and people in general. They have the churches to thank for that."

"What do you mean?"

"Demons cannot actually possess a person. They are physical beings. But demons have control over a host of evil spirits, which they can use to possess someone else."

Kailey frowned. "All of the demons do?"

"Not all. It depends upon their level of power. Like with vampires, there is a hierarchy within the legions of demons. The most powerful ones inside Nocturnal Trinity are never seen by mortals or most of the nightclub's council."

"Why not?"

"They aren't social beings. They're there, but trust me, should they ever make their presence known, it's Hell on Earth, if you'll pardon the pun."

"What about Jinn? I've seen him a couple of times."

Jaclyn laughed softly and shook her head. "Jinn? He's a player. A front man, so to speak. He's *not* one of the six in the circle. He represents them, but that's essentially it."

"So a demon cannot possess us, but they can use evil spirits to possess others?"

"Yes."

Kailey frowned, taking in the information. "The witches fear the demons using these spirits to possess them?"

"Of course. No witch would ever want a demon totally controlling her and her magic. Magic released can never be recalled, and neither can spells used for evil. For any witch that does harm to another person, the punishment is threefold."

"Even if a demon cast the spell through the witch?" Kailey asked.

Jaclyn nodded. "Yes. That's why my mother and the others refused to leave. They didn't want to risk such repercussions."

"But wouldn't their aid in helping boost the demons' power contribute to the demons casting spells in their name?" Brady asked.

"For some reason it doesn't."

"So the witches are basically being held hostage and that is what has caused the rift?"

"It's the major reason for the division. Resentment has grown, but not enough yet to break the ties that hold them together. The vampires need to be brought down, or at the very least that unity needs to be broken. Once they are weakened, their power lessens a hundred fold or better. But alone, there's little I can do."

"Do you think the witches would side with an outside source that seeks to break the unity?" Brady asked.

Jaclyn thought for a few moments. "There's a strong possibility that they would, or at least my mother and two of the witches might."

"Wouldn't that be enough?" Kailey asked.

"Perhaps. But there's no real guarantee."

"There are a lot of others plotting to destroy the circle and stop Nicodemus," Brady said.

"Really?" Jaclyn asked.

Brady and Kailey nodded.

Kailey said, "You see, they took my friend Raven hostage last night and are holding her in exchange for the key. But I'm afraid that it might be too late for us to save her."

"Why?" Jaclyn asked.

"She enchanted a pendant for me, and ..." Kailey took the pendant and showed Jaclyn. "It no longer has her magic upon it. I dreamt she was turned into a vampire. But right before this pendant was charred, I heard her voice crying for help."

"In your nightmare?"

"No. I heard her while I was awake and showering."

"That is concerning," Jaclyn said.

Brady pulled the squad car into the credit union parking lot, turned off the engine, and looked at Jaclyn in the mirror. "We're here."

Brady got out of the car and opened the back door for Jaclyn.

As she stepped out of the car, she said, "Other than you being an officer, there's another reason why all this interests you, isn't there? I sense something different about you."

Brady smiled and shrugged. "We all tend to have our little secrets."

"Ah, mystery," Jaclyn said with a playful smile. She squeezed his arm. "What does it take for me to know *those* secrets?"

Kailey felt her stomach turn with uneasiness. She had never suffered from jealousy before, but suddenly found herself confronted with a new enemy rising within her.

Brady shook his head. "If this ... *Grimoire*, as you call it, proves to be a useful tool, you'll learn far more than what you expected today."

Jaclyn smiled. "There's something more I've not told you about this book that you'll find quite useful."

"What's that?" he asked.

"My mother kept a detailed journal of the debaucheries the circle has committed for decades. Damning evidence, and all the more reason why the Circle of Unity needs to be ripped asunder."

CHAPTER 40

A few minutes after Kailey, Jaclyn, and Brady stepped to the teller counter with the key, Cassie stepped through the door behind them.

"I believe you have something that belongs to me," Cassie said coldly. "It would be best that you hand it over before things get nasty."

Kailey and Brady turned. An arrogant smile widened on Cassie's face. Death couldn't wear a smile any more beautiful than hers. She winked at Kailey, which sent chills down Kailey's back.

Kailey's hands formed fists without her even thinking about it.

Jaclyn whispered to Kailey, "That's Cassie?"

"Need you ask?" Kailey replied with a slight nod.

Cassie wore a tight black dress with black heels. Her complexion was much darker than when Kailey had seen Cassie at the cemetery. Her makeup and elegantly styled hair were perfect, giving her a regal professional look. Her posture commanded attention. Her eyes sparkled with a strange captivating radiance. Nothing about her hinted she possessed any flaws.

Parked long-ways in the parking lot was the silver limo.

Kailey took a deep breath. Her heartbeat hammered. She whispered, "They followed us."

"So it seems," Brady replied. His hand instinctively rested on the butt of his 9mm. He didn't show any fear of her, despite her being a succubus. Did he know something she didn't or were all werewolves arrogant when it came to fighting or threats?

Kailey noticed Cassie glance toward Brady's gun and tilt her nose upward, almost as if she dared him to use it. Kailey wondered what might happen if he did shoot Cassie. Could a bullet kill her?

Ignoring Brady, Cassie extended her hand, palm upward. "The key, please."

Kailey shook her head. "No. The key is mine."

The husky teller with long hair frowned as she stared back and forth at each of them. She appeared quite uncomfortable. "Is there a problem?"

Kailey faced the receptionist, leaned closer to the young lady, and whispered, "I need to open my box. 612, please."

"She has *my* key!" Cassie said, intentionally making a scene and drawing the attention of the other tellers and customers.

Brady's fingers unsnapped the strap on the outside of his gun, but he didn't draw the weapon.

The teller looked at the key in Kailey's open palm. "This is your box?"

"It was my brother's," Kailey replied.

"Who was my husband," Cassie said, pushing her way toward the counter, but Brady stepped between Cassie and Kailey, stopping her from getting any closer.

Kailey scooped up the key and held it inside her tightened fist.

The teller, whose nametag identified her as Sharon, looked from Kailey toward Cassie. "Ma'am, do you have a copy of the will that states you have the right to the key and the contents of the box?"

Cassie took a frustrated, deep breath. "No. The will states no such thing."

Sharon said, "Then I cannot help you. You will have to go through the probate office and get an order before I can allow you access to the box. Sorry."

Jaclyn stepped beside Kailey, still using Brady as a human shield, and looked at the teller. "Is there a name listed as the joint renter?"

"One second and let me check," Sharon said. She typed the box number into the computer. "Uh, yes. For a ... Kailey Yates."

Kailey faced Cassie with a mocking smile and winked. Cassie's jaw tightened. The sparkle in her eyes flickered like small red-orange flames, but apparently she reined her succubus self back in, turned and headed for the door with brisk steps. Her heels clicked her anger with each step she made.

"This isn't over," Cassie said, pushing open the door.

"It's over," Brady said, following her to the door with his hand on his gun.

She turned and ran her tongue across her lips. "You still fantasize over our kiss, don't you? Get me that key, and I promise you more pleasure than your heart can take."

His hand shook. "You'd best be going. *Now.*"

She grinned and made a purring sound before exiting through the door.

Brady stood there until she reached the limo and got inside. She paused long enough to catch his frown before the driver shut the door.

Without shouting from the glee rising inside her, Kailey released a sigh of relief, and shuddered inside. *One tiny victory, but this war is far from over.* "Can you show me where the box is?"

"You're Kailey?"

"Yes."

"Just as soon as you show me your identification, I can take you to the box."

Kailey slid her driver's license from her wallet.

Sharon gave a relieved smile. "Okay. Right this way."

Sharon led Kailey to the vault. Brady stood with Jaclyn in the lobby. When Kailey returned to them, she hugged the leather-bound Grimoire against her chest tightly. The last thing she wanted was for Cassie to pop up and yank the book away.

Kailey expected the limo to still be outside, but it wasn't. Although she was relieved, she expected the vampires and Cassie to be waiting somewhere nearby. She hoped Brady's approach had been a stern enough deterrent to keep them away.

"They left?" Kailey asked.

Brady nodded.

"I still don't understand why the vampires would risk coming out during the daylight hours," Kailey said, following Brady to the door.

"The windows have layers of mirrored tinting, which reflects ninety-nine percent of the sunlight," Jaclyn said. "But we don't really know that the vampires are inside the limo. Or *what* might be in the limo with Cassie."

"That's true," Brady said, pulling open the door. "Let's get back to the bay."

"The bay?" Jaclyn asked. "Why?"

"You'll see soon enough."

"Planning to reveal your secret?" Jaclyn said, picking up her pace to stand beside Brady.

Kailey stepped between them and handed the Grimoire to Jaclyn.

"Lots of them, but we need to pick Skye up first," Brady said, opening the passenger door for Kailey.

"Skye?"

Brady said, "Coven leader that came from Boston with Raven."

"Boston? What would bring them out here?"

"Me," Kailey replied.

Jaclyn frowned with confusion and shook her head. "And I thought that I had enough problems trying to figure out the Circle of Unity and how to help free my mother from Nocturnal Trinity."

"Believe it or not, it's all related. I came here for my brother's burial, found out about the nightclub and that I might find Cassie there, and the next thing I know, someone sent a demon to my apartment in Boston to attack Raven. She and Skye were on the next flight out."

Kailey's cellphone buzzed. She checked her messages. "It's Skye. She said that she'll meet us at the ferry dock."

"Why? Micah and the others are supposed to meet at the magic shop."

Kailey scrolled through a few more messages. "Apparently Micah and the majority of the pack went back across the bay. He wants us to all return there. She didn't say why."

Brady grinned. "He wouldn't tell her the reason."

Kailey texted a short message back to Skye.

"Hmm. I wonder if Skye discovered something to help us," Brady said. "If so, that might be the reason for the quick return to Micah's estate."

"Maybe that's why she's waiting for us there. So we can tell Micah quicker."

Brady shrugged. "Maybe."

"Micah? You keep mentioning his name. Who is he?" Jaclyn asked.

"He's the Alpha."

Brady gave Kailey a harsh side-glance.

"Sorry," she said, her face reddening.

"Alpha? Wait," Jaclyn looked from Kailey to Brady's gaze in the rearview mirror. Her eyebrows rose. "Werewolves?"

Brady sighed. "Guilty."

Jaclyn chuckled and then for a half minute, she lost herself to a deep belly laugh. When she grasped control of herself, she wiped away tears.

"Problem?" Brady asked.

"Oh, goodness no! This day just keeps getting better and better."

"How's that?"

"For the first time ever, I think the Circle of Unity can be broken. Wait. *Micah*? Oh, he's the one ... Nicodemus killed his wife?"

Kailey and Brady nodded.

"Pardon my laughter."

"No, that's fine," Brady said. "Because after we attack, laughter will be scarce for some time, especially inside Nocturnal Trinity."

"So you've heard about him?" Kailey asked.

Jaclyn said, "The story seemed more legend than reality. But, honestly, I thought he moved far away from Seattle. Not much has been said about him for a long time. The only werewolves I hear about are in Oregon. But a woman leads that pack. Lydia is her name."

"Contrary to what you've heard," Brady said. "Micah has never left Seattle and his pack numbers have grown to include me."

"I *knew* there was something different about you."

Brady smiled. "Well, just as much as you'd like no one to know you're a necromancer, that's how our pack members feel about what we are."

"Oh, I understand the secrecy. Really, I do," Jaclyn said. "But who would I blab to? You cannot get much more solitary a witch than myself."

"Well, after Micah exacts his revenge, the whole city will know about our existence. We might have to find another place to locate."

"Understandable," Jaclyn said. To Kailey, she said, "May I see your pendant?"

Kailey nodded. She unlatched the protective glass divider and slid one pane over. She passed the charred pendant to Jaclyn.

Jaclyn closed her eyes and held the silver piece between her fingers. A few seconds later, she rubbed the pendant between her thumb and forefinger.

"Do you sense her?" Kailey asked.

"No."

Kailey's chest grew tight.

"Would you mind if I cast a new spell upon this?"

"What kind?"

"Another protection spell."

"Sure," Kailey replied.

"I'm certain the credit union won't be the last place where you'll cross paths with the succubus."

Kailey gritted her teeth. "It will prove to be her last."

Brady cleared his throat. "Never become overconfident. It impairs your judgment. I'm certain your training instructor taught you that."

Kailey nodded meekly. "You're right."

Jaclyn set the pendant on the seat beside her. She glanced at Kailey. "If you'll close the glass and give me a few minutes of privacy, I'll enchant your pendant."

Kailey smiled and shut the glass. She turned to face the street of traffic ahead of them. According to the sign, they weren't too far from the ferry, but as she noticed on the previous passage, the waiting took more time than getting there.

Her mind drifted toward Raven. For some reason she couldn't picture her best friend without fangs and a glare of pure hatred on her face. As much as she wanted to return to Nocturnal Trinity to destroy the Circle of Unity and perhaps Cassie as well, Kailey dreaded returning to see Raven. Her roommate with the massive love crush for her was *not* the same Raven she had left behind. Regardless of what Flora had said over the phone, Raven was a vampire.

She thought of Brady's friend bound inside a casket and how Brady was unable to kill her. Tears formed in Kailey's eyes. Again, she wondered if she had to kill Raven would she be able to do so?

As angry as Raven was with Brady, once Raven discovered Kailey and Brady were lovers, Raven's ensuing rage couldn't be quenched by words. Raven would probably try to kill him or Kailey or both of them. Either way, Kailey would have to fight back. Fists and feet weren't enough. Wooden stake through the heart.

Kailey cringed at the thought of what that required.

Even though Raven was undead, Kailey didn't think she'd be able to consider that to be true. She'd picture Raven as her friend and would plead for rationality where it no longer existed. For all that she hoped and believed, she wanted to find Raven still human. But her gut insisted the friend she had known for four years no longer existed. Instead, she might face a greater enemy than what she had viewed Cassie to be.

CHAPTER 41

*W*hile they rode across the bay on the ferry, Brady contacted his supervisor and requested the rest of the day off. Afterwards, he logged in to his work computer in the car and requested next three days off. Were things really that bad and demanding?

Kailey had texted a quick message to Skye to look for Brady's police car before they headed across the bay. Skye had replied back that she was on the upper deck and wanted to view the water while they crossed.

"So who's the tall silent type that hangs around Micah?" Kailey asked.

"The tall bald guy?"

She nodded.

"That's Clive. He's Micah's bodyguard."

"Awfully quiet."

"I've never heard the man say one word."

"Really?"

Brady nodded. "Yep. I don't know that he *can* talk."

"Creepy."

"I agree."

As the ferry pulled into the island port, Jaclyn tapped on the protective glass. When Kailey turned, Jaclyn held up the pendant and smiled. Kailey slid open the glass and took it.

"Wear it, especially when you reenter Nocturnal Trinity," Jaclyn said.

"Thanks."

Jaclyn smiled. "Don't mention it."

Brady checked his watch. "Still haven't seen Skye. What's taking her so long?"

"She's somewhere around."

Someone pecked against Kailey's window. She looked. "Here she is."

"Have her get in the back with Jaclyn."

Kailey motioned toward the back door. Skye replied with an insulted expression. She cocked an eyebrow and reluctantly shook her head. The gentleness in Skye's eyes remained, but Kailey was curious as to what the old woman had done during the night. Skye appeared older, more wrinkled, and extremely weary. She was stooped when she walked and now used a cane to steady herself. Kailey had learned from Raven during the past few years that some spells taxed the body readily, sapping strength and apparently vitality. In every way, Kailey regrettably saw the similarities between Skye and the old crone images that misinformed artists had drawn years ago.

Skye opened the door and sat down, setting her handbag on her lap. Her labored breathing rasped and wheezed. She offered a wry smile. "I understand that you don't know me that well, but I never expected to be riding in the *backseat* like a criminal."

Jaclyn grinned.

Brady shook his head. "Sorry for the accommodations, Skye, but this car is faster than the one Kailey had rented."

Skye chuckled softly. "I'm only teasing."

Kailey turned in her seat. "Did you find out anything about Raven?"

"Nothing except cold silence. I've never encountered anything like that before. It's almost as if there's a magical barrier preventing me from contacting her. How about you?" Skye said.

Kailey didn't know how to explain what she feared might have happened to Raven. She knew she could never offer a lie to Skye for two reasons. One, Kailey's facial expressions gave her away, and she still hadn't discovered how to form the proper poker face. And two, lying to a witch was not the smartest move anyone could make, not with the likely repercussions of when the truth finally surfaced. Although the witches practiced, 'Do no harm,' Kailey believed karma played havoc to those who deliberately set out to deceive. Maybe not immediately, but somewhere down the line the deception would bite her on the ass.

Skye leaned forward in the seat and pointed. "Kailey, what happened to the pendant that Raven had given you?"

With tears burning in Kailey's eyes, she explained the chain of events about her nightmare, Raven's cry for help, and how the pendant almost burned her.

Brady flipped on the car's flashing lights after they pulled out of the ferry, causing the drivers ahead of them to pull aside and let him through.

Skye eased back from the seat, lowered her head, and rested her head in her hands. "Oh, dear Goddess."

"We did find what Cassie wanted," Kailey said.

Skye rose. Her feeble hands trembled, but she pushed herself back against the seat. "What is it that she wanted?"

"This," Jaclyn said, showing the book to Skye.

"And this is?"

"A Grimoire."

"Ah." Skye's eyes widened.

"And it's a partial journal, too," Kailey added.

Skye smiled. "Even better. So this is what your brother had hidden?"

Kailey nodded.

"How did he get it?"

"Me," Jaclyn replied.

"And you are?"

"Jaclyn."

Skye smiled and offered her shaky hand. "I'm Skye, as I'm certain you're aware of now."

"Blessed be," Jaclyn said.

"And blessings to you, young lady."

Jaclyn smiled. "Not as young as many might believe."

"Age is a number tagged to these ol' flesh coverings, dear. Life is eternal in one form or another."

"That is true."

"Seems I may be getting close to what lies after this one," Skye said with a tired voice.

"You probably just need some rest," Kailey said.

Skye opened the Grimoire and leafed through the pages. "So Jaclyn, how did you get ahold of this book?"

"It is my mother's."

"She left it to you?"

Jaclyn shook her head, told Skye who her mother was, and why she had to *borrow* the book. "My mother wants out of her alliance with the Circle of Unity. At least two other witches want out as well."

"Wouldn't that be enough to break the circle?" Brady asked.

"Yes, if it wasn't for the fear of what the demons would do," Jaclyn replied. "Abandoning the cause of the circle would be much easier if not for that."

"Then, child, we shall do whatever we can," Skye said. "They have Raven, who is like a daughter to me. But I fear that even if we arrive in full force by the deadline, we will be too late to save her, from what Kailey has experienced and from my inability to connect with her spirit overnight."

"Never give up hope," Jaclyn whispered.

With tears in her eyes, Kailey faced Skye. Neither said a word, but they gave a single nod, both in agreement that Raven was probably gone forever.

"We shall be at Micah's estate in a few minutes. He should have a plan for us to discuss."

CHAPTER 42

*K*ailey was surprised to see the entire pack gathered around the outside pavilion while Jacob and two others grilled.

"Is that all you do? Eat?" she asked as Brady parked the squad car.

He grinned. "We have high metabolisms."

"I know. You told me."

"Seeing is believing," he replied.

Micah sat on the rock wall facing the bay. Clouds darkened the horizon. Cold wind whipped across the white-capped waves and blew against Micah. The brisk temperature didn't seem to bother him or the others.

Kailey and Jaclyn followed Brady while Skye remained inside the car. She had said that it was too cold, and she'd rather sit in the car for a bit. Kailey was concerned about Skye's health. She didn't look well.

Micah's eyes were closed when the three of them stepped between him and the bay. The sudden block of wind caused Micah to open his eyes. After his vision focused, he smiled. "Rain's moving in again."

"It's Seattle," Brady said. "What do you expect?"

Micah shrugged. "Did you find what we're looking for?"

Brady nodded.

"Good."

Brady stepped back and motioned toward Jaclyn. "This is Jaclyn."

Micah's eyes widened with surprise. "I *know* you."

Brady and Kailey exchanged glances.

"That would have saved us a lot of time," Kailey said.

Micah laughed softly. "You're right. I should have said that I recognized her instead. I didn't actually know her name though."

"So where have you seen her?"

Micah grinned. "She frequents my shop. Very quiet, reserved."

"It's best to be such in one's solitary path," Jaclyn replied. "You learn more by listening than speaking."

"Very true. From the things you often purchased, I'd say that you participate in necromancy?" Micah asked.

She nodded modestly.

"Divination, scrying, or actually bringing the dead back to life?"

"Depends upon the circumstances," Jaclyn replied.

Micah remained silent for several moments as his eyes studied Jaclyn's. Her eyes reflected a mysticism and darkness that Kailey had never seen before. She could see the power in Skye's gaze, and occasionally something similar in Raven's. But with Jaclyn ... the look was much different. Since Micah had insisted that he could not rightfully kill due to being a shaman, Jaclyn, on the other hand, was everything their group needed to successfully do so.

Kailey glanced toward the grill and caught Ashley watching Micah. The she-wolf's eyes were filled with longing. Kailey didn't understand why Ashley didn't move on. Jacob was handsome and didn't seem attached. But he was also high strung and impatient. The young woman's patience was being whittled away by her obsessive infatuation, and while it wasn't completely clear that Micah would choose Ashley after he found justice for the murder of his wife, he let her ache and hope.

Brady said, "Jaclyn holds the book that Nocturnal Trinity seeks."

Micah extended his hand. "May I?"

Jaclyn nodded and offered the book to him. He studied the binding carefully. Gently he placed his palm to the cover and closed his eyes. His body visibly shook. He quickly handed the Grimoire back to her.

"What's wrong?" Kailey asked.

"There's much magic bound to that book," he replied.

Jaclyn nodded.

"Where did you get this?"

"My mother, Eva."

"The witch who is a member of the Circle of Unity?"

"The same."

Micah stared into Jaclyn's eyes for a long while. Neither blinked. Kailey wondered if he was able to look into her soul or vice versa. He was a shaman, and she wasn't quite certain what all he could do. But he looked at her with more than his eyes. She felt what seemed to be a slight pulse of power webbing between the two.

"After we eat," Micah said, "We're going to discuss our battle plan."

Brady rubbed the stubble on his chin and nodded. "Sounds good to me."

"Everyone we have is here. I've reached out to neighboring ..." Micah glanced at Jaclyn momentarily, "groups for assistance. Perhaps five more will be here later today, which is why we headed back while you two searched for Jaclyn and the safety deposit box."

"She knows what we are," Brady said.

"Ahh. You told her?"

Kailey shook her head. "He didn't. I let it slip. Sorry."

"No, that's perfectly fine. She'd have to know before tonight anyway," Micah said. "We hold no secrets from our allies."

"You don't know me well enough to consider me as such," Jaclyn said with an inquisitive stare.

"The fact you're here speaks volumes. You've even shown us this Grimoire, which reveals their weaknesses and your power."

"My mother's as well."

Micah nodded. "Go eat. We head in after nightfall. That's not necessarily the best time to fight vampires, but the darkness of night draws less attention from the mortals in Seattle. The only problem is getting inside since Kailey is the only one with a membership card, and she can invite one person inside."

"There are the underground passages where you can get inside," Jaclyn replied.

"I thought those had collapsed decades ago," Micah said. "We scouted there a little over a year ago. Huge chunks of asphalt, steel beams, and bricks still had it sealed off."

"Illusion spell."

"Really?" Micah asked.

"Yes. Courtesy of the witches."

"It looks so realistic."

Jaclyn smiled. "Of course. It has to. Otherwise, Nocturnal Trinity could be invaded by all the desperate wannabes that wait outside for an invitation to get inside."

"Damn. We could have already taken care of the vampire problem had we known that. Then we wouldn't have our present problem with rescuing Raven."

Kailey's throat tightened. Remorse overwhelmed her. Her knees shook and suddenly became weak. Before she fell down, Brady wrapped his arm around her and balanced her.

"Are you okay?" Brady asked.

"I just need to sit down," she replied.

"Come on," Brady said. "I'll fix you a plate."

Kailey shook her head and grinned. "I'm not even hungry."

"We eat early," Micah said. "Because tonight, we're not going to have time to even think about food."

"Where are Blaze and Luna?" Kailey asked.

"Watching the magic shop. They're safer there. Besides, they can't go back to Nocturnal Trinity after the holy water incident."

"That's true."

Micah stood and offered his arm to Jaclyn. "Let me introduce you to the others."

Jaclyn accepted and draped hers over his, allowing him to escort her to the pavilion. Kailey caught Ashley's glare toward Jaclyn and Micah. When Ashley looked into Kailey's eyes, Ashley stormed away from the grill and headed toward the house.

Kailey rose on tiptoe and kissed Brady. "I'll be back in a few minutes."

"You sure? You nearly passed out."

"I'm fine. Be back in a few minutes."

As she headed toward the house, Micah made Jaclyn's introduction to the group seated beneath the pavilion. While it looked like they were progressing in some areas, Micah's treatment of Ashley was in shambles.

Kailey found Ashley sobbing at the kitchen windows that overlooked the bay. Ashley covered her face with her hands, and her body shook.

Easing up beside her, Kailey gently placed a hand on Ashley's arm. Tears streaked her face. She lowered her hands and faced Kailey.

Kailey leaned forward and hugged Ashley.

Ashley tightly wrapped her arms around Kailey. Still sobbing and shaking, she said, "Why doesn't Micah want me? Am I not attractive enough?"

"You're a very beautiful woman," Kailey replied.

"Apparently not enough for him."

Kailey pulled back from Ashley and wiped away her tears. "He still grieves for his wife."

"He's overly friendly with whoever you brought here."

Kailey shook her head. "No, he's welcoming her to our group and making introductions. Nothing more, I assure you."

"How can you be so sure?" Ashley asked, sniffling.

"Micah seems to be the type of person who will truly devote himself to one person, and he cannot offer that type of devotion to you while he is still dealing with his loss. He also seeks vengeance, and I believe he's torn inside. Jaclyn's someone who can help us get justice. Nothing more. Micah doesn't want to kill because it is opposite of what his spirit is, and he's struggling with that, too. Does that make sense?"

Ashley nodded.

"Once he gets past her death, I believe he will be different and give you his love and devotion."

"Do you think he'd pick me to be the Alpha female?"

Kailey frowned and studied her eyes. "That's not the reason you're wanting to be with Micah, is it?"

"No. What I meant is do you think he'd view me as strong enough to be his Alpha?"

"Of course. You're the toughest young woman I've ever seen. I'm glad you're on my side. I certainly never would want to go against you in a fight. When you and I first met, I immediately thought you were the female Alpha."

"Really?"

Kailey nodded.

"I've worried for some time that he is interested in meeting the She-Alpha Lydia in Oregon," Ashley said with a worried expression. "From the stories we hear, she'd be a better mate for him."

"Legends are sometimes just ... hyped up stories. You're worrying far more about the situation than you should be."

"Not if she's what they say she is."

Kailey shrugged. "Are there no politics between separate packs?"

"Possibly. She's mentioned a lot in our circle."

"Then wouldn't she have a male Alpha to be partnered with?" Kailey asked.

"From my understanding, this Lydia just showed up to the pack and attacked the leader, beating him in the fight, and refused him or any of the males as her Alpha. Micah said that she's the only female pack leader he knows of."

"Really?"

Ashley nodded.

"And does he ever mention that he's interested in her as a way to join your packs?"

"No, but I wonder if this is why he stays single, and not from his grief."

"My guess is that it's highly unlikely."

"I hope so."

Kailey smiled. "Be patient."

Ashley thought for a few moments, nodded, and then said, "I understand that you're quite accomplished in martial art fighting."

Kailey crinkled her nose and then smiled. "Accomplished isn't the word I'd use, but I do hope to eventually fight in the ring."

"You're short, but you do have that tough girl attitude, which I kinda like. You can hold your own, I'm certain."

"Thanks."

Ashley had regained her composure and her sniffling lessened. Her cheeks were still flushed, but she stepped to the window and looked down toward the pavilion. Micah no longer stood close to Jaclyn, and she seemed to be talking to others in the pack.

"Who is she?" Ashley asked.

"That's Jaclyn."

"The one you and Brady went to find?"

Kailey nodded.

"You found her a lot quicker than Micah and the others expected."

"More by accident than anything else."

Ashley placed a hand on Kailey's shoulder. "At least you found her."

"Yep. Can I ask you something?"

Ashley shrugged. "Sure."

"How long have you been a werewolf?"

"Six years."

"Wow."

"Yeah."

"How did it happen?" Kailey asked.

The question made Ashley uneasy. She crossed her arms.

"It's okay, if you don't wish to tell me," Kailey said.

"It's hard to talk about, but something you should know since you're dating Brady."

Kailey swallowed hard and her stomach turned.

Ashley released a long sigh and sat at the kitchen table where they had a great panoramic view of the bay. Kailey took the seat beside her.

Ashley folded her hands atop the table. "I went on a blind date with this guy, Bill. A coworker—Benita—I think that was her name. She had set us up when I first moved to Oregon. He seemed like a great guy, so we made plans to go hiking the next day at a wildlife refuge area. We each drove because he said that they have miles of hiking trails and it might get dark before we made it back out."

"That'd make me nervous. Being out in the woods with someone after dark that I hardly knew."

"Oh, trust me, I was nervous about it, so I brought a small Taser in my pack, just in case he got handsy and tried something."

"Good idea."

Ashley shrugged slightly and took a deep breath. "The Taser is probably what saved my life. When we arrived at the park, we noticed a couple of posted signs that wolves had been spotted a few weeks earlier and for hikers to take precaution. Wolves aren't predatory toward humans and generally can be spooked away. Too many people are misinformed and think they will attack humans at a moment's notice, but the majority of them don't. But anyway, we headed out with a map of the trails. Other than being a bit nervous, the day was gorgeous. Perfect temperature. Light breeze. Leaves changing colors. It was magnificent. And Bill was every bit the gentleman. Then we got lost."

"With a map?" Kailey crinkled a curious frown.

Ashley laughed. "We lost the map *first*. A sudden gust of wind sucked the map out of his hands. Instead of it attaching to a tree or getting caught in briars, the paper was blown straight up above the treetops and carried away like a kite. We headed off the trail in the direction it had blown but found ourselves in a darker area of the woods where it was muddier."

"What did you do?"

"Bill stopped and playfully pinned me against a tree. He kissed me, and I didn't resist because by then I was rather attracted to him. You know how after a hour or so whether or not an individual is someone you want to be around, right?"

Kailey nodded. "Yep."

"He seemed okay until ..."

"What?"

"During the kiss, his hand went up under my shirt, and *that's* when I resisted."

"Oh my God. Really? He didn't keep going, did he?"

Ashley shook her head. "I pushed him away, and he didn't persist. He apologized."

Kailey gave a sigh of relief. "That's good."

"That he decided to behave himself was good. What happened next ... wasn't so good."

Kailey started to ask, but Ashley held up a finger.

"That's when the wolf showed up about fifteen feet or so away. It was the biggest wolf I had ever seen. It rushed us without warning. Bill stepped between the wolf and me. The huge beast mauled his right forearm by clamping down its jaws and jerking back and forth. I heard the bones in his forearm snap." Ashley winced, closed her eyes, and collected herself. "I had never heard anyone scream like that, and I would have never expected the sound to come from a man.

"I dug in my pack, trying to find the Taser because I figured the electrical shock would be enough to make the wolf run away if it didn't succumb to the voltage."

"Did it work?"

"No. I wasn't fast enough to get it out. The wolf pressed Bill to the ground and went for his throat. With his one good arm, he fought the wolf long enough that I was able to get the Taser, but by the time I reached the wolf, it turned and gnashed me with a snappy bite. It was enough to break through my skin and apparently enough to make me a werewolf."

"It just left?"

"After it nipped me, I thrust the Taser into its side and jolted the hell out of it. It yelped and fled through the trees. I swear part of its fur caught on fire."

"Did Bill survive?" Kailey asked.

"No. His throat was slashed. I held the wound closed with one hand and called 911 on my cellphone, but well before they ever found us, Bill had died. The whole time that I was waiting for the paramedics or the game warden, I kept expecting that damned wolf to come back."

"Damn. What did you do then? I mean, God, seeing Bill die and then your first transformation?"

Tears formed in Ashley's eyes. "It was ... bad."

"I imagine so."

"Yeah, since I was new to the area, I had no one that I really knew. Benita was just someone I worked with, so I didn't talk to her much, especially not after Bill's death. We avoided one another. But the last thing I expected to discover was that I was going to change into a werewolf at the first full moon."

"Where did that happen?" Kailey asked.

"At the house I was renting in the country ... luckily. God only knows what would have happened if I had changed in public place. But the first transformation was the most painful thing that has ever happened to me. I've never felt pain so severe. There aren't any words I can say to describe it. That's why I'm warning you. If you're dating Brady, or around any of us when we change, it doesn't take much to get the virus we carry that changes us. And tonight is a night we will all change for the first time in months. Our aggression will be high scaled."

"I understand."

Ashley shook her head. "Wait. I'm not finished. Rumor is that whatever spell we were under and after it was reversed last night, we might be able to transform outside of the full moon."

"Really?"

Nodding, Ashley said, "And if that's true, when you're having intense sex with him, he might change *during*."

Kailey's eyes widened.

"I'm not trying to frighten you, but you need to be aware. While the first transformation was so painful, the next one wasn't as bad. Then, month-by-month, you no longer fear the coming pain because it is no longer pain. You *crave* the change. The pain is pleasurable, like a drug, and it's like a euphoric high when it comes. Because with the change comes strength and power like you've never known before. You saw everyone the night of the full moon?"

"Yes."

"They needed the change. They wanted it. Had Micah not reversed the spell that was holding our wolves inside, I think Jacob and several of the others were planning to attack him."

"I got that feeling, too."

"Let me add one more thing about being a werewolf."

"Okay."

"That first change is the worst part, but for all the benefits you gain, it's worth it."

Kailey frowned. "Are you suggesting I become a werewolf?"

"I'm just saying that everything is better. Your sight, hearing, and smell. Food tastes better. Sex is heightened far greater than you've ever had in the past. Even last night." She winked.

Kailey laughed. Her face reddened. "I'll take your word for it."

Ashley smiled at Kailey and took her hand. "Thanks."

"For what?"

"For being here for me. Listening. I do hope that you plan to stick around once this is all over."

"I hope to."

"I'm sorry that I acted like such a bitch to you when you came to talk to Micah about the nightclub," Ashley said. "I ... I get territorial sometimes."

Kailey smiled. "I understand, but that's what packs do, isn't it? I was the outsider."

"Yeah, but still ..."

"Don't worry about it. We're passed that and are friends now."

"I'm glad of that."

Brady's shoes clicked across the hardwood floor as he approached the table. "What are you two doing?"

"Girl talk," Ashley said, beaming a smiled.

"Well, food is done," Brady said. "Micah wants everyone together while we eat. Visitors are supposed to arrive sometime soon."

Kailey rose, took Brady's hand, and then she took Ashley's. For the first time in a long while, she was finding herself surrounded by friends that were more like a family. Things seemed too good. Nightfall was coming. She never liked what came after the sun set.

CHAPTER 43

As the western afternoon sky had hinted, rain set in for the evening. The cold temperatures became colder, and wisps of fog drifted along the surface of the bay like ghostly appendages of a long dead, giant sea monster. Micah had decided to hold their meeting in the dining room instead of outside around a modest bonfire. His invited guests had not arrived, but he attended to the matters at hand without waiting any longer.

Clive stood behind Micah's chair. His narrow eyes were watchful. He never seemed to blink.

"I don't know what's holding them up," Micah said, lighting another candle. "Perhaps they will show by the time we're ready to leave."

Jaclyn sat beside Skye on the opposite end of the long table from Micah. Skye looked worse for wear. She was fatigued, and even in the faint glow of the candles one could tell that her health was getting poorer with each passing hour. Micah had offered to take her to a hospital, but Skye waved him off, insisting that Raven was far more important.

Kailey sat between Brady and Ashley. Jacob sat to Micah's right with three thick rare steaks on his plate. Hunger and eagerness glinted in Jacob's wolfish eyes. He kept tightening his hands into fists, and his chest and shoulder muscles seemed to swell. His breaths were deep, and he exhaled shallow growls. Kailey tried to force herself to look into his eyes, but found that she couldn't. His impatient actions were unpredictable, and she wondered if he'd make it through the night's meeting without changing.

Micah rose at the head of the table, wearing his moon patterned blue robe. He clasped his hands together and slowly gazed from one to the next all the way around the table. "We've already discussed what this night brings. Nocturnal Trinity took Raven last night for ransom, and what they want in return for her, they cannot have. But by using the spellbook, we can weaken them and perhaps break the Circle of Unity once and for all. Tonight is not a night for cowardice, and though some might believe it is about vengeance, it is not. This night is about justice. Nothing more and nothing less."

Jacob made two fists and gently slammed them down on the table. Plates and dinner utensils rattled atop the table. "Yes!"

"We are a pack. A family. Blood will be shed tonight. Some people will die. Some here may die as well. None of you are obligated to make such a sacrifice, nor am I requiring you to go. The choice is yours. No ill will be thought of you should you decide to stay behind. Understood?"

Everyone nodded, including Skye and Jaclyn.

"Now, for a show of hands. If you're going, raise your hand," Micah said.

Jacob's hand rose before Micah had even finished the sentence. Others rose slowly as they looked from one another, perhaps calculating the risks. Eventually, all had volunteered to go.

Micah smiled and nodded. "Very well. Now, I open the floor for any who have questions or comments."

"Getting Raven is our ultimate goal?"

"Yes," Micah replied.

"And then what?" another member asked.

"Destroy any vampire or demon that gets in your way," Micah replied.

Jacob said, "How are we going to get inside without membership cards?"

Micah grinned. "Glad you asked. Jaclyn? If you would explain."

Jaclyn stood. "If you've lived in Seattle for any amount of time, you're aware of the hidden passageways and tunnels beneath parts of the city. One set of tunnels actually ends beneath Nocturnal Trinity. That's how we will enter."

"We've searched them before," Jacob said. "They are blocked."

Micah said, "They *look* blocked."

"The six witches of the Circle of Unity cast an illusion spell, which gives the appearance of a blocked tunnel, but trust me it's open. That's how my mother and I have visited one another after they banished me. Well, until I took her Grimoire."

The eldest pack member cleared his throat. "So you're giving us permission to *kill* the vampires?"

Micah shrugged slightly. "They're already dead, Barry."

Barry ran his hands through his thick mane-like grayish brown hair, shook his head, and then he rubbed his face with the palms of his hands. "But they're not even our enemies."

"After tonight, they'll all become our enemies," Jacob said.

Micah folded his arms, took a stern look at each member of his pack, and said, "Again, you're not obligated to do this. No hard feelings should you opt out."

"I'm not opting out," Barry said in a low, gravelly voice. "But do we really want a powerful band of enemies like we're about to stir up? We've been living it up fairly nicely by keeping to ourselves."

"I know, and the pack's consensus was that you wanted me to release you from the bondage spell. That alone puts you up for greater exposure now."

"How's that?"

"Instinct. The draw of the transformation. That ache inside to turn into your wolf. Under the power of the full moon you'll have even less resistance," Micah said.

"Only then?" Ashley said. "I thought after our release that we could change at any time."

Barry and Jacob looked at her in surprise.

"Is that true?" Barry asked, staring at Micah.

"I think it is now possible," Micah replied. "I had to make some adjustments on the spell that released us."

"What adjustments?" Brady asked.

"The full moon had passed, and we couldn't wait another month to get Raven. So ... we should be able to change anytime during the month."

Barry grinned and bellowed a deep laugh.

Micah's eyebrows rose. "Why's that funny?"

"It means that we're even more powerful, and the hell with pissing off a few vampires. I'm in!" Barry slapped Jacob's back hard.

"Glad you're aboard, Barry. Just remember the goal," Micah said.

"Rescue the girl."

Micah nodded. "And within our group we have several among us that aren't werewolves or vampires, so be aware of where they are during our attack. Don't scratch or bite them during a frenzy."

Everyone around the table laughed except Ashley. While Micah spoke her eyes stared solely at him with respect, love, and great admiration. Micah had to be blind if he didn't read the look in her eyes. Kailey had no doubt that Ashley would die for him and his cause because it was the same exact look Raven had toward Kailey when she had foolishly rushed off after Cassie.

"I'm serious," Micah said.

The roar of laughter quieted.

"The main reason I had to adjust our transformation is because we don't have time to wait until the next full moon to change, which is a bonus. So consider that a gift from me, but act responsibly. We have to act tonight."

Kailey looked at Micah. "And if they've turned her into a vampire?"

"We kill the one that did it," Skye said in a weak tone.

"Agreed," Micah said.

Barry's eyes flicked from person to person. He folded his thick muscled hands on the table. "Just out of curiosity's sake, what kind of numbers are we going up against?"

"Six major demons and six elder vampires," Micah replied. He glanced at Jaclyn. "The witches?"

Jaclyn gazed around the table. "My mother despises her allegiance to the Circle of Unity and will side with us. Rose and Debra aren't fond of their servitude to the vampires and demons, either. The three male witches? It's questionable which side they will choose or if they'll even participate at all."

"Why's that?" Micah asked.

"They tend to follow whatever means suits their desires the most. That's how the circle benefits those who have unified together. Being inclined for the sexual favors the demons have offered them, the male witches don't mind exchanging magical courtesies in return for incredible sex," Jaclyn replied.

Barry's eyebrows rose. "Really? How good could it be?"

Jaclyn smiled and gave a modest shrug. "I've never had sex with an incubus or succubus, so honestly, I cannot tell you from personal experience. However, I can tell you that those in such relationships are enraptured with such ecstasy that they no longer seek sex from humans ever again."

"Damn!" Barry said, pounding a fist on the table and grinning. "Maybe I'm on the *wrong* side of this."

The pack members seated around the table chuckled. Micah did not. His eyes became cold and his facial expressions were solemn. "I know you love to cut up, Barry, but I find no humor in that statement. What we're about to do will cost people lives. Preferably not ours."

"Sorry, boss," Barry replied, waving his hands in surrender.

"Getting back to the question of opposing numbers," Jaclyn said. "Of the Circle of Unity, I'd say we'll face fifteen at the most, but one never knows if everyone is in attendance each night. Some designate one night a week to visit, like a personal holiday to drink and look for a new sexual partner. The only time they all meet together are for specific influence or radical spells to alter major city changes in Seattle. Laws or elections. But, from what my mother has told me over the years, the six vampires within the circle are known to *father* or *mother* new children to their fold."

"How many of those do you estimate?" Micah asked.

She shrugged. "Not certain, but dozens might be an underestimation."

"Shit," Barry mumbled. "Vamps are increasing their numbers by that much? Micah, I knew that you were fixed on getting Nicodemus, but you never mentioned they were building an army."

"Some things I've kept to myself and a select few," Micah said, crossing his arms. "Until we had enough evidence. But Dale's death and Raven's abduction are two things that have forced my hand. They are why we must attack tonight."

Brady nodded. "Exactly. As a police officer, it's no secret from me that people have been oddly disappearing for years. Families post posters of missing teenagers on windows and poles throughout the city. Those flyers disappear almost as quickly as the people put them up. The problem is that it's covered up by the high ranking officers and city council members because some of them are vampires, too."

"Damn," Barry whispered, glancing at Jacob.

Jacob nodded. His fists tightened and looked much hairier than fifteen minutes earlier. He growled softly. "They will suffer for what they did to Dale."

Other pack members nodded and gnashed their teeth like angry wolves.

Let's get this damn meeting over with! We don't have much time before they all shift. Kailey nervously edged forward in her seat, looking for the quickest exit.

"So you see," Micah said, "where the greater threat lies. They're spreading their power by actively recruiting."

"Who'd even want to be a vampire?" Barry asked.

"There are hundreds," Kailey said. "All you have to do is stand outside Nocturnal Trinity and you'll see all the naïve individuals ready to offer themselves to the Circle of Unity. It's a lustful dream come true."

"Until it happens," Brady said. "You've heard of buyer's remorse? There are those who are turned into vampires that wish they could go back to being human."

"That's why they keep them underground," Jaclyn said.

Someone knocked on the patio door so hard that the windows in the dining room shook. The vibrations were like thunder rumbling and the sky shaking during a violent storm during the summertime.

Micah tilted his head back and smiled. "I see our guests have arrived. Excuse me for one minute."

After Micah stepped from the room, the pack commenced to whispering amongst themselves. They talked about what was coming. The fights. Bloodshed. Crazed glows overshadowed their eyes. Their inner beasts craved violence and Kailey sensed it.

Kailey became uneasy and nervously reached beneath the table and took Brady's hand. She squeezed, but he didn't react to her touch. A look into his eyes alarmed her. The growing frenzy was building inside him as well. He was feeding off the pack's fury and his eyes held a yellowish tint around his hazel irises.

Dammit!

She had hoped that since he was a police officer that he might be able to contain the rage, but she realized that she had been foolish to think so. The inner animal was taking control, and she didn't think it mattered what someone's occupation was or his mannerisms, the beast got what it wanted *when* it wanted it. Hell, a werewolf priest couldn't contain the monster inside whenever it decided to emerge.

No mere worded vow prevented the change, but Micah's spell had somehow caged them until the point where he had to release them because they kept *begging* for him to do so.

How much longer can they hold back?

What had she gotten herself into?

Raven. Think of Raven.

And the more she did, the sadder she became. Kailey truly believed Raven was a vampire. She needed to close the door on her remorse and unleash her anger. That was the only way to survive through the coming night.

The floor shook. Moments later, Micah stepped into the dining room with three rough-looking individuals. The man in the center was a human mountain of a man with long curly brown locks that hung down over his collar. His thick wiry beard came halfway down his chest. His oilskin Aussie hat set low on his head and with the hat tipped slightly forward, seeing his eyes was difficult, which made him even more intimidating, not that his size alone wasn't frightening enough. Remnants of rain dripped from his hat and down the sides of his heavy trench coat.

Kailey had never seen a man so large. He stood nearly seven feet tall and weighed well over three, possibly four, hundred pounds. A wall of a man, he had barely squeezed through the door to get into the dining room. His chest, shoulders, and arms were thick and muscular. The man's legs were the size of tree trunks and his fists the size of hams. His midsection was narrow, as best she could tell with his trench coat tied around his waist. His steps were swift, sure, and *heavy*.

The massive man held a huge wooden briefcase in his right hand. The outside was rugged with a silver cross fastened to the topside panel. Deep grooves were carved along the edges. Aged brass brads held the large hinges in place. He heaved the briefcase over Kailey's head and set it firmly down on the table with a heavy thud. The case was at least two feet thick. The cross gleamed in the faint candlelight.

He smiled through thick his beard. In a voice deeper than any Kailey had ever heard before, the man said, "I understand you're looking to kill some vampires. Forrest Wollinsky, Vampire Hunter, at your service."

CHAPTER 44

The members seated around the table stared incredulously at Forrest and then exchanged glances with one another. Kailey almost chuckled because their facial expressions weren't much different than a dog that had tucked its tail between its legs. Fear and uncertainty loomed around them. Clive was the only one that kept an even stare at the giant visitor and remained unimpressed.

Kailey felt uncomfortable about having the huge man stand directly behind her, but the reflection off the china cabinet allowed her to see what he was doing.

The trio smelled like wet leaves, mossy dirt, and pipe tobacco.

"Trip took a bit longer than we anticipated," Forrest said with a grin.

One of Forrest's partners shook his head and smiled. "Hard to find a pontoon boat this late in the day. He almost sunk the motor boat, so we had to turn back."

"Pipe down, Gunner," Forrest said in a gruffer tone. "They don't need to know the *exact* details for our delay."

"We were *taking* on water!" Gunner exclaimed with a high-pitched voice. "Lots of it."

Forrest turned with a harsh glare and raised the back of his hand.

Gunner cowered but laughed softly, which produced a whistling sound through his gnarled, yellow teeth. He pulled back his stringy hair from his dirty face and grinned. Kailey had to look away. All she could picture were those novelty Hillbilly teeth she had seen in souvenir shops. She never imaged some people actually suffered from such severe dental problems. But looking at the other man beside him, who must have been Gunner's identical twin, she worried because his were actually worse. She winced.

"Where are you from?" Jacob asked.

"I was born in Romania and lived in Victoria, British Columbia," Forrest replied. "But I'm seldom there. I travel more than I stay in one place."

With his brow furrowed, Jacob glanced toward Micah.

"I've asked them here," Micah said, "because he's an expert in killing vampires worldwide and has weapons that he is willing to loan us."

"We've talked many times over the phone," Forrest said, "but this is the first time we've been able to meet in person. I tend to be overseas ... hunting." He beamed a broad grin.

"He's only showing us weapons? He's not going to help us?" Jacob asked.

Forrest laughed heartily. "Oh, I'm *going* to help. No doubts about that. Nothing gets the adrenaline pumping like hunting vampires and putting them to rest. Besides, I need to carve a few more notches on this side of my box."

There were so many notches along each side of the box that it was a wonder the box hadn't fallen apart.

"Good to know that you're fighting by our side," Brady said. "You pack a lot of muscle and brute strength. Something we need."

"Weapons arc what you *need*," Forrest said with a wink. "At least that's what Micah told me. Vampires move swiftly, so you need something that's quicker than they are and effective."

Forrest opened the rugged case. Everyone around the table rose with curiosity to see the items this vampire hunter kept inside the case. Since the candlelight didn't offer enough light to see the weapons, Micah stepped to the edge of the room and turned up the lights.

An old wooden mallet, stained with blood and age, rested beside three crude cross-shaped wooden stakes. The tips of these stakes were also blood-stained. Both ends of a set of rosary beads were connected to a silver cross, which appeared to be something a person could wear as a necklace. Labeled vials of holy water, garlic oil, and silver nitrate were fitted nicely inside plush cotton-lined slots to prevent breakage. A worn Holy Bible was fastened into place with leather straps. Candles and other supplies were also stashed in between the larger items.

Forrest popped out a panel to reveal an old rustic pistol. Lined in a row above the weapon were a half dozen wooden stakes that were small enough to fit into the gun's barrel. A small powder flask was strapped beside the stakes.

Since Kailey was seated directly in front of the hunter's box, her view of the items was better than anyone else around the table. Although the gun appeared well over a hundred years old, the bottom of the butt had been modified with some type of valve where another apparatus could be screwed into the gun. She had never seen a gun like that and wondered *what* connected to it.

Forrest cleared his throat with several deep, harsh grunts, apparently coughing up thick phlegm. "There are several ways to kill vampires. Wooden stake through the heart works best, but it's seldom that you're fortunate enough to find one at rest, especially these younger ones nowadays. They tend to be too restless here in America. I blame the highly caffeinated blood most Americas have and their short attention span." He laughed as did most seated around the table. Then Forrest glanced at Micah. "You have any axes?"

Micah nodded. "Out in the toolshed I have several."

"Good," Forrest said, opening the right side of his trench coat. He slid an ax from its sheath and firmly held it with his right hand. Two sets of silver handcuffs hung on his belt. "Decapitation is much better if you're precise. Machetes work wonders too. Not many creatures can recover from losing their heads."

Gunner and his brother grinned, snickered.

Forrest set a dozen small vials of holy water on the table and instructed them to take one. "Holy water burns them, but it doesn't kill them unless you inject it into them. Only use this as a painful distraction if you're being overpowered. Stake them in the heart while they try to rub off the water."

Kailey took a vial and tucked it into her purse while others grabbed vials.

If Forrest's presentation were a college course, Kailey would have called it, Vampire Killing Tactics 101. She studied the ax Forrest held and thought how cumbersome that would be for her to use as a weapon. A machete, on the other hand, was a weapon that might prove more useful for her since she had learned sword training in Aikido. Of course, moving targets were much different than slicing through melons atop mannequins.

"Silver won't kill vampires," Forrest said, pulling a three foot silver chain from the box. All the werewolves backed away from the table. Forrest chuckled. "Ah, sorry, didn't mean to startle you. But silver slows them down, giving you a better chance to stake one. Taking a chain like this and draping it over a vampire's body at rest will slow it long enough for you to hammer a stake through its heart. But, of course, werewolves can't exactly use these. For those who aren't, feel free to use them."

"What kills a demon?" Kailey asked, turning in her seat and looking up at him.

Forrest frowned. "What type of demon?"

"A succubus."

Forrest reached into the deep pocket of his trench coat and pulled out a dagger. The black blade glistened in the light. "This obsidian dagger I had blessed by a monk in the Western Ghats Mountains of India in exchange for killing a vampire that stalked travelers. I suppose you could say that it is very expensive since that was perhaps one of the hardest vampires I've ever hunted and killed."

"Why?" Barry asked, combing his beard with his hand.

"That vampire was good at hiding. Damn near invisible. Took me three months to finally get him cornered inside a small mountain cave. After that, child's play."

Kailey extended her hand toward the dagger. "May I?"

Forrest handed her the dagger. He cocked one brow, studying her. "And how do you know this particular demon?"

"She killed my brother," Kailey replied softly.

"Then, my dear young lady, consider this a gift."

"Thanks, but—"

Forrest shook his head. "No returns. But I must caution you. Use the blade wisely."

"What do you mean?"

"It has a one-time usage. Once you kill the succubus, or I should say *any* succubus, the essence of the dagger is gone ... forever. The blade vanishes with her into the abyss, never to be seen again. In other words, strike to kill the specific one, if you happen to get surrounded by such demons."

"Okay. Thanks." Kailey held the blade handle and shifted the knife in simple offensive maneuvers. Light reflected off the chipped blade surface. It was almost a shame to destroy such a beautifully crafted weapon, but she'd use it if she managed to get close enough to Cassie.

"So it only works on a succubus?" she asked.

Forrest shrugged. "It probably works on demons closely related to succubae, but there's no guarantee. I asked for a specific blessing since I was in an area where succubae were known to prey upon sleeping men in the village during the night. Of course things are often lost in translation."

Kailey's cellphone rang. She read the screen. "Shit."

"Flora?" Brady asked.

She nodded.

Micah stepped closer and raised his palms. "Everyone be quiet. Kailey, put it on speaker."

She hit the button and put the phone on speaker, then she answered, "Yes?"

"Time's almost up, Kailey," Flora said. "Are you going to make the trade?"

"I'm on my way."

"Good."

"Please let me talk to Raven," Kailey asked.

Skye stood. Her jaw tightened. Micah raised a finger toward her, cautioning her to remain quiet.

"You'll see her soon enough. As much as you love one another, I'm certain your reunion will be ... emotional."

Kailey opened her mouth to reply, but Flora disconnected the call.

"She will die!" Skye said, steadying herself against the table. A second later, she clutched at her heart, winced, and seated herself.

Jaclyn quickly attended to her. Skye took several deep breaths and waved Jaclyn away.

"I'm fine," Skye said. "Let me catch my breath."

"Who was that?" Forrest asked.

"Flora is the vampire holding Raven hostage."

His eyes held recognition at the name. He frowned. "Why?"

"It's a long story, but that's why we need your help. To rescue her."

"Sounds like fun and games to me," Forrest replied with a grin.

Micah patted the back of Forrest's massive arm. "Thanks for coming." He turned toward the others. "I have some newly sharpened stakes setting on a table out in the toolshed. Anyone who wishes to use an ax, feel free to do so."

Brady raised a hand. "But remember to keep any weapons concealed. Police aren't going to tolerate our group roaming the docks and streets with axes and machetes. Keep a low profile until we're under the streets."

"Good points," Micah said. "And one other thing, no one transforms until *after* we're underground. Understood?"

Several groaned in reply.

"Is that clear?" Micah said, frowning.

"Yes," they replied in unison while nodding.

"Then let's get our weapons and get ready to cross the bay." Micah glanced at Forrest. "I'm guessing you did get that pontoon boat?"

Forrest laughed and nodded. "Yep."

"Any room for some of the pack?"

"Actually, we could use about half the group to help balance the boat," Gunner said.

His brother nodded. "Forrest's heavy. He is. Imagine scrounging up enough food for 'em each day."

"Ian—" Gunner said, shaking his head.

"It's true."

Micah smiled. "I just need to make certain we can get everyone across at the same time."

"We have more than enough room," Forrest said. "Micah, how's Jacques?"

"My father?"

Forrest nodded.

"I've not seen or heard from him in a long time."

"Same here," Forrest replied with a grim face.

Micah checked the clock on the wall. "Get everything together and meet at the shoreline in five minutes. Five minutes or I'll assume you're staying behind."

Ashley hurried around the table and took Micah's hand. "Where do you need me?"

"Ride with me?" he asked, taking her hands into his.

She smiled broadly. "Of course."

Micah looked into her eyes. "I'm sorry for the distance I've kept between us, but I want you to stay close to me during all of this tonight."

She smiled and nodded. He pulled her close and hugged her.

Most of the pack headed out the patio door toward the toolshed while the others exited toward the walkway that led to where the boats awaited them.

Kailey hurried to Skye. "Are you okay?"

Skye nodded. "Old age and anxiety. Never a good combination."

"Perhaps you should remain behind?" Jaclyn suggested.

"No," Skye said, vehemently shaking her head. "No. I have to be there for Raven. Regardless of what might have happened to her. She needs me."

Jaclyn flicked her gaze to Brady and then to Kailey. Kailey shrugged.

"I understand how important Raven is to you—" Brady said.

Skye shook her head. "No buts. *I'm going.*"

Kailey bit her lower lip to prevent a smile. She loved how crabby the older lady was.

"Very well," Brady said.

Kailey leaned closer to Brady and whispered, "There's no way that any of us can constantly keep an eye on her."

"We'll do what we can up until that point, but once the pack turns ... you, Jaclyn, and Skye need to be outside of our reach. The fever to fight is getting stronger, as I'm sure you're aware."

"I know."

"You and Jaclyn help Skye to Forrest's pontoon boat. I'll help Micah and the others get weapons."

Kailey nodded.

In so many ways she wished she could convince Skye to stay, but she knew Skye would protest. With Raven's welfare at hand, human or possibly vampire, she understood how Skye would never stay behind. That was how strong love was. Love could cause a person to risk her own life in order to save another. By the end of the night, she wondered how many sacrifices would have to be made.

$\mathcal{A}$t the docks on the mainland near the ferry, Brady and the pack members got off the pontoon boat at the marina. Micah, Ashley, and a few others climbed off the small fishing boat. All wore long trench coats to hide axes and machetes.

Kailey helped Skye along the narrow floating dock. "Are you sure you're going to be okay?"

"I can have paramedics out here in a few minutes," Brady said, sliding out his cellphone.

"No, please don't fuss over me," she said with a stern frown while waving a feeble hand. "Just help me get to the underground tunnels, and I'll catch up to you."

Brady shook his head. "Nocturnal Trinity is blocks from here. You'll never make that walk. The best thing to do is to take a cab and get dropped off a block away from the nightclub." He took his phone and searched for the local cab service and then called them. Looking at Skye, he said, "The cab will be here in a few minutes. Wait for us at Pine Street. Someone will come up and get you."

Skye offered a frail smile and nod.

"Sorry, but it's the best we can do right now," Brady said.

"As long as it gets me there when you find Raven."

"We'll do what we can, but once the pack members turn and the fights ensue, there's little we can guarantee."

Skye shrugged. "I understand."

Kailey and Brady helped Skye to a bench at the edge of the street where she could wait for the cab. Kailey hugged her tightly, and Skye whispered a blessing into her ear.

"Be careful," Skye said softly.

Kailey smiled. "I will, and I'll find you at Pine Street."

Brady took Kailey's hand and hurried across the street to where Jaclyn stood clutching the Grimoire to her chest. Half of the pack members were half a block down the sidewalk, following Micah and Forrest.

"Things are going to get nasty," Brady whispered.

Jaclyn nodded but said nothing.

"I expect the worst, but either way, I'll do whatever is necessary for Raven and Vincent," Kailey said. Anger rose in her chest. She needed her rage to grow even more because she was always nervous before a fight. Only, she had never been *this* nervous before.

Micah led the pack several blocks before they turned into a dark alley. "While there are tourist groups that take people on tunnel tours, the tunnel that leads to Nocturnal Trinity is not a part of any of those attractions. I could have sworn this was the alley where we could go underground."

Jaclyn pointed. "It's been years since I entered here, but this opening is about midway down this alley behind one of those dumpsters."

Micah instructed two of the pack members to slide a dumpster away from the wall. They did so. Behind the dumpster were two metal doors. They were painted green with a heavy padlock securing them.

"Those are the doors," Jaclyn said.

Micah inspected the lock and then he slammed it down, agitated. "Dammit!"

"Here," Forrest said. He reached down, squeezed the lock tightly in his hand, and then he twisted. The latch bolts that fastened between the doors snapped off. He grabbed the door handle and pulled. The rusty hinges screeched. "There you go."

"Thanks," Micah said, cocking a brow with the slightest hint of intimidation. "Okay. Who wants to go first?"

Barry found the rungs of the ladder and lowered himself into the dark tunnel first. A few seconds later, several bats flittered out the doors and spiraled upward into the night sky.

Gunner and his twin brother, Ian, followed Barry.

Kailey looked up at Brady. "No flashlights?"

Brady shook his head. "I didn't think to bring any. Once the pack transforms we have perfect night vision, so we don't need them."

"Here little lady," Forrest said. "I keep a couple on me at all times. I tend to be in dark places more than light."

"Thanks," she said, nodding her appreciation.

"Don't mention it." Forrest pulled some odd looking goggles down over his eyes.

Kailey motioned for Jaclyn to join her. "We should be close to the front, don't you think?"

"Yes. I will need to reverse the illusion spell so they can find their way to the stairwell that leads into Nocturnal Trinity."

"I told Skye that I would go up to get her."

Jaclyn sighed. "Do you really think that's such a good idea? She's in bad shape."

"I know, but I promised her. Never lie to a witch or demon." Kailey winked.

"I see your point. But don't get yourself killed because of her, okay?"

"I'll be careful."

Kailey took the first rung. It was wet, sticky, and cold. The next few were slicker with moisture. The smell of the garbage dumpsters hung in the air, making her hold her breath as she descended several rungs. When she reached the bottom, the floor of the tunnel was uneven and wet. She turned on the flashlight and shone it up the metal ladder so Jaclyn could see the rungs.

"Toss me the book?" Kailey asked.

"No. I must keep it close. Some of the pages are loose, and we cannot afford for any of them to get lost."

"Okay. I understand."

Jaclyn reached the last rung and carefully stepped onto the floor. Kailey waited for Brady. When he reached the bottom, she asked for the machete. He handed it to her.

When he reached the bottom, he stood beside her. "You two need to hurry ahead. Jaclyn, do you know the way?"

Jaclyn nodded. "Yes. We're fourteen or fifteen blocks away."

"You both need to run. After Micah and the others all get down here, we begin our transformations. Trust me, you don't want to be anywhere near us. While we will try to maintain our control, your scents will be fresh, and there's no telling how some of the members will behave since we've not changed in two years. Our inner beasts being restrained for that amount of time ... there's no guarantee as to what we might do. Pent up aggression will be released. Gods help the innocents that happen to get into our way."

Kailey took a deep breath and held it. The gentleness in Brady's eyes was altering. Behind the kindness crept the lurking animalistic need to run, to destroy, and to kill.

Brady leaned close to Kailey and kissed her lips. She wrapped her free arm around him and squeezed, not breaking the kiss. She suddenly feared this might be the last intimate moment they shared. Neither of them was assured they'd survive the attack against the Circle of Unity.

Finally, he pulled away. "Micah told us that since we had held back our wolves for two years that we would be more powerful than ever. I'm not exactly sure why he believes that. But, just in case, both of you need to find Raven as quickly as possible. We'll take care of the demons and vampires."

"And if she's a vampire?"

"Either kill her, or run like Hell."

Forrest reached the bottom rung. The rusted old ladder creaked and his foot broke through the rung. He gazed up the ladder. "Heads up, I broke the bottom one!"

Gunner was halfway down and shouted, "I told you that you should have gone *last.*"

Forrest shook his head. Gunner released the next to last rung and dropped to the tunnel floor beside Forrest. Ian plopped beside him.

Taking a deep breath, Forrest looked at Gunner and nodded. "Vampires are nearby. I smell them."

Kailey frowned as she studied Forrest. "You can really smell them?"

Forrest nodded.

"How?"

"When you've hunted them all over the world for as many years as I have, the stench of the undead is quickly identifiable, especially when there's a large number of them."

"I don't smell anything that resembles death. Just musty air," Kailey replied.

"Nor do I," Brady said.

Forrest smiled. "When it's your life or theirs, believe me, you'll learn to recognize the scent or you'll be dead before you can see them attack. The smell isn't like a rotten carcass. It's much milder or else they'd have little hope to attract others to them. That's part of their glamour."

"Makes sense to me," Kailey said.

Forrest looked at Brady. "You need to understand that it's important that we kill *all* of them."

"That's the plan," Brady replied.

Kailey's eyebrows rose. "All of them?"

"Every ... single ... one," Forrest hissed out each word for emphasis. "You cannot trust them to keep a promise. If you allow them to live, they will bring their disease to the surface. Once they get a foothold in a city's population, people flee and desolation follows. They prey upon anyone that remains behind."

Brady nodded. "Like Micah and I have told you, Kailey, that's happening in Seattle right now. The vampires have become bolder and taken government office seats, key positions in the police force, and even the mayor's office. Their subtleness is fading, and they will soon make more noticeable advances. Seattle's a large city and a good breeding ground."

Jaclyn eyed Forrest. "How long have you hunted vampires?"

"Going on thirty years."

"Who trained you?"

"My father and my cousin, Jacques."

Jaclyn cocked an eyebrow, watching his facial expressions. "Your accent doesn't sound American or Canadian."

Forrest chuckled. "I'm native to Romania. My father and I have scoured all sorts of dark towns, villas, and cities, trying to eradicate the vampire infestation. But their disease isn't something a couple of people can effectively destroy."

"Where is your father?" Kailey asked.

Forrest looked away. "Dead."

"Sorry."

Micah and the remainder of the pack stood around them. Some of the pack snarled and gnashed their teeth.

"What happened to him?" Brady asked.

Forrest cleared his throat and his jaw tightened. "My father's death is the reason I said that you cannot trust a vampire. We made the mistake of trusting a vampire in the mountains near the Black Forest in Germany because he had paid us to find a lair of vampires and destroy them. What we didn't realize was that he had hired us to wipe out his opposing hierarchy, giving him the rule of the area. After we had accepted partial payment for our services to kill his opponent, we headed up the narrow mountain trail in the dead of night. Strange bat-like creatures swooped from the mountainside and landed in the leafless tree branches over the narrow path. I found out later that these were the same creatures he had sent with us to destroy his rival, only he had never mentioned them to us. But now they had come to kill us. To make a long story short ... after we had fought with every weapon we had, we were surrounded and my father was killed."

"How did you survive?" Kailey asked.

"One of the winged creatures grabbed me and flew off with me. I fought with it and plummeted over the edge of the rugged bluff. The creature didn't want to die and used its wings to slow our descent. I slit its throat with a dagger and grabbed its hand-like appendages on its wings to use its wings to glide into the rushing river. Gunner's brother, Ian, pulled me from the frigid waters, which prevented me from drowning or being thrashed to death by rocks under the rapids."

Micah glanced at Kailey. "Flora won't wait past the deadline, if I know how the founders of the Circle of Unity behave."

Jaclyn nodded. "Micah's right."

Micah said, "My pack is growing restless. I cannot ask them to hold back their beasts any longer. My suggestion is that you get through the tunnel as swiftly as possible."

Kailey looked at Jaclyn. "You ready?"

Jaclyn nodded. "I've not jogged in a long time, but a pack of aggressive werewolves behind me is enough incentive to run a marathon if necessary."

Brady took Kailey's hand. "You're going to hear some ferocious snarls and yelping. The most dominant will nip at the lessers. Trust me, we're not killing one another, although it might sound like it. Don't stop. Just keep running. Get to where the tunnel looks blocked." He glanced at Jaclyn. "How long will it take for you to remove that spell?"

"Since the Grimoire has the original spell written out, and my mother also wrote a reversal spell, it won't take but a few minutes."

"That's good. Then the two of you get inside Nocturnal Trinity quickly. Both of you be careful."

Kailey smiled and nodded.

"Run!" Brady said.

The intensity in his voice jolted Kailey and was more motivating than a firing pistol at the beginning of a race. She and Jaclyn tore into a sprint without glancing back. Kailey held the machete at a safe angle while she ran, so that if she fell, she wouldn't impale herself.

Jaclyn tucked the Grimoire tightly beneath her arm while she ran, and Kailey tried to keep the flashlight's beam on the path directly in front of them. Bats acrobatically swooped between their heads. Little red eyes occasionally appeared in the light. The fat sewer rats squeaked and waddled into the shadows, fearful of the two women's pounding footsteps.

CHAPTER 46

Growls, snarls, and bellowing roars echoed in the dark tunnel behind Kailey and Jaclyn. Chill bumps covered Kailey's arms and back. Her body quaked from what sounded like a zoo in total chaos a couple of blocks behind them. She ran faster.

Occasionally she glanced over her shoulder to see Jaclyn panting hard, but the determined woman keep jogging, albeit much slower than earlier on. Kailey was glad that she was in top shape. Part of her daily workout regiment was to jog four miles, which gave her an advantage over Jaclyn, but probably none over the growling werewolves running in their direction.

Kailey watched for the manhole ladders as she ran. She paused at each one and washed the light over the sign attached to the wall, which indicated what street they had reached. They still had not come to Pine Street, and she wondered if Jaclyn was right about not bringing Skye down into the tunnel. The elder witch was in rough shape. Kailey couldn't see any way that Skye could pick up the pace for another block to escape the rush of the pack.

Nearing the next manhole, the flashlight lit up "Pine Street."

Kailey was half elated and half fearful to be heading up. Stopping long enough to go up the ladder gave her some time to catch her breath, but the amount of time also granted the werewolves the ability to catch up to their position.

"I'm going up to get her," Kailey said, stopping at the ladder. She handed the flashlight to Jaclyn.

Instead of the argument she expected Jaclyn to give, Jaclyn nodded, grabbed a ladder rung, and panted. "Okay. Hurry. I'll keep watch."

Lines of sweat ran down Kailey's cheeks. She gasped slightly, handing the machete to Jaclyn. She then grabbed the rungs and hurried up the ladder. She slid the manhole cover to the side, peering up enough to see whether any traffic was coming. Nothing, so she braved rising higher. On the street curb, Skye sat on a bench.

"Skye!"

The witch raised her head and looked toward the open manhole.

"Hurry!"

Skye used her cane to brace herself and rise from the bench. She hobbled between two parked cars and groaned as she crouched down, trying to sit on the pavement so she could find the ladder rung with her feet.

"Hand me the cane," Kailey said. Skye did so. "Meet you at the bottom."

Kailey reached the bottom of the ladder and found Jaclyn reading the spell for the illusion. The snarls of the wolves grew closer. Kailey looked up to check Skye's progress. The older woman was coming downward much faster than Kailey or Jaclyn expected. When Skye was within their reach, Jaclyn and Kailey helped the woman balance on the floor between them.

Snapping jaws and brazen growls neared.

Skye's eyes widened. "That's them?"

Kailey nodded. "Yes. We don't have much time."

Jaclyn looped her left arm in with Skye's right arm while Kailey looped her right with Skye's left. They hoped by holding her between them, they'd reach the illusion barrier with enough time for Jaclyn to reverse the spell before the pack was upon them.

"I think I have the counter spell memorized," Jaclyn said.

"Good," Skye said. "That will save some time."

"It's hard to estimate, but my guess is that they are two blocks or so behind us, which isn't a lot of time," Kailey said.

"Sorry I'm slowing you down," Skye said.

Kailey leaned her head toward Skye's and patted the older woman's shoulder. "I promised to get you there."

"If it comes down to your lives, leave me behind and go rescue Raven."

"Nonsense," Kailey replied.

"You can't rescue her if you're dead," Skye said. "None of us can."

"Let's hope that it doesn't come to that. There's the chance that the wolves will recognize our scent."

Jaclyn said, "I've not dealt with shape-shifters before, so I can't tell you whether or not that's true."

"Brady knows our scents well, as do Micah and Ashley. I don't think they will attack us, and they probably will defend us should any of the others try," Kailey said.

"I wouldn't bet on it, and I don't want to find out the hard way," Jaclyn said.

"I'll keep moving with Skye," Kailey said. "You go on ahead and start the spell reversal."

"You sure?"

Kailey nodded.

"Okay." Jaclyn carefully unhooked her arm from Skye's. Once she was certain that Skye had her balance, Jaclyn handed the machete to Kailey and sprinted ahead into the darkness with the Grimoire and flashlight.

The darkness swallowed Kailey and Skye. The approaching pack was more intimidating in the pitch-blackness.

Kailey continued moving forward with Skye. "Can I ask you something?"

"Sure," Skye replied.

"What happened to you last night?"

"What do you mean?"

"You seem to have aged ten years or more. Your health was completely depleted in only a few hours. Raven had told me many time that some spells can be taxing on the body and mind, requiring days, sometimes weeks, to recover. Is that what happened?"

"Yes. I was trying to aid Raven."

"How?"

A sliver of light shone through a metal grating at the edge of the sidewalk above, offering little light but alleviating the impenetrable darkness.

Skye coughed and held a hand for Kailey to stop a moment. "Sorry. Having difficulty breathing in this dank old air."

"It's okay. We can rest in the light for a minute. What happened?"

"I cast a blood spell, hoping to send the essence of my spirit to Raven to give her strength to add to her magic since I had no way of contacting her. By doing so, her powers would increase and she would have had more power to fight Flora or whoever else might be holding her captive."

"Do you think it worked?" Kailey asked.

Skye shook her head. "Not for Raven. But someone intercepted the spell and drained me, not only my magic but my health as well."

"Someone else?"

"Yes. One of our enemies is now more powerful because of my foolishness, which is why your premonition is probably true."

"About Raven being a vampire?"

Skye nodded.

"So Raven never received your blessing or communication?"

"Sadly no."

"Oh, Skye ..." Kailey wrapped her arms around Skye and hugged her.

Several long howls reverberated through the tunnel.

"Shit," Kailey whispered. "They're getting too close."

"Leave me."

Kailey shook her head. "I could never do that. Hang on."

Kailey scooped Skye into her arms and cradled her, and then she ran.

"You're going to hurt yourself," Skye said.

"No, I won't. But I hope the jarring won't hurt you. We have less than a block to go."

"I'm fine."

Ahead, the flashlight glowed at Jaclyn's feet. Behind them, the werewolves were swiftly approaching. Kailey wasn't certain if she'd reach Jaclyn before the wolves reached her. She tried not to think about it. Instead, she simply ran harder and faster.

CHAPTER 47

When Kailey reached Jaclyn and set Skye down safely, Jaclyn stood in the tunnel where beams, concrete, and other obstructions blocked the path. Kailey picked up the flashlight.

Kailey whispered, "For something that's not real, it definitely fools me."

"That's the power of magic," Skye replied softly.

Jaclyn extended her hands with her eyes closed. She chanted the spell over and over. While she recited the incantation, the sound of the frenzied wolf pack was closing in behind them. After the seventh recital, the illusion faded but a new danger presented itself. On both sides of the tunnel were several dozen coffins.

Metal shelves attached to the walls were spaced adequately apart so the coffins could be stacked three high with enough room in between to open the lids.

Jaclyn opened her eyes.

"What's this?" Kailey asked, pointing at the caskets. "Another illusion?"

Jaclyn shook her head, grabbed the Grimoire, and backed toward Skye and Kailey. "No. These are new."

"Someone else's illusion?" Skye asked.

"They're real coffins," Jaclyn replied. "There's no magic on them."

Kailey swallowed hard. "Why are they here?"

"Young guards for the elders' fortress would be my guess, but my mother has never mentioned these. Of course with the contention growing within the circle, she might not have even known about this. We've not talked in a long time."

Coffin lids creaked opened slowly. Kailey shone the flashlight toward stairwell.

"Shit!" Kailey said. "What do we do?"

"Stay close," Jaclyn said. "The pack is almost here. Once they arrive, we must stay out of the way. Although Barry thought it a joke, Micah was dead serious. Any bite or scratch from the pack will alter us. Not immediately, but even my magic cannot reverse the infection."

"And vampire bites?" Skye asked.

Jaclyn said, "I'd avoid those, too."

"Where do we go then? There's nowhere out of the vampires' reach here. Going back simply puts us in the pack's direct line of attack. What do you suggest we do?" Kailey asked, taking Skye's hand.

Kailey washed the light around the tunnel and then back toward the stairwell. The two coffins nearest the stairwell were open and the young vampire occupants stood at the bottom of the stairs. The male looked like any number of the male Goths she had seen standing in the line outside Nocturnal Trinity a couple nights earlier. The female wore a low-cut silken gown, which stopped short of exposing her nipples. Her death complexion needed no makeup to fit in with the emo or gothic wannabes, and her seductively thin, see through tight gown was enough to mesmerize any young horny male or female. The rate of recruitment for vampires was probably higher than any religion or other type of organization in the world.

The two vampires' eyes gleamed with hunger, need. They bore fangs in an instant. The glare of the flashlight didn't seem to deter their advance.

"Don't make eye contact with them," Jaclyn said. "They're young, but they are still capable of compulsion."

Jaclyn stood between the two vampires and Kailey and Skye. She held her arms to her sides like a fence to prevent Kailey or Skye from advancing past her.

"Where are your stakes?" Jaclyn asked.

"I have one tucked behind my belt and one in my purse."

"Mind if I borrow one?"

"Not at all," Kailey said, pulling the one from behind her back and handing it to Jaclyn. "Help yourself."

Jaclyn took a deep breath. "You know, the entire time I've been a guest at Nocturnal Trinity to visit with my mother, I've never had to stake a vampire. It's honestly never been a thought in my mind. I truly never believed I'd have to."

"Would you rather I try?" Kailey asked.

Jaclyn shook her head. She took one step toward the male vampire, and an instant later, he held Jaclyn in his grasp, reared back his head to bite her neck, his sharp fangs glistening in the flashlight's glow.

Kailey's hand tightened on the machete, but she didn't see any possible way to decapitate the vampire without removing Jaclyn's head as well.

One second later his head rolled across the tunnel floor. His body dropped to the concrete and disintegrated into ash. The fluid movement occurred so quickly that Kailey had momentarily thought she had done it with her own mind.

Jaclyn shrieked, dropping the stake, and falling to her knees. Kailey quickly grabbed her, and pulled her back.

The pack had arrived.

The noise of their arrival awakened the other vampires. Coffin lids opened all around them. Vampires rose. Some of the awakening vampires were staked and died before they ever got the chance to climb out of their coffins. Several positioned themselves near the stairwell while a half dozen more pressed to encircle Kailey, Skye, and Jaclyn from behind.

The most frightening snarl roared a few feet away from Kailey. A massive beast lunged over them and lopped the heads off three vampires in one powerful swipe. The giant claws resembled small swords. Before the heads struck the floor, the grizzly bear barreled headfirst into the other three, separating their heads from their shoulders with a second swipe of its huge paw.

"Where the hell did the bear come from?" Kailey asked.

Jaclyn grabbed Kailey's arm and jerked her and Skye into the shadows. "I do believe the bear must be Forrest."

"Seriously?"

"Yes. Apparently he's a bear-shifter."

"Didn't know such things existed," Kailey said. "But he certainly has the build for it."

Hell, I didn't know werewolves and vampires existed, either.

Blurs of fur rushed past Kailey, Jaclyn, and Skye. Apparently, Kailey's assumption was correct, at least for now. The werewolves either recognized the women's scents or their disdain toward the attacking vampires kept their focus on destroying the undead instead of the living.

The pack members were half human and half wolf. The way Brady and the others had talked, she had visualized them simply turning into large wolves, but they were hybridized, having the characteristics of both man and wolf. And somewhere within the attacking undead and monstrous wolfmen, two odd weasel-like creatures were gnawing at the throats of other vampires. She guessed these two were Gunner and Ian since the grizzly bear was Forrest.

Kailey found herself wishing that she was drunk because at least then the explanations for what was occurring around her would make more sense.

As werewolves grappled with vampires, the path to the stairwell was cleared.

Kailey nodded. "We have an opening. Let's go."

"I think the pack has everything under control," Jaclyn said. "But understand that these younger vampires are unseasoned and much weaker than anything we will encounter as we head upward. With vampires, power comes with age."

They were almost to the stairs when a young male vampire suddenly appeared at the foot of the stairwell. Jaclyn readied her stake and advanced. She swung the stake overhead and downward, but the vampire caught her wrist and twisted.

She cried out in a high squeal, dropping the stake again.

"Duck," Kailey said.

Jaclyn leaned forward. Kailey took the machete handle in both hands and swung. The vampire's head separated from its body. Blood sprayed.

Kailey felt her stomach twist with sudden nausea. "How the hell does someone do this for a living?"

"Watch out!" Skye yelled.

Another vampire lunged forward, but Kailey wasn't prepared. She took a step to the side, but was at an impossible angle to use the machete. The vampire slammed into her, knocking her to the tunnel floor. She tried not to scream or panic, but lost on both counts.

Rolling quickly to the side, she slung the vampire partway off, exposing enough of his chest for Jaclyn to plunge the stake into his chest. The vampire's eyes widened for a moment, and then he fell to dust.

Jaclyn extended her hand down to Kailey and helped pull her to her feet. She glanced around and watched the pack tearing into other vampires. A few of the werewolves were being overpowered, but the path to the stair-well was open again.

"Come on," Jaclyn said. "Hurry."

Kailey knew the power Flora had. She had felt it, and she feared it.

"What's our best approach on going up?" Kailey asked as they reached the stairs.

"Get Skye out of the commotion here, and I need to find my mother. She needs to know we're here."

"She'll help us?"

Jaclyn nodded. "I'm hoping she can tell us where Raven is. She should have some idea."

"And Cassie?"

"The succubus?"

"Yes."

"One thing at a time," Jaclyn said. "Rescue is one thing. Revenge is some-thing completely different. Which is more essential to you?"

"Saving Raven, of course."

"Then that's where you focus first. Unless Cassie presents herself beforehand."

"Okay."

Kailey wiped blood from her face and then helped Skye ascend the spiral stairs. As they rounded each level, the snarls and growls grew softer. She wondered why Forrest had spent so much time discussing the different weapons when it seemed the grizzly had enough power and strength to dispose of several vampires in a couple of swipes. The fact that he was a bear-shifter brought many more questions to her mind.

Skye panted and leaned into a corner off the stairwell. "I can't go up any farther."

Kailey looked at Jaclyn with concern. "How much farther?"

"A couple more turns."

Skye shook her head. "No, Kailey, I'm spent. Give me a few minutes and I'll try to work my way on up."

Jaclyn nodded at Kailey. "She's right. I hate to say it, but she is slowing us down."

"I hate leaving you," Kailey said.

"I'll be fine. Once I catch my breath, I'll make my way up."

Kailey fought tears. She leaned forward and embraced Skye. For some reason, Kailey thought it would be the last time she'd ever hug the old woman. "I'll find Raven."

"Blessings, child, and courage."

Kailey smiled and pulled away from Skye. Her heart ached leaving Skye behind. They were so close. But in Skye's condition, the witch wasn't strong enough to even cast a spell. The poor woman was fighting for her breath.

Skye eased down to the corner of the wall, took a deep breath, and closed her eyes.

Kailey turned and hurried after Jaclyn.

Jaclyn tucked the Grimoire inside her robe and tightened her belt. "The last thing we need is for them to get their hands on this book."

"Why would you bring it into Nocturnal Trinity? Wouldn't it have been safer to hide it down in the tunnel?"

"No. I still need it."

"What for?"

"To cripple the circle's power. Plus, I hope to destroy their summoning circle. If I can accomplish that, it would prevent the demons from calling other powerful demons out of the abyss. That's why I need to find my mother. With her help and the aid of the other two witches, we'll have enough power to perform the ritual."

"Where should we look first?"

"At this hour, my mother is normally in the VIP lounge preparing the festivities for any guests the founders have chosen."

Kailey explained the practical joke that was played on her that first night and how she had been granted the consolation prize of membership. "Do they tend to do that sort of thing often?"

Jaclyn shrugged. "Several have warped sense of humors, especially the demons. They love practical jokes and thrive on mockery at times. I've learned to ignore them when I was allowed to visit."

The stairwell stopped at a dark corridor. Music pulsed, slightly vibrating the walls.

"Where are we?" Kailey asked.

"Outside of one of the dance floors. I think we're in the demon section. Follow me."

Jaclyn turned left and eased along the edge of the wall. Kailey followed close behind, using the flashlight to illuminate the floor.

A whispering sound made Jaclyn stop walking. She turned and pressed an index finger to her lips. "Turn off the light."

"What is it?" Kailey whispered.

"Somebody's up ahead."

Kailey flicked off the light. In the narrow corridor ahead of them, red demonic eyes glowed. The demon laughed with mockery. She had no doubt that it was Cassie.

"That's her," Kailey said, darting around Jaclyn.

"Kailey, don't! We need to stick together."

"This won't take but a minute."

"Kailey!" Jaclyn shouted, hurrying after her.

CHAPTER 48

Kailey's determination, much like her sudden foolishness, kept her blind to realizing her actual dangers. She was doing the very thing she had scolded Raven for doing. By the time Kailey thought of the damage the demon had done to her before, she stood in a small room with the succubus. Several sconces lit the room.

"Kailey!" Jaclyn shouted from the corridor.

Cassie waved her hand and the door slammed shut, housing Kailey with the demon in the small room. The door on the other side was still open, but Cassie stood at it.

Jaclyn beat on the closed door.

"It's easy for me to feel your hatred toward me. You wish to kill me."

Kailey nodded.

"If this is what you wanted," Cassie said, "let's finish it."

Cassie's tail looped around Kailey and flung her toward the wall. Instinctively, Kailey placed her hands before her to cushion the impact. Pain rattled from her hands to her elbows. She dropped to her knees, her hands numb. The machete clanged and bounced on the floor. Cassie's tail swiped the blade across the room, well out of Kailey's reach.

She wanted to pull the blade from her strapped-on purse, but her hands felt as though a million needles were stuck in them. She rose and turned.

"I'll give you one last chance to leave me alone," Cassie said, "and you can live."

Kailey's jaw tightened. "You are the one that's going to die."

Cassie pursed her lips and shook her head in disbelief. "You'd think a girl would learn. Of course, you *are* human. I guess that makes you a bit dumber."

Anger consumed Kailey. In spite of what her trainers had taught her over the years to never react out of anger or verbal assaults, she ignored the wisdom and rushed straight at Cassie.

Cassie mocked a yawn, patting her hand over her open mouth, taunting her.

When Kailey was midway across the room, Cassie's tail wrapped around Kailey's waist, lifted her off the floor, and brought her face-to-face with the demon.

Kailey's hands still tingled, but she had enough feeling to make fists. With a solid right, she struck Cassie's left jaw, rattling the demon off balance.

"Uh!" Cassie said, falling back and covering her face with her hand. Her tail loosened its hold, releasing Kailey. Cassie rubbed her cheek. "Damn, girl. You sure you're not part demon? That hurt!"

Cassie lowered her hand, revealing a huge bruise.

Kailey smiled.

So you do bruise. I wonder if you bleed, too.

Cassie staggered and shook her head. Before she totally gained her balance, Kailey moved in closer and jabbed several punches into the demon's stomach, pressing the demon against the wall. Cassie bent forward in pain, hissed, but before Kailey noticed, Cassie used her tail to sweep Kailey's feet out from under her.

Dammit! Watch the tail.

Kailey hit the floor hard, winced, but shoved herself up while Cassie was still in pain. She knew from her bouts to never stay down. Doing so gave the advantage to her opponent. But she also needed to stay clear of the demon's tail.

Kailey stood in a defensive pose with both fists raised.

Cassie studied Kailey for a moment. "Why is your rage and hatred directed toward me?"

"You know why."

Kailey rushed forward and struck Cassie again. Blood leaked from the demon's lips. The demon wiped away the blood with her hands, looked at it, and licked it from her fingertips. She hissed again, baring jagged teeth, and then all the beauty that Kailey had ever seen in the demon vanished, quickly becoming a most hideous creature. She couldn't help but wonder what Vincent would have thought if he'd known she looked like this beneath the surface.

Cassie released a shriek that reverberated through Kailey's body, causing Kailey to recoil in sheer agony.

"You don't know what you're fighting, do you?" Cassie asked. "All I've asked is that you let me be, and yet, you continue attacking me. Your persistence has brought you a quick death."

Cassie no longer stood on two feet. She lowered to the floor and became a scaly creature with four legs. Almost like a lizard, but little horns protruded along her spine and appendages.

Kailey had never believed in a hell, and only partly accepted that the abyss was where the demons had come from, but seeing this demon form, she no longer doubted a horrid realm like an abyss existed. How else could one explain it?

How was she supposed to fight this thing?

Then it dawned upon Kailey. Illusions, magic. Such had kept the pack from heading through the tunnel because it looked like it had collapsed and was blocked. The succubus took many forms, as had Jinn. Surely, this was just another way Cassie could alter herself to manipulate an enemy.

Kailey clenched her fists tighter and ran toward the creature. Its eyes widened. Instead of punching, Kailey brought up a harsh kick to its jaw with enough strength that it rose off the floor and crashed its back against the wall.

The lizard form dissolved, bringing Cassie back into her succubus form. "Damn, doesn't *anything* frighten you?"

Kailey didn't reply. She threw continuous jabs into Cassie's abdominals. Cassie helplessly tried to block the blows, but Kailey crouched lower and kept punching.

In desperation, Cassie brought around her tail, but this time, Kailey was prepared. She stomped her boot onto the tail and twisted the toe of her boot back and forth.

Cassie screamed, but the pain didn't deter her. Instead, it ignited the strength of the demon. Cassie thrust forward with both hands, striking Kailey in the chest and knocking her back about ten feet. Before Kailey caught her balance and reset her feet, Cassie swung her tail full force, smacking Kailey's jaw, and spinning her into the air. Kailey landed face-down on her elbows.

Pain tore through her. Everything spun, darkened.

Jaclyn beat harder on the door, shouting for Kailey.

Kailey thought it was over, and the demon was going to kill her.

She struggled to get up, but her head splintered in agony. Her ears rang. She'd never taken a punch like that before by a contender or trainer, and she'd never been knocked unconscious before either, but she assumed that she was close to dropping or tapping out.

"Why don't you leave me alone?" Cassie asked. She took several deep breaths, steadying herself against the wall. "I didn't want to kill you, but you really have left me no choice."

Kailey shook her head, wincing, and pushed herself into a seated position. The dim room seemed darker, but she fought to stay awake. She leaned forward with her hands on her knees, trying to clear her head and hoping that the incessant ringing in her ears would cease. She looked up enough to see where Cassie was. A slight few moments of vertigo set in and the room kept moving, making her stomach churn. The succubus had stepped away from the wall and was slowly dragging her feet across the floor, heading toward Kailey. Apparently Kailey had disoriented the demon somewhat as well.

Kailey eased the obsidian dagger from the side of her strapped on purse and held it in her palm where she hoped Cassie didn't see it.

Cassie paused long enough to take several more deep breaths. "Honestly I don't know why you're bent on fighting me."

Kailey grunted and forced back her pain, taking one last charge at Cassie. Since her vision was still coming back into focus, she aimed at the Cassie in the middle of the three swirling Cassies before her. Luckily, she hit her target.

Surprise widened Cassie's eyes as Kailey shoved her weight against the succubus and slammed her against the wall. Before Cassie could attempt to counter the attack, Kailey put the dagger to her throat.

"You want to know why I keep coming?" Kailey seethed.

"It really would be nice to know," Cassie replied in a whisper as her fearful eyes peered down at the dagger.

"Because my brother is dead."

"I understand that it's hard for anyone to lose a loved one."

"Really?"

"Yes."

"Is that why you made such a mockery at his funeral?" Kailey asked. "Trying to seduce his coworker into coming home with you?"

"What? What the hell are you talking about?"

"You know exactly what I'm talking about. I was there. I watched your pitiful act of trying to make everyone feel sorry for you. You were hitting on Frank only moments after the prayer."

Cassie eyed Kailey and attempted to shake her head. "Honestly, I don't know what you're talking about."

The pleading tone in Cassie's voice was convincing, but she was also a demon. If a demon was capable of changing her appearance for the art of deception, she was well able to also sound genuine, even when she was lying.

Kailey pressed the blessed obsidian dagger against Cassie's throat and pinned her into a corner of the room. "I'm sick of the lies."

"Kill me, if you believe it will make you feel better," Cassie hissed through her sharp teeth. "But doing so won't bring him back."

Kailey smiled. "Let me clarify something for you. This blade was created and blessed to destroy succubae, which means, once you're sent to the abyss, you cannot come back. You're trapped there for eternity."

Cassie's eyes showed deeper fear. Her lower lip trembled, but she kept her fangs visible. "Go ahead if you must, but know that if you do, you'll never get out of Nocturnal Trinity alive."

"That's where you're mistaken," Kailey replied. "I didn't come here alone."

"One witch won't do you much good though."

"I know. That's why I'm not so worried."

Cassie studied Kailey but she didn't reply.

"Why did you kill Vincent?" Kailey asked. Tears burned her eyes, but she refused to give the demon the satisfaction of seeing them trickle down her face.

"I never killed your brother," Cassie said softly. Tears welled in her eyes, too. "I truly loved him. I loved him more than anything, and I would never have hurt him."

Kailey gnashed her teeth and growled, pressing the blade firmer against Cassie's throat. "You admitted to killing him when you confronted me in his office."

"No," Cassie said. "No. I didn't kill him."

"You said that you did!"

"That wasn't *me*."

Kailey rolled her eyes and huffed. "You have to be kidding? How can you expect me to believe this after you have already told me that you did? Then you tried to kill me when I brought this pendant too close to you."

"I have no fear of your pendant." She reached up cautiously, her eyes staring at the dagger pressed against her throat, and held the silver pendant between her index finger and thumb. Nothing happened. "See?"

Tears rolled down Kailey's cheeks. "No, when you tried to kill me the pendant was blessed by my roommate, Raven. This is not the same spell."

"Raven?"

Kailey nodded. "You know of her?"

Cassie shook her head. "No."

"Stop lying! Raven is gone," Kailey said. "Flora had you take her."

"What?" Cassie's stunned expressions showed that the demon was confused by the accusations. "Take her where? *Why* would I take her?"

And the Oscar goes to ...

Kailey's tone lowered. "You vanished with her. I have witnesses."

"What reason would I have?" Cassie said with pleading eyes.

"For the same reason you attacked me at Vincent's office. You wanted the key that I found."

Cassie blinked absentmindedly. "What key?"

"Stop with your amnesia bullshit! Don't act like you don't know what I'm talking about."

The succubus bit her lower lip. Tears spilled down her cheeks. She totally relaxed against Kailey. Her eyes indicated she was searching for reasoning and understanding, but her dominant blank expression remained. "I honestly don't know."

Frustration built inside Kailey. She pressed the dagger harder, making an indention in Cassie's skin. Kailey eased back slightly because she feared she might prematurely stab Cassie. Could it be the succubus was telling the truth?

"If I can assist you in any way, I will," Cassie said.

"Help me? When I came toward you in Vincent's office, you flung me across the room and then you disappeared in a mighty explosion. *You tried to kill me.* How can you expect me to ever believe anything you say?"

"Please, either kill me or lower the blade so I can explain what I *do* know, okay?" Cassie's crimson eyes were wide and striking. The veins in her neck were swollen. Even with horns and fangs, she was a beautifully exotic creature, and she saw perfectly why her brother had been attracted to her.

"I'll lower the blade if you will open the door for Jaclyn."

Cassie gave a slight nod. The door opened, and Jaclyn burst through. She frowned. "What the hell is going on?"

CHAPTER 49

Jaclyn gave a perplexed glance toward Kailey. "Why haven't you ended her?"

"Information," Kailey replied.

"Ah," Jaclyn said, her jaw tightening. "Are you having any luck with that approach?"

"Hard to say. I can't tell whether she's telling me the truth about some things or not."

Cassie said in a soft, pleading voice, "Please, the blade? You promised."

Kailey was hesitant to lower the blade. Jaclyn's spell on the pendant ensured Kailey protection from a magical attack and the obsidian dagger could kill the succubus should Cassie lunge at her. All Kailey needed to do was to stab the succubus.

Should she trust a demon?

"I promise that I won't attack either of you."

Jaclyn grinned. "You're really not in any position to cause us any harm. I'm certain Kailey told you what the blade is capable of doing."

"Yes." Cassie swallowed hard and then licked her lips. "You can trust me."

"And my magic can do worse by making you suffer immense pain *before* she stabs you," Jaclyn said.

Kailey eased the blade back from the succubus' throat. The indentation remained on her skin, but she took a deep breath and exhaled slowly. Kailey backed a few steps away from the demon.

Cassie straightened and rubbed her throat. Fresh tears leaked from the sides of her eyes. The bruise and cut lip that Kailey had gifted the succubus with were still there. In fact, the bruise appeared to be swelling.

Demons must be slow healers ...

In spite of the bruise, the demon still possessed unequaled beauty. Kailey found it difficult to stare at her for too long. The seductress might not need to attack physically when she could use lust in her favor.

"Talk. We don't have any time to waste," Kailey said. "Why tell me that you killed my brother and now deny it?"

"First, Nicodemus betrayed me."

Jaclyn frowned. "Nicodemus?"

"How?" Kailey asked.

"They used the summoning circle and ..."

"To summon you?" Kailey asked.

Cassie vehemently shook her head. Tears spilled from her shimmering crimson eyes. She wiped them away. "No. I've been here for years. Nicodemus said that they needed me to help them perform a ritual. They promised that if I cooperated, they'd release me and allow me to stay married to Vincent. They lied."

"What did they do?"

"They told me to stand in the center of the summoning circle. The eighteen council members of Nocturnal Trinity focused their individual talents, magic, and energy toward the circle. When the portal opened, they conjured up shadow demons. Instead of granting me my freedom, they bound the shadow demons to me. These demons controlled me, and I couldn't break free of their bonds. Some of the things I did happened under their control, and I don't know what I did during those times."

"When was this?" Kailey asked.

"A couple of months ago."

"Marvelous, fantastic story. I'd love to believe you—"

Cassie nodded, closed her eyes, and more tears flowed. "I understand. It's okay. Kill me if you don't believe me. Without Vincent, I'd rather be dead anyway. So finish me. I won't put up a fight." She placed her hands behind her head and tilted her head upward, offering Kailey the easiest place to use the dagger. A second later, her long tail vanished, lessening her advantage of inflicting harm upon Kailey.

Jaclyn said, "Kailey, she's telling the truth."

Kailey turned sharply and looked at Jaclyn with surprise. "You believe her?"

"I do."

"When did these shadow demons stop controlling you?" Kailey asked.

"Last night."

Kailey struggled with what to do. She wanted to avenge Vincent, but if the succubus was telling the truth, Cassie hadn't actually killed Vincent. A dark force or demon through her probably had killed him. Was Cassie capable of deceiving Jaclyn, too? That was the more important question, wasn't it? Since Kailey trusted Jaclyn and not the succubus, the demon won through deception.

You're overthinking again ...

But if Cassie had genuinely loved Vincent and had done him no harm, Kailey would be the true murderer if she killed the succubus with the blessed dagger. That wasn't something Kailey could live with. Even if it was a demon, it was still murder. The one who set Cassie up was the guilty party and that was the person, demon, or vampire that should pay.

Kailey sighed. "Raven told me that Vincent was being drained. That's what a succubus does, right?"

Cassie slowly opened her eyes and lowered her hands. "Usually, yes. But we'd never kill or totally drain a lover unless he or she had done something vile or unfaithfully pursued another demon or human lover. Vincent was a kind, sweet man, Kailey. He loved me. I loved him."

"You never fed from him?" Kailey asked.

"I never drank his blood. He fed me in a *different* way."

"How?"

Cassie cocked one brow and pursed her lips. "You really *want* that information?"

Kailey's eyes widened, realizing what the succubus was suggesting, and she blushed. Kailey shook her head. "Never mind. I get it."

Jaclyn laughed softly.

Tears flowed from Cassie's eyes. "Vincent was so proud of you, Kailey. He was looking forward to you coming to Seattle. And while you probably don't believe it right now, I couldn't wait to meet you."

Hot tears burned in Kailey's eyes. "If you didn't kill him, when did you learn of his murder?"

"Last ... night. They told me how he was found. While I cannot prove it, I believe Nicodemus is the one responsible."

Kailey lowered the blade from an offensive position, and held it to her side, just in case. "Are you still being controlled by the shadow demons?"

She shook her head. "No."

"Where are these demons now?" Jaclyn asked.

"Inside Nicodemus. He took them into himself, consuming their powers, and making himself one of the most powerful vampires ever. Possibly invincible."

"Why don't they control him?"

Cassie smiled. "The witches cast spells to prevent them from rebelling against him. They are bound to him in such a way that he has access to their power, whereas I was controlled by them."

Jaclyn frowned and looked at Kailey. "I can't see how my mother allowed herself to get involved in casting such a spell. We cannot allow this. Nicodemus must be stopped."

"I'll do whatever I can to help you," Cassie said. "Because of Nicodemus, Vincent is dead. I ache inside without him, his touch."

Kailey stared at Cassie. The succubus was broken. Grief weighed upon her.

"I miss him, too," Kailey said softly.

Jaclyn said, "She doesn't know where Raven is, even though she was the one who grabbed Raven and then vanished with her?"

Kailey and Cassie shook their heads.

Cassie said, "Like I told you. Whatever those shadow demons made me do, escapes me."

Jaclyn frowned but after a few seconds, she nodded slightly. "Okay, I'll accept that for now but it sounds awfully convenient an excuse."

Cassie sighed. "I recognize that it does, especially after what's happened. All I can do is offer my help and hope to gain your trust."

Kailey tucked the dagger back into her purse. "Jaclyn, is there any spell you could cast on Cassie to help her remember where she took Raven?"

"None that I can think of."

Kailey grieved inside. She wanted to be absolutely certain that Cassie was being truthful. Since Kailey had built up so much animosity inside about Cassie, she found it difficult to suddenly begin trusting her, but she wasn't left with much choice. Given the information about what Nicodemus had done to increase his power, that was the greatest threat against all of them. That was also information Cassie wouldn't have revealed if she truly was an enemy.

"Cassie," Jaclyn said. "Are you really interested in proving yourself to us?"

Apparently, Jaclyn felt the same way.

Cassie nodded. "Yes."

"There is something I need you to do."

"Anything. Name it."

"Without alerting any vampires or demons of our arrival, I need you to find my mother, Eva, and tell her that we're here. Tell her to bring the other two female witches with her."

"Why?" Cassie asked.

Jaclyn held up a finger and shook her head. "If you can do that, without any of the others knowing we're here, you will have earned my trust, and we'll believe everything you've told us," Jaclyn replied. "But it's essential that only those three witches meet us here. No male witches, no vampires, and no other demons. Okay?"

Cassie nodded. She smiled and looked a little relieved. "I can do that, but do you have any idea where your mother would most likely be?"

"Try the witch VIP room first. If she's not there, you may have to search the dance floors. She's not much for dancing, but she does like to watch."

"Okay." Cassie closed her eyes. A small circle of smoke rose and drifted around the succubus. Seconds later, Cassie vanished.

The circle of smoke wasn't like Kailey had witnessed when Cassie had taken Raven and vanished. No evil faces floated in the smoke like before. Had Cassie told the truth and the faces Kailey had seen were actually faces of the shadow demons?

Kailey shifted her gaze toward Jaclyn. "Do you trust that she will do what you've asked?"

Jaclyn offered a shrug and gave a slight smirk. "Time will tell. If demons or vampires enter before my mother comes, we shall know whether we can trust Cassie or not."

"What do we do until then?"

"The pack will find us. We tell them why we're waiting here and about the power Nicodemus wields. If what Cassie said is true about the shadow demons, it might require more than our numbers to stop him."

"You think he'd be that strong?"

Jaclyn nodded. "Yes, and when my mother gets here, she has some important questions to answer and a *lot* of explaining to do."

CHAPTER 50

Kailey's temples were squeezed with an unseen viselike pressure. She winced and leaned against the wall quickly.

"Are you okay?" Jaclyn asked.

Kailey couldn't answer.

"Where are you?" Flora demanded. *"Time's up."*

Jaclyn rushed to Kailey. "What's wrong?"

"Flora," Kailey whispered, squinting her eyes tightly, trying to drive out the pain. The undulating agony was like needles being stabbed into the sides of her head.

"I sense that you're close, but where? Something blocks me from seeing your whereabouts," Flora whispered. *"I thought you loved Raven more than this."*

I do, you wicked bitch! Get the hell out of my head!

"Now, now. That's no way to speak to your elder," Flora replied.

You're not my elder.

Without realizing it, Kailey's eyes had turned up in her head, showing only white.

"Damn," Jaclyn whispered. She placed her right hand onto Kailey's forehead and whispered a spell.

"Damn you!" Flora screamed inside Kailey's mind, releasing her hold on Kailey.

Kailey staggered and fell forward. Jaclyn wrapped her arms around her, holding her up until Kailey had the strength to steady herself.

"Are you okay?"

Kailey nodded. "Thanks. What the hell happened? She's talked to me like this before, but never did the pull seem so severe."

"She must be close by. Did she compel you before?"

Kailey nodded slowly. "Yes. Without my consent or knowledge."

Jaclyn grinned. "Vampires don't bother with consent. Most believe they can do whatever they wish."

"She's going to flaunt her power one time too many."

"What did she say?"

"Just that she knows I'm near, but she cannot locate me."

"Good. My blessing on the pendant worked somewhat, but you see that she still has incredible power."

"More than she deserves."

Jaclyn nodded. "Agreed. Another problem we have is that we don't have much time."

"If Flora is this powerful, can you imagine how strong Nicodemus must be?"

"It's a frightening thought."

Several soft chuffs came from the corridor.

Jaclyn steadied Kailey and both looked toward the door at the darkness on the other side. Several pairs of glowing wolf eyes peered in at them.

Even though Kailey knew the pack members, she held her breath, afraid to move. The wolves panted heavily, standing right outside the door, watching. The front wolf's eyes narrowed, but a lighter gray wolf nudged it, and walked past. What she had assumed to be a regular wolf wasn't, but they were the hybrid wolfmen she had seen in the tunnel now walking on all fours.

The grayer wolfman approached Kailey, its eyes keenly staring into hers. When she gazed into its eyes, she knew it was Brady. She didn't know exactly why or how she knew, except that she sensed him.

"Be careful, Kailey," Jaclyn said.

Brady turned toward Jaclyn and sniffed the air. His eyes narrowed for a moment, and then he returned his attention back to Kailey.

Kailey didn't know quite what to do. Seeing the man she had fallen for as a werewolf left her uncertain of what he might do. She and Jaclyn had been warned not to get scratched or bitten, and they had done the best they could to avoid it. But now, the pack was outside the room with the exception of Brady who had stopped only a couple of feet away from her.

There was the other door, but running ... they'd never reach the door in time. But the wolfmen didn't seem interested in harming them.

Slowly, one by one, several of the pack members entered the room. Micah was the first to shift back into his fully human form. The transformation took about five minutes as his massive claws shrank. His jaw and snout popped and snapped as they reshaped, returning him to human form. Joints popped. Muscles decreased in size. The extra digits on his fingers vanished. Small growls and groans came from Micah's mouth, a mixture of pain and pleasure, much like Ashley had described. Instead of being nude like Kailey expected, he wore spandex briefs. He lowered himself to his knees, panting and sweating.

Brady suddenly arched back. He snarled, showing his large yellow canine teeth. He shook his head and gazed at Kailey, taking a step toward her.

"No!" Micah said, pushing himself to his feet and standing between her and Brady. Micah pointed a stern finger. "Back away, Brady."

Another of the pack eased closer, sniffing Jaclyn and then gazing toward Kailey.

"Jacob, no," Micah said. He rubbed his hands together and said words that Kailey didn't understand. While he kept repeating them, radiance balled around his hands. He flung his hands outward and all the pack members whimpered and lowered their heads.

"What's wrong?" Kailey whispered.

Micah shook his head. "Since this was their first transformation in two years, they are too energized and have little self-control. The good thing is that Brady recognizes you in his alternate form. In a few minutes they should return to their human forms. Seems that small spell has settled them somewhat."

The pack members crept into the small room and lay on their sides. Their bodies writhed slightly as their wolfish appearances receded.

"Were there casualties?" she asked. "Where is the rest of the pack?"

"We lost two pack members. They were some of the youngest ones."

"I'm sorry."

Micah shrugged. His eyes saddened. "We all know the risks."

"Where are the rest of them?"

"I asked the remainder of the pack to remain in the tunnel just in case we missed any vampires. We don't need stray vampires sneaking up behind us to attack."

"I agree." She studied him for a bit. "What's with the spandex?"

Micah smiled. "It's a rule I implemented. Speedos are a bit more comfortable on the eyes should we happen to change back into human form near a public place. Less questionable, and no calls to the police for indecent exposure."

Jaclyn laughed. "I could see where that might pose some issues."

As the wolves transformed back to human, Forrest stepped into the room with his vampire killing kit. He was already human. Of the pack, Ashley, Brady, Barry, Jacob, and Micah had come up from the tunnel, leaving all the others behind.

"Why the holdup here?" Forrest asked, setting his heavy case on the floor.

Jaclyn explained.

Forrest looked at Kailey a bit harshly. "You ask for a weapon to kill this succubus and then you simply let her go?"

"Given the circumstances ..." she started to reply.

"No," he said, shaking his head. "Like vampires, you cannot trust a demon. They are masters of deception."

The intensity in his eyes and furrowed brow caused her to look away. Her eyes glanced to the recovering pack members. Now that their fur was gone, she could see claw and bite marks on several of them. None of the wounds were bleeding and the injuries seemed to be knitting together except for Ashley.

"Sometimes, you have to take those chances," Kailey said.

"Well, you do that young lady, and you'll find your death much quicker."

Jaclyn stepped beside Kailey. "She's right, Forrest. Not every demon or vampire is purely evil."

"It's that in between, witch, where you find what you believed to be your friend is actually a deadly foe," Forrest replied.

Kailey bravely studied Forrest's eyes. In with his anger was the same type of sadness she had with the loss of her brother. "With how you and your father were set up by the vampire that hired you, I understand your distrust. Betrayal is unforgiveable because trust cannot be re-earned, no matter how much we insist it can be. But we cannot live our lives more afraid to chance discovering a friend or an ally because we automatically ordain them to be enemies based upon the type of creature they are. You're unique to the rest of us. You've sided with werewolves and witches to destroy vampires and demons. Is that just convenience or will you turn on the rest of us after this battle ends?"

Forrest smiled and roared with laughter. "I didn't come here to kill demons. I came for the vampires. The weapon was *your* request. Not mine."

"I know—"

Forrest waved his hand. "No. Listen. Vampires are soulless beings who know no mercy. Demons practice deceit. I'm simply informing you that creatures will say anything to convince you that they're on your side when you have them cornered and ready to kill them."

Jaclyn nodded. "That's true, and we understand that. But from what I've discerned about Cassie, what happened wasn't her doing. She was controlled by the shadow demons that now reside inside Nicodemus, who is a powerful vampire in his own right. Since he controls the shadow demons, his power is even greater. He will be one of your greatest challenges in a while."

Forrest smiled eagerly at the thought.

"But to draw him out requires Cassie's aid."

"How do you figure?" Forrest asked.

"I'm a target in this nightclub. None of the pack has a pass to get inside. Kailey was ordered to bring the key or this book to get her friend released, but we're all intruders. We had no open invitation." Jaclyn looked at Micah. "I assume that all the vampires in the tunnel are dead?"

Micah nodded.

"Oh, very dead," Forrest added, showing the vampire blood and ash on his hands.

"So add that to our encroachments of Nocturnal Trinity," Jaclyn said. "Now Nicodemus and the other elder vampires will want to kill us."

"Over them?" Forrest said. "They were fodder. A simple obstacle to scare off the normal humans who happened upon them. Nothing more."

"Maybe so," Jaclyn said, "but it will still attract the attention of Nicodemus or whichever vampire fathered them."

"I'm ready," Forrest said, holding a stake and his heavy wooden mallet. He glanced around at the sprawled five pack members and shook his head. "Already tuckered out? We've only started."

Ashley moaned. Her left shoulder was scratched and she crawled forward on her hands and knees until she dropped on the floor beside Micah. Blood leaked from the deep claw marks. She looked like she had been mauled.

"Is she okay?" Kailey asked, kneeling beside her.

"She'll heal."

"No, Micah, look," Kailey said. "The bleeding isn't stopping."

Micah knelt beside her. "Give her time."

Ashley smiled up at Micah. He placed a gentle hand on her forehead. Closing his eyes, he mumbled words. Power flowed through his hand into Ashley, leapt off her, and flowed past Kailey toward the open door.

Skye eased through the door, propping slightly against the frame. Although she still looked worse for wear, some color had returned to her cheeks. Kailey guessed that Micah's healing spell had gone to those who needed it the most. While Kailey feared being clawed or bitten by the werewolves, she wondered what consequence, if any, werewolves suffered from a vampire's bite.

None of the male werewolves seemed the slightest bit fatigued by the battle, but Ashley and two of the other wolves were much weaker.

Skye stood a bit more upright and didn't drag her right foot like she had when Kailey had helped the woman down the manhole and through the tunnel. Now that Skye was in this small room, Kailey worried about their small group being surrounded and trapped inside. So many dangers existed that could be the end of her and the pack.

Fire, poison, and six elder vampires rushing inside and snapping necks were a few of the ghastly images that came to mind. Anything might happen should Cassie fail to carry out Jaclyn's request. And who knew what else might lurk in the tunnel below that could kill the other members of the pack? If Kailey had to guess, she'd say that the pack members in the room with her were the strongest ones, and if so, the rest of the pack might be at the mercy of other enemies they weren't yet aware of.

Ashley stood, shook her head, and wrapped her arms around Micah's neck.

"It's not over yet," Micah said.

Forrest laughed. "The best part is yet to come."

CHAPTER 51

*E*va entered the room and immediately went to Jaclyn. The two embraced fiercely, and then kissed one another on the cheek. Two ladies followed Eva and suspiciously looked around the room.

Plus one for Cassie.

"Jaclyn, do you mind telling us who these intruders are?" The one lady wearing a dark robe asked.

"Rose and Debra," Jaclyn said, waving toward the group. She quickly introduced Forrest, Micah, and Brady and then the rest of the pack.

Debra wore a light blue robe much like Micah had when Kailey had met him at the shop. Both witches looked uncertain about being in a room filled with werewolves.

"What is the purpose of bringing all these were-creatures here?" Eva asked.

Before Jaclyn could respond, Kailey said, "Flora took Raven."

"Your friend?" Eva asked.

"Yes. Where did she take her?" Kailey asked.

Eva shook her head, confused. "We've not seen her."

"Nor Flora for some time," Debra added.

Jaclyn pulled the Grimoire from inside her robe.

"So you do have it?" Eva asked.

Debra turned and faced Jaclyn. "You have some nerve stealing that book and then returning here with these ... beasts."

"Careful where you hurl your insults, lady," Forrest said, holding his hammer and pointing it toward her.

Debra took a deep breath and held it, studying the mountainous man with curiosity and suspicion.

"The nerve, as you say," Jaclyn said, "is on the three of you."

"Hold your tongue, young lady," Eva said. "You—"

"Mother," Jaclyn raised her right index finger with authority and power. She narrowed her gaze. Eva's eyes widened, as did the other two witches. They feared her and visibly shook. "Explain why you three foolishly granted Nicodemus such power. I am appalled that you'd give the vampires the greater balance of power within the Circle of Unity."

"What power are you speaking of?" Eva asked, crossing her arms.

"The ritual where you had the succubus stand in the center of the circle while you freed her from the shadow demons."

"That's all it was," Debra said. Her eyes pleaded for everyone to believe her. "Nothing more."

"According to Cassie, Nicodemus now harnesses and has access to control those shadow demons. They are inside him to do his bidding."

The three witches gazed at one another. Their complexions grew paler.

"We were informed differently," Eva said.

Forrest stepped toward them. "You were part of the ritual. How could you *not* know?"

Rose, dressed in a scarlet robe, bit her lower lip. "No incantation was given. We simply added our power, our magic."

"Blindly so," Forrest said. His jaws tightened.

"Apparently," Eva replied. "They deceived us."

Debra said, "We thought we were helping Cassie. She had married a human—"

"My brother," Kailey said.

"Oh, dear," Debra said. "Well, from what we were told, she received a curse and was plagued by the shadow demons. Nicodemus asked for our assistance, to freely grant our magic to aid her."

"Fools," Forrest said. "Naïve fools. People like you should never be trusted with magic."

"We never thought we had contributed to any such spell," Eva said. "We certainly would have never done so had we known."

"You see why you cannot trust vampires?" Forrest asked, glaring at Kailey. She nodded.

"What happened to Cassie?" Kailey said, looking around the room. "She never returned."

Rose shrugged and glanced toward the door. "She was right behind us."

Eva reached toward Jaclyn to take the Grimoire. Jaclyn pulled it away and shook her head.

"I need my book," Eva said. "It's the only way we can make this right."

"You've proven you cannot be trusted with it," Jaclyn replied.

"Daughter, don't—"

"It's not *yours*," Debra seethed.

"Do you really want to go against the three of us?" Rose asked.

Jaclyn offered a slight smirk. "Do the three of you wish to provoke me?"

Eva gasped. "We're elder witches. Show respect."

Jaclyn frowned and opened her mouth to reply, but Micah stepped forward.

"Ladies," he said. "While skirmishes exist almost everywhere, this isn't the time for you to rehash your petty differences. We came here to find Raven. Until we do that, the book remains with Jaclyn. Is that clear? Should you protest, you might want to consider my alternative."

"What's that?" Debra asked with a cold tone.

"Do you really want to go against all of us?"

Forrest held his mallet in both hands and grinned. The five pack members formed a semicircle eyeing the three witches with intense glares. The witches glanced around for a few moments but showed no obvious fear.

"I appreciate your input, Micah," Jaclyn said. "But it wasn't necessary. They know my power and since I hold the Grimoire I can strip them of their magic for the rest of their lives." She glared at her mother and the other two witches. "Can't I?"

Eva shook her head. "You wouldn't?"

Jaclyn raised her right hand.

"Wait!" Debra said. "She would. Don't test her, Eva."

"Banishment from the nightclub didn't weaken me. It aided my resolve. All I want is for any one of you to give me a reason, just one," Jaclyn said, eyeing each witch. "And I'll peel away every thread of magic you possess. From your irresponsibility with Nicodemus, I'd say that would be justified."

Micah looked at Jaclyn incredulously.

"I agree," Forrest said.

"Don't be hasty," Rose said. "We had no part of your exile."

"She's right," Debra said.

"Does any of that matter now?" Jaclyn asked. "I didn't come here for revenge against the three of you. I came to help a friend who died as a result of Nicodemus. Since I am now friends with his sister, I will carry out my oath."

Cassie stepped through the door with her head held downward. She was unable to make eye contact with anyone.

"Where have you been?" Kailey asked.

Flora stepped in behind Cassie. She beamed a smile and then pointed at Jaclyn. "That book. I have need of that."

CHAPTER 52

"You lied to us?" Kailey asked.

Cassie shook her head and kept her gaze upon the floor. "No."

"Then why is Flora here?"

Flora replied, "I came because I sensed you were here, Kailey. For some reason, I have this special link that draws me toward you. Funny how that works, huh?"

"No. I detest it."

"Well, no matter," Flora said. "I'm here because we had a deal."

"Not a *voluntary* one," Kailey replied. "Where's Raven?"

"The book first."

Jaclyn frowned. "No. The book is ours. You cannot have this."

"We all need the book," Flora said, her eyes firm, icy. "Nicodemus has betrayed us all."

Debra, Rose, and Eva looked at Flora in surprise.

"So what Cassie said was true?" Eva asked.

"About his unmatched power?" Flora said.

They nodded.

"I'm afraid so."

Forrest looked at Kailey. "This is the vampire?"

"One of them."

Flora turned toward him. "Who are you?"

386

"Odd. You don't remember?" Forrest asked.

She stared at him for several long seconds and then her eyes widened with recognition. "Forrest?"

Kailey glanced at Flora and then back to Forrest. "You know one another?"

"Yes. Flora, I am the bringer of your eternal death," he replied, tossing a long silver chain at her. "I told you that I'd find you eventually."

The chain wrapped around Flora's neck before she could move, singeing her flesh. She shrieked in agony, tugging at the silver, which burned her hands in the process. Kailey held no pity for Flora. Seeing her squirm and struggle gave her a giddy feeling, and for a moment, she felt ashamed for taking joy in the vampire's suffering.

Flora dropped to the floor, screaming. Her flesh blistered. The three witches stood in horror, watching Forrest approach with a huge stake and the mallet in his hands. Micah stood while the other pack members sat on the floor still regaining their strength but their eyes stared with intense interest.

"Spare me," she pleaded, looking up into Forrest's eyes as he loomed over her, preparing to position the stake.

"I've never spared a vampire, nor do I intend to start now," he replied, straddling his knees over her narrow waist. "Remember how your father betrayed me? I want that to be your last thought."

"Please, Forrest, spare me, and I'll give you Nicodemus."

Forrest shook his head. "I'll find him on my own."

She shook her head. "No. No, you won't."

Forrest's small chuckle birthed into a belly laugh. "Oh, the lies vampires give to not be driven back into the earth."

"You kill me," she gasped, "and he'll flee. We're joined by blood. All six of us. If one of us dies, the rest of us know. He'll flee, but if he doesn't, he'll know you're here. And he'll be ready. Let me leave and I can get you—all of you—to where he is."

"She's not lying," Cassie said.

Forrest stared at Cassie. "Of course she's not lying. She and her siblings fled when I stake their father. They didn't have enough backbone to come to his defense."

Flora pushed at the silver chain. Blisters bubbled on his palms and fingers. "He told us to flee. But Nicodemus … I'll give him to you."

"You'd sacrifice your own brother?" Forrest asked, looking into Flora's eyes.

She nodded, still pushing at the thick silver chain with her blistered fingers.

"So much for blood ties and family loyalty."

"Like I told you, '*he* betrayed us all.'"

Kailey watched Forrest put the tip of the stake above her left breast. In seconds her alabaster skin would be splattered momentarily with crimson. She found that she couldn't look away. For the mental torment Flora had caused, Kailey believed she needed to see the vampire's death.

Flora's eyes flicked from the stake toward Kailey. "Nicodemus has Raven."

The statement shook Kailey, awakened her from the want of seeing an enemy killed.

"Stop!" Kailey said.

Forrest glanced in Kailey's direction. His eyebrows rose. "Are you serious?"

Kailey nodded. "Yes."

"If he kills me, you have lost any chance of getting her back," Flora said in desperation.

"Please, Forrest?" Kailey said.

Forrest grimaced. His jaw tightened. He eased back on his heels, removed the silver chain from around Flora's neck, but he kept the stake pressed against her skin. With a narrowed gaze, he peered into Flora's eyes. Her eyes darkened, and Kailey half expected him to fall under her power.

He laughed. "Don't even start trying to compel me. You have no hold over me. You didn't when we first met, and you don't now. But before I release you, you must swear an oath."

"What kind of oath?" she hissed.

"That you'll not attack or compel anyone in our party here. If you violate the oath, you are dead. I've killed over two hundred vampires all over the world, including your father. I have so many different ways of killing you in a split second, so don't even think about breaking your word."

So much for not ever trusting a vampire. Kailey smiled.

Forrest said, "Micah and Jaclyn, bind her to her statement with magic."

They nodded.

"Now swear it," Forrest said.

"I promise that I won't attack or compel anyone in your party," Flora said.

He glanced at Micah and Jaclyn.

"It's done," Micah said.

Jaclyn nodded.

With huge disappointment in Forrest's eyes, he rose to his feet and tucked the stake into a narrow band on the inside of his trench coat. He leaned over and offered his huge hand to Flora. She looked somewhat surprised but reluctantly accepted. He pulled her to her feet in one swift tug.

Flora sighed and ironed out the creases on her dress with her hands. She looked at the welts on her fingers and palms. Tears edged at the corners of her eyes. She glanced into Forrest's eyes. "Will these blisters heal?"

"You've never touched silver?" Forrest asked.

She shook her head. "I know better."

"They will fade. Quicker if you … drink blood. Now, where's your brother?"

Flora smiled and coldness reclaimed her voice. Her eyes shimmered icy blue. "I hope that you're a god-fearing man, and that he or she has mercy upon your soul."

Forrest shrugged. "While most vampires fear the synagogues and temples as holy ground, the majority of the mortal world has realized the sanctuaries of old were nothing more than stage acts led by popes and priests to control the kings, queens, and kingdoms of the world. Finding true faith nowadays is almost as rare as finding a vampire in a lost city."

"Then why all the trinkets and holy water in your case?" Barry asked.

"Mostly for show, but the holy water and crosses work if the vampire is old enough to have genuine faith. What was once considered holy a half century ago is no longer taken seriously by the younger generation in America. However, in the old countries like Romania, Croatia, and Italy, all holy relics and charms work without fail because they people are brain-washed … *raised* to believe."

"How can a disbeliever effectively use a cross or holy water?" Kailey asked.

"As I said, if the vampires believe, that's really all it takes."

"And if they don't?" Micah asked.

Forrest smiled and ran fingers through his beard. "Those vampires take a bit longer to subdue and kill."

The pack members stood. Brady came to Kailey and Cassie.

Micah said to Flora, "Why does your brother have Raven?"

"I'm not certain. He took her from where I had confined her, but he never gave any reason why he wanted her."

"So that's why you wouldn't allow me to talk to her?" Kailey asked.

Flora shrugged. "What could I say? If I told you I didn't have her and didn't know where she was, I feared that you wouldn't come. We do need the book to stop him."

Jacob approached Flora. She looked up into his angry eyes. "My brother was killed here. Dale was his name."

The mention of the name caused Flora to tremble. "He's dead?"

Jacob stepped closer. "He was drained of his blood. You mind telling me who was responsible?"

Micah said, "It looked like his death was part of a ritual."

Eva looked nervous, as did the other witches.

Kailey glanced around the room. It looked like all the exposed iniquities of Nocturnal Trinity were about to send the occupants of the pack into a violent rage. Only Cassie seemed unimpressed.

Flora sighed. "It was a blood ritual instigated by Nicodemus. Dale was not supposed to die, but once my brother discovered he was a werewolf, he must have drained him the rest of the way."

"You were a partaker of my brother's blood?" Jacob said, his hands balling into fists.

"Yes."

"Then you shall die."

Micah placed a gentle hand on Jacob's shoulder. Looking at Flora, Micah said, "Explain the reason you partook."

"You may not believe me, but Dale volunteered to be the donor."

"Bullshit!" Jacob said, fuming.

"I swear it's the truth."

Micah nodded. "It probably is."

"What?" Jacob asked. He growled low in his throat. His eyes shifted darker like a wolf.

"We needed to find the summoning circle," Micah said. "That is where the ritual was held, right?"

Flora nodded. "Yes."

"Dale volunteered to get us information."

"But he wasn't supposed to die," Flora said. "Nicodemus was the one who killed him after he dismissed all of us because Dale was still alive when I left."

"Then he is the one who will die," Micah said. "Not you. Show us where he is."

With tears brimming in her eyes, she nodded. "Follow me."

CHAPTER 53

Flora led the pack, the witches, and Kailey through a long labyrinth of passages. Cassie stayed close to Kailey. The succubus seemed genuine about her love and devotion for Vincent. And she might eventually prove to be an asset none of them had ever expected to have.

However, at times, Kailey expected they were being set up by Flora because, after all, how many people would willingly sacrifice their own flesh and blood, a sibling, regardless of what horrible act he or she had done?

Kailey had read many times about parents pleading a court judge over a mass-murdering son's death sentence because *some* good must still reside somewhere deep inside the child they had raised. People are often blind to crime whenever love is involved. She imagined it was difficult for some parents to view their child as an adult since they had been the ones to feed and nurture him, change his diapers, and helped educate him. Seeing the monster instead of the child was accepting part of the blame for apparent mistakes they might have made in the rearing process, even if none of the responsibility for the warped devious behavior of the murderer was their fault. Some people were simply born with mental problems, no fault of the parents or society in general.

But this situation with Nicodemus was different. He had lived more than two centuries. How many ruthless things had he done during that amount of time? How many murders? Rapes? The lists of carnages could be limitless.

Despite immortality, Kailey wondered how age affected one's mind after two centuries? Did a vast time period increase instability? Did it lessen one's morals?

And Flora? What about her mental stability?

Nocturnal Trinity was a front for no telling what kind of heinous crimes. Once the Circle of Unity garnered the support of the police, clergy, and political offices, they were no different than a mafia organization, but operating in full sight. Money, power, and sex were the biggest reasons for political corruption. Destined cover-ups protected otherwise reputable officials, as long as it was necessary for both sides. Apparently Nocturnal Trinity possessed ways to protect all the founders and its members.

Flora stopped at the end of a set of stairs. Flickering sconces lit the sides of the staircase that lofted up in what seemed to be a couple of stories high. Dusty spider webs swayed along the ceiling and an occasional bat flitted and swooped from one hidden recess to another. Kailey would have thought the furry winged creatures were excellent stage props, but she knew they were real. Most likely they had found their way from the underground tunnel into the nightclub, and based upon the scruples of those longing to get inside, seeing bats wouldn't alarm them. The winged creatures of the night added to the overall mood and effect.

"I shall bid you good luck," Flora said, heading away.

"No," Forrest said, wrapping the thick silver chain around her neck like a leash. "You're not leaving."

She winced at the burning pain but fought against the urge to scream. Her jaw tightened, making her speak in a low angered tone. "You promised not to kill me in return for my brother."

"I'm not the one who made that promise. I delayed staking you as a favor to Kailey. So since you're still alive, you shall lead the way through the door."

Her nervous eyes searched his. "Why?"

"Your brother needs to know where you stand," Forrest replied.

Genuine tears leaked and meandered down Flora's pale cheeks.

Betrayal was worse than death for some.

"And where are your siblings?" Jaclyn asked.

"Away," Flora replied.

"They had best be," Forrest said, pulling the chain tighter.

"Why's that?"

"Unless you wish them to be amongst tonight's casualties."

Flora offered a smirk in spite of having the silver wrapped around her neck. She reached for the doorknob. "I guess you will find out, won't you?"

"Wait!" Jaclyn said, lifting her hand. The witch trio beside her cowered.

Flora paused and looked at Jaclyn. "What?"

"Is Nicodemus the only vampire in that room?"

Frustrated, Flora nodded. "Yes."

"None of your siblings are in there?"

"No, they are not. He should be alone."

"Should be?"

"If he has company, it *isn't* family."

Jaclyn's eyes darkened. "If you're lying, you don't need to worry about Forrest killing you. I'll do it with words and watch you crumble painfully to dust right where you stand."

"Your boldness increases as I am bound by this chain. Don't be foolish with idle threats, little witch."

Jaclyn smirked. "I don't make threats I won't carry out. Ask them."

Flora considered the words, weighed them, and then shot a glance to the three witches. The fear in the witches' eyes indicated that Jaclyn was true to her word.

Kailey marveled.

Jaclyn was petite and dainty compared to Forrest, but she incorporated more fear with her gaze and the tone of her voice than Forrest had when he had nearly staked Flora. Now she seemed more perturbed than fearful of having his silver chain wrapped around her neck for a second time, even though her skin was blistering, Flora kept her composure.

Kailey wondered exactly how much power Jaclyn possessed. She had said that she was a necromancer, which as far as Kailey understood meant that Jaclyn could raise the dead. What more could she do? Jaclyn's mother feared her as did the other witches and even Flora. With all the contention and division among the ranks of the Circle of Unity, she was surprised that they ever accomplished casting basic spells.

Flora glanced around the corridor at the werewolf pack, Forrest, Kailey, Cassie, and the witches. Her last gaze returned to Jaclyn. The sternness in Jaclyn's stare made Flora gasp. She acquiesced with a humble nod, turned the doorknob, and pushed the door inward. The tired old hinges groaned a soft gritty shrill.

Cold air spilled from the room and enveloped everyone standing in the narrow hallway. Candles flickered inside the room from the sudden release of air into the hallway.

Flora glided into the room where her brother stood. She stopped less than a foot inside the threshold. "Nicodemus."

He turned with a wine goblet in his hand, regarding her with raised eyebrows, and his regard glanced behind her to everyone standing in the hallway. "Ah, sister. What brings you ... here ... and with uninvited guests, too."

"Pardon my intrusion, brother." She offered a humble curtsy. When she rose, she brushed her black hair from her eyes.

"You know my chambers are off-limits to outsiders. That is *not* something new." His eyes darkened and a blood droplet dripped from his mouth, spattering lightly on the cold marble floor. He set the goblet of blood on an antique table and cocked a brow, looking past her. "Something about your guests disturbs me, sister. *Why* have you brought them here? I never fancy myself to offer entertainment toward groups. There are so many more activities for them to gain in the upper sections. Bit drab here, don't you think?"

"Apologies, again, but we have matters of grave importance to discuss," she replied.

"Like what? Our council is not due to convene for another week yet. You know this."

"They have come for Raven."

"Have they now?" He sounded greatly amused.

In the candlelight, his face was a sickly pale and his wavy hair was blacker than the night. There was bewitching beauty in his features, in such a way that men and women would easily be drawn to him. He held a regal air in the tone of his voice, and his perfect posture proved a family that thrived on manners and proper etiquette had raised him. He wore an elegant black vintage suit and even had a handkerchief neatly tucked into his breast pocket. He was quite slim, and his charm flowed with every movement he made.

"Yes," Flora said firmly.

Nicodemus waved his right hand with a single motion. "Send them on their way. She was a difficult one to break, even with the power of my compulsion, but her virginity became mine. She stays with me to be by my side forever."

Flora's mouth gaped. "You wish to take *her* as your mate?"

"No. I have already done so."

"She's human ... she must not be turned—" Flora gasped. "Damn you! You didn't?"

Skye released a sharp whine and dropped to her knees in the hallway. Kailey placed a hand on her shoulder, crouched down, and turned so she could keep an eye on Nicodemus.

"Not such a horrible thing now, is it?" he asked, stepping toward her. His buckled boots clicked on the marble floor. "Eternal life. It's what every person longs for."

"Why her?" Flora asked, shaking her head. "When you have had dozens of young beautiful women who have begged to be taken by you."

Nicodemus laughed softly. "Ah, but you know it's the ones you can't have that are the most desirable. And oh what a fight she put up. Feisty little thing. I do love a good challenge."

Skye sobbed louder.

Kailey's hands tightened into fists. She headed for the door to enter, but Jaclyn shook her head and grabbed Kailey's arm and yanked her to the side.

"No. You'll be killed," Jaclyn said.

Cassie placed her hand on Kailey's arm. "Let us do the fighting."

"He raped her," Kailey hissed.

Flora swept through the door and stood beside Kailey in an instant. She shook her head. "The virginity he speaks of taking wasn't sexual. He turned her despite her aggressive fight to prevent him from doing so."

"Is that not a rape in its own way?" Skye asked, rising to her feet. The elderly woman's eyes leveled a cold harsh glare. Anger replaced her tears, and vengeance flowed around her every expression.

"How did you hear—" Kailey looked at Flora.

Flora smiled. "Vampires have remarkable hearing, and you and I sort of have a connection."

Kailey started to reply, but a second later, Flora was gone. She had returned to stand near her brother. "What does she mean by that?"

Cassie shrugged.

Jaclyn stepped into the room, followed by Micah and Forrest.

Nicodemus crossed his arms, watching their bold approach.

"The challenge you have sought is much worse than you can ever imagine," Jaclyn said.

"And why is that, little sister?" Nicodemus asked, ignoring Jaclyn's statement and the others making their way into the room. He saw the silver around her neck and his eyes widened slightly, but for only a moment. "Silver doesn't become you, Flora. Really, it doesn't."

"I didn't exactly pick it out," she whispered bitterly.

Nicodemus offered an amused smile, stepped beside her, and faced his intruders. "So, I take it that our guests think it sporting to invade a vampire's lair to mock him and his family? Well, sister, let us show them how dreadful a mistake they have made."

"Not *us*. You," Flora replied.

He frowned and eyed her, studying her. "So you're not going to partake in this?"

She shook her head.

"Pity. We do so well working together."

"I brought them here to *kill* you."

The statement stunned him. His facial muscles creased deeply, momentarily showing his age. Betrayal struck deeply. "Have you now?"

"Yes." Flora looked emotionally torn between sorrow and regret.

Kailey really began to wonder if Flora would keep her end of the agreement. Perhaps Forrest was testing her to find out the same thing.

"And your purpose for doing that would be?" Nicodemus asked.

"You betrayed us by taking control of the shadow demons that you told us we were excising from Cassie."

"Ah, you discovered that?"

Flora nodded.

"That wasn't information you were to know. I was saving that for a later surprise."

Flora sulked and shook her head. "As the oldest you've always wanted to be the most powerful, even at the expense of others, including your family, but everyone inside our circle needs to remain equal. That was what kept us unified. With your actions and deception, the Circle of Unity no longer is."

"Our world that we've grown accustomed to is forever changing. Not for the better, sister. Things evolve, but we must take control and ensure that society progresses forward. Humans cannot do this without our guidance," Nicodemus said.

Forrest held his mallet and drew a stake from his trench coat. "You know what I hate about the elder vampire generations?"

Nicodemus took a step toward him, unconcerned about Forrest's weapons or his size. He didn't seem to care about the pack members gathering into the room, either. "Do tell."

"Your damn sanctimonious attitudes. The world over, it's always been the same. You believe your undead qualities are better than the living."

"I'm betting you cannot name a way they *aren't* better," Nicodemus sneered. "But no matter. What I hate are those who enter someone's abode without a proper invitation."

"Probably because that's the only way your kind can go inside another's home." Forrest made the statement with so much distaste for what Nicodemus and Flora were that Flora cringed. "I'll only ask you once before I tear a hole through your heart with this dagger. *Where* is Raven?"

Only Kailey, Cassie, and Skye remained in the corridor. Edging to the threshold, Kailey watched and listened, fearful of seeing Raven as a vampire, but desperate to know, all the same.

Nicodemus held himself with such arrogance and defiance that Kailey could imagine how Raven had fought and resisted his attempted charm and compulsion, which probably had infuriated him to the point of *making* her submit. If he had bitten Raven and turned her, it would have had to be against every fiber of her being. Raven had never once hinted that she was attracted to any male, nor had she ever complimented a man as being handsome.

Kailey recognized Nicodemus' power. It flowed off him in waves, much stronger than any energy she had ever felt from Flora, or the werewolves, and that frightened Kailey.

Flora pressed the back of her hand to her forehead and seemed suddenly weaker.

"Sister," Nicodemus said. "I will bid you one last favor before I entertain you with your guests' bloodbath." He unwrapped the silver chain from around her neck, and let it fall to the floor.

"Thank you."

Nicodemus stepped past her and faced the pack. "You wish to see my young bride?"

Micah stepped beside Forrest. "We do. She's the one we came for."

Kailey scanned the room, hopeful that Raven was nearby. At the far end of the bedroom was an antique four-poster bed. The canopy curtains were black and closed. Perhaps Raven was in there?

Skye coughed and cleared her throat. Raspy sounds rattled as she exhaled. Everything about this elderly witch seemed broken. The shattered look in Skye's eyes, the frailty in her voice, and the fading color of her complexion indicated that this woman as well as her magic was nearing death.

A large oriental rug lay at the side of the bed. Near the bed were a massive mahogany wardrobe, a small dark table with an oil lantern set on top, and two high back, hand-carved chairs. Candles flickered all around the room, creating dancing shadows and mystery. Kailey noticed the beauty of the simplistic lighting and how modern fluorescent lights would have killed the mood of the room.

Several aged bookshelves rose from the floor to the lofty ceiling and were lined with musty old books. Toward the center of the room, what looked like another oriental rug, but smaller and rounder, caught her attention. After staring at it for nearly a minute, she realized it wasn't cloth, but an elaborate stained glass design patterned into the floor. She found the architecture quite odd, but the beauty captivating. Why was it there and what did it represent?

Kailey's curiosity almost made her step into the room, and she would have, had the area inside the door not been nearly blocked by the pack members and witches. Cassie held Kailey's arm tightly.

"I wasn't able to protect Vincent, but I will do everything possible to keep you alive," Cassie said. "You have my word."

Nicodemus retreated toward the bed, but Flora didn't move. He stood next to the bed, watching the pack and the witches, and waited.

The pack and witches in turn did the same.

Kailey wondered why they were all stalling, except perhaps to size one another up. The group didn't seem to intimidate Nicodemus at all, and the werewolves were waiting for Micah to signal the attack.

Perhaps Nicodemus wasn't stalling at all. Maybe he was waiting for the pack to let their guard down.

Energy churned inside the room, growing in intensity like storm winds gathered to produce a deadly tornado.

Then Kailey recognized the look in Nicodemus' eyes. It was the same look she had seen and even used when she stood eyeing an opponent in the ring. Nicodemus was sizing up his intruders, looking for the weakest first, and considering what his best approach would be. No fear resided in his eyes. Only coldness and death.

Kailey opened her mouth to warn Brady and the others, but before any words escaped, Nicodemus made his move.

CHAPTER 54

One second Nicodemus had stood beside Flora and then in the next, he was on the other side of the room in a blink. He grabbed and snapped Barry's neck in a fluid motion before the rest of the pack or Barry had a chance to react. Nicodemus held the unchanged werewolf a second longer, smiling, and then let the older wolfman drop to the floor.

Micah, Jacob, and Brady transformed in an instant. Bearing fangs, sprouting fur, they growled and lunged at a surprised Nicodemus but missed.

Nicodemus was back beside Flora, shaking his head. "Hiring out for a pack of wolves? I must say that I underestimated your sudden hatred for me, little sister."

"It's festered and grown for over two centuries, Nicodemus. That's not *sudden.*"

He shrugged. "What are two hundred years in an eternity?"

"Allowing yourself to consume the power of demons to exert your authority over the rest of us let me know that you're more evil than I ever believed you capable of being. Perhaps much worse."

"Flattery, sister, doesn't appeal to me."

Forrest rushed across the floor toward Nicodemus. The thin vampire didn't move or attempt any defensive stance, as most people would do. He waited. When Forrest came close enough, Nicodemus grabbed Forrest by the collar and flung the giant man over the vampire and high into the air as though the bear of a man weighed nothing. Forrest crashed through the bed canopy. The black sheet and splintered posts dropped upon him, burying him.

Nicodemus wiped his hands together as if he were removing dust. Flora ran toward the wardrobe, trying to get outside of the radius of the snarling wolves.

The werewolves growled and lowered to all fours, ready to attack.

"Wait!" Nicodemus said, raising a hand.

A second later a woman screamed from beneath the broken canopy. The mattress sagged and creaked as Forrest fought to find his way off the bed.

Raven rolled off the bed, startled, and stood with her back against the wall. She wore a tighter bustier, which made her breasts look even larger. She stood in black lacey lingerie, and Kailey knew that someone else must have dressed her that way because it wasn't attire Raven would have ever worn, especially not in front of males. But her clothing wasn't the most disturbing detail.

Raven's eyes were full black. No irises. Not a hint of white. Just wide, black, and soulless eyes. She looked like she had just awakened, and perhaps she had, from life to death to now being one of the undead.

Kailey teared up. She wanted to wrap her arms around Raven and hug her; to make things go back to what they were a week ago before the supernatural terrors had become a part of their lives. But wishful thinking and time machines didn't work or alter history.

Raven held her hand to her throat. When she lowered it, two prominent puncture marks were there, swollen and pink. Dried blood streaks ran past her neckline.

"Oh, God, Raven," Kailey said, stepping out of the shadows of the hallway and partway into the room.

Raven's hissed, seeing Kailey. "You! You betrayed me! How could you leave me and let them do this to me?"

"No," Kailey replied.

Cassie took Kailey by the hand and whispered, "Careful. She's not the woman you knew."

"You wished to meet my bride," Nicodemus said. He elegantly waved a hand in Raven's direction. "Behold!"

Raven glanced around the room, but she stood perplexed. Her hand touched the tender wounds on her throat. The fierceness in her brow tightened, and she growled in response to the werewolves approaching Nicodemus.

Nicodemus flashed a brief smile, showing fangs. At the vampire's feet a black ripple of smoky fog grew. Three sets of crimson eyes rose within the building black smoke. As the circle of smoke widened, the creatures became more solid. The trio of demons stood knee high with clawed hands, long pointy tails, and wings. Their tiny mouths were filled with jagged teeth. Long forked, pink tongues spiraled downward from their mouths. Drool dripped from the sides of their mouths.

Brady eyed Micah and Jacob. "What the hell do you make of those?"

"I think you have their origin right. Other than that, I haven't a clue," Micah replied.

Jaclyn held the Grimoire in her left hand and raised her right. Light shimmered on her fingertips, but before she harnessed the power of her spell, Nicodemus pointed. One of the winged demons flew straight for Jaclyn.

"You have the book," Nicodemus shouted, enraged. "Hand it over."

Jaclyn shook her head.

The demon sped through the air like a tiny black blur. It reached for the book, but Jaclyn snatched the winged imp from flight by its wings and squeezed tightly. Little bones snapped and its wings crumpled. The little shadow demon squalled, snapping at her, but her hand was outside of its reach. Its long tail swung upward and lashed at her hand, striking its razor-sharp tip into the back of her hand.

"Dammit!" She slung the creature at the wall. Before it collided with the wall, the demon puffed into a black ball of smoke, immediately reappearing at Nicodemus's feet, uninjured.

"Get him." Micah rushed at the vampire. Brady followed, swiftly and more aggressively. With a wave of his hand, Nicodemus shoved Micah off course without even touching him. Micah fought to turn, to correct, but his momentum thrust him into the wall. He half yelped and half cried out.

Brady leapt upward before Nicodemus braced for the collision. Brady knocked the vampire backwards, landing atop him. Brady snarled with his large yellowed teeth exposed. The tiny shadow demons glided upward, produced sharp-tipped weapons, and stabbed into his back. Out of instinct, Brady cocked his head and looked over his shoulder to kill the imps, and that's the moment Nicodemus took advantage of Brady's distraction.

Nicodemus caught Brady around the throat and choked. Brady shook his head back and forth, trying to jerk free, but Nicodemus was too power-ful. In desperation, Brady used his hands to try to pry himself free. Even after his transformation, Brady wasn't strong enough. His face went from deep red to a darkening purple.

"No!" Kailey said, trying to pull her hand free of Cassie's.

Cassie tightened her grip and shook her head. "No, you wait here with Skye."

"He is going to kill Brady."

"Stay here and live, or expose yourself and die."

Kailey huffed and gritted her teeth.

With lightning speed, Cassie vanished from beside Kailey and reappeared near Nicodemus' head. She swiped her tail, slashing across the vampire's wrists with enough force to break his grip. Brady shoved both fists against Nicodemus' ribcage and pushed himself away. Ribs cracked.

Nicodemus winced in obvious pain. Apparently the demons granted him their power, but they didn't offer a protective shield. He rolled to one side. The bed creaked. From his peripheral vision a large shadow moved.

Forrest.

The massive man shook his head, grabbed a stake, and then he grinned. His heavy boots thudded onto the floor. He took labored strides toward Nicodemus.

"Leave him alone," Raven hissed. She pushed away from the wall with fangs reared. Her full black eyes haunted Kailey, making Kailey look away.

Forrest batted Raven away with little effort and knocked her onto the broken bed. He seemed less interested in her, perhaps because she was a new vampire. His attention focused on Nicodemus who was a challenge for Forrest to conquer. He approached more cautiously this time. He seemed to have enough sense to realize that if a thin vampire was capable of hoisting a giant with such ease as Nicodemus had, the vampire had excessive strength and needed to be dealt with accordingly.

Forrest widened his stance like a wrestler, but Nicodemus shook his head, unconcerned.

The vampire turned his hands palm upward. The three shadow demons cocked their heads, looking at him. Without any delay, the demons flew into him. Nicodemus' eyes glowed greenish-yellow. His fingernails lengthened, as did his fangs. The charismatic expression that he possessed when they had first entered his chambers was gone. Evil creased around his eyes. His delicate jaw tightened with fury. He no longer held the aristocratic appearance.

Jacob ran upon all fours, snarling and growling. His muscled body moved with power. His mouth widened as he approached the vampire.

Nicodemus threw a solid punch into the werewolf's mouth. Jacob's lower jaw careened and struck the marble floor hard. Teeth spewed from his mouth and scattered across the floor like crude bloody dice. He released a quick bark of pain, sliding past Nicodemus.

Although the vampire smiled in triumph, Nicodemus clung to his ribs where Brady had struck him earlier. He turned to face Forrest.

"It's been a long time, Forrest Wollinsky, stalker of vampires," Nicodemus said in a deep unnerving voice.

Flora crouched into the corner beside the wardrobe. Although she had led them to her brother, she was taking no part in killing him or getting killed.

"Stalker?" Forrest laughed heartily. "That's better than what I'd call you."

"And what is that?" Nicodemus asked.

"As when we met years before, you fled when I slayed your father. You're a coward."

"Coward? A lot has happened since then. Just know that you cannot slay vampires from the afterlife, which is where you shall find yourself soon enough."

Raven struggled to get to edge of the bed.

"We shall see," Forrest said.

Jaclyn knelt beside Barry with one hand pressed to his forehead and the Grimoire resting upon his chest under her other hand while she chanted softly. His eyelids flittered. Opening his eyes, he glanced around the room, apparently trying to figure out where he was.

Micah and Brady stood side by side at Nicodemus' left side as Forrest approached from the right.

"No," Forrest said. "This is my fight."

"This isn't a game," Micah replied. "Nicodemus must be destroyed. We cannot make mistakes that will allow his escape."

Jacob rose from the other side of Nicodemus, placing the vampire directly in the center of them. Barry sat up, but he wasn't in any condition to join the fight. Jaclyn turned and extended her right hand toward Nicodemus.

"My fight," Forrest repeated.

"He's far more powerful than you know," Jaclyn said, "since he took the demons back inside himself. All of us fighting him together will have a difficult enough time as it is."

Forrest laughed. "At least let me try."

Nicodemus tilted his head backwards. His haughty attitude returned. A light airy, yet mocking, laughter flowed from his mouth. "Fools!"

He extended his hands far apart and clapped them together. An explosion of air thrust all of them against the walls of the room. Deafening thunder followed. All the furniture wobbled, candles flickered wildly, and books dropped from their shelves. The gorgeous chandeliers shattered, swayed back and forth, making their metal attachments creak. Shards of glass rained down.

The vampires, wolves, and witches dropped to the floor, slumped and held their heads in pain. Kailey and Skye were spared, partly she believed because of the doorframe. Flora remained crouched. Raven was still somewhere on the bed.

Cassie had been unaffected by the blast and appeared behind Nicodemus. He turned and looked at her in surprise. Her tail looped around his waist like a snake wrapping its victim. His eyes widened. "You forgot that I'm immune to demon spells, didn't you? It's time you pay for taking Vincent away from me."

Cassie lifted Nicodemus off the floor and slammed him headfirst through the circular stained glass on the floor. The glass shattered and he dropped into the room below. Cassie immediately went down after him.

Raven looked to her left where Forrest was shaking his head and brushing himself off. She bore her fangs and hissed. He pushed himself to his feet and picked the stake off the floor. Before he staggered close enough, she sprinted to the hole and dropped down after Nicodemus and Cassie.

Micah stood and helped Brady to his feet. Then he grabbed Jacob's hand and pulled him up. Jacob rubbed his jaw. He was missing a lot of teeth.

Ashley crawled to Micah, panting and squinting.

"Are you okay?" Micah asked her.

She nodded slightly.

Micah turned toward Jaclyn who lay on the floor beside her mother and Debra. Rose was unconscious. Blood dripped from her nose and ears. Eva and Debra cradled one another. Both looked in pain, but Debra was injured badly, too. Jaclyn scooted her back against the wall.

"What's down there?" Micah asked.

"The summoning circle," Jaclyn replied, rising to her feet and picking up the Grimoire. "Cassie did the best thing for us by throwing him down there."

"Why's that?" Brady asked.

"The summoning circle is where we can kill him the easiest."

Micah turned toward Ashley. "Can you stay with Kailey and Skye?"

She nodded.

"Help them get downstairs safely." Micah faced Brady and Jacob. "Ready?"

They nodded.

Micah leapt through the narrow opening. Jacob followed, and then Brady.

"Dammit!" Forrest said, picking up his Hunter box. He marched toward the hallway. "No way in hell I'll fit through that damned hole."

Jaclyn tried to run toward the corridor and met him at the door. She limped more than she actually ran. "Follow me, and we'll be there in a few minutes."

"This vampire will be a distant kill. No way I'll be able to pierce the dagger through his heart close up."

"You sound disappointed," she said.

"Well, yeah. Nothing's more reassuring than seeing their eyes go dim when the dagger is driven through their hearts."

"As long as he's dead, Forrest, I'm happy with whatever method works without getting us killed in the process."

He chuckled, heaving the heavy case in his left hand. "As much as it pains me, I'll use the gun-staker."

Kailey followed behind them while Ashley helped Skye to her feet. "What happens to Raven after you kill Nicodemus?"

"She dissolves to dust," Forrest replied.

Kailey bit her lower lip. "Please, no. We can't do that. It's not her fault. There has to be a way to kill him without her dying."

"There is no other way."

"Actually," Jaclyn said, "there might be."

"How?"

"The summoning circle, and this book has some spells. The book is something that Nicodemus wants badly. He sent one of the demons to take it from me."

"Seems a lot of people want that book."

Jaclyn nodded. "That's why it stays with me."

"Even when all of this is over?" Kailey asked.

"Yes."

"What purpose will it give you then?" Forrest asked.

Jaclyn smiled. "I'm sure you have little secrets of your own that you don't wish to disclose."

He shrugged. "Don't we all?"

$\mathcal{A}$s Kailey stepped onto the spiral stairwell with Forrest and Jaclyn, Ashley remained at the top of the stairs with Skye. Skye motioned that she needed to rest.

"Is she okay?" Kailey asked Ashley.

"Leave me here," Skye said, placing a hand over her heart. She was pale. Pain creased her face, making her look even older than she actually was.

"I can't. Micah insisted that I stay with you and Kailey," Ashley said.

Ashley had released herself from her inner wolf and was human. Whatever had weakened her during the earlier bouts had lost its hold on her. She no longer looked fatigued. Color had returned to her cheeks and confidence set in her eyes. She leaned down and scooped Skye up. "Hold around my neck. We'll follow Kailey and the others down to the next floor."

Skye nodded and wrapped her tired arms around Ashley.

"We're right behind you," Ashley said to Kailey.

Kailey glanced up and nodded.

Kailey stared at Forrest as he took his gun from the hunter kit. He fumbled around with a nozzle that was connected to a tiny metal canister on their way to the bottom. Once they stepped off the stairs, he stepped to the side, still making connections.

"What are you doing?" she asked.

"Ramping up the power." He grinned.

"How?"

"You'll see."

Down the hallway, snarls and growls echoed. Jaclyn gave a simple nod. "The summoning room is that way."

Eva limped toward Jaclyn. "What the hell are you doing?"

Kailey wondered how Eva had beaten them to the bottom. She looked around for another door, but she didn't see anything. Quite possibly Nocturnal Trinity had a lot of hidden passageways that only the Founders were aware of.

"Going to correct your wrongs," Jaclyn replied.

"Haven't you done enough damage already?" Eva asked with a harsh frown.

"What do you mean?"

"Rose is dead. I think Debra is dying."

Kailey covered her mouth with her hand. "Seriously?"

Eva nodded while she continued glaring at Jaclyn.

"Blame Nicodemus, not me," Jaclyn said with a cold stare.

"If she dies—"

"It's not my doing. It was his. I cannot believe that you just left her," Jaclyn said. "Why not heal her?"

"You have my book, for one. You need to give it back to me. It's mine."

Jaclyn shook her head. "You should have shown more responsibility with your magic."

"Dammit," Forrest said, working with the gun. He grumbled more words beneath his breath.

"You've already destroyed the Circle of Unity," Eva said. "What more needs to be done?"

"Are you suggesting that Nicodemus should live?"

Eva remained silent, thinking. "Not at all, but he is our leader."

Kailey turned toward Eva and crossed her arms. "He killed my brother and turned Raven into a vampire. He dies."

"I guarantee it," Forrest said, attaching the hose around his belt and adjusting the canister.

"How could you choose to practice the darker forms of magic?" Eva asked.

"Seems, mother, that your magic slants heavily toward the darker realms. You really have no grounds to judge me. The products of your magic are proof enough."

Eva opened her mouth to speak, but Jaclyn pointed a stern finger at her.

"You're fortunate that what happened to Debra and Rose didn't also happen to you," Jaclyn said. Her voice became icier. "But the night isn't over, is it, mother?"

Eva took a deep breath and bit her lower lip.

A wolf yelped from down the hall.

"We'd best hurry before Nicodemus kills any more pack members," Forrest said. Leaving his Hunter box on the floor, Forrest took to running. Kailey and Jaclyn hurried after him. Eva hesitated, but then followed slowly, which was obviously deliberate and not due to injury.

The summoning room was dark, other than the dim chandeliers over-head. A large circle was carved into the granite floor. It was identical to the Nocturnal Trinity symbol outside the nightclub. Power seemed to flow from it, and Kailey was hesitant to enter.

Micah rose to his feet, still fully in his wolfman exterior. Brady and Jacob lay sprawled on the other side of the room, breathing and barely conscious. Both were injured and turning human. Raven edged her way toward Brady with hatred in her eyes.

"I'm going to kill you for taking Kailey away from me," Raven seethed.

Brady rolled to his stomach and fought to push himself up, but he struggled to move. He was weak, tired.

"Raven, don't!" Kailey shouted.

"What?" Raven said with a mocking innocence. She placed both hands dramatically over her mouth. Then her eyes filled with hatred. Her mouth tightened. "You worried about your pet? This *mongrel!* You often said that you liked dogs. Never once did I think you'd be fucking one."

Raven kicked Brady in the side hard enough to lift him into the air and flip him over. Brady moaned, clutching his stomach.

Turn back into your wolf form.

Kailey didn't know the procedure for how and why they were able to shape shift, or what prevented them from doing so when they absolutely needed to. She had missed most of the fight. No telling what Nicodemus was capable of doing or the little shadows demons as well.

"Raven," Kailey said in a sorrowful tone. She hoped pleading might reach whatever humanity still resided within Raven. "What happened to you shouldn't have occurred. We were told that they wouldn't turn you into one of them. Flora promised, but Nicodemus is to blame. *He* did this to you."

"A little late for pretenses, love. You had your fun with Brady just like I thought you wanted to. I see it in your eyes. I can't explain how, but I smell his scent on you, so don't deny that you spread your legs for him. I guess that was easy enough after you got me out of the way. Now, I'm going to have my turn with him. Not sexually, but he will bleed and suffer for your teasing betrayal. Then he dies."

Nicodemus stepped from the shadows with a broad sneer on his face. He laughed and gazed directly at Micah. "I simply love when old friends get reacquainted, don't you?"

Kailey placed a hand on Forrest's left forearm. "Stop her, but please don't kill her."

Forrest pumped a wooden stake into the gun, pulled the trigger, and the gun made a loud popping sound. The stake struck deeply into Raven's right shoulder, pivoting her backwards. She shrieked and yanked at the dagger until she pried it free. A hole remained. Dark blood filled it and seeped out.

"How dare you," she hissed. She strove toward them, and Cassie appeared behind Raven. She swung her tail, knocking Raven's feet out from under her. With the flat end of her tail, she smacked Raven hard in the face several times. Raven's eyes lost their rage. When she looked at Cassie, the succubus pointed for her to move across the room.

"You're *sure* you want her left alive?" Forrest asked. "Because she's rather pissed now."

Kailey nodded.

"Nothing you do will ever win her favor. You know that, don't you?"

"I'm being hopeful."

"Hope is going to get you killed," Forrest replied. He held the aim on Raven until she was across the room. She sat down on a step and tended to her injury. Cassie remained between Raven and the two injured wolves. "Eventually, she's going to come for you, and she will attempt to kill you. Best if I stake her now before she grows stronger."

"Please?"

Forrest shrugged, but the anger on his face didn't lessen. It was obvious he wanted to kill Raven, but Kailey struggled internally. She hoped somehow Raven could find redemption.

Micah, still in werewolf form, gave a cold hard stare into Nicodemus' eyes.

"You're a brave wolf," Nicodemus said. "Trying to hold my gaze."

"You don't remember me?" Micah asked in a scorned tone.

Nicodemus frowned, long and hard. Finally, he shook his head. "No. Should I?"

"If you love when old friends get together, how do you feel about meeting an old enemy who wants to kill you?"

Nicodemus shrugged. "I'm sorry. Still not making a connection."

"You killed my wife, Jeannine."

Nicodemus' eyes flicked with sudden recognition. "It's been a long time, Micah. I had heard that you moved away."

"No. I've remained in Seattle, masking my presence, until now."

Nicodemus smiled, nodding. "So you decided to invite a number of friends to help you."

"We each have our reasons for wanting you dead. A general consensus, so to speak."

"I don't like the odds in number, here," Nicodemus said. "Mind if I set things in order a bit?" He waved his hands and a dozen young vampires rushed from the shadows and headed toward the center of the room.

Forrest smiled, turned, and began firing wooden stakes in rapid succession. Kailey was surprised at his precision with the swift moving vampires. He dropped each one that stepped into the circle. They shrieked before falling into piles of ash.

Nicodemus narrowed his eyes. "I'm a tad bit tired of your large friend."

Micah laughed. "He's just racking up points."

"What?"

"Notches to carve into his Hunter box."

"Ah, I see."

"He's an expert vampire hunter. And if you're waiting for your vampire guards from the underground tunnel, they aren't coming. We killed them first."

Nicodemus mockingly applauded. "All this over one dead she-wolf?"

"It's much more than that," Jaclyn said, moving across the granite, summoning symbol. She held the Grimoire beneath her left arm.

The vampire looked quickly toward her and then back at Micah.

"Getting a bit nervous, Nicodemus?" Micah asked.

"Come at me, if you believe you can beat me. Unless, of course, you *need* your friends here to do it for you."

Micah's teeth grew larger, his eyes darker. The lust for revenge he had held back for so many years surfaced, overtaking his Shaman attributes as a healer. His muscles thickened, and he was two feet taller, more massive than any of the others in his pack. "I've waited for this for a long time."

Nicodemus grinned but no fear showed in his expressions. "I never understood why you refused to allow her to become a vampire and live forever like me?"

"It's not what she would have wanted."

"You didn't know what she wanted, did you?"

"Meaning?"

"While you lay in your drunken stupor, you missed all the things she *begged* me to do to her. I acquiesced, of course. She had wild needs, and believe me, it was tempting not to turn her even against your wishes."

Micah's eyes were black and swirled with murderous intent. For some reason, Kailey didn't believe what Nicodemus had said. She believed this vampire knew how to push buttons to send people into a rage. He thrived upon that, perhaps even fed off their fury.

Before Nicodemus blinked, Micah drove his sharp claws into the vampire's chest, clawing and shredding through the suit and into Nicodemus' flesh. Already suffering from cracked ribs, Nicodemus jerked back and placed a hand to his chest. When he pulled his hand up, blood coated it. The lacerations were deep.

A circle of black smoke encircled Nicodemus. The little demons swirled with the smoke. Before they could break free, Jaclyn raised her right hand and chanted. The demons vanished from sight.

Micah snarled and lurched forward again. He was more animal and less human. With a harsh swipe of his claws, he raked four gashes down Nicodemus' left cheek.

Nicodemus scrambled, backing away, retreating. He was overflowing with immense fear.

"Don't kill him," Kailey said. "Raven will die."

Micah's rage was beyond pleading words. He thrashed Nicodemus again, cutting more grooves into his face. Then he hit the vampire with such power that Nicodemus fell backwards. Micah pursued.

Kailey glanced at Brady with pleading eyes. Brady forced himself to stand, and hurried to stop Micah from ripping Nicodemus' head off.

"Raven," Brady whispered. "Think of Raven."

Micah's eyes reverted from the evil blackness. He shook his head slightly.

Nicodemus gazed upward. Blood leaked from the deep gashes. "Don't have it in you, do you?" He forced himself to stand. "Go ahead and kill me. Doing so completely nullifies your existence as a shaman doesn't it?" He grinned and laughed.

"It would." Micah glanced toward Jacob and Brady. "Sometimes, it pays to have good friends. Forrest?"

With a stunned expression, Nicodemus glanced toward Forrest right as the bear of a man squeezed the trigger.

"No!" Kailey cried. "Raven!"

The stake pierced through Nicodemus' heart. He clutched his chest, dropped to his knees, and then fell face forward onto the cold granite floor.

"You shouldn't have done that," Kailey said, hitting Forrest's arm over and over.

"He's not dead yet," Forrest said. He rubbed his arm. "Good solid punches."

Confused, she looked at Forrest and then at Nicodemus. He lay perfectly still, but had not turned to dust. "What happened? What did you do?"

"He's paralyzed."

"How?"

"Silver dagger. But it won't hold him more than a half hour. Well, in his current condition, the dagger might hold him longer than that. So, Jaclyn, what's your plan to keep Raven ... alive," Forrest asked, somewhat bitterly.

Flora glided into the room, stopping beside Micah. "Is he dead?"

"No, he's paralyzed," he replied.

"If you're going to kill him, do it quickly. I received word that my brothers and sisters are coming. While I'm certain they'd agree with me about Nicodemus' fate, you never know how they might react."

Jaclyn motioned to Micah and Forrest. "I need his body placed on the vampiric symbol. I need Cassie to stand upon the demonic symbol, and a witch to stand at the witches' mark."

Forrest grabbed Nicodemus by the shoulder with one hand and dragged him to where Jaclyn had indicated. Cassie stood on the demonic symbol.

"You're planning to perform a human sacrifice?" Eva asked, walking toward Jaclyn.

Kailey felt her stomach turn from the shock of what the spell required. "No."

"It's the only way the spell will work."

"I don't see it written anywhere that a human sacrifice is necessary."

"Of course not. That's why this book will do you little good. Not everything is included in the details. That was my safety net in case it ever got stolen."

"It'll have to do without such a sacrifice."

"It *won't* work."

"What kind of devious practices have gone on here?" Kailey asked. "Human sacrifices? And you think Jaclyn practices dark magic?"

"You have no idea exactly what Jaclyn is, do you?"

Kailey wanted to ask, but she was fearful to gain the knowledge.

"Besides," Eva said. "I never said that any have occurred."

Jaclyn smirked. "It's *your* Grimoire, so it has your notes. You have contributed to Nicodemus' causes for many years, willingly or not, so if what you're saying is true and you deliberately left that part out, you must have performed one sometime."

Eva's guilt reflected in her gestures.

"I thought so. Now back away," Jaclyn said.

Eva shrugged. "Without a human sacrifice, it isn't going to work."

"I'll sacrifice myself," Skye said, forcing herself to hobble into the summoning room.

"No," Kailey said.

"For Raven, yes," Skye said, nodding.

"But she's a vampire now. You only prevent her from turning to dust. She won't be the same," Kailey said.

"Having second thoughts?" Forrest asked.

Kailey nodded and whispered, "A little."

"Perhaps she won't be," Skye replied, looking into Kailey's eyes. "But at least she'll be on this earth. Besides, I'm dying. I sense it. With all the stress, my heart is giving out. I don't think I have but a few more hours."

"Skye ..." Kailey reached for her.

Skye shook her head and waved Kailey away. She looked at Eva. "Where do I need to lay?"

Sadness and uneasiness washed over Eva. "The center of the circle."

Skye sighed heavily and kept hobbling until she reached the center. Before she crouched to sit, her eyes met Raven's.

Tears formed in Raven's eyes. Her lower lip quivered. She rose to her feet but Skye shook her head and motioned for Raven to stay where she was.

"Start the ritual, Jaclyn," Skye said, lowering herself to the center of the circle and then lying back on the cold granite. She slid her sharp dagger from the sheath on the inside of her robe and placed the tip right over her heart, waiting for Jaclyn to start the incantation.

In tears, Kailey walked out of the summoning room. She couldn't watch. She just couldn't. All these horrible chain of events had occurred for the Grimoire that Jaclyn now possessed. First, Vincent had died. Raven had come from Boston with Skye to protect Kailey, but Raven had become a vampire. And now Skye was offering her own life in order for her vampire ex-friend to be spared. None of it was fair. Life wasn't fair.

Into the shadows of the corridor she walked. Life would never be the same, and she feared that she might not be strong enough to handle the memories or endure the losses of the past few days. She kept walking until she reached one of the dance floors. She ignored the music, the dancers, and she headed toward the front door.

CHAPTER 56

The next day Kailey sat on the outside patio at a coffee shop. The air was crisp, but the sun was out, and she preferred being out in the open instead of being seated in the midst of other people.

"Mind if I join you?" Cassie asked. She wore snug yoga pants that revealed the perfect roundness of her ass and her muscled thighs. Her tight top hugged her breasts perfectly. Her curly hair was pulled back in a pony-tail. Her hair was red. She looked like she had just come from a gym, but Kailey knew the succubus had no need to work out. Her form would always be of perfection, and that made Kailey somewhat envious. Women worked their asses off in the gym to look a fraction as good as Cassie.

Kailey motioned to the seat across from her. "Please, by all means. Help yourself."

Cassie sat down and set her coffee on the table. "Thanks."

"Don't you ever get cold?"

She crinkled her nose and winked. "Really? You'd ask that. You *know* where I'm from. Besides, it'd be a *sin* to cover up a body as gorgeous as mine."

Kailey reached across the table and placed her hand atop Cassie's. "I'm really sorry for misjudging you and thinking that you'd ever hurt my brother. I'm also sorry for hitting you."

"I know that you were acting out of emotion. Of course it didn't help that I was being controlled by the shadow demons that Nicodemus had bound to me. I'm certain that by all accounts, I looked every bit as guilty as you suspected, and you know, I think maybe that was part of Nicodemus' plan."

"Why's that?"

"To make you kill me. My death erased the evidence of the shadow demons and his scheme to gain more power. After I was released from them, I was beginning to wonder if I had been the one to kill Vincent because I honestly couldn't remember what I had done. Flora finally told me last night that Nicodemus was the one that had killed Vincent in the swimming pool and to cover it up, he put the syringe into his arm."

"Again, I'm so sorry. I can tell that you really loved him."

"Kailey, please don't worry about it. I heal fast, and since we both loved Vincent, I cannot hold a grudge against you. You are his sister, and I consider you to be something I've never really had before Vincent. You're family."

"Thanks."

"Have you talked with Jaclyn since last night?" Cassie asked.

Kailey sipped her espresso and nodded. "I have. She called me early this morning."

"So she told you that Forrest had the pleasure of staking the bastard?"

"Yes." Kailey grinned. "He was rather pleased as she told it. Did you stick around after the ritual?"

"No. Like you, I found the mood too depressing. Once I knew Nicodemus was dead, I had no other reason to be there."

"I didn't know Skye that long, but I couldn't—"

"I understand," Cassie said, softly. She changed the subject. "Hey, what are your plans now? Are you moving back to Boston?"

"There's nothing for me to return to there. I need to hire some movers to haul my belongings out here though."

"You can always stay with me until you get settled in," Cassie said, smiling.

Kailey liked the way Cassie's eyes sparkled in the morning sunlight. And she tried to maintain eye contact rather than glance at the succubus' gorgeous body. She couldn't fight her attraction toward men and women, but she was loyal to the one she was with, and never promiscuous.

"I appreciate that," Kailey said.

"Or are you staying with Brady?" she asked with a wink.

"I did last night."

Cassie smiled. "So you think he's the one for you?"

Kailey blushed. "It's too soon to say, but he wants me to move in with him."

"I'm guessing you're not fighting to get away."

"Of course not. I suppose you'll be on the dating scene soon?"

Cassie looked down with sadness in her eyes. She shook her head. "No time soon. Even demons grieve."

Kailey gave an even smile and stirred her coffee with the tip of her finger. "Jaclyn told me that the Circle of Unity has been dissolved. They are making a new council with twelve members, but the name of the nightclub will remain the same. Three are from each of the factions—witches, vampires, demons, and werewolves. Micah apparently insisted that he was going to be on the board."

"That's good, though. He's level headed, has morals, and can be trusted. Did she mention what her mother will be doing?"

"All I know is that Eva was banished from the nightclub, and basically, Jaclyn told her mother that she had best leave the city if she wanted to keep her magic."

Cassie sipped her coffee. "So Jaclyn kept the Grimoire?"

"Yep."

"Good."

"Jaclyn is on the council. Debra and Rose both died. What will happen to Raven?" Kailey asked.

Cassie bit her lower lip and studied Kailey for a few moments. "I have some disturbing news about Raven."

Kailey swallowed hard. Her stomach twisted. "What?"

"I talked to Flora, and well, you just need to know. Raven has vowed to kill you if she ever sees you again."

The day suddenly seemed colder. "Kill me?"

"Understand that Raven will never be the person you once knew. Never. She's a vile monster spawned by Nicodemus. She has lost her humanity. You would have been better off allowing Forrest to kill her."

"I just couldn't," Kailey said, shaking her head. "I felt responsible for leaving her with Flora."

"I know. But here's the thing. She might eventually seek to find and kill you. When that occurs, are you willing to kill her?"

"I don't know."

"That hesitation right there will get you killed. If you ever tangle in a fight with her, you'd best kill her or she will kill you. She hates you, to put it mildly."

Hot tears brimmed in Kailey's eyes. She refused to release them.

Cassie placed a gentle hand atop Kailey's. "The good thing is Flora said that she would train Raven to control her temper and her urges to feed on people outside of Nocturnal Trinity. And I'll be near anytime you need me, okay?"

Kailey nodded slowly, but no words came. She didn't know what she could say. Raven had been the best friend that Kailey had ever had, and now Raven was her mortal enemy. That was hard to accept, and would take some time to register. How did you kill someone that was a dear friend?

Hatred, for starters. Such a vile emotion allowed one to forget love and compassion. But she didn't hate Raven. More than anything, she pitied her.

The most troublesome part of the whole ordeal was understanding how quickly Raven's love had turned to hatred. That radical change had not simply occurred from Nicodemus turning her. This resentment must have always been buried deep inside Raven. It had to have been. The second Kailey had chosen to give her and Raven a chance at an intimate relationship, Raven's true nature emerged. Jealousy, resentment, and unrelenting control possessed Raven and immediately soured Kailey from staying in the relationship. Not long afterwards, Flora took her and held her for ransom. Raven's spark of resentment blazed into an inferno.

Suddenly it dawned upon Kailey. The demon had appeared at their apartment in Boston, and then the strange chant that had come from Raven's cellphone. Had the intruding demon possessed Raven before she and Skye left Boston and came to Seattle? That was possible, but nothing Kailey did now could ever make Raven human again. As a vampire, the demon might still reside inside of her.

Had Forrest not been there in the summoning room, Raven planned to kill Brady to spite Kailey. Thankfully she had failed.

"You okay?" Cassie asked.

"Yeah. Just deep in thought."

A female server with a heavy fake fur coat brought a large piece of chocolate cheesecake, two forks, and set it before Cassie. Cassie handed Kailey one of the forks as the server walked away. "Here. I ordered this before I came out. Put some fat on your thighs."

Kailey forced a laugh. She wondered if she'd ever genuinely laugh about life ever again. "Cheesecake for breakfast?"

"Don't act so surprised. Besides, chocolate is a woman's cure-all."

Kailey took the fork and cut a bite off the cake. "I have to ask you something."

"What?"

"You keep changing your appearance each time I see you. You do that with your demon spells or do you have to dye your hair?"

"I can be whatever I'm in the mood to look like, and whatever race I'd like to be. All because I'm a succubus. But, I can disguise as a male, too."

"Really? Wow, now I'm super envious."

Cassie smiled. "Why?"

"Great disguises for whenever you don't want to bump into someone you don't like, or a quick way to run out on a scary blind date."

"It has its benefits."

Kailey sipped her coffee, which was getting cold fast due to the winter morning air. "What attracted you to my brother?"

"His eyes. They reflected the honesty of his soul."

"Do you have a thing for humans?"

"He was the only human I ever dated. I steered clear of most men simply because they knew what elation a succubus could give them sexually. That was one of the main reasons businessmen become members at Nocturnal Trinity. Rumors of the exotic pleasures the succubae gave made us a popular item. But Vincent, he was different. When he met me, he treated me like a lady. No mention of sex for the first few weeks."

"Did he know you were a demon?"

Cassie nodded. "He complemented me on my beauty the first time I brought him a drink. I thought that he was going to be like all the other humans that had hit on me or thrown out the corniest lines, but he didn't. He asked if I'd like to go out to dinner and see a movie. First man at the nightclub that had ever made the suggestion, so I accepted. Few men are like he was, Kailey. He was sincere, courteous, and opened doors for me. He made me feel special and important."

Kailey took Cassie's hand and squeezed. "So how did Nicodemus get you mixed up with the shadow demons?"

Cassie bit her lower lip and looked away. After a few moments, she said, "I was a waitress at the nightclub, and I was contracted to work three years without pay to repay the Founders for summoning me out of the abyss. Sort of an indentured servant, so to speak. When I quit to marry Vincent, Nicodemus offered to void the contract and allow my freedom if I did one summoning spell. He had me convinced that he was summoning a replacement for me, but instead, all the other unfolded."

"You being bound by the shadow demons?"

Cassie nodded. "They are shadows of the beast sent by Lucifer himself, offering great power to the one who yields to their control, which I never did. They controlled me without my knowledge until Nicodemus found the right spell to bind them to him."

Kailey frowned. "So ... what happened to them after Nicodemus died?"

Cassie's eyes widened and she shook her head. "I really don't know."

"That might be a problem."

"They did try to emerge when Micah was fighting Nicodemus, but Jaclyn prohibited them from breaking out."

Kailey nodded. "But they should have still been inside him."

"When Forrest drove the stake through Nicodemus' heart, the demons never surfaced."

"You think they might have returned to the abyss since their master died?" Kailey asked.

"Maybe."

"I hope so. But the good thing is that Jaclyn used the Grimoire to seal the summoning portal, so no other demons can be summoned. She might have also sent the demons back."

Cassie nodded. "Great. So since you plan to move to Seattle, what will you do for a job?"

"I'm starting a supernatural blog to report the occurrences that happened during the past few days, and how the founders of Nocturnal Trinity were behind a lot of it."

"Aren't you putting yourself at risk by doing that?"

Kailey grinned. "I will write under an alias and charge a modest online subscription fee. If the blog takes off, it can turn out to be a full-time job. I earned my degree in investigative reporting, so I can possibly get leads about other strange occurrences from readers. It would be fun researching."

"If you need help, let me know. That sounds sort of dangerous, so I'd be happy to provide you with some backup."

"I'll let you know."

Cassie stood. "You need a ride somewhere?"

"No," Kailey replied, glancing at her watch. "Brady will be here soon. We're going to visit Jacob in the hospital. Nicodemus did quite a lot of damage to him. He healed fairly quickly, but he will still need dentistry work."

Cassie winced.

"We also have to report Skye's death to the police. Brady said that if he includes Nocturnal Trinity in the report that it will most likely be swept under the rug, but we still have to make arrangements to get her body or ashes back home, if we can find relatives."

"That's sad. You know where I live, so stop by anytime. Or call, and I'll come pick you up."

"Thanks," Kailey said, standing.

Cassie leaned close and hugged Kailey. She whispered into Kailey's ear. "If things don't work out with you and Brady, we could be lovers, you and I, after my grieving process is over. I know you have a thing for women, too. I saw you checking me out before I sat down. But what I can give you, no man or woman can ever match."

Kailey pulled away, looked Cassie in the eyes, and shook her head.

"Wait, close your eyes," Cassie said in a soft, gentle tone. "Let me show you the forbidden pleasures I can give you."

Kailey's heart raced as she viewed herself and the succubus on the bed. Both were nude, wrapped in one another's arms, kissing, touching, and caressing. Excitement rushed through her as their lovemaking intensified and Cassie showed Kailey how she could shape the end of her tail, and *what* she could do with it.

Kailey felt herself getting wet. Her face flushed and her mouth suddenly salivated. She swallowed hard, feeling her hips gyrate involuntarily. Her knees weakened.

Kailey gasped and pushed away from the succubus. "Sorry, Cassie, no. You're a gorgeous creature, one of the most beautiful women I've ever seen, but you were my brother's wife and his lover. I really cannot see sharing myself with someone he loved. If you can understand that?"

Cassie winked and kissed her cheek. "I do. But ... after what I've shown you ... you'll never forget me and what you could have with me."

"While I'm certain of that, I'm content with Brady."

Cassie grinned. "You'll think about it. More than you ever expected to. Trust me. Who knows? Maybe you'd like to invite Brady for a threesome?"

As Cassie turned and walked away, Kailey watched the perfect body saunter with such teasing motion that Kailey fought to look away.

Dammit!

After Cassie was through the door and out of sight, Kailey's heart fluttered with lust and want. Brady pulled into a parking spot and hit the horn, pulling her from the lustful fantasy for a moment, only to find herself imagining what a threesome would be like.

Regardless of how much she craved making love with Brady, she knew

Cassie was right. She'd never get the image and need of what Cassie had shown her out of her head, but she'd damn near try.

Kailey grabbed her purse and headed toward Brady's car. They had won a few victories the night before, but they had also suffered losses. Time would tell whether such confrontations ever rose again, and she hoped that they didn't. With the supernatural she knew one thing.

Expect the unexpected.

THE END (Next in Series: Raven)

AUTHOR'S NOTE

Thank you for purchasing this novel. If you enjoyed this book, please check out my website and join my mailing list at www.leonarddhilleyii.com to receive a free digital copy of Forrest Wollinsky: Vampire Hunter.

If you could also take a moment and leave a review, it is greatly appreciated!

Blessings to you and yours.

ABOUT THE AUTHOR

Leonard D. Hilley II grew up a quiet, shy kid with an inquisitive mind. Learning to read at an early age, he fell in love with books. He read every book he could get his hands on and stacks of dark comics about ghosts, monsters, and creepy things that stalk the night.

Like a lot of boys, he caught beetles, wooly bears, butterflies, and had an ant farm. When he was ten, his interests in science increased even more after seeing a professor's insect collection. Soon he set out on his quest to build his own collection. He also learned to rear butterflies and moths to obtain perfect specimens. He learned botany, gardening, and set his goal to become an entomologist.

At eleven, he watched the original Star Wars on the big screen. His imagination soared. Soon after, he discovered Roger Zelazny's Chronicles of Amber. Six months later, he had written the first draft of a novel. A novel he later discarded, but the characters stuck with him. Years later, these characters came to life in Shawndirea, which Hilley intended to be a novella for Devils Den. The characters, however, refused to be ignored and took the opportunity to unveil Aetheaon in their first epic fantasy. Lady Squire: Dawn's Ascension was quick to follow.

Shawndirea was Hilley's farewell to butterfly collecting, and those who have read the novel understand why. He has taken Ray Bradbury's advice to heart: "Follow the characters." He does. He follows, listens, and take notes—often never knowing where they're going to take him, but he's never been disappointed in the results.

Hilley earned a B.S. in Biology and an MFA in Creative Writing to combine his love of science and writing.

Sci-fi Titles: Predators of Darkness: Aftermath, Beyond the Darkness, The Game of Pawns, Death's Valley, The Deimos Virus.

Epic Fantasy: Shawndirea (Aetheaon Chronicles: Book One), Lady Squire (Aetheaon Chronicles: Book Two), Frosthammer (Aetheaon Chronicles: Book Three), Shadowfae (Aetheaon Chronicles: Book Four), and Devils Den.

UF/PR: Succubus: Shadows of the Beast (Nocturnal Trinity Series: Book One), Raven (Nocturnal Trinity Series: Book Two), A Touch of the Familiar (Nocturnal Trinity Series: Book Three)

YA UF/Paranormal: Forrest Wollinsky Vampire Hunter; Forrest Wollinsky: Blood Mists of London; Forrest Wollinsky: Predestined Crossroads.